Ch...
Mine

All these 'Dads' have to do is reach out and their children will run into their arms…and the 'Mums' don't seem to be able to resist these virile, rugged hunks of masculinity either!

Dear Reader,

Welcome to this month's fantastic selection of Desires.

We continue the MILLIONAIRE'S CLUB mini-series with a two-in-one volume entitled **Millionaire Men** including a provocative tale from Cindy Gerard called *Lone Star Knight*. This is joined by *Her Ardent Sheikh* from Kristi Gold, giving you a double helping of mesmerising, rich, honourable men. Look out for the next volume, **Millionaire Bachelors**, next month.

There is a fabulously royal air about us this month with our first ROYALLY WED volume for this year. **Royally Wed** includes two wonderful books, *The Expectant Princess* by Stella Bagwell and *The Blacksheep Prince's Bride* by Martha Shields. Visit the Stanbury dynasty to enjoy these magnificent weddings!

Child of Mine is our third two-in-one volume and puts together two sinfully rugged, gorgeous men and their newly acquired children to tug at your heart-strings with *Cowboy's Secret Child* by Sara Orwig and *The Rancher and the Nanny* by Caroline Cross.

We hope you'll enjoy them all.

The Editors

Child of Mine

**SARA ORWIG
CAROLINE CROSS**

SILHOUETTE
DESIRE

DID YOU PURCHASE THIS BOOK WITHOUT A COVER?
If you did, you should be aware it is **stolen property** as it was reported *unsold and destroyed* by a retailer. Neither the author nor the publisher has received any payment for this book.

All the characters in this book have no existence outside the imagination of the author, and have no relation whatsoever to anyone bearing the same name or names. They are not even distantly inspired by any individual known or unknown to the author, and all the incidents are pure invention.

All Rights Reserved including the right of reproduction in whole or in part in any form. This edition is published by arrangement with Harlequin Enterprises II B.V. The text of this publication or any part thereof may not be reproduced or transmitted in any form or by any means, electronic or mechanical, including photocopying, recording, storage in an information retrieval system, or otherwise, without the written permission of the publisher.

This book is sold subject to the condition that it shall not, by way of trade or otherwise, be lent, resold, hired out or otherwise circulated without the prior consent of the publisher in any form of binding or cover other than that in which it is published and without a similar condition including this condition being imposed on the subsequent purchaser.

Silhouette, Silhouette Desire and Colophon are registered trademarks of Harlequin Books S.A., used under licence.

*First published in Great Britain 2002
Silhouette Books, Eton House, 18-24 Paradise Road,
Richmond, Surrey TW9 1SR*

CHILD OF MINE © Harlequin Books S.A. 2002

The publisher acknowledges the copyright holders of the individual works as follows:

Cowboy's Secret Child © Sara Orwig 2001
The Rancher and the Nanny © Jen M Heaton 2000

ISBN 0 373 04739 8

51-0202

*Printed and bound in Spain
by Litografia Rosés S.A., Barcelona*

COWBOY'S SECRET CHILD

by
Sara Orwig

SARA ORWIG

lives with her husband and children in Oklahoma. She has a patient husband who will take her on research trips anywhere, from big cities to old forts. She is an avid collector of Western history books. With a master's degree in English, Sara writes historical romances, mainstream fiction and contemporary romances. Books are beloved treasures that take Sara to magical worlds, and she loves both reading and writing them.

With love to Hannah, Rachel and Ellen…and with special thanks to Debra Robertson, Joan Marlow Golan and Maureen Walters. And to Patricia Smith, my new editor and a wish come true…

One

On a Monday during the first week of June, Jeb Stuart sat quietly in his car beneath the shade of a tall elm on a residential street in Dallas. He waited, his calm manner belying his churning emotions. He glanced at his watch, and then his gaze returned to the shady street. Ten minutes later his pulse jumped as a black car rounded the corner, slowed and turned into the drive of a small red brick house across the street. He saw the riot of the driver's red hair before she disappeared up the driveway.

Still waiting, he looked at her surroundings, noting that she lived in a nice neighborhood. Farther down the block, sprinklers turned in silvery arcs on lawns. Her yard had flowers and trees and looked idyllic. In a few more minutes he was going to disrupt her peaceful life, much like a bomb going off in the neat red brick house. From all the difficulty he had in locating her, he guessed that she had expected him to come searching for her and had taken precautions against his ever finding her.

Then the front door opened and another woman came out. From the detective's reports, Jeb knew she was the nanny. Dressed in jeans and a red T-shirt, she sauntered to a parked car, slid inside and drove past Jeb without a glance.

He had waited long enough. He stepped out and crossed the street. With each stride his heartbeat quickened, until it was thudding in anticipation when he climbed the porch steps and rang the doorbell.

The door swung open and only a screen door separated him from the woman he had watched turn into the driveway earlier. Dressed in cutoffs and a blue T-shirt, Amanda Crockett looked up at him and their gazes locked. Jeb stared into wide crystal-green eyes that were enormous and seemed to grow larger. For a moment he was caught and held, but only for a moment, and then he remembered who she was and what she had done.

During the past two months he had rehearsed what he would say when this moment came. Yet now, as he looked down through the screen door into her green eyes, words failed him.

Then he realized it wasn't going to be necessary to say half of what he had intended because all color had drained from her face, and she looked as if she were going to faint.

Fainting would not win her any of his sympathy, he thought, but as he watched, she raised her chin. Even through the screen door, he could see the spark that came into her eyes and he wondered if he was in for a fight. If so, he relished it because he wanted to let her know how much pain she had caused him. He watched her grasp the door, and her knuckles were as white as her face. Had she really thought she could get away with what she had done?

While her world shifted, Amanda Crockett gripped the solid door. As she looked at the tall stranger glaring at her, she could feel the most precious thing in her life slipping away. The moment she had dreaded for three years had come. One look at his face and she knew without a doubt that the stranger before her was the father of her son. In a grown-up version of three-year-old Kevin, she saw the same bone structure, the same straight nose and wide forehead, the same dark eyes and black hair that Kevin had. She knew now how Kevin would look when he was a man.

She tried to get her breath and fight the dizziness that threatened. The stranger hadn't said a word, yet his dark eyes said everything. Determination, anger—there was no mistaking his feelings.

He towered over her, and his broad shoulders were as formidable as his height. Yet it wouldn't have mattered if he had been slender and lightweight—he would have carried the same dreadful threat. More than a threat. The end of her world.

Her stomach constricted as if he had slammed his fist into it, and her head swam. Clutching the door, she gulped deep breaths of air, but words wouldn't come. She had to invite him into her house. From his expression, she knew he would get inside whether or not she invited him, but for Kevin's sake she needed to be civil, even though everything in her screamed to slam the door and run. Grab Kevin and keep running.

"Come in," she whispered.

He opened the screen, and the hinge squeaked as he

swung it wide while she stepped back. When he walked inside, he seemed to fill the hall. Dressed in a white shirt, jeans and western boots, he was rugged and handsome and an overpowering presence.

He turned to face her. "I'm Jeb Stuart. Cherie's ex-husband."

While Amanda fought a knot in her throat, her tears welled up. Nodding, she closed her eyes.

"Are you all right?" he asked gruffly.

"Yes," she said, opening her eyes, thinking he looked as if he would like to lock his hands around her throat and squeeze. She tried to gather her wits and catch her breath, but she failed. She reminded herself that he gave up all rights to his child a long time ago.

Feeling shaky, she closed the door and moved ahead of him. As she ushered him into her small living room, she heard his boot heels scraping the oak hardwood floor.

"Have a seat," she said, perching on the edge of a walnut rocker while he sat on a dark blue wing chair facing her. Looking at him, she became aware that he was very handsome, with riveting dark eyes, sexy, thick lashes, broad shoulders and long legs. When he glanced around the room, she wondered if he thought her home adequate for his son.

She looked at her simple furniture in maroon and navy, her plants, the books on the shelves and the prints that hung on the walls. Kevin's little books were on the oak coffee table. Whether Jeb Stuart liked it or not, this was Kevin's home. She locked her fingers together in her lap while the silence became thick and tense.

"I guess you already know that I'm Amanda Crockett, Cherie's cousin."

"Yes. I've talked with my lawyer and I hired a private detective—that's how I found you."

Amanda struggled against the ridiculous urge to beg him to leave her alone. And then she thought about all Cherie had told her about her ex-husband and anger mixed with fear. She would get her own lawyer; she would fight for Kevin.

"What changed your mind about your son, Mr. Stuart?"

"Changed my mind?" he asked, frowning, a note of incredulity in his voice. She noticed that he gripped the arms of the chair until his knuckles were white. He leaned forward slightly, narrowing the distance between them. "Look, lady, you've got my child. I'm his father and I'm entitled to my son."

"You abandoned him, Mr.—"

"Abandoned!" The word was snapped like the crack of a whip. His face reddened, and even though his voice grew even quieter, it was laced with fury. "I did not abandon my son."

"You may say that now, but at the time—"

"Oh, no," he interrupted, rage blazing deeper in his dark eyes. "I didn't abandon him," he said slowly, with emphasis. "I didn't know Cherie was pregnant with our child. She kept that from me when we got divorced."

Amanda's head reeled again, and the worst of her suspicions were turning out to be the truth. Every word he said was a knife thrust into her heart. Was he lying or telling the truth? If he was lying, he was a good actor. His gaze was direct and his tone held conviction.

Amanda's stomach churned. Deep down she had always wondered if her cousin had lied to her.

"She said you didn't want your child and you left her and joined the army. Where have you been these last three years?"

"I've been in the army," he answered stiffly. "But when I left for the army, I didn't know I had fathered a child. We divorced in October 1997. I haven't seen Cherie since right after our divorce. In January 1998, I went into the army and got out in January of this year. In April I learned about Kevin."

"Who was born the twenty-second of May three years ago." With her anger and fear growing, Amanda wondered who was the truthful one. She knew Cherie wasn't always truthful, but she didn't know whether Jeb Stuart was truthful, either. After all, he married Cherie. What kind of man would marry her cousin? As swiftly as that question came, Amanda knew that most men would be drawn to Cherie.

"Cherie told me that you abandoned her and that you didn't want your child. She didn't want the baby and she knew that I would. She asked me if I would adopt him when he was born. So I went to court and adopted Kevin. I'm his legal mother."

"Legal adoptive mother," Jeb reminded her. "I didn't know about my son. I found out through a friend who knew Cherie and me. Three months after I got out of the army, I just happened to see her. She knew Cherie had been pregnant, but she didn't know Cherie didn't keep the baby."

"Look, I've raised Kevin as my son. You'll tear his life to pieces if you try to take him from me now," Amanda said, growing more certain of the rights she had and angry that he would barge in and expect her to hand over her child.

"Lady, I'm his *father*."

"I have a letter from Cherie saying that you abandoned her when she was pregnant and you knew she was pregnant. Any judge will look at that. I can get Cherie to testify."

"We both know what her testimony is worth!" Jeb's anger surfaced again at the lies Cherie had told.

"You're not going to take my son," Amanda said defiantly.

"Yet you want to keep my son from me," Jeb shot back. He wanted to reach out and shake her and tell her that he had missed his son's babyhood because of her and her cousin.

"Mama?"

At the sound of the soft voice, Jeb turned. A small boy holding a blue blanket stood in the doorway. Dressed in a green T-shirt and jeans, he was barefoot. His thumb was in his mouth.

As Jeb looked at the child standing across the room, he felt as if a fist had clamped around his heart. The rest of the world vanished, leaving only the child. Awe and love and uncertainty filled him. He wanted to touch his child, just touch him. And he saw why Amanda Crockett had recognized him when she opened the door. The resemblance deepened Jeb's awe. This was his son! He wanted to take the boy's hand and say, "I'm your dad, and you're coming home with me," but he knew it was not going to be that simple. The child was wide-eyed, looking from one adult to the other.

"Come here, Kevin. Did you just wake up?"

Amanda's voice was transformed, sounding calm

and sweet and filled with love, carrying so much warmth that Jeb turned to study her before looking back at his son.

Kevin cast a wary eye at Jeb as he scurried across the room to his mother and climbed into her lap to hold tightly to her. While Amanda gently rocked him and stroked his back, Jeb's heart received another blow.

For the past two months, from the moment he had discovered Cherie's deception and the loss of his child, he had been filled with rage and hurt that was compounded when he saw how completely the woman who had his son had vanished. She had left no trail, as though she had known full well that she was doing something underhanded. Now as he watched Kevin wrap his thin little arms around Amanda Crockett's neck, Jeb's pain deepened. For the first time, he wondered how he could take his son from the woman who was truly a mother to him.

She gazed over Kevin's head at Jeb, watching him carefully, and when he looked into her eyes, she gave him a searching stare.

"We need to talk some more," she said quietly, "but we can't right now."

"I can come back," he said, his voice as quiet as hers, yet he knew that her emotions were as much on edge as his. She seemed to think this over, looking down at Kevin, stroking his hair from his face and patting him. Was she a good mother? Jeb wondered.

"If you want to stay for dinner, Kevin goes to bed around eight and we can talk then."

Surprised that she offered dinner, Jeb wondered if she wanted him to see her with Kevin to press her point that she was his mother and they loved each other. She didn't need to, because Jeb could already see they had a close relationship. Was she good to him? he wondered again. Even if she was a marvelous mother, he didn't want to walk out of his son's life and give up all rights.

"Thanks. I'll stay because we do need to talk."

She gave him another one of her cool, level looks, and he experienced a flicker of admiration for her because she had weathered a big shock and was now in control of her emotions and ready to fight for her rights. At the same time, he didn't want to admire her or like her or find her attractive. So far he had succumbed to two out of the three and he wondered whether, if he stayed for dinner, he would also begin to like her.

His anger was transforming into a dull, steady pain, and all his plans for getting his child and watching him grow were going up in smoke. The woman facing him was causing him to readjust his thinking. And, adding to his turmoil, he was too aware that she was damned attractive. His gaze flicked over her in a quick assessment that took in the wild red hair that was an invitation to a man to tangle his fingers in it. His gaze lowered to his son's tiny hand resting against her breast with trust and love. Yet, at the same time, Jeb couldn't keep from noticing the lush fullness of her breasts beneath her clinging blue T-shirt.

"Kevin, this is Mr. Stuart," she said.

Kevin twisted slightly to stare at Jeb.

"Hi, Kevin," Jeb said quietly, feeling another knot in his throat.

Kevin held his small blanket against his face and gazed steadily at Jeb for a long moment until he ducked his head against his mother again. She smoothed his straight black hair. "Sleepy?" she asked him.

He nodded without answering her.

She rocked him slightly, stroking his head while she glanced at Jeb, and he could feel the clash of wills between them. They both wanted the same child. Jeb thought he was entitled to his son, yet for all his young life, the one person Kevin had known as his parent was Amanda Crockett. Jeb realized he was going to have to face that and deal with it in a way that wouldn't cause a lot of pain to his child.

Why had he thought that he could show up and demand his son and she would hand him over? He had expected a fight, but he hadn't stopped to think about her being locked into his son's affections. He had thought of Amanda Crockett as he thought of his ex-wife, Cherie, and Cherie would have given up a child by now. She had given this one up at birth.

"Do you have a grill?" Jeb asked.

"Yes."

"I'll go get some steaks and grill them, and then you won't have to go to so much trouble." He stood, feeling a deep reluctance to leave. He wondered if he would ever get enough of looking at Kevin. What a marvel the child was! His big brown eyes watched Jake solemnly. Oh, how he longed to touch his son, to hold him. "Anything else you'd like?"

"Thank you, no," she answered politely. She stood and picked up Kevin and shifted him to one hip.

As Jeb followed Amanda to the door, his gaze left his son and drifted down over her; he noticed the slight sway of her hips and her long, shapely legs. She opened the door and stepped back for him to leave. When he was outside, he looked back again at Kevin.

"I'll be back in a few minutes," he said. She nodded and closed the door. Jeb felt as if she had slammed it shut on his hopes and dreams.

He shopped quickly, and as he drove back to her house, logic told him she would be there, getting dinner. But his emotions churned and he half expected to come back and find her house empty. Too easily, he could imagine her taking Kevin and running away.

Why hadn't he stopped to think what he would do if she was a wonderful mother to Kevin? Kevin. Jeb liked the name. According to the detective, the child had his adoptive mother's last name, Crockett.

When Jeb returned to her house, her black car was in the drive and relief poured over Jeb. He parked behind it and picked up the sack of groceries. On impulse, he went to the back door and knocked.

She opened it and motioned to him. "Come in."

He entered a kitchen that had mouthwatering smells of hot bread and a blackberry cobbler. He was even more aware of Amanda as she gazed up at him with those compelling crystal-green eyes. Her tangle of red hair and the tiny beads of perspiration dotting her brow gave her a sultry earthiness that was appealing. She blinked, and with a start he realized that he was staring at her. She waved her hand.

"Set the groceries there," she said, motioning toward a space on the countertop. "Kevin isn't into steaks and salad. He gets macaroni."

Jeb placed the grocery sack on the counter and took out the steaks to unwrap them. All the time he worked, he was conscious of Amanda moving around him, of her perfume, of her steady, watchful gaze. She looked at him as though she had invited a monster into her kitchen. Her house was comfortable and appealing, but the kitchen was small, and when he brushed against her accidentally, he was acutely conscious of touching her.

"Sorry," he muttered, glancing at her. She looked up and once more they were caught, gazes locked and sparks that he didn't want to feel igniting. Her lips were rosy and full, a sensuous mouth that conjured up speculation about what it would be like to kiss her. He realized where his thoughts were going and turned away, bumping a chair.

What was the matter with him? He was reacting to her like a sixteen-year-old to a sexy woman, yet Amanda Crockett had done nothing to warrant any blatant male attention. He needed to remember that this woman was tearing up his life and that he was getting ready to tear up hers. If only she would do the right thing, acknowledge that Kevin was his son and simply hand him over. She had no right to take his child from him.

Hope began to flicker that she would be reasonable, realize she had taken a child from his father. Then he glanced across the kitchen into her eyes, which held fire in their depths, and he was certain that wasn't going to happen.

Dinner was a silent, strained event with little conversation by anyone. Jeb began to wonder about his son, who seemed shy and too quiet. Kevin was the only one with an appetite and he ate his macaroni, his bread and butter, and drank his milk.

"You've been in the army?" Amanda asked.

"The Eighty-second Airborne. I was a paratrooper."

She inhaled sharply. For some reason he had a suspicion she didn't approve, yet she probably didn't approve of anything about him.

"Do you and Cherie keep in contact?" he asked.

"Very little," she added, carefully. "I haven't seen her in three years," she said glancing at Kevin, and Jeb wondered if Kevin thought Amanda was his blood mother.

"She's a country-western singer. I've seen her CDs in stores."

"I've seen them, too," Amanda replied, "but I haven't seen Cherie. She's remarried."

"Right, for the third time," he added dryly. "To the actor, Ken Webster."

"You know a lot about her."

"I hired a detective. I got all this information from him." As Jeb talked, only half paying attention to their conversation, he tried to think what he could do about his son. His attention slid back to Kevin. "How old are you, Kevin?" he asked quietly, knowing the answer.

Kevin held up three fingers.

"Three years old. That's getting very big. Do you go to pre-school?"

Kevin shook his head.

"Not yet. He's enrolled for next fall," Amanda said, touching Kevin. She constantly reached out to pat his shoulder or brush his hair from his forehead, and Jeb wondered whether she was affectionate all the time or whether she was giving Kevin attention out of worry now. Jeb leaned back in his chair. He had little appetite, and she didn't seem to have any, either. Yet he was happy to be with Kevin, even though the child seemed inordinately shy.

"Is macaroni your favorite food, Kevin?"

Kevin shook his head while Amanda answered, "His favorite is chocolate ice cream. Maybe chocolate cake is a second favorite and then chicken drumsticks." Her answer was perfunctory, her thoughts still churning.

Glancing over the food on the table, Amanda could hardly eat. What kind of battle lay ahead of her? Was Kevin going to be one of those children she had seen on the television news and in the paper—a child who had two people battling over him while he was always pictured as crying and unhappy?

She was sick at the thought. Every time she looked into Jeb Stuart's brown eyes, she could see his determination, and every time he looked at Kevin, she could see his longing. He wanted his son.

That knowledge tore at her because at the time of Kevin's birth, when Cherie wanted Amanda to take the baby, Cherie had sworn Jeb hadn't wanted his child. Had he had a change of heart or was he telling her the truth—that he really hadn't known? Amanda suspected that he was telling the truth. He looked earnest enough.

She couldn't imagine having one of those horrible battles that hurt Kevin badly. She felt as if Jeb Stuart wanted to cut her heart out and take it with him. She realized he was staring at her, and she guessed he must have asked her a question.

"I'm sorry. What did you say?"

"I see a child's swing in your backyard. Will there be time before Kevin goes to bed to go outside with him and play?"

"Sure," she answered easily. "We're finished. As soon as I clean the kitchen, we'll go outside. Want to?'' she asked Kevin, and he nodded. He started to stand.

"Wait. What do you say?"

"May I be 'scused?"

"Yes, you may," she answered, and Kevin slid off his chair and ran to get his toys.

When she stood, Jeb Stuart rose also and picked up dishes. "I can clean up," she said.

"This is no trouble," he answered politely, and she thought how civil they were being to each other, yet what a sham it was. She knew he was doing it for Kevin's sake, just as she was.

In her small kitchen she could not avoid bumping against Jeb. Each time she was intensely conscious of the physical contact. Every nerve tingled. Jeb Stuart looked full of raw energy, and she wondered if he would make her as nervous if Kevin weren't the connection between them.

Making a rumbling noise like an imaginary motor, Kevin sat on the floor, playing with one of his toy cars. He was so little, too vulnerable. While she watched him, her eyes blurred. She couldn't give up her child! As pain came in waves, she fought a rising panic. Trying to gain control of her emotions, she didn't want to cry in front of Jeb Stuart. *I'm Kevin's legal mother.* But she had seen the pain in Jeb's eyes and she knew he was entitled to his son. She was losing Kevin! She felt queasy, as though she were going to lose the little she had eaten for dinner. She turned on the cold water and ran some over her hand, then patted the back of her neck and her forehead.

"Are you all right?"

His voice was quiet and deep and he was right beside her. She looked up into his inscrutable dark eyes and wondered if they were both headed for dreadful heartache. She feared that no one was going to win in this situation, least of all Kevin.

"I'm all right," she said stiffly, turning to blindly rinse a plate and place it in the dishwasher. A hand closed gently on her wrist. Feeling his touch to her toes, she looked up at him.

"Go outside with Kevin. I'll finish this and join you."

She didn't argue. After drying her hands, she took Kevin's hand and headed outside, thankful to escape her kitchen, which now seemed smaller than ever and filled with the electrifying presence of the most disturbing male she had ever encountered. She still tingled from that casual touch of his hand on her arm. At the kitchen door, she glanced back over her shoulder.

Jeb stood watching her, and the moment their gazes met, another lightning bolt of awareness streaked through her. His midnight eyes were riveting and sexy. She felt a raw edginess around him that she suspected she would have experienced even if Kevin had not been a factor in their relationship. As they gazed at each other, the moment stretched between them, tense, breathtaking, until she turned abruptly. Hurrying outside, she tried to catch her breath and ignore her racing heart.

When Jeb joined them, she was swinging Kevin, and the child was smiling. Jeb stood watching and she was grateful for his patience and caution around Kevin. She knew Kevin was shy, and he became even more withdrawn if someone forced attention on him.

Time seemed to stretch into aeons until they went inside. She bathed Kevin and tucked him into bed.

When she kissed him good-night, she held him close. He hugged her and then lay on his pillow. "Mama, who is Mr. Stuart?"

"He's a friend, Kevin," she answered slowly, wondering how to tell Kevin the truth. *He's your father and he's come to take you from me* ran through her mind while she looked into a pair of dark eyes so much like those of Jeb Stuart.

"I like it better when you don't have a friend here."

"You like it when Megan or Peg come over."

He thought this over and nodded. "I like Megan better than Mr. Stuart."

Amanda merely nodded and hugged Kevin again and fought tears because she didn't want to cry in front of him. As though he sensed something amiss, he clung to her. She kissed him again and tucked him in.

"One more story, please."

She relented and told him another story until his eyes closed and his breathing became deep. Reluctantly, she squared her shoulders, then tiptoed out of Kevin's room and closed the door behind her.

In the small family room, Jeb Stuart stood with his back to her, staring out a darkened window at the night. She knew he was lost in his thoughts because there was nothing to see outside.

"He's asleep."

Jeb turned around and studied her, flicking a swift glance over her that she felt as much as if he had brushed her body with his fingertips.

"Is he always so shy?"

She shrugged and crossed the room to sit down on the sofa, folding her legs beneath her. "He's shy, but he's even more shy with you because he's seldom been around men. He sees me and his nanny, his Sunday school teachers, my friends and, on rare occasions, my aunt, and they're all women."

She received another assessing gaze. "You're pretty," Jeb said.

"Thank you," she answered perfunctorily, because she suspected he was going somewhere with his remark, and her wariness increased. Even as her defenses rose, on another level, she was pleased by his assessment.

"You're too attractive to be single unless there's a good reason. I know this is a blunt question, but you and I are going to have to do some serious talking. Why haven't you married and had your own children?"

She raised her chin. It had been a long time now since she had thought about marriage, and having Kevin had taken most of the sting out of the question, because Kevin had helped her lose a lot of her feelings of inadequacy.

"Why haven't you remarried and had more children?" she shot back at him.

"I had one unhappy marriage, and I'm not ready to marry again. So back to my question—why haven't you married and had kids of your own?"

Like a lot of other people, she had secrets she didn't care to share. Jeb Stuart's question was personal, and she knew she could refuse to answer him or give him one of the two or three casual replies she had given on dates, but she saw no reason now to be anything except totally honest.

"I can't have children of my own," she replied, looking him squarely in the eye, feeling an old familiar pain.

Two

"Sorry. And I'm sorry to pry into your private life."

She nodded, appreciating his apology and fighting an urge to like him. "When I was engaged, my doctor discovered a tumor and I had to have surgery. I'm fine, except I won't ever be able to have children. My fiancé decided that I wasn't really a complete woman, and he broke our engagement."

As Jeb closed his eyes and looked as if he had received a blow, she could guess what was running through his mind. "That was one of the reasons I agreed to adopt Cherie's baby, but it has little to do with why I love Kevin so much now."

"But you'll be much less willing to give him up because of it."

She bristled and swung her legs to the floor, coming to her feet to face him. "I'm not willing to give him up now because he's my son! He's my son as much as if I had given birth to him. I got him when he was a day old. Cherie didn't even want to see him! She hated being pregnant. I love him because he's my baby and has been since he was born!"

Jeb rubbed his forehead. "Lord help us both," he mumbled, hearing her agony and watching tears stream unheeded down her face. He hurt, too, and he couldn't give up his son. "What do you want me to do? Walk out that door and forget that I have a son?"

They stared at each other, and he knew her emotions were as raw as his. She was shaking and white as snow again. She had a smattering of freckles across her nose, and when she became pale they stood out clearly. As she clutched her stomach and ran from the room, he felt as if he had just beaten her.

While he was alone, he paced the room and wondered whether he should just go and try to get back with her later, but that was only putting off what was inevitable. They were each going to have to give or else they would end up hurting Kevin, and Jeb didn't think she would want that any more than he did.

When she returned, she looked even more pale. She moved to the sofa and sat with her feet on the floor. She looked small and hurt and defiant and he felt like a bastard for what he was doing, but he wasn't going to give up his son to save Amanda Crockett's feelings. He pulled a chair to face her and sat down. "We'll have to work something out."

"I don't know anything about you."

"I grew up on a ranch in Saratoga County. I have three brothers—Cameron, a rancher, lives near here with his wife, Stella, on the family land. It's ironic that you left Houston and moved close to my family and home. My brother Selby and his wife, Jan, live in

El Paso. He's with the DEA. The youngest brother, Burke, leads wilderness treks. He and his wife, Alexa, have a home in Houston, so they're not far away."

"You were a paratrooper, you have a brother with the DEA and another who leads wilderness treks—your family is a little on the wild side."

He shrugged. "I'm settled now. I bought land southwest of here and I'm raising horses. I hoped to take Kevin there."

"You weren't a rancher when you were married to Cherie, were you? I thought she told me she had married someone who worked in Houston."

"I did. As soon as I graduated from Tech, I was hired as a salesman for a Houston feed company. After the second year I was promoted to district superintendent, then in another couple of years, director of marketing. That's when I was married to her. I couldn't have afforded Cherie before then." He looked away as if seeing his past, and she wondered if he was lost in memories and talking out loud. "When we met, Cherie was charming, seductive, adorable. As long as she got her way, she stayed charming, but when I quit work and wanted to become a rancher, that's when her true personality emerged. I was wildly in love with her when we married because she seemed to be everything a man could want."

"I can imagine," Amanda said quietly, knowing her beautiful cousin could be delightful as long as things went her way, but when they didn't, she could be dreadful.

"Why did you decide to become a rancher?"

Jeb shrugged. "The corporate world was not for me. I grew up on a ranch, too, and I wanted to get back to that life."

He studied her, and silence stretched tensely between them. "If you thought I had abandoned Kevin and Cherie, why did you cut all ties to your past and hide your tracks when you moved from Houston to Dallas?"

As she flushed and bit her lip and looked guilty, he wondered if she had been leading him on with an act. How much was she like Cherie? he wondered again.

"I guess deep down there was a part of me that doubted Cherie," Amanda said, so softly that he had to lean forward to hear her, yet leaning closer was a tactical error because he could smell her perfume, see her flawless skin, watch as her tongue slid slowly across her lower lip. His body heat rose and momentarily he lost awareness of anything except a desirable woman sitting inches away. He had to fight the urge to reach out and touch her.

She twisted a string from her cutoffs in her fingers. "I wanted to believe her when she said you didn't care and you had gone, but my cousin has never been a stickler for the truth. She tells things to suit herself. I was scared of just what's happening now. That someday the doorbell would ring and there would be Kevin's father—you—wanting him back." She looked Jeb in the eye. "Maybe I shouldn't have made it difficult for you to find us, but from all indications, you weren't a man I wanted to get to know."

"I suppose not, since I can take him from you."

"I don't think you can," she said coolly, and he realized she was pulling herself together more and more as they talked. "Cherie has gotten mixed up with people in the past that I didn't want to know. Her choice in men would never be mine. Sorry, that doesn't sound complimentary, but Cherie and I are very different."

"So I'm noticing," he remarked dryly. He wondered if she realized exactly how guilty she looked. But she was different from Cherie. Cherie was a charmer when she wanted something, flirting and using her feminine wiles to sweet-talk someone into doing what she wanted. He had been charmed completely, but marriage had brought reality and another side to Cherie that was far from charming. Cherie would never have been as forthright as Amanda.

Amanda caught another string on her cutoffs and twisted it back and forth between her thumb and forefinger. Otherwise, she looked quiet and composed. He watched her hand, noticing that her fingers were delicate and slender. She did not wear any rings and wore a simple watch with a leather strap circling her wrist.

"I suppose we're going to have to work something out to share him," she said stiffly, and each word sounded wrung from her in agony. "Unless you're still intent on going to court and trying to take him from me completely. If you do that, I'm going to fight you and we'll just end up hurting him."

"I agree."

She let out a long breath and closed her eyes. "Thank you!" she said. "We agree on that much. Kevin should come first."

"If he came first completely one of us would give him up."

She opened her eyes to look at him and he could see the speculation in them. "Maybe not. Maybe he needs a father as well as a mother. But I have to know how you'll be with him. There are things I don't approve of."

Jeb's temper flared and he leaned closer. "Lady, I'm his father. Whether you approve or not, I'll do what I think is best for my son. I won't abuse him, but I suspect I'll let him do things that you and that nanny and the other women in his life would be afraid to let him do. He acts scared of his shadow now."

"He's just shy," she said defensively. She studied him as if trying to figure him out. "Would you strike a child?"

"Never. It shouldn't ever be necessary." Green eyes searched his, and he gazed back steadfastly.

"I hope you're telling me the truth," she said. "Is there any way that you can prove to me that you knew nothing about Cherie's pregnancy? How do I know that you didn't abandon him and now that Cherie has a successful career, you've decided you want your son after all?"

"I can find the person who told me, and you can talk to her. It was Polly McQuarters. She knows I wasn't putting on an act. And what difference would it make to me whether Cherie's career is soaring? You've legally adopted her child."

"She's set money up in a trust for him."

"I don't need or want Cherie's money. I'll bring you records of my income and my net worth."

"You don't have to do that," Amanda said, rubbing her temples.

"I told you about my brothers. There's another family member I haven't mentioned—my mother."

"Kevin's grandmother," Amanda whispered, closing her eyes and experiencing a blow to her middle. A father and now another grandmother. She could feel her child slipping away from her, yet she knew she couldn't fight to shut those two important people out of his life. She opened her eyes to discover Jeb watching her intently.

"I haven't told Mom about her grandson yet. I want you and Kevin to meet her."

"Of course, Kevin should meet her." Amanda laced her fingers together. "It's a shock—to open the door and find Kevin's father and learn he has three uncles and a grandmother. Is there anyone else you haven't told me about?"

"Nope. My father's no longer living. My mother is Lila Stuart and she's raised four boys and she was a damned good mother. She lives in Elvira, a small town near my ranch and Cameron's. She's Elvira's mayor."

"How will I break this to Kevin? He's shy around men. Could you just start coming over and getting to know him and then I tell him?"

"I think it would be better to tell him from the start and then I get to know him. Either way it's a shock, but he's only three. Little kids accept life as it comes."

She caught her lower lip in her small white, teeth. As she gazed into space beyond him, Jeb studied her, thinking she must have been engaged to a real jerk. He thought of Cherie and he could see little resemblance between the cousins. Cherie was a blue-eyed blonde, drop-dead gorgeous, with a lush figure. Her cousin had a more earthy look with her riot of red hair and a smattering of freckles, but, in her own way, she was a beautiful woman. He pulled his train of thoughts away from her and focused on Kevin.

"What have you told Kevin about being adopted?"

"I've told him the truth, but he's only three and I don't think he cares or understands. I always tell him how much I wanted him and how much I love him."

"Can you be more specific about 'the truth'—what did you tell him about me?"

"I told him his mother had to give him up because she moved far away and that she's my cousin. He hasn't seemed to realize that he's never even seen her since the day he was born. I told him that his father was in the army and far away. And I told Kevin I wanted him badly and loved him with all my heart. It's pretty simplified, but he accepts that, and when he gets older and wants to know more, I figured I would explain more. At this point in his life, he doesn't seem to care."

"Sounds good enough," Jeb said, thinking over her answer. "What about Maude—Cherie's mother?"

"Kevin knows Aunt Maude is his grandmother, and she's seen him five or six times, but since she remarried and moved to California, she's out of touch and she doesn't seem deeply interested in him. She's more interested than Cherie is though, because she sends him birthday and Christmas presents and calls him once a year. At the time I adopted him, she went to court with me. Aunt Maude said I'd make a better mother than Cherie."

"I'm sure you do." He thought about the rest of the week. "Would you like to come out to my ranch tomorrow night and bring Kevin? I'll pick you up, take you out there for dinner and bring you home early so he can get to bed."

"Are you that close to the city?"

"It's a long drive—about an hour and a half—but I don't mind. I think we'd better start getting acquainted."

Nodding, she gave him another searching stare. "Are you dating anyone?"

"No, and I don't intend to marry again."

Her eyes widened in surprise and she shook her head. "You look like a man who likes women and vice versa."

"I do like women, but I don't want to get married. Or at least not for a long, long time. Maybe someday, because I'd like more children. I was a fool about Cherie and I don't ever want to go through all that pain again," he said, being completely honest with her because they were going to have to work something out. "Our marriage was wonderful for a time, but then it went really bad." Jeb stood. "I'll leave now and pick you up tomorrow evening. Is half past five too early?" he asked, knowing she got home before that time each day.

"That's fine," she said, standing and walking to the door with him. The top of her head came to his shoulder, and as he looked down at her, conflicting emotions warred in him. He didn't want to find her desirable. He wasn't happy that he wanted to touch her and soothe her and stop hurting her.

"We'll work it out. Kevin is the main consideration, and we'll just have to share him."

"I can do that," she said, but she sounded worried. "I want to know that you'll be good to him. I don't know anything about you except that you married Cherie and fathered Kevin."

"You and I will get to know each other." He hesitated. "Do you have a picture of Kevin I can have?"

"Yes," She left to return in minutes with a picture in a small frame. "I have a lot of pictures. Here's one you can take. I'll look for some more and give them to you tomorrow."

"Thanks."

They both looked at the picture of the smiling child. "He was two when that was taken," she said softly. Jeb noticed that when she talked about Kevin or to him, her tone filled with a special warmth. "He looks very much like you."

"Even I can see a resemblance," Jeb said. "There's no mistaking he's mine," he added grimly, knowing that Cherie hadn't been faithful to him. He glanced at Amanda. "Thanks for the picture."

"I have another copy of it in a scrapbook."

"I'll see you tomorrow evening."

She opened the door and he left, striding down the walk to his car. Jeb drove away, his emotions still churning. Nothing had gone the way he had imagined it would. Why hadn't he stopped to think how attached his son would be to his mother? He supposed hurt and anger got in the way of reason. He was going to have to share Kevin. It could be worse, and Amanda Crockett might be a very nice person. How much was she like her cousin? So far, damn little, or she wouldn't have taken Kevin in the first place.

The boy was too shy. Jeb hoped Kevin would get over his shyness. From the looks of it, he needed a man in his life. Jeb's thoughts shifted to Amanda Crockett and her broken engagement. He could hear the hurt in her voice and he knew why she had taken Kevin. She would fight to keep him because he would be the only child in her life. The ex-fiancé was a real jerk, Jeb thought again.

Amanda Crockett. Jeb thought about the statistics the detective had brought him about her: parents deceased, only child, no family except an aunt, Maude Whitaker, and a cousin, Cherie Webster, twenty-eight years old, an audiologist, no men in her life, attends church each week, a large circle of friends, a broken engagement two years after college. Now he knew more—her perfume, whose scent lingered in his memory, her tenderness with Kevin, her full red lips and long slender legs, and that mass of unruly red hair that had to mean there was a less serious side to her. He had to admit that when they touched or looked into each other's eyes, some fiery chemistry occurred. Sparks flew between them, and he suspected she didn't want to feel any attraction, either, but in those moments, he had seen the change in the depths of her eyes, the sultry intensity. He had felt a tightening in his body, a sheer physical response to nothing more than that exchange of looks.

"Forget it," he growled under his breath, trying to concentrate on the problems ahead.

When Jeb reached his ranch, a full moon spilled silver beams over the sprawling land. Feeling restless, he put the car next to his black pickup in the garage and began to walk, heading toward a pasture where some of his horses were. Two of them raised their heads and came to the fence near him. He stopped to talk to them, wishing he had brought an apple with him.

He moved on, knowing sleep wasn't going to come. How would they divide their time with Kevin? Half a month with one parent, half with the other? Weeks with one, weekends with the other? They would have to go to court, get lawyers involved and get it all settled legally, and he dreaded the entire process. The disruption in Kevin's life wouldn't endear him to a man who had been a complete stranger until half past five this afternoon.

Jeb swore, striding fast, turning and going back to

his house to get his running shoes. He switched on lights in his kitchen, which was big and roomy and had oak cabinets and stainless steel equipment. He thought about her tiny kitchen, remembering the times he had brushed against her. The lady sizzled effortlessly. She had an effect on him that set his pulse racing. *"Think about something else,"* he told himself.

In February he had bought the ranch—including the house, which was only four years old—from a family moving to Arizona, and he had spent little time doing anything to it. He strode down the hall to his big bedroom. He had a king-size bed, a desk and little else.

Pulling on his running shoes he left the house, breaking into a jog. His nerves were ragged, his emotions still churning. Cherie.

What a bitch she had been! Hiding her pregnancy from him and letting him walk out without knowing about his baby. Giving the baby away instantly. Jeb wondered why she hadn't had an abortion, knowing she would have no qualms about it. Maybe she didn't realize she was pregnant until it was too late to get one legally. He was still surprised that had stopped her, but then he remembered Cherie had told him about a good friend in high school who had died from a botched illegal abortion. Maybe fear had deterred her. His thoughts jumped to Kevin.

Tomorrow night he was bringing his son to the ranch! The thought of having Kevin cheered him immeasurably and he began to plan. He would barbecue a chicken and get extra drumsticks since Amanda said that was one of Kevin's favorite foods. He thought of Popcorn, a small, gentle pinto mare. Maybe Kevin would like to ride her.

Jeb yanked off his shirt and tossed it over a bush

beside the road where he could pick it up on his way back to the house. Sweat poured off him as his thoughts danced around the possibilities. This Friday he was riding in the county rodeo. Would Amanda let Kevin come and watch? Jeb suspected that Amanda was going to be less than enthusiastic to learn about his rodeoing.

How would they divide the time? Kevin was so accustomed to being with Amanda, would he resent having to be with Jeb?

Question after question swirled in Jeb's mind as he wondered about the future and went over the past few hours, from the moment he had first looked up and had seen Kevin standing in the doorway, staring sleepily at Amanda.

When his muscles were aching, Jeb jogged back home, knowing he was no closer to answers to his questions than he had been when he started. As he passed the barn and bunkhouse, a tall figure emerged from the shadows.

"Kinda late run, isn't it? How'd it go with your son?"

Jeb slowed and wiped sweat from his forehead with his shirt as he faced Jake Reiner, a fellow saddle bronc rider and horse trainer who was working with some new horses Jeb had bought. Jake was shirtless, wearing jeans, with his shaggy black hair hanging loosely on his shoulders.

"Not like I expected."

"When does anything go like you expect it to?" Jake drawled, lounging against the corral fence.

"I saw Kevin and talked to him a little. He's shy."

"He just doesn't know you. What about his mama?"

"I'm sure she hates me, but she's being cooperative, all things considered."

"Cooperative? When you left here, you sounded as if you would storm her house and bring your son home with you."

"Yeah, I know. I didn't stop to think what I'd do if she and my son were very close and he loved her deeply. Which seems to be the case. And she was told that I abandoned him. My ex-wife was a congenital liar."

"I've seen Cherie. Most men wouldn't care whether she was a congenital liar or a kleptomaniac. She is one beautiful woman. Is her cousin as beautiful?"

"Not in the same way."

"In other words, no." Jake shook his hair away from his face. "So where is your son?"

"I'm bringing them both to the ranch for supper tomorrow night. Want to join us?"

Jake grinned. "No, thank you. I'll leave the family gathering to you. She may look at you as possible marriage material."

"No, she won't. She was hurt by an ex-fiancé, and I think she's as uninterested in marriage as I am."

"If she is, she'd be the first female I've ever known. 'Course, I don't know her yet, but there's no such thing as a woman who doesn't want to marry."

Jeb laughed. "I should have come and talked to you instead of wearing myself down with all my running. Sure you don't want to join us for supper?"

"I'm sure. I'm not much for the domestic scene."

"If you change your mind, come to the house about seven. We should be here by then."

"Sure."

"How's Mercury?" Jake asked, referring to a wild two-year-old sorrel he had acquired.

"He's gentling down. Give me another day."

"Good. You can't sleep, either."

"Naw. Some nights are good, some aren't."

Jeb nodded. "See you," he said, wondering again about Jake's past and what demons plagued him. They had known each other from the rodeo circuit and then they had grown close when they had been together through scrapes in the army. Jake had saved Jeb's life once when Jeb had been shot rescuing an American diplomat who had been taken hostage in Colombia. Yet as close as they had become, there was always a part of Jake shut away from even his best friend. Whatever it was, that dark secret kept Jake on the move.

Jeb turned and jogged to the house, glad Jake was with him, because his friend was one of the best horse trainers in the country. Jake wouldn't put down roots anywhere long enough to really build up his reputation with horses. Jeb knew he couldn't worry about Jake's wanderlust—when Jake was ready to move on, he would move on.

Thinking about Amanda, Jeb showered and sprawled across his big bed, sleep as elusive as ever. Neither one of them was going to like dividing Kevin's time between them.

Jeb stared into the darkness, his thoughts racing over possibilities. What if he talked Amanda into moving to his ranch? With three bedrooms and three baths, there was plenty of room. During the day when she was at work, he would be as good as any nanny. While he worked, he could take Kevin with him, and if he couldn't, he had Mrs. Fletcher, who cooked and cleaned for him four days a week. She was a grandmother to ten kids, so she would be good to Kevin.

Jeb sat up and rubbed the back of his neck. He slid off the bed and began to pace around the room, switching on a bedside lamp as he thought about the idea of having Amanda Crockett share his house and his life. If they weren't married or dating, they probably wouldn't get in each other's way and they could share Kevin. His ranch house was sprawling and roomy. They would have to share their lives, but maybe they could manage it for Kevin. All week she would be gone during the day. He would be gone all day Saturday.

He shook his head at the thought of a woman underfoot all the time, and he guessed she would take an even less enthusiastic view about having him around. He sat on the edge of the bed and ran his fingers through his hair. Scratch that idea.

Half an hour later the idea came back to him and he mulled it over until the first rays of daylight grayed the night and spilled through the windows. He debated with himself about talking it over with her, but the thought of presenting the idea of them living together at his ranch gave him a queasy stomach. And he could imagine it would take her all of three seconds to kill the notion.

Tuesday evening he was again on Amanda's porch, his nerves jangling as he punched the doorbell. When she opened it and smiled, his pulse jumped. Revealing her even white teeth, her smile held so much warmth, he wanted to reach out and touch her.

"We're ready. Want to come in a moment while I get my purse and Kevin's things?"

"Sure," Jeb answered, and stepped inside. Without the screen door between them, he could get a better look at her. She motioned him toward the living room. "I'll get Kevin."

She wore a blue sundress that left her pale shoulders bare, and with her hair tied in a ponytail, she looked about twenty years old. She didn't have the breathtaking dazzle her blond cousin did, but she was incredibly good-looking.

"Hi, Kevin," Jeb said warmly when the little boy ran into the hall. Instantly Kevin slowed and looked up at Jeb.

"'Lo," he said. Amanda appeared and took his hand.

"I'll lock up, so go ahead and we'll be right out."

Jeb nodded and stepped outside to wait.

Amanda locked the house, switched on the alarm and took Kevin's hand. Dressed in a yellow sunsuit, Kevin clutched his blanket and a small book. As Amanda strolled toward the car, carrying Kevin's car seat, Jeb took it from her, their hands brushing. "I'll buckle this in."

Opening the door, Jeb put the car seat in the back, and Amanda went around to the other side to help.

"These aren't the easiest things to fasten in place," she said. When her hands brushed his again, a current shot through her, and she looked up to meet his gaze.

He was only inches away from her and his dark eyes bore into her. While he studied her, there was no denying that she felt something, yet she didn't believe in chemistry between men and women and she didn't want to feel any magic with this man.

With an effort she looked down at the seat and tried to catch her breath. Jeb had placed a strap in the wrong place and she took it from him, too aware of each contact with his warm fingers. She fastened the strap quickly. "Come on, Kevin."

He climbed into the seat and buckled it while she fastened her own belt and Jeb slid behind the wheel.

"My ranch is southwest of town. It's in the direction of your office."

"You know where I work? Oh, the detective you hired told you. I forgot for a minute. I suppose you know a lot about me."

"A lot of statistics. Where you work, where you go to church, that from all indications you're a good mother now."

"How could a detective decide I'm a good mom?"

"The statistics prove that—you take Kevin places on the weekend, see that he gets to visit his friends, have him on a waiting list for private school, that sort of stuff."

She turned slightly in the seat to look at Jeb. Dressed in a pale blue shirt and tight jeans, he was ruggedly handsome. He didn't seem as intimidating as he had during those first few hours, although he was blatantly masculine. She glanced at his long legs and then shifted her gaze outside.

"Will I see horses?" Kevin asked.

"Yes, you'll see horses, and we have a pond with ducks and baby ducklings," Jeb replied.

Kevin clapped his hands, and Amanda twisted in the seat and saw a sparkle in his dark eyes.

"He's going to have fun," she said solemnly, turning back to look at Jeb again. Was he going to win her son's affections swiftly? With a twinge of guilt, she wondered about jealousy, but she knew that, instead of jealousy, it was more fear that she felt, fear that she might lose Kevin completely. But that was ridiculous. Jeb might be very good for Kevin, but she didn't see how she could ever lose the bond she had with her son. She didn't know what his teen years would hold, but she didn't have to worry about them yet.

Later that evening the same fears and questions rose in her mind as she watched Jeb playing ball with Kevin in his backyard. Laughing, Kevin kicked a big red ball and it rolled along the ground, hit a rock and bounced beneath the rail fence. Jeb's long legs stretched out as he dashed to retrieve the ball. He jumped the fence easily, scooped up the ball and threw it back to Kevin. She watched Jeb leap back over the fence with ease and realized how strong and agile he was—how very male. Kevin needed a man in his life, and Jeb Stuart was going to be good for her son. That thought both tore at her and cheered her. But *she* didn't need a man in her life and she didn't want to find Jeb attractive or appealing or allow him to become an important part of her life.

Later, she perched on a fence and watched Kevin ride Jeb's gentle pinto mare. Next, they went to the pond to see the ducks, then walked back to the house where they had bowls of ice cream. Afterward, they moved to the family room and Kevin got out a coloring book Amanda had brought for him. In seconds he was asleep on the floor.

"It's time for us to go home," Amanda said. "I suppose we should have left when we finished the ice cream, but he was having a good time. You won him over tonight with the horseback ride and the ducks and playing ball with him. He's always loved to play ball."

"He's a great kid, but then I'm prejudiced."

"Yes, he is," she said, looking at Jeb. He was seated in a large leather chair, his booted feet propped on an ottoman in front of him. He appeared as relaxed as Kevin until she looked into his brown eyes. His determined gaze made her heart a skip a beat.

"Kevin is already asleep, so why don't we take this time to talk about what we're going to do. I thought about it all last night."

"So did I," she answered quietly, wondering if he had slept as little as she had. She wished she could put off ever making decisions about how she would share her son with this forceful stranger.

"Good. I'd like to tell him that I'm his father."

"Isn't it a little soon?"

"I don't think so. Kids accept life as it comes to them. I want him to know the truth. Can I come get both of you and bring you here for dinner again tomorrow night and tell him?"

She knew it was useless to tell him that he was rushing her. She gazed into his dark eyes and could see the steely determination, so she merely nodded. A knot burned her throat once again. She wished she could just gather up Kevin and run too far away for Jeb Stuart to find them. He was talking to her and she tried to focus on him.

"Kids adjust to whatever life hands them. You'll see."

She knew he was right, but she was having difficulty adjusting to anything concerning Jeb Stuart. There was, however, no point in postponing the inevitable. She nodded. "Fine."

Jeb stood with an easy grace. "I'll be right back. I have something to show you." He left, and she looked around the large family room that she could almost fit half her house into. The stone fireplace was immense. Bookshelves lined one wall—all empty. He said he had only lived here since February and he hadn't bought much furniture. That was an understatement. He had a large leather sofa and a big matching brown leather chair, two end tables, lamps and nothing else. The plank floor held a shine and everything looked neat and clean, but the room was so bare it looked as if he had moved in yesterday. She thought about her home, which was filled with pictures and books and plants, and wondered if he found it cluttered.

She was already saving money for Kevin's education and she didn't want to use her savings. In any case, she would have to hire a lawyer to help her with the legalities of whatever arrangement they worked out. She rubbed her temples. She had had a dull headache since yesterday when she had opened the door and looked up at Jeb.

Boot heels clicked on the polished floor and then he swept into the room and handed her a folder. "Here are records showing what I'm worth, a sort of résumé that tells as much as I could think of about me, the phone numbers of my brothers. You can talk to them and their wives."

"I suppose we need to know all this about each other," she said reluctantly. She ran her hands over the folder in her lap. "Shall I look at this now or take it home with me?"

"Go ahead and look and then take it with you. The information is yours. I'll put Kevin on a bed."

He picked him up easily, the tender look that came over Jeb's face making her breath catch, and in that moment she knew he would never hurt Kevin. She told herself not to go on hunches or feelings, but Jeb's expression was so filled with love and longing, it was painful to see.

He left the room, holding his son as if he carried fragile china, and her hurt mushroomed. For Kevin's sake, if Jeb were a loving, caring father, she had to share her son's life with him.

Reluctantly, she opened the folder and began to read, surprised by how much Jeb was worth. She thumbed through more pages, seeing the decorations he received while he was in the army. When he returned to the room, she glanced at him and met his shuttered gaze. Returning to her reading, she reached the information about his bronc riding and looked up at him.

"You're a champion saddle bronc rider."

"Yep. That's where some of the money came from, and I've invested it since I was eighteen years old."

"Bronc riding is dangerous, isn't it?"

"So's daily life."

Wondering about him, she lowered the folder and ran her fingers over its smooth cover. "Everyone has secrets. What are your secrets, Jeb?"

"What are yours?" he shot back.

"I've already told you mine. I don't usually tell new acquaintances about my physical limitations, that I can't have children."

"My secrets? My life's pretty open. I have regrets about my marriage. I regret that I was such a sucker for your cousin because that turned out to be one shallow marriage."

Jeb was studying her intently, and she had an uneasy feeling. Intuition suddenly told her that she didn't want to hear what he was going to say next. There was a speculative gleam in his eyes and that look of determination was back in his expression.

"I've been thinking about what we can do, and I have a proposal."

Three

Amanda mentally braced herself. Whatever was on his mind, he didn't look too happy about it himself. "Let's hear your idea."

"I've been trying to think how we can divide up the time." He rested his feet on the floor and propped his elbows on his knees. "Now, hear me out, okay?"

"Sure," she said, her gloomy feelings deepening.

"You said you don't date and you don't expect to marry. I told you I didn't want to marry again for a long time, if ever. I don't like the idea of taking Kevin on weekends, while you have him all week or vice versa or anything like that. If we have to, okay, but I had another idea. Why don't you and Kevin move in here?"

"On your ranch?" Stunned, Amanda stared at him. She almost laughed out loud, except he was so earnest and her son's future was at stake.

"Just listen," Jeb said quietly. "This isn't impossibly far from your work. I have a housekeeper, Mrs. Fletcher, who is a grandmother. She's good with kids and she cooks and cleans for me four days a week. She could be a nanny if I need one, but most days when I work, I could keep Kevin with me. We could share our lives with him so much better."

"I'm sorry, but that's out of the question!"

"Why? You think about it a little. We wouldn't have to divide up the time between us—"

"We can't live here together! I'm sorry, but I'm very old-fashioned about some things."

"We wouldn't be living together in a sexual way. It's like living in the same apartment complex."

"I don't think so," she said, beginning to wonder about his mind. "The world would think we were sleeping together," she said, her nerves jangling at even saying the words. "You know that's what everyone would think."

"Who cares?"

"I care. And I care for Kevin's sake," she said, and Jeb looked startled, as if it hadn't occurred to him that the arrangement might not be the best for Kevin. "I don't want to do that. And suppose you have a date and bring her home for the night. What would you do—introduce me as the mother of your child and a woman who just happens to live here, but oh please, ignore her?"

Suddenly a flicker of amusement danced in his dark eyes and her heart lurched because it made him even more appealing.

"I haven't had a date I wanted to bring home with me in a long time."

"That doesn't mean you won't in the future. I'm

sorry, but it's out of the question, and I think you would have major regrets. You'll fall in love again and marry again. Men like you don't live alone."

The moment the words were out of her mouth she wanted to yank them back, and a flush burned her face. He tilted his head, his dark eyes watching her intently, and something changed in their depths. Her half-dozen words had instantly charged the atmosphere with electricity.

"Men *like me*—now, what do you mean by that?" he drawled, his voice lowering to a husky, sexy level.

She looked away because she didn't want to look into his eyes, which seemed to see too much already. "You're an appealing man," she admitted swiftly, the words almost running together, "and I suspect women are easily attracted to you, in spite of your 'not having a date you wanted to bring home' lately. That will change."

Silence stretched until she was compelled to look around. He was sitting still as a statue, studying her as intently as ever.

"Maybe you and I should try dating."

She did laugh then, and his eyebrows arched. "I don't think so! Neither of us wants that."

"We might fall in love," he said, a sparkle dancing in his eyes.

Now he was flirting, and she experienced a bubble of excitement she hadn't known in a long time. "That's impossible. I don't want to fall in love. You don't want to, either. Besides, if you married again, you'd want another child, wouldn't you?"

The sparkle in his eyes vanished and he stood, crossing the room to her to pull her to her feet. The moment he touched her, tension crackled between them. While his hands rested on her shoulders, he gazed at her solemnly.

"Don't sell yourself short. You adopted one child. You can adopt two."

"Don't give me your sympathy," she snapped, too aware of him and too aware of her racing pulse.

"I'm not, Amanda," he said softly, in a deep voice. He was only inches away and his gaze was locked with hers. Her pulse raced and then her breath caught when his gaze lowered to her mouth. His hands slid slowly down her back.

"Don't complicate our lives," she whispered.

"I'm not. How long since your last date?"

She knew she should move away, but she was rooted to the spot, unable to do anything. Could he hear her thudding heart? Did he know the effect he was having on her? She suspected he knew full well.

"Too long to remember," she whispered, an inner voice screaming to move and stop him.

"Same here," he said, although she didn't believe him.

"Don't lie to me, Jeb," she whispered. He leaned down, and she thought she would faint. How could he have this devastating effect on her? Was it because she was so incredibly vulnerable? Was she that lonely and hadn't realized it?

"I'm not lying. I won't lie to you." Watching her intently, he leaned closer.

His lips brushed hers lightly and time stopped. She closed her eyes and inhaled, her lips parting as she swayed. His hands tightened on her waist. *Stop him, stop him* came the voice of wisdom. Was he doing this just to win her over to his way of doing things? Did he have a hidden agenda, or did he just want to kiss her?

His lips moved slowly, so slowly over hers, and she wanted to tighten her arms around his neck and kiss him back, but she knew she shouldn't.

"Oh, don't," she whispered against his mouth.

"Shh, Amanda." He tightened his arms around her, pulling her hard against him, leaning over her to cover her mouth with his. He opened her mouth and his tongue stroked hers and a wave of desire washed through her.

Heat flared in her, desire awakening swiftly. Her hands flew to his arms and she felt his muscles and his smooth skin. He laced his fingers in her hair while his other arm tightened around her waist and he leaned over her, his kiss deepening and driving all thought and caution from her mind. She wound her arms around his neck, feeling the textures and strength of him, smelling soap and aftershave, feeling his heart pound with hers. He was at once danger and desire, awesome strength and sexy confidence. For how many breath-stopping moments did she kiss him back?

Finally, she pushed against him. He released her at once and she gazed up at him. He looked as dazed as she felt, and she attributed their reactions to the fact that neither of them had dated in a long time. He was looking at her as though she were the first woman he had ever seen in his life.

"We shouldn't kiss," she said in little more than a whisper. "Sex will only complicate a situation already too complicated."

"It wasn't sex," he said in a husky voice as his fingers drifted lightly over her shoulder. "It was only a kiss. You and I are both old enough to kiss without the world changing."

She turned away from him to put some distance between them and to keep him from seeing too much in her expression. It hadn't been only a kiss, she thought. It hadn't been like any kiss she'd ever had before. Instantly she tried to ignore that realization and shifted her thoughts to Kevin. "We should go home."

"Don't get your feathers in a ruffle," Jeb said easily. "Sit down and we'll talk."

"We're not moving in here."

"All right. What do you suggest? Shall we get our lawyers together and see what they can hammer out?"

"I don't like that idea, either."

"Nor do I."

Silence stretched between them, and he waved his hand. "Sit down and we'll discuss what we can do."

She sat on the sofa, kicked off her shoes and placed her legs beneath her, too aware that he was watching her every move. "I don't know what's customary in divorce settlements. I have a friend whose children stay with their father two weekends out of every month."

"I want to see Kevin more than two weekends." Jeb crossed the room and sat on the other end of the sofa, facing her. She drew a deep breath, feeling that he was too close. Her pulse quickened, and she tried to focus on what to do about dividing their time with Kevin.

"I want to see him grow up, teach him things, be with him like tonight."

"If you and Cherie had stayed married, you wouldn't have seen him often. You would've been away in the army."

"No, I wouldn't have. I would never have gone into the army if I'd known. I was running away from a failed marriage, from hurt, maybe from myself. Now I'm back home. I know what I want to do with my life, and I want my son."

She had a feeling they were going to end up in court and she hated the thought. "I don't want to fight you over this."

"I don't want you to." He reached over to catch her hand, holding it casually and looking at her fingers as if he had never seen fingers before. "You don't wear much jewelry."

She shrugged, aware of his fingers running lightly over her knuckles, causing tingles.

"I want Kevin to meet my mother as soon as possible. How about all of us going to the rodeo Friday night?"

"You're rushing everything."

"Why postpone life? I want to know my son, and my mother is going to be overjoyed. How about Friday, Amanda?"

"Very well. We'll go to the rodeo with you."

"Good. I'm riding in the saddle bronc event, so I won't be sitting with you part of the time."

"That's all right. I'm sure Kevin will like seeing a rodeo. I've never been to one, either."

"This will be a fun one. I've been thinking about our situation and there's something else I'd like to do. Instead of having a nanny with Kevin next week while you work, let me come get him and bring him out here. I'll pick him up and I'll bring him home. You'll be with him as much as ever, and I'll get to be with him a lot. Surely, you can give me the time with him that you let the nanny have."

Turning cold with concern, she pulled her hand away from his. "I don't know you that well. Give me some time. I don't have a detective to find out everything about you, and I can't just turn Kevin over to a stranger."

"If I take you to court, you'll have to. I'll wait to bring him out here without you, but not too long. He's old enough to tell you if he doesn't like it here."

She bristled at his answer. "You know as well as I do that any adult can frighten a small child enough that he won't tell what the adult does."

"I'm not abusive to small children," Jeb said quietly. "You're scared I'm some kind of monster. Call my brothers, ask them if I can be trusted."

"I don't think that would prove much."

"All right, let me bring the nanny out here. She can hang out with us."

Suddenly Amanda had to laugh at the thought of Caitlin Shore having to follow a cowboy around all day. Then she thought of his sex appeal and knew that Caitlin probably wouldn't mind at all.

"What's funny?"

"Caitlin Shore is my nanny, and I laughed at the thought of her following you around, but then, knowing Caitlin, she'd probably enjoy it because she's sort of man-crazy."

"I will not make a pass at your nanny. No problems there."

"Maybe not for you. I'll think about it." She studied him. "Not all men would be this interested in a child they had known nothing about. I'm surprised you are. You don't look like the type to be wild about a baby."

"He's my son. That's important. Our family was

important to all of us. My dad died when I was nineteen, but Mom held us all together. There are four boys and we have aunts and uncles and cousins. We are a close family and all of us think family is the mainstay of life." He ran his fingers across her knuckles.

"Jeb—"

"There's a law against touching?"

"No law, but I still don't think it's wise. I told you, we have enough complications."

"A little harmless flirting, a few harmless kisses won't complicate anything," he said in that sexy, husky voice that was as soft as melted butter.

"Flirting, kissing, you want me to move in with you. You know it can get terribly complicated. I had a broken engagement and you have a broken marriage. I don't want another heartbreak."

"Scared of falling in love with me?" he asked softly.

She knew he was teasing because the sparkle was back in his dark eyes, but he was taking them into dangerous waters. "You're flirting again, and I think it is definitely time to go home."

"Whatever the lady wants," he said, standing when she did. "I'll get Kevin," he said, and left the room.

She watched him walk away, her gaze drifting down over his broad shoulders and trim hips and long legs. That had been some kiss, and flirting with him was more fun than she'd had in a long time. She shouldn't even think about it. Or about his offer to move to his ranch. Yet she had to think about how they would divide their time with Kevin.

When he returned with Kevin curled in his arms, she knew she was going to have to guard her heart because this man was getting past her defenses in ways that no other man ever had.

If Jeb was this crazy about a son he had never seen until yesterday, he would want more children. For an instant the old feelings of inadequacy taunted her, but she had long practice in dealing with them.

She picked up her purse, gathered Kevin's things and went out with Jeb. She waited in the pickup with her sleeping son while Jeb locked up his house and came back. As she watched him stride toward her, his long legs eating up the ground, she remembered his mouth on hers. What had been his motive in kissing her? He was bound to realize the effect he had on her. Was he just doing it to charm her into getting his own way?

As they drove away, she turned slightly to look at him, seeing the illumination from the dash highlight his prominent cheekbones and throw his cheeks in shadows. "I suppose we've made progress. We got along better tonight than last night."

"What about a month with me and a month with you?"

"No. I couldn't bear a whole month without seeing him and that's too disruptive for him. What happens when he falls and gets hurt or gets sick and wants me to hold him?"

"He may get where he's satisfied to have me around."

"Maybe, but he won't right away."

They were slipping back into the clash of wills, and she couldn't stop it. She'd had fun sometimes tonight, but there was no forgetting that she wanted her son with her and Jeb wanted Kevin with him. No matter how much he had them out to his place and how civil they were to each other, she suspected they were going to end up in court battling, and it depressed her to think of that.

As they drove home, she wondered if Jeb was as tense and worried as she was. Even though he hadn't acted too concerned this evening, she knew he was. And while he seemed trustworthy, she couldn't bring herself to trust him yet with Kevin.

At her house, he carried Kevin to his room. As she watched him go ahead of her, her heart lurched at the care with which he placed Kevin in bed. They looked so right together. He pulled off Kevin's shoes and socks.

"He's all right dressed the way he is. If he stirs, I'll get him into his pajamas," she said.

Jeb brushed a lock of hair away from Kevin's forehead and she turned away, knowing she couldn't be soft or too sympathetic because Kevin's happiness was at stake.

She went to the front door and held it open for Jake. Watching her in that hawklike way he had, he paused in front of her and ran his finger along her jaw. "Don't look so worried. We'll work out something that we can both live with. We both want Kevin to be happy, and I know he needs his mother."

She nodded. Jeb bent and brushed her cheek with a kiss. "Stop worrying," he repeated. "We'll work it out."

Then he was gone, striding away. She hadn't thanked him for the dinner or the evening, yet she couldn't bring herself to call thanks to him. She had a knot in her throat and tears in her eyes. She suspected that she was losing Kevin. Jeb Stuart had enough money and resources to fight a tough court battle. He was the blood father and he had rights.

Amanda swiped at her eyes as she locked up, then, after checking on Kevin, she went to her room. She remembered standing in Jeb's arms, kissing him. She didn't want to remember, but she did in total clarity, her lips tingling. His kiss had been devastating. "Don't fall in love with him," she whispered.

She wondered whether he even remembered their kiss.

Wednesday evening Jeb's nerves were taut even when he played with Kevin after supper. They kicked a ball back and forth, and he was aware that Kevin was more talkative with him. He had hung a child's swing on a limb of a tall elm, and later, he sat and watched Amanda swing Kevin. Tonight she wore a red sundress and sandals and had her hair piled on top of her head. She looked even more appealing than she had last night. He wanted to pull the combs out of her hair, let its silky mass fall over her shoulders and run his fingers through it.

All day long he had looked forward to having Kevin at the ranch again, but he had to admit to himself that he had looked forward to another evening with Amanda. Was she getting to him because he was lonesome? Or because she was part of Kevin's life? Or simply because she was an attractive, sexy woman he found interesting?

He wasn't happy about any of the reasons, but he did like having her around and he liked watching her and he wanted to kiss her again. *Cool it,* he told himself. She was right—they should avoid complications, but last night he hadn't been able to resist kissing her.

He had passed it off to her as nothing spectacular, but that hadn't been the truth. Her kiss had ruined his sleep and was tormenting him now. That and the prospect of telling Kevin the truth. How would the child react? Would he hate Jeb for interfering in his life?

It wasn't until dusk had fallen and Kevin was sprawled on the glider on the porch that Jeb scooped the child up and sat down with him on his lap. As Jeb's insides knotted, he took a deep breath. "Kevin, your mother and I have something to tell you."

Kevin glanced at her and looked at Jeb expectantly.

"Would you like to be alone with Kevin?" Amanda asked, standing and moving toward the back door.

"Stay out here with us. I want you here," Jeb said.

Surprised that he wanted her present, she sat down near them and watched Jeb smooth locks of Kevin's hair back from his forehead. All last night and today she had wondered how Kevin would take the news. Every time father and son were together, she knew this was right and good for Kevin, even if it meant that she was losing him a little. She looked at the two of them together—Kevin in his rumpled T-shirt and faded cutoffs, Jeb in a cotton shirt and jeans. The cowboy and his secret son. She should have known someone would tell Jeb about his baby.

"I love you, Kevin," Jeb said in a husky voice

"I love you, too," Kevin replied politely, and Amanda wondered what he really thought about Jeb.

"Kevin, I've been away in the army and now I'm back home to stay, and I came home to find my little boy."

"You have a little boy?"

"Yes, I do, and I love him very much."

Kevin nodded solemnly, and Amanda could hear the

catch in Jeb's throat and knew he was having trouble controlling his emotions. She laced her fingers together tightly and waited.

"Kevin, I have a surprise for you," Jeb said. His voice cracked and he paused. Amanda saw that his eyes were red, and she felt like an intruder, yet he had asked her to stay.

"I'm your daddy, son, and you're my little boy."

"You're my daddy?" Kevin asked, his eyes widening. When he looked at Amanda, she nodded her head.

"Yes, he's your daddy, Kevin."

Kevin looked at Jeb and then he broke into a smile and Jeb hugged him. When Jeb swiped at his eyes, Amanda stood and walked away, giving them privacy, knowing Jeb would pull himself together swiftly.

"I love you, Kevin," Jeb repeated softly, but Amanda heard him.

"Now I have a mommy and a daddy, don't I?"

A knot burned her throat because she could feel Kevin slipping from her. She tried to reassure herself that she wouldn't lose him and that he would gain from having a loving father.

When she heard Jeb laugh, she knew he was back in control of his emotions, so she returned to her chair, feeling relieved that Kevin had accepted Jeb's announcement so easily.

"Yes, indeed you do. A mommy and daddy to be here always for you."

"Will we all live here together now?" Kevin asked, and Jeb glanced at her before smiling at Kevin. "That's something your mother and I haven't worked out. We're talking about it."

"Are you going to leave again?"

"No. I'm here to stay. I'll always be here for you, Kevin," Jeb said solemnly, and Amanda's heart lurched. This man would forever be part of their lives. What kind of arrangement could they possibly work out that would avoid hurting Kevin?

"Kevin, there's one more thing I want to tell you. I have a family, too, and since you're my little boy they're your family now. My mother is your grandmother. My three brothers are your uncles."

Kevin thought that over for a few quiet minutes. "Am I going to see them?"

"Yes, you will. Particularly your grandmother. She wants to see you badly. Okay?"

"Okay," he repeated solemnly, glancing again at Amanda. Amanda had to admit that Jeb imparted all the facts to Kevin in a quiet, forthright manner the child seemed to accept. He looked pleased to have a daddy. "Are we going to meet tonight?"

"No, but we will Friday night. I'm going to take you to a rodeo and she'll be there. Okay?"

"What's a rodeo?"

"Mostly people riding horses."

Kevin nodded. "Will you read me a story?"

"Sure. Get your book."

Kevin scrambled to get several books they had brought, and the moment the door slapped shut behind him Jeb glanced at Amanda.

"He took it pretty well. He seems happy to learn he has a dad."

"I'm sure he is. Every little kid wants a dad. You were good in breaking the news to him."

"Thanks. He just accepted it with no questions."

"That's because of his age and because you've won him over."

"That's because I love him and he knows it."

They gazed at each other and she knew they both wanted to keep Kevin. Once again she could feel the silent clash of wills, and she couldn't bear to think about giving Kevin up part of the time to this man who was all but a stranger. They sat in an uneasy silence until Kevin dashed back and climbed into Jeb's lap.

Jeb read three little books, and then Amanda stood and announced that it was bedtime even for a summer night in the country.

Jeb drove them home and Kevin was asleep fifteen minutes into the drive. Riding in silence, Amanda looked at moonlight splashing over the sprawling land. Her son's life was changing—Jeb's cowboy influence was going to be strong.

"Penny for your thoughts," Jeb said quietly.

"I'm just thinking about the influence you'll be in Kevin's life. This is all new."

"That doesn't mean it's bad."

She merely nodded and looked out the car window again, feeling hot tears sting her eyes. They would go out again Friday night and Kevin would meet his other grandmother.

"You're worrying."

"Of course I'm worrying. You've turned my life upside down!"

"It hasn't been bad, though, has it?"

"Not altogether," she said stiffly, and lapsed into another stony silence, wishing again she could run away with Kevin but knowing that was impossible.

On Friday night, her pulse began to race as she opened her door and faced Jeb. He was dressed in a deep blue western shirt, jeans and boots and his broad-brimmed black hat. In his hands was a box.

"Come in," she said, stepping back, her heart skipping beats the moment she looked into his eyes. He was handsome, exciting, and she was more on edge than ever because she had mixed feelings about the evening.

Kevin came in and stood shyly in the doorway.

"Hi, Kevin," Jeb said easily, and Kevin smiled at him.

"Hi."

"I brought you a present," Jeb said, handing Kevin the large box.

Kevin took it and looked at Amanda. "Thank you," he answered politely, and Amanda wondered whether Jeb was going to try to bribe his way into Kevin's affections, but then she realized that was unfair because this was his first gift.

"Want to open the box, Kevin, and see what you have?" she asked, knowing Kevin was shy and still not at ease instantly around Jeb.

Kevin nodded and sat down on the floor to take the lid off the box. He pulled out a miniature broad-brimmed black western hat like the one Jeb was wearing, and a grin spread over his face.

"What do you say?" Amanda reminded him.

"Thank you," Kevin said politely, running his small fingers over the hat.

"Put it on," Amanda said, once again having mixed feelings and telling herself it was only a hat and not a new way of life.

Kevin put the hat on his head and smiled at her. He wore black slacks and a blue cotton shirt, and now, with the hat, he looked like a little cowboy.

"Go look in the mirror," she said to him, and he ran off.

"I hope you don't mind, but I thought he'd like to wear it tonight."

"He'll love it."

Jeb nodded and touched her red collar. "You look good in jeans. You look pretty."

"Thank you," she answered, warming, yet feeling that constant caution around him because she didn't know whether he was sincere or merely trying to charm her into accepting him.

"Are you ready to go? Mom checked into the hotel at about five."

"Why didn't she stay with you and ride in with you?"

"She's independent and she likes to do her own thing."

Amanda suspected that Lila Stuart's son had inherited the same traits. "Let me get Kevin and my things."

They drove to a large hotel in downtown Fort Worth and all went inside. Amanda couldn't conjure up an image in her mind of Jeb's mother. He was too tall, too male and forceful. So she was totally unprepared for the woman who came strolling toward them.

Four

Tall, black-haired, with a short, casual hairdo that loosely framed her face, Lila Stuart looked forty years old and had as much commanding presence as her son.

"That's your mother?"

"Yeah. Mom looks younger than she is."

"She looks like your older sister!"

Then she was close, smiling at Jeb, and Amanda was astounded that Mrs. Stuart hadn't remarried after the death of Jeb's father. She was a stunning woman and couldn't fit any grandmotherly image Amanda knew.

"Mom, meet Amanda Crockett. Amanda, this is my mother, Lila Stuart."

"How do you do," Amanda said, trying to not sound cold or angry.

"I can't tell you how much this means to me," Lila Stuart said, taking Amanda's hand. "I hope getting to know Jeb and our side of the family hasn't been too hard on you, but for me it's fantastic to discover I have a grandson," she said.

"Kevin, this is my mother and your grandmother, Lila Stuart. Mom, this is Kevin."

"Kevin, I'm so glad to meet you," she said warmly, making no move toward him.

When he stared at Lila Stuart shyly, Amanda prompted, "Say thank you, Kevin."

"Thank you."

"Let's go eat and we can talk," Jeb said, steering them toward the door.

Amanda soon realized that she was dealing with a woman who knew boys. Lila Stuart ignored Kevin until halfway through dinner, then as they ate, she began to talk quietly to him, and in minutes, he was telling her about his toys.

After eating, Jeb drove them to a sprawling building that held the rodeo. When they walked through the large building both Jeb and his mother constantly saw people they knew and paused to say hello and introduce Kevin and her. She realized that the Stuarts were friendly, outgoing charmers who had a wide circle of acquaintances. They would broaden Kevin's life.

Jeb had seats for them in a box along the front row, and while they had the best view of the arena, Amanda wished they were farther away from the action. The place smelled of sawdust and horses. Entering the box, she held Kevin's hand as she moved to the fourth seat in the row, next to the side of their box. Kevin sat beside her and bounced in his seat with excitement. Lila sat next to him with Jeb at the opposite end. Even with the distance between them, Amanda was constantly aware of him.

While they waited for the rodeo to start, Lila pulled a coloring book and crayons from her purse, and in seconds, Kevin scooted closer to her. Then Jeb stood and lifted Kevin into his seat and hunkered down to talk to Kevin about his coloring while Lila leaned over him, too. In minutes Kevin was happily coloring with Lila commenting on his efforts while Jeb came around and swung his long legs over the row to drop down in Kevin's vacated seat next to Amanda.

"Your mother's a charmer, too," Amanda said without thinking as she watched her son talking to his grandmother.

"Too?" Jeb asked, turning to study her.

She faced him. "You know you charm people," she said, amused by his innocent act.

"I didn't know it in this case. I'm glad to hear that you think so," he said, leaning forward with his elbows on his knees, effectively putting his back to his mother and Kevin and enclosing Amanda in a very private space, in spite of being surrounded by people.

"Don't push your luck."

"I'm not pushing anything," he drawled. "I'm sitting here doing nothing."

"You're flirting and getting your way. Look what you've done in a week. Kevin has a father and a grandmother and a whole new family. That's pushing. You've done everything—pushing, flirting, kissing."

"You've done a little of all that yourself."

"Sometimes those things make life more fun," she said in a suggestive voice, unable to resist.

He grinned, revealing even white teeth and looking incredibly appealing. "Aah," he said, "here's a good side to you I haven't seen."

"And the side to me you have seen was bad?" she

asked, teasing him and enjoying the banter and knowing it was like playing with a tiger.

"You don't have a bad side," he drawled, his gaze drifting down to her waist and back up to meet her eyes. "I should have said it's just another intriguing facet to you—one I'm going to explore," he said, his husky voice flowing over her in its own caress. He stroked his finger along her forearm and across her knuckles, and fiery tingles danced over her nerves.

"We'll both have some exploring to do," she said softly, letting her gaze rest on his mouth and wanting him to kiss her again. She was playing with danger and she knew she should stop. Although flirting with him was fun, she suspected that this was not a man to toss idle challenges to. Not unless she wanted him to act on them. Yet, at the moment, they weren't idle; she did want his kiss. She didn't understand her own reactions to him, except that she couldn't remember how long it had been since she had done something reckless, something purely for herself alone.

"Actually, I never dreamed it would be fun to flirt with Kevin's mommy, but it is. You blush easily, you know."

"I know that. And you know which buttons to push to get the reaction you want."

"I hope so," he said, lowering his voice. "It's fun to discover which buttons I get to push and play with," he drawled.

"You can't stop flirting, can you?" she asked, smiling at him, yet feeling her pulse pound with his remarks and the velvety voice that was like a warm caress.

"Not with you. You bring all this out in me."

"And every other female under thirty doesn't? Oh, please!" she exclaimed, laughing softly.

"No, they don't," he said flatly.

"I don't believe that for a minute. Now, behave yourself and put Kevin back in this seat between us. How did we all get moved around like this, anyway?"

Jeb grinned at her. "Around you, I can't behave."

"You're going to be good tonight."

"Now you've given me a challenge."

While she gazed into his dancing eyes, her pulse drummed. How long since she had had anything like this in her life? Since any man had made her feel desirable? "When you and I flirt, I feel as if I'm toying with a tiger."

His brow arched wickedly and his eyes sparkled. "Maybe there's a little excitement in living dangerously."

"My life is quiet and peaceful and I don't need any excitement."

"Uh-huh," he drawled. "I think I want to see how you like excitement. I can't help but wonder just how you'd react. My imagination just runs away with me," he said softly, and she knew he wasn't talking about excitement at all, but about making love. Her pulse skittered and she was giddy from his flirting, yet it was a dangerous pastime for both of them.

"Imagine all you want because that's all you're going to do." Why was she flirting right back with him? Yet she knew why—it was dangerous and it was fun and he was irresistible.

"Another big challenge. Maybe and maybe not. The evening's far from over, and I won't forget," he said, brushing her hand lightly with his fingers. It was the slightest, most casual touch, yet the contact with him was searing, and her breath caught.

She stood and leaned over to look at Kevin's coloring. "That's great, Kevin. Come here and let me see your picture."

Kevin came immediately, proud to show his artwork, and she sat back down, touching the arm of Jeb's chair. "You sit here, Kevin, and Jeb can move over where you were. Then you'll be between your grandmother and me and we can both watch you draw."

Jeb gave her a mocking smile and moved easily. When he stood, his hip was at her eye level, and for an instant, she was intensely aware of his tight jeans and long leg only inches away. Even after he sat down at the end of the row with Kevin and Lila between them, Amanda was still acutely aware of him.

The rodeo started with a parade of men and women mounted on sleek, prancing horses, and Lila Stuart slipped the crayons and coloring book back into her purse as Kevin scooted to Jeb's lap to watch everything.

Jeb sat with them through the calf-roping event and the barrel racing. When he left them, Lila Stuart leaned across the empty seat between them to talk to Amanda.

"I want to thank you for the way you're sharing your baby with us," she said quietly. "I can't tell you how fantastic it is to suddenly learn that I'm a grandmother. I had about given up on my boys, but now—this is truly wonderful and I'm grateful for any time I get with Kevin. He's adorable and I know this has all been hard on you."

"I'll have to admit Jeb's appearance was a shock."

"Jeb can be forceful and very determined to get his

way. It looks as if you're holding your own, though. He's my oldest and has a tendency to take charge because, with three little brothers, he had to take charge at home while they grew up."

"We're trying to work things out," Amanda said.

"I know you are, and everyone wants what's best for Kevin. If I can ever keep him just for an hour or two while you go out—I would absolutely love it," Lila said, looking at Kevin. "Anytime I can. Just call me."

"Thanks, but I imagine your life is pretty busy as it is."

"Being mayor of Elvira isn't nearly as important as being a grandmother. I'll come if you call. I would love it."

"I'll take you up on that sometime," Amanda said, unable to resist the mother any more than she had resisted the son. Lila Stuart was warm, understanding and trying to cooperate.

Then Amanda's attention shifted to the arena as she heard Jeb's name announced and saw him climb into a chute and slip into the saddle. Breathlessly, Amanda watched, her fingers knotted together as Jeb's horse leaped out of the chute and seemed to land stiff-legged on springs to bounce up again.

Man and horse fought a wild contest, the horse bucking and kicking, Jeb hanging on. At the first buck Jeb's hat flew off. Amanda was torn between wanting to close her eyes and a fascination that kept her gaze glued on him. When the buzzer sounded, he swung his leg across the horse and jumped to the ground, landing like a cat on both feet and striding away while cowboys corralled his horse. Grabbing up his hat, Jeb slapped it against his leg to shake off the dust. Then he combed his fingers through his disheveled hair and set his hat on his head.

As Jeb strode across the arena toward them, her pulse raced. Kevin was clapping and jumping up and down. She hadn't seen him that exuberant in a long time.

More than ever, vitality and strength radiated from the tall cowboy, and desire scalded Amanda as her gaze flicked down his long, lean frame.

Jeb was a new factor in her life, and he was a dangerous one because he flirted and charmed and he could break her heart easily. And was he sincere? Or was he being so appealing to get what he wanted from her—to take Kevin? Was she being taken in by a smooth-talking charmer?

He seemed physically fearless, a daredevil cowboy who wanted her most prized possession, and she knew she had to guard against losing not only Kevin, but her heart.

When the event was over, Jeb was announced the winner.

"Congratulations," Amanda said. "Another win."

"This time. Jake isn't here tonight. When he competes, I have a tougher time."

"Jake is a bronc rider?"

"Yep. That's how we first met when we were teens."

"You have a wild streak, Jeb."

"I'm beginning to suspect that you do, too," he said, touching her hair lightly.

She smiled at him and turned to watch the next event.

They enjoyed the rodeo, but Amanda was too aware of Jeb, who had regained his seat beside her and continued to flirt the rest of the evening. After the rodeo they stopped at an ice cream shop and then he took his mother back to her hotel. Jeb drove Amanda and a sleeping Kevin home, where he carried Kevin to bed.

"Want a glass of tea or a cup of coffee before you go home?"

"I'll take the coffee," he said, tossing his hat on a chair and following her to the kitchen to sit down and watch her while she moved around the room. Aware of his watchful gaze, she put a plate of homemade cookies in front of him and sat down across the table from him while the coffee brewed. Even with a table between them, she was too close to him, too aware of his presence. He looked relaxed, but anytime she met his gaze, a crackling tension snapped between them and it was difficult to look away.

"Mom was in heaven tonight." While he talked, he unbuttoned the top three buttons of his shirt in an idle way. She didn't know if he was even giving any thought to what he was doing, but she was too aware of his muscled tanned chest beneath the open blue shirt, the smattering of dark chest hair. She couldn't keep from glancing at his chest, and the room had grown hotter and she tried to keep her attention focused on his face.

"I don't know whether you have any idea how thrilled she was to learn about Kevin, but I couldn't have made her any happier."

"She told me. She offered to baby-sit anytime," Amanda said, shaking her head. "It's hard to imagine her baby-sitting."

"She meant every word. Call her and you'll see." He leaned forward, narrowing the gap between them, and she drew a swift breath. "Don't worry about the way she would treat him. I can promise you, she'll be good to him."

Amanda nodded, still wary of leaving Kevin with anyone she didn't know well.

He leaned back. "Mom has wanted a grandbaby probably since Burke went off to college."

"Now she has one."

"I had a good time tonight, Amanda," he added quietly.

"So did I, except for watching you ride. You like taking risks, don't you?" She glanced at the coffee, saw that it had brewed and stood to pour them both cups.

"I drink it black," he said as she placed his cup in front of him. "Life is full of risks and some of them make life more interesting. I like challenges and I remember some tonight from you. They were a lot more exciting than that bronc I rode."

Her pulse was racing and she tried to ignore him and her reaction to him. "Have a cookie. I made them because Kevin likes them."

She sat down across from Jeb again, and when she glanced at him, he gave her a mocking smile. He leaned forward and took her hand. His thumb ran lightly back and forth across her knuckles, sending tingles through her.

"Jeb—"

"Your pulse is fast, Amanda."

"This is crazy. We have enough to worry about without flirting with each other. Or are you doing this to soften me up so you'll get your way about Kevin?" she asked, feeling desperate because she liked what he was doing too much.

"Soften you up?" he drawled in a husky whisper,

his gaze drifting down over her. "I expect you're as soft now as any man could hope for."

"Jeb, stop playing with me!"

"I'm not playing with you yet, and when I do, you'll know it. And I hope you won't ask me to stop."

She yanked her hand away. "Jeb," she threatened, and he leaned back, smiling at her.

"What's this school you have Kevin signed up for?"

"Hillcrest? It's a private school. I visited it and had an interview with the principal. It wasn't the only one I went to," she said, going on to tell him about the other schools, yet too aware of him. Her hand still tingled from his touch and his comments echoed in her mind, giving her a bubbling excitement.

He drank his coffee and stood, stretching lazily. "I should go home." He looked at her speculatively as she stood. "I remember your saying something tonight about how I could imagine all I wanted because I wasn't going to get to know your reactions to—excitement." He walked around the table as he talked and her pulse jumped.

"Jeb, I mean it. We don't need to complicate our lives."

"Scared?"

"Scared senseless," she whispered as he reached her and rested his hands on her waist. She should step away. She should do all sorts of things except stand still and gaze up at him and want to walk into his arms.

"We're not—"

"Yes, we are," he interrupted, leaning down to kiss her. He slid his arms around her and pulled her tightly against himself as he leaned over her. Her head spun and her insides turned upside down. She wrapped her arms around him and kissed him as passionately as he kissed her. Their tongues met and stroked and touched, hot, wet and silky, and she was on fire.

When she pushed against him, he raised his head, studying her intently.

She wriggled out of his embrace. "Kisses are fun, but with you, they're a dangerous complication I don't want."

He gazed at her solemnly and nodded, turning to leave the room. She followed and watched while he got his hat and strode to the door.

He turned to her, touching her collar lightly. "Maybe you're right after all," he said quietly. "It was a fun evening, and you've made my mom unbelievably happy. Thanks, Amanda. See you in the morning."

Then he was gone, striding down the walk. "Thanks, Jeb. We had fun, too. It's good for Kevin to have a grandmother."

He waved, looking over his shoulder at her, and she wondered what had changed his mood so swiftly.

She closed the door and leaned against it, remembering his kisses, wondering what was going through his mind now.

As Jeb drove away swiftly, he swore. He was on fire, aching with need, hard, wanting her and too aware that he had complicated everything tonight, but dammit, the woman had been fun to flirt with.

"Keep your distance. Keep it businesslike, Stuart," he told himself, knowing he wasn't going to take his own advice.

All evening long he had been unable to resist her.

And she felt something, too. From the first day, they both had.

He thought about his mother and her joy when he'd broken the news to her about Kevin. Nothing he could possibly have given her would have made her as happy as a grandson.

What were Amanda and he going to do to share Kevin? Over and over the question repeated itself in his mind.

What could they do? How could they divide Kevin's time?

The following Thursday at dawn, Jeb came to a conclusion. He hadn't slept twelve hours total for the past week, and he had to do something. He loathed the idea of a court battle and knew that Amanda did, too.

He drove into town, ran a few errands and called Amanda to ask if he could come over and bring dinner tonight. With a note of reluctance in her voice, she agreed. He knew she wished he would simply vanish out of her life as swiftly as he had come into it, but he wasn't going to.

That night, as he got ready to leave for Amanda's, his stomach churned, and he wondered whether he was making another enormous mistake. But at the thought of Kevin and going to court over visitation rights, he knew he was doing the right thing. Then he remembered kissing Amanda. Her kisses had stunned him because they had stirred him in a way that he couldn't recall happening before, and he felt uneasy again.

Dressed in jeans and a starched white cotton shirt, his excitement building, he drove into town. On Amanda's street he slowed, enjoying the cool spring night, the shady trees and lawn sprinklers swirling, the sounds of kids playing in front yards. He turned into Amanda's drive and stopped the pickup behind her black car.

For the next two hours, his pulse hummed with nervousness as he played with Kevin and chatted with Amanda. His gaze flicked over her casual sleeveless navy blouse and cut-offs, down her shapely legs. As he watched her, his pulse speeded even more because she was a beautiful woman. He had sworn he would never give his heart to another woman and he wasn't ready yet to change. Was Amanda really as warm and loving as she appeared? Or was he being taken in again? His defenses came back up, and the queasy feeling returned to his stomach.

When Amanda had Kevin bathed and dressed for bed, Jeb settled in Kevin's rocker, lifting the boy onto his lap and opening a book. He began to read, aware that Amanda was seated on the foot of Kevin's small bed, watching him as he read to his son. Their son.

Their son. Kevin was hers as much as he was Jeb's. Jeb and Kevin had blood ties, but Amanda and Kevin had heart ties and maybe those went even deeper. As Jeb read, he glanced at her and met her speculative gaze. It seemed to him that they continually sized each other up like two combatants about to go into a fight.

His gaze drifted down over her crossed legs and instantly he jerked his attention back to the book. Kevin's small hand was splayed on a page, and as Jeb read and turned the page, he glanced at Kevin, who lay back in his arms, content to listen to him. A surge of love for his son filled him and he leaned down to kiss the top of Kevin's head, knowing that it would be worth the struggle to work out something that would allow them to share Kevin. Would Amanda feel that way, too? he wondered.

As Jeb read, Amanda listened to his deep voice. How had he moved into their lives so swiftly? She was dazed and wary. Two weeks ago she hadn't known of his existence, and now here he sat with Kevin in his lap while he read to him. And each hour she spent with Jeb, she grew more attracted to him. She had changed clothes three times tonight before she was satisfied with her simple blouse and cutoffs.

She ran her fingers across her brow. The cowboy was a forceful dynamo, getting his way about too many things. He sat in the rocker, one long jeans-clad leg propped on his opposite knee while he rocked Kevin. As she watched them, Jeb leaned down to brush a kiss on the top of Kevin's head.

Too many questions were still unanswered. Would he be as good to Kevin when she wasn't present?

When Jeb finished the story, she tucked Kevin in and kissed him good-night.

"Good night, Kevin," Jeb said softly.

"Night," he answered faintly, and Amanda could hear the drowsiness in Kevin's voice.

Jeb and Amanda walked back to the living room, where he began to turn down lights until only one small one was left.

"What are you doing?" she asked, sitting on the sofa. She was both amused and annoyed that he was taking charge in her house.

"Getting soft lights." He crossed the room to her and pulled her to her feet. "I've been thinking and thinking."

"And I'm sure you came up with another plan," she said, aware of his hands still holding her arms and his dark eyes watching her closely. He hadn't kissed her since the night of the rodeo and his touches had been casual, yet his restraint had made her even more aware of him.

"As a matter of fact, I did," he said solemnly. "I've thought about it all this week. I haven't been hasty or impulsive, and I've weighed the pros and cons."

"Well, now I am curious," she said, wondering what it was and why he was taking such care in telling her.

"You will listen, won't you?"

"Yes, of course." With growing curiosity she waited while he reached into a pocket, pulled out a box and handed it to her. It was a ring box and she stared at it, puzzled. She looked at him questioningly and then looked at the ring box.

"Open it."

She did and a dazzling diamond ring caught the light, sparkling, catching her breath with its glittering possibilities. Shocked, her gaze flew to his. "You're crazy!"

"No, I'm not. I've given this a lot of thought, Amanda. Will you marry me?" he asked.

Five

Stunned, she stared at him, thoughts scrambling in her head. It was impossible. A ridiculous solution. Married to this virile, appealing male, who no doubt would fall in love with someone else in the next few years? It was an absurd solution, a stopgap that wouldn't really solve anything. In spite of the barrage of doubts, her pulse jumped and something inside her wanted to cry out *yes*. How simple it would be to accept his proposal. Marry him and solve so many problems. But create so many new ones.

She remembered that first day when he had sat facing her and told her he wouldn't marry again for a long time—not until he decided he wanted more children. Marriage now would only be a fleeting solution that could vanish like smoke.

"I think marriage would be another complication in our lives."

"One that would be worth the rewards," he said, stroking a tendril of hair away from her cheek. With his warm fingers brushing against her, she tingled and wondered whether he knew the effect he had on her. Was he trying to sweet-talk her into this union? "I know it'll be a marriage of convenience, but that should be all right for both of us."

"Marriage—even one of convenience—is too important to be entered into lightly."

"I agree."

"Then how do you think this can work? You don't even know me."

"I know enough about you, and if you'll consider my proposal, I think you'll see that marriage would be workable."

"I live in the city—you live in the country—"

"I've thought about that. Come here," he said in a husky, coaxing voice. Taking her hand, he led her to the sofa where he sat down and pulled her down beside him, turning to face her. She held the ring box in her lap as she studied him. He was a forceful, appealing man, and she suspected that he was very accustomed to getting his way. *A marriage of convenience?*

Convenient for whom? "I can't move to your ranch."

"Hear me out. As an audiologist, you run your own business. I'll pay you for two days' work so we can live on my ranch. That way you can still work in town by commuting the other three days, or keep your house and live here those three days. It would give you two more days with Kevin than you have now."

"That's rather expensive for you," she said,

shocked that he would go to such lengths to get what he wanted.

"I can afford it and I want to do it. It would be good for Kevin, and I think it would be fair to you. I know I can't ask you to give up your work and I don't want to. I'm just asking you to cut back."

She looked down at the sparkling ring resting against a deep blue velvet lining. A marriage, even in name only, would solve their dilemma. It would give Kevin a father and give her more time with her son. The diamond glittered, a far bigger stone than would have been necessary—no stone was necessary at all— yet in its dazzling depths lay unforeseen pitfalls. She raised her head to meet his gaze, looking at midnight eyes that gave no hint of his thoughts, yet seemed to see everything in her head. She studied him openly, looking at his full lower lip, his well-shaped mouth. His nose was straight and his prominent cheekbones gave a rugged handsomeness to his face. A small, pale scar ran along his jaw. She had no idea how he got the scar and she thought again how much a stranger he still was to her.

"I don't know anything about you. I don't know what causes you to lose your temper and how you would treat Kevin if you were exasperated with him. I don't know what you like, or what you don't like. I don't even know your age."

"Thirty-one."

"I don't know your ambitions. You've given me facts and figures about your income, but I don't even know if those are accurate."

He nodded. "I can give you the name of my accountant and my attorney and tell them to answer any questions you ask. I have nothing to hide from you. I'll never knowingly hurt Kevin."

"You got into a bad marriage the first time. Now you're racing headlong into a second marriage that's loveless. Aren't you making another mistake?"

"I don't think so. This is completely different."

"What happens when Kevin is grown?"

Jeb reached out to run his finger along her knuckles, brushing them lightly, stirring those tingles that astounded her. She hadn't reacted this way to other men she'd dated. Even with Darren, there hadn't been this powerful physical attraction. What if she fell in love with Jeb?

"We can worry about that a few years down the road."

She barely heard his answer. This man was sexy, virile, and he wanted more children. He would eventually fall in love and then what would happen? And if she fell in love with him, she would be hurt far more than she had been when her relationship with Darren ended because Kevin would enter the equation.

"What happens when you're married to me and you fall in love with someone else?"

"I won't."

Annoyed, she tossed her hair away from her face. "You can't know that, and you can't avoid falling in love just because it would be inconvenient. Loving another person isn't a calculated, rational thing. It's an affair of the heart, not the mind."

"Kevin is the most important person in my life. I won't jeopardize my relationship with him."

She heard the force in his voice and saw the muscle working in his jaw. She looked at his broad shoulders, the T-shirt clinging tightly around muscled biceps.

One hand still rested on hers; his other hand was splayed on his knee. A hand-tooled leather belt with a silver belt buckle circled his narrow waist. As she pulled her gaze up to meet his again, heat rose in her cheeks.

"What about sex? You don't intend to stay celibate all the rest of your life."

He studied her and the heat enveloping her seemed to burst into flames. Tilting her chin up, he lowered his gaze to her mouth. She couldn't get her breath and her pounding heart was deafening. He was going to kiss her again—she could see it in his eyes. She wanted to stay cool and collected and keep things neutral between them, yet words and thoughts failed her.

"You feel something now, the same as I do," he whispered, leaning closer. Her hands came up to rest on his shoulders and she felt the hard muscles. Then he was too close, his mouth covering hers. Her eyes closed as he pulled her into his embrace. His fingers tangled in her hair and he opened her mouth, his tongue stroking hers while her insides constricted and heated.

Unable to resist, she slipped an arm around his neck, catching the soapy scent of his skin. Her fingers brushed his hair as he tightened his arm and kissed her deeply. Her pulse raced, and a dizzying rush of longing tore at her.

She was lost in kisses that stormed her senses and melted her reserve, and she ignored an inner voice nagging dimly at her. Lifting her into his lap, he leaned over her and cradled her in his arms. Her hand slid down to his solid chest. How could she like kissing him so much?

Struggling to hang on to common sense, she finally

pushed against him and opened her eyes. He paused, raising his head slightly to study her. She wriggled free, sliding off his lap and sitting beside him, overcome with embarrassment and surprise. The ring box had tumbled to the floor. She knew he was watching her. His breathing was as ragged as her own and she had felt his wildly beating heart when her hand had slid down against his chest.

He picked up the box with the ring.

"I'm human," she said. "You've proved I like to kiss." She didn't add that he was the only man she had ever reacted to so intensely and swiftly.

He turned her to face him and she met his gaze. "You're a very desirable woman," he said quietly.

She shook her head. "I can't have a relationship without love."

A shuttered look closed over his features, making her feel as if another barrier had come up between them. "I can't love again, not anytime soon. Your cousin killed that in me. So if that's what you want, I can't give it to you."

"Then we're at a stalemate," she said firmly, watching the muscle in his jaw clench. "I don't want a physical relationship. Sex without love isn't my idea of happiness."

"Fine by me. We'll do what you want."

"You're not going to want to stay celibate." She touched the ring, still nestled in the box that now rested in his hand. "I don't think a marriage of convenience would work."

"Don't say no so fast. Think about it. There doesn't have to be any sex, no intimate relationship if you don't want it." She looked at him, meeting his inscrutable dark gaze. "But there's an attraction between us."

"One that neither one of us wants. Are you ready to fall in love again?"

He looked down at the box in his hand, turning it so the ring reflected the light. "No, I'm not." He faced her and stroked hair away from her face. "I was hurt badly and I don't want to go through that again."

"There you are. I don't, either."

"Well, I still think our marrying is the best thing for Kevin. We're both going to be involved in his life from now on. I say, let's give this a try. We'll leave sex out for now. A marriage on paper and two parents to give Kevin what he needs. We'll share him the simplest way possible. You'd see him far more than you do now."

She couldn't argue that point. It was so tempting, because if she said no, she suspected that Jeb would be a powerful opponent.

He removed the ring from the box and picked up her hand to slide the ring on her finger. Her gaze was trapped by his and she had another dizzying spin, feeling as if she were losing control of her life. "I have to know you better," she blurted.

"Fine. We'll get to know each other, but start making plans and I will, too."

"You're moving too fast."

"I want my son in my life. I've lost three precious years of his young life—his babyhood. I don't want to idly wait now. Will you marry me soon? Think of Kevin, Amanda. I'll be a good dad to him."

She suspected that was the truth, and so far he had been fair with her.

"Marry me," he coaxed in a husky voice that washed over her like a caress.

"Yes," she whispered, wondering if she was destroying a chance for future happiness or heading down a path to lose Kevin. Or would this give them some good years together while Kevin was young and impressionable?

"Yes, I will," she repeated, feeling that she was stepping off a cliff at midnight.

"Great!" Jeb hugged her lightly. "How about lunch tomorrow so we can make some plans?"

She thought about her schedule. "I don't have patients scheduled from noon until half past one."

"Good. I'll pick you up at the office. Think about where you want to get married. We can go to a justice of the peace, a minister, whatever you would like." He stood. "I'll go now and see you tomorrow."

He sounded jubilant—and why shouldn't he? she thought. He had gotten what he wanted. Heading to the door with him, she didn't even hear what he was saying as her thoughts spun and doubts bombarded her.

At the door, he turned her to face him with his hands resting lightly on her shoulders. "Stop worrying. I can practically hear the wheels clicking and I can see worry in your big green eyes. It'll be good, Amanda. I don't ever want to hurt Kevin."

When she nodded, he brushed a kiss on her forehead, his lips warm against her skin. Leaving, he took the steps in one long stride.

She closed the door and leaned against it, holding her hand out before her and looking at the glittering solitaire. "What have I done?" she asked aloud. "You got your way again, Jeb Stuart." She thought about his passionate kisses and her eager response. Was she that love-starved that she had melted and lost her judgment?

Would a marriage of convenience work? Goodness knows, it would be good for Kevin, giving him both a father and a mother. It would save a court battle and dividing time with Kevin between them. And she would have more time with Kevin while he was still preschool age.

On the other hand, it seemed like the most impossible arrangement. Jeb Stuart was a virile male and not one to remain celibate. And she didn't want a relationship without love. Would they fall in love? The thought made her tingle, though it seemed absolutely impossible. She couldn't give him the children he wanted.

She ran her fingers across her brow. Why wasn't there a simple way out of the situation!

She went to her room to spend the next hours restlessly tossing and turning, drifting to sleep near dawn.

At half past eleven on Friday Amanda was in her examining room testing Mrs. Mallory's hearing when her intercom buzzed. "Sorry to interrupt you, but I thought you'd like to know that Mr. Stuart is here. He said he has an appointment with you at twelve for lunch."

"That's right, but it'll be another thirty minutes, Julia, before I'm through here. I'll see him then."

She glanced at the closed door to the reception room and could imagine Jeb in her office, probably pacing the room and looking into every nook and cranny. With an effort she turned back to Mrs. Mallory, who was waiting patiently.

Thirty minutes later when Amanda emerged from her examining room, chatting with her patient, her gaze flitted to Jeb and then back to her patient as she told her goodbye. Then Amanda glanced at him.

"Want to come into my office?"

He rose and followed her into the office. She slipped out of the white cotton coat she was wearing, hung it on a hook, then turned to face him. His gaze flicked over her simple dark blue dress with a straight skirt that looked tailored and prim. Her hair was fastened in a knot on top of her head, but wild, curling tendrils escaped, a reminder of the mass of loose curls that usually cascaded over her shoulders.

"I'll have an hour, and then I need to get back because I see another patient at half past one and I want to get ready for my afternoon patients."

"Sure. You pick the place," he said easily, looking at the diamond on her finger and feeling the same mixture of nervousness and satisfaction. He wanted the marriage and he didn't want it, but it seemed the only solution. The sooner they did it, the more he would like it and that's what he intended to discuss over lunch.

In minutes they were seated in a nearby restaurant on a glassed-in, air-conditioned porch that overlooked the busy street.

While he ate a cheeseburger, she ate a few dainty bites of a Waldorf salad, and he suspected she was as nervous over the coming marriage as he.

"Let's set a date. I brought a calendar."

"This is June. What about the end of July?"

He winced and shook his head. "Let's not put this off. We don't have to plan a honeymoon. Only a wedding ceremony. I was thinking one day next week."

"You're rushing things!"

"No, I just want to be with my son. And I don't see any good reason to put it off. Did you want a big church wedding?"

"Heavens, no! I haven't really thought about our wedding." The moment she said *our wedding,* flutters in her stomach took the last of her appetite. Looking relaxed and self-assured, Jeb sat facing her. Today he wore a long-sleeved navy western shirt, jeans and his black boots. With his black hair and dark clothes, he looked as ruggedly handsome as he looked dangerous.

"Next week," she repeated, her mind reeling at the prospect, yet what good reason could she give for putting it off? Any ceremony they had wouldn't be elaborate or take much planning.

"I made an appointment this morning to talk to your accountant," she said, feeling as if she were prying into a total stranger's business. "I don't want to sell my house right away. For now, I'm not going to do anything with it so I'll have it here if I want to stay in town after work."

"Good idea."

"There are some of my things I'd like to bring when I move to your ranch."

He nodded. "Fine. You've seen my place. There's plenty of room, and as far as I'm concerned, the house is in your charge—do what you want with it, except my office and my bedroom." He grinned, a half smile that was crooked and so appealing it took her breath away. "I assume we'll each have our own bedroom."

"Of course!" she snapped.

"Do what you want." He reached into a hip pocket and produced a tiny notebook and flipped it open.

"Here's a calendar. When and where would you like to get married?"

She still couldn't believe what was happening to her, yet the man waiting for an answer was real and earnest. Dazed, she stared at the month of June.

"I have three or four very close friends I'd like to invite to our wedding. This is as close to a real wedding as I ever expect to come," she said, looking out the window. He reached across the table to take her chin in his hands and turn her to face him.

"You can't tell what the future will bring."

She shrugged. "I don't have any family to attend. I'll call Aunt Maude, but she won't come from California. What about your mother and your brothers?"

"I hope all of them will be there. Mom and Cameron definitely will. Pick a date and I'll let them know."

"Since this is a sham wedding, I suppose a justice of the peace will be fine."

"It's still a legal, binding arrangement, so if you want to marry in your church, that's fine with me."

She looked away, watching traffic flow past on the street outside, but not really seeing any of it while she thought about what she wanted. "Let me call my minister." She looked at the calendar. "I'll ask him if a week from tomorrow is convenient and call you."

"Would you like to call from here? I have a phone."

She nodded and he produced a tiny cellular phone. In minutes she had arranged for a wedding at ten o'clock, the morning of the twenty-third of June. As she handed the phone back, she looked up into his dark eyes. "I haven't had contact with Cherie in three years, but I think we need to let her know."

Anger flashed in his eyes, and his jaw tightened. "I don't owe that woman anything."

"I'll call and tell her."

"Suit yourself. My men and I can move your things to the ranch this week."

She laughed, and his brows arched quizzically.

"That's funny?"

"When you want something, you really go after it, don't you?"

"I suppose I do." He reached out to touch the corner of her mouth, a lazy stroke of his fingers that was tantalizing. "You have a nice smile, Amanda. I hope I can see it often."

"That depends on what you do," she said, unable to resist flirting with him a bit.

His eyebrow arched wickedly this time and a gleam came into his eyes.

"I'll try to think of ways to coax more smiles," he said, his velvety voice lowering another notch. "Maybe getting to know each other is going to be fun after all. Think so?"

"It already is," she answered, throwing caution to the wind.

He drew a deep breath, and his chest expanded, and for the first time, when she looked into his eyes, she could read his thoughts because pinpricks of blazing desire had burst to life in the dark brown depths. While her heart pounded, she was caught and held in his gaze, unable to breathe, unable to look away. Thought processes stopped and her skin prickled with a hungry need while she fought the overwhelming urge to touch him.

"I think I've waded in over my head here," she said breathlessly, barely able to get out the words.

"I won't let you drown." His dark gaze consumed her, and still she couldn't look away. The silence crackled with tension. Watching her with that mesmerizing look, he took her hand, raising it to his mouth to kiss her palm, his warm breath a feather-light touch.

"We were talking about moving," she tried to say with some force in her voice, knowing she was failing. Pulling her hand away from his, she broke eye contact and looked down at her hand in her lap. She could still feel his warm breath on her palm. So light, so devastating.

"I think the subject was my moving to the ranch," she repeated, and looked up to find him still watching her intently, and she suspected that she had subtly changed their relationship, no matter how much she told him she wanted to keep things platonic.

"Come out to the ranch tonight," he said, drawling lazily in a coaxing voice that sounded more like an invitation to bed. "While I cook, you can look the place over again and decide where you want to put your furniture. I really don't care what changes you make, and if you want to buy new furniture, that's all right, too. I'll give you my credit card."

Surprised, she studied him. "How do you know I won't make outrageous purchases that you'll hate?"

"I trust your judgment," he said in a silky voice.

"You're still flirting, Jeb," she accused.

"You started it."

"There's something in you that brings recklessness out in me."

"I can't wait to find out what else I can bring out in you."

"Now, we've got to stop this foolishness."

"Aah, don't. This is getting interesting. Don't stop now."

"Jeb—"

He laughed softly. "I can see the redheaded stubbornness appearing. Do what you want with the ranch. Just don't do the house in pink. I've seen your house and it's attractive. I meant it when I said I trust your judgment."

"Thank you," she said, thinking how polite and flirty they were, yet she didn't want this sham marriage and she was certain he didn't, either. Silence fell between them while she wished there was some alternative.

"For Kevin's sake, we're going to make this work," Jeb said in a deep voice. She met his steely gaze and suspected that if she battled him, she would regret it.

"I need to get back to the office."

Nodding, he rose and came around the table to take her arm. When she was seated in his car, she watched him walk around to get behind the wheel, noticing his snug jeans and trim hips. Realizing how she was studying him and where her imagination was going, she turned her head, but she was acutely aware of him when he got into the car. Why did she find him so appealing? The question taunted her.

Six

Sunday afternoon after church Amanda and Kevin watched while Jeb parked his pickup in her driveway. Another man followed, backing a flatbed truck up the driveway. Both men climbed out.

Kevin was excited, looking forward to the prospect of moving to the ranch, and he raced to Jeb, who swung him up onto his shoulders easily.

A tall, black-haired, broad-shouldered man walked beside Jeb. He was rugged, slightly thicker through the shoulders and chest than Jeb, with powerful muscles. The moment she met his dark-eyed gaze, she knew he was aware of the situation and didn't approve of her.

Kevin laughed, winding his fingers in Jeb's thick hair. "How's my boy?" Jeb asked.

"Fine," Kevin answered, looking happy, and she thought how swiftly father and son had bonded.

"Amanda, this is Jake Reiner. Jake, I've told you about Amanda."

"How do you do," he said politely, and she greeted him politely in return.

"And this is Kevin, Jake. Kevin, this is Jake Reiner." Jake shook hands with Kevin.

"Where shall we begin?" Jeb asked, ending any idle talk. For the next two hours, the men were busy carrying out her furniture. Jeb let Kevin help in tiny ways and put him in the bed of the truck while Amanda helped with lighter belongings. Once, while she stood in the kitchen packing a box, Jeb passed through the room.

"Where's Kevin?"

"Jake's watching him. He's good with women and animals, so he ought to be good with kids."

"This is the superb horse trainer you've told me about?"

"He's the best. You should see him tame a wild horse. The wildest melt for him. So do most women," Jeb added dryly.

"He doesn't approve of me."

Jeb shot her a curious glance and shrugged. "Jake doesn't approve of marriage. I don't think it's personal. He'll never tie himself down to marriage. Hell, he won't tie himself to a job more than a year at a time."

"Why not?"

"I don't know. Besides my brothers, he's my best friend. We're really close, but there are some things I don't know about him. There's something that keeps him from sinking roots anywhere."

"Well, this is one time when I think his dislike is personal. I still don't think he approves of me."

"If he doesn't now, he will. You're irresistible," Jeb said with a sexy leer, and she smiled.

As soon as everything had been loaded, Amanda and Kevin rode to the ranch with the men, and Amanda supervised the unloading of the pickup and truck. It was one in the morning when Jeb drove Amanda and Kevin back to the city.

After carrying a sleeping Kevin to bed Jeb left, hearing the door close behind him.

When he returned to the ranch, he unlocked the back door and entered. He could smell her lingering perfume. Already his life was changing and his house was transformed into unfamiliar surroundings. He walked through the rooms, looking at her furniture. Emotions clashed in him: joy over the prospect of getting his son, worry over a marriage that wasn't a union of love. Were they going to regret this—or would it work out?

On the twenty-third of June, these questions still plagued Jeb as he entered the church. His brother Cameron saw him and came forward to shake his hand. "I wasn't sure you'd show up," Cameron said quietly. "You were supposed to be here thirty minutes ago."

"I didn't want to stand around and wait. Let's find the minister and see if everyone is here. I'd like this wedding to start now. Have you seen my bride?"

"Yep. She's been here almost an hour. Maybe she's anxious."

"I think she's supposed to get here early. Where's Kevin?"

"With Mom. I hope you know what you're doing."

"I do. This will be good for Kevin."

"Jeb, he's three. He'll be grown in fifteen years—fifteen good years of your life. Then what will you do?"

Jeb grinned. "I have fifteen years to figure that one out. Stop worrying. Look at Mom and Kevin. This is the best gift I could have given her."

"That's the truth, but you could have done it without marrying. I think Mom had given up ever having a grandchild, but Stella and I are hoping to give her one."

"I'm sure you will."

Cameron smiled, but the worry didn't leave his eyes. "I hope you'll make it. I still can't believe you're doing this. The wives went off to talk to Amanda. That's one thing—they all seem to like her."

"Good," Jake replied absentmindedly while he glanced at his watch again.

"Here comes Jake. I wish I could get him to come work for me when he leaves you. Then again, maybe this time he won't leave you. Maybe he'll settle."

"When pigs fly."

Jake joined them, shaking hands with Jeb and then with Cameron. "You can't talk your brother out of this?" Jake asked Cameron, who shook his head and grinned.

"You know how mule-stubborn he is."

"The hell with you two."

"I'm going to find the good reverend and get this over with," Jeb said, and walked away. Jake watched him. "I hope he knows what he's doing."

"From what's he told me," Cameron said, "she's as uncertain about this whole marriage deal as he is."

"Am I doing the right thing?" Amanda asked herself for what seemed like the millionth time as she stared in the mirror in the room designated by the church for brides and bridesmaids. When someone knocked on the door, Amanda's thoughts shifted from Cherie. Her best friend, Megan Thorne, entered and smiled radiantly. "How's the bride? Jittery?"

"Of course I'm jittery! There's no way to know whether I'm doing the right thing or not." They had discussed this coming marriage at length, and Megan's cheerful acceptance of Amanda's decision was both a relief and an annoyance. She almost wanted someone to try to talk her out of marrying Jeb.

"You've seen Jeb at his best," Amanda said darkly. "He can be charming when he wants to be."

"He's marvelous, Amanda! I say go for it!"

Amanda nodded and turned to look at herself again. She knew the time for hashing over this marriage decision was past. Within the hour, she would be Mrs. Jeb Stuart.

She studied herself, straightening a lock of hair and feeling so fluttery that she wondered if she really would faint for the first time in her life.

She wore a white silk, knee-length sheath with high-heeled white sandals. Her hair was twisted into a knot on top of her head, tendrils framing her face. In spite of some blush, she thought she looked pale and her freckles stood out more than ever.

"You look beautiful."

"Thanks, Megan." She reached for a bottle of perfume and knocked over a jar of lotion. Taking deep breaths, she set the jar upright.

"Calm down," Megan said cheerfully.

"All my soon-to-be sisters-in-law have been here to see me. I met them last night."

"And...?"

"They're nice and they act happy, but I can see the curiosity in their eyes. I don't see how any of them can approve of this."

"You said his mother does."

"Goodness, yes! She gets her grandson, so she's happy."

A knock at the door interrupted them and Megan opened it, talking to someone briefly and returning with a bouquet in her hands. "This is for you from the groom."

"We weren't going to have any of the trappings. I said I wouldn't have any flowers," Amanda said, taking the fragrant bouquet of cascading white and red roses, white carnations, a few deep purple iris and baby's breath. "It's beautiful!" she exclaimed, inhaling deeply the fragrance of the roses. She looked at herself in the mirror with the bouquet in her hands and thought that, with the flowers, she did look like a bride.

"I think this is going to be a good marriage, Amanda."

Amanda lowered the bouquet and smiled. "Because he sent beautiful flowers? You're an optimist." She glanced at her watch. "I guess it's time to go."

Megan smiled broadly. "Come on, Miss Crockett, soon to be Mrs. Stuart."

With a deep breath Amanda held her bouquet and crossed the room.

As soon as she stepped through the door of the church, entering to one side of the altar, her gaze met Jeb's. He came from a door on the opposite side of the church. He was dressed in a dark suit and tie, and the sight of him took her breath away. He was incredibly handsome. Her pulse drummed, and she was fluttery all over. She knew that with the intense physical reaction she had to him, she was going to complicate her life by marrying him.

Megan followed Amanda while Jeb's blond brother Cameron followed him. Amanda glanced at Kevin sitting in the front row, looking solemnly at her. She smiled at him and he smiled and waved in return. She saw him slip his hand into his grandmother's and suddenly she felt better. A grandmother for Kevin was a blessing.

Her gaze shifted back to Jeb, and she looked into his unfathomable dark eyes. He looked relaxed, confident, certain of his world. The only thing that betrayed his emotions was a muscle flexing in his jaw. At every step that brought her closer to him, her pulse seemed to jump a notch until it roared in her ears and drowned out all other noise. Finally, they stopped and turned to face the minister.

When Jeb took her hand, his fingers were warm and strong. She glanced down at his hand and wrist; a white cuff showed slightly beneath the dark sleeve of his suit. As he moved his wrist, a gold cuff link glinted.

Repeating her vows, Amanda felt stiff and cold and as if she were committing a crime by agreeing to this sham marriage.

"I now pronounce you husband and wife, Mr. and Mrs. Jeb Stuart. You may kiss the bride."

She looked up at Jeb, who gazed into her eyes solemnly. Then his gaze trailed to her mouth. He leaned down to brush a warm kiss across her lips.

After the brief kiss, he took her arm and together they turned to smile at friends and to go to Kevin. The simple, bare-bones ceremony was over. There was no music, no walk back up the aisle together as a married couple, but Jeb had wanted pictures for Kevin when he was grown, so there was a photographer taking shots of everyone. As she turned, her gaze met Jake Reiner's. He sat staring at her, his dark eyes cold and grim, and a chill ran down her spine.

"Welcome to the family," Lila Stuart said, and hugged Amanda lightly, her brown eyes warm and friendly. She smiled at Amanda and looked down at Kevin, who slipped his hand into his mother's. She suspected that he knew something momentous was occurring, even if he didn't understand what it was. Then the rest of the family swarmed her to hug and wish her well until the photographer interrupted them.

"Mrs. Stuart, Mr. Stuart, if you're ready, I'll take a few pictures here and then take some more at the reception."

Mrs. Stuart. How long would it take her to grow accustomed to being Mrs. Stuart, Amanda wondered as she turned to face the photographer Jeb had hired. They posed for pictures, with Kevin in all but one. Finally Jeb waved his hand, motioning to his family.

"Let's head out for the party," he said easily. "We can talk there and get more pictures then."

Lila Stuart and Kevin rode with them to the reception. Jeb had rented a restaurant for the next three hours and it had a glassed-in area overlooking a small lake. A band played, and for the guests it seemed to be a festive party. Jeb was charming, and when he asked her to dance, Amanda moved willingly into his arms for the first even slightly private moment with him during the entire day. His arm circled her waist and his warm hand held hers. They danced to the slow number and she moved easily with him, looking into his dark eyes and feeling her pulse drum.

"You look beautiful," he said quietly.

"Thank you. You look very handsome."

"Are you doing all right with all of this?"

"So far, yes. But this is easy and you have a very nice family."

"We'll take it a day at a time. I learned the hard way not to plan too much for the future."

"Thank you for the beautiful flowers."

"I thought you should have flowers. We don't know where we're going, Amanda. Maybe we'll fall in love and want memories of this day."

His words rippled over her nerves, and she wanted to believe what he said, but she knew better. This man someday wanted a wife who could give him more children, and she couldn't. She tilted her head to study him. "I thought you didn't want to fall in love again."

"I don't, but as you said, that's something the heart does and not the head. Wisdom and logic don't rule the heart. Besides, we're married, anyway, so why not?"

She smiled and shook her head. "Love isn't ever a convenience."

"Those sound like words of a starry-eyed romantic. You continually surprise me."

"I imagine we're going to continue to surprise each other. We're little more than strangers now."

"We're a lot more than strangers," he said in a soft voice, tightening his arm around her waist. "We don't have to worry about the future now. Today is all we have to face, and enjoying this party with family and friends. And at the moment, I like dancing with you," he said, pulling her closer.

"Aunt Maude called me this morning again to wish me well. She likes you very much."

"She called me, too. She said you're the woman I should have married in the first place."

"Sometimes she doesn't get along with her own daughter."

"I'm sorry she couldn't be here."

"I'm accustomed to being without a family, except now I have Kevin and you and a very big family." She wanted to close her eyes, follow his lead and forget all her worries. And maybe he was right. Take the moment and don't worry about tomorrow. Yet as she gazed into the dark depths of her handsome husband's eyes, she suspected that she should guard against falling in love with him if she didn't want heartbreak.

The party went on until two in the afternoon, and by half past two, everyone had gone except Jeb's relatives, and one by one, they said farewell until only the brothers, their wives and Lila were left. The brothers and their wives were staying at Cameron's ranch until their planes left on Monday morning, so they all drove to Cameron's place. As a result Amanda wasn't alone with Jeb until midnight, when Jeb stood and announced, "I better take my wife and son and go home."

The words made her acutely aware of the awkwardness of their situation. Through the goodbyes and as she watched him carry a sleeping Kevin to the car, her insides grew more fluttery. When they reached his ranch, he carried Kevin toward the house. Following him, carrying Jeb's coat and tie, Amanda watched him be so careful with Kevin. His broad shoulders looked like a bulwark for her son, his long stride easily covering the ground while he seemed to carry Kevin effortlessly.

They moved through the darkened kitchen, and she walked ahead of him to switch on lights.

"Drop my things on a chair, and I'll get them later," Jeb said. Earlier in the evening he had pocketed his cuff links and rolled up his shirt sleeves. His crisp white shirt was unbuttoned to his waist.

They moved into Kevin's room, his familiar furniture now in Jeb's house. "It's not cold. I'll strip him down to his underwear," Jeb said, slipping off Kevin's shoes and socks. She helped, and in minutes, she was leaning over Kevin to kiss him goodnight.

Jeb did the same and they tiptoed out of his room. When they stepped into the hall, Jeb took her hand.

"Let's have a drink," he suggested.

She was tempted to say no, but one look into his dark, coaxing eyes and she nodded. Deep in her heart, she knew she not only wanted to be with him, but after a day with him, dancing with him and constantly being touched by him, she wanted to kiss him.

In the kitchen Jeb opened a chilled bottle of champagne and she watched the pale, golden liquid bubble in the fragile glasses. He carried their drinks outside to his porch where a new monitor was turned on so they could hear Kevin if he woke. Jeb handed her a glass of champagne. As he stood facing her, he raised his glass in a toast. "Here's to our future."

She touched her glass to his, sipped and then raised hers. "Here's to tonight," she said softly, knowing she was once again tempting fate. "For better or for worse, we'll remember this evening forever."

"I think there are some things we've still left undone," he said in a husky voice, taking her drink and setting both glasses on a table.

Seven

Her pulse pounded and an inner voice cried out warnings, but she ignored them. It had been a magical day and night, and she'd had more fun today with Jeb than she'd had in years.

Slipping his arm around her waist, he drew her to him and she came eagerly into his arms. As she looked into his eyes, her pulse leaped. His gaze shifted to her mouth and then he leaned down. His mouth covered hers and desire burst within her, white-hot and all-consuming.

As his tongue stroked hers, he tightened his arm around her. Her hands went to his chest and she pushed away his shirt, which he had long ago unbuttoned, and then her hands were on his bare chest, sliding around to his smooth, muscled back.

Dimly she felt his other hand in her hair and was

aware of pins falling, her hair tumbling over her shoulders.

"Mandy," he whispered, bestowing the first nickname she'd ever had in her life; yet said by him it was instantly special. His gaze held hers. "This is good," he said roughly, and then his arm tightened, holding her pressed against him while his mouth covered hers in a fierce, hungry kiss that turned her to jelly.

Trembling with need, she clung to him, returning his kisses wildly, the fingers of one hand winding in his hair while her other hand moved down his back to his narrow waist, stopping when her fingers touched his belt.

He was warm and strong, all solid muscle. His kisses were hot, heady and demanding. Who was this man who had stormed into her life and swept her into marriage? Kevin's father, now her stranger-husband. Dynamic, sexy, he was a whirlwind, rushing her headlong with him into what? Another heartbreak? Rapture?

He tugged at the zipper of her white silk dress and pushed it off her shoulders. She was only dimly aware of what he was doing because his kisses had shut out reality. His tongue stroked hers, thrust deeply into her mouth, moving in a rhythm that made her think of complete union with him. Her hips pressed against him and she trembled, aching and wanting so much more of him, wanting to touch and kiss him and relish his maleness.

He shifted and his hand pushed her dress to her waist. While he cupped her breast, his thumb caressed her nipple. Moaning with pleasure, she stroked his back, then slid her hand around to his chest as he leaned down, taking her breast in his mouth, his tongue stroking where his hand had been seconds before. Gasping with pleasure, she clung to him.

Jeb shook, trying to hold back, his body raging with desire. He wanted this tall, red-headed woman who was a mystery to him, and who intrigued him. Now she was his wife. Legally married—yet he had agreed to avoid making love. And here he was on their first night, before their vows were twenty-four hours old, breaking that agreement. She was incredibly desirable. Was he making the same mistake again, being swept off his feet by a woman he truly didn't know? Yet in his heart, he couldn't imagine that she wasn't as good as she seemed. Three years of mothering a little boy was a true test of character. And did that make her even more desirable to him?

All day long thoughts had swarmed through his head. When he'd watched her walk into the church, her green eyes wide and solemn, with self-assurance in her walk, his heart had missed a beat. The white silk clung to her slender figure. She had looked elegant, poised and so desirable that he had broken into a sweat and had to turn to look at Kevin and think about his son.

Then through the party, when he had glanced across the room at her or saw her laughing with friends, he wanted to go claim his new wife and take her away where he could be alone with her. When she had stepped into his arms to dance, her green eyes darkening, his desire had compounded. Tension had sizzled between them, racing along his nerves like heat lightning.

Again, when he danced with her, holding her close, he wanted to dance across the room and out the door and take her away with him where he could kiss her.

At last she was in his arms and she was all he had dreamed about and so much more. Trembling, returning his kisses eagerly with her hands sliding over him as hungrily as his moved over her, she was incredible.

Plans, logic, caution were gone. She was a beautiful, desirable woman, and he wanted her. Promises or not, he wasn't stopping until she indicated that she wanted him to.

He inhaled the intoxicating perfume she wore, winding his fingers in her cloud of silky hair. He wanted to strip away her dress and lacy underclothes and carry her to his bed, but he tried to hold back.

Then she pushed against his chest lightly. Reluctantly, curbing his desire, he raised his head and looked down at her. Her green eyes were stormy, her mouth swollen from their kisses and her face flushed with passion.

She reached to pull up her silk dress, but he caught her hands lightly and feasted his gaze on her high, firm breasts, which he had freed from their lacy constraints.

"You're beautiful, Mandy," he whispered, stroking her breast so lightly.

With a gasp, she pulled up her dress, holding it in front of her. "We're going way too fast, Jeb." Her words were breathless and slow, her voice lower and raw with need as her heated gaze ran over his bare chest and he felt as if she had stroked her hands over him.

When she ran her tongue across her lips, he ached to lean forward and catch her tongue lightly with his teeth. Desire burned in her eyes and fueled his own longing.

"A month ago today, I didn't even know you," she continued.

"We're married," he reminded her, wondering why words that usually came so easily failed him now. He wanted her with a driving force that consumed him like a raging fire. His brain couldn't focus on persuasive arguments and he was just trying to hang on to his control. All he knew was that a beautiful, desirable woman stood only inches away, and she had responded eagerly to his touches and kisses and now she wanted him to stop.

"We agreed to keep things platonic, at least for a while. This is too fast for me."

"You liked kissing. Tell me you didn't," he said huskily, running his fingers along her bare arm, over her shoulder and across her nape.

"Yes, you know I like to kiss, but I don't want to get deeply involved in a physical relationship. Not until I know you better." Her voice became even more shaky.

"You feel something every time we touch," he reminded her quietly.

"Yes. I know I can't hide my responses and I don't really want to. At the same time, I don't want to rush too far, too fast and make a terrible mistake that will hurt all of us."

Wriggling with seeming ease, she slipped back into her dress. When she struggled to zip it up, he turned her around. "I'll do that."

"You're making things worse."

"I can't resist," he whispered, leaning forward to brush kisses on her back before he began slowly to draw her zipper up. He heard her intake of breath, and he wanted to unzip her dress instead.

He trailed kisses up, following with the slow tug of the zipper, and then he brushed her hair away to kiss her nape. She turned to face him, taking his upper arms and holding him lightly.

"We have to get to know each other. There are too many things from both our pasts to ignore. We've both been hurt before and don't want to be again. I think the sensible thing to do is to tell you good-night and go to *my* room now," she said, emphasizing the *my*. Swiftly she stood on tiptoe and brushed his cheek with a kiss. "Thanks for so many things today." Then she was gone, hurrying away from him with that sexy walk of hers, and he wanted to go after her and haul her into his arms and kiss away every protest, but common sense said she was right.

Sleep would be impossible and he looked around, wondering if there was anything he could do to wear himself into physical exhaustion and try to forget the only thing he wanted to do. He went down the hall, too aware of passing her closed door, imagining her lying in bed and wondering if she could sleep. He swore under his breath and stopped at Kevin's room to tiptoe inside. The adjoining door to her room was open and he wanted to swear again, thinking how easy it would be to go the few yards to her bed.

Instead he walked to Kevin's small bed and looked at his son sprawled asleep. Smiling, Jeb touched Kevin's hand, brushing his fingers across his son's fingers, and he was thankful she had agreed to the marriage. Now that he had his son, the world was much better. Jeb tiptoed out and went to his room to change to jeans and running shoes. He wondered how long he would have to run to get his raging body to cool down and to get erotic thoughts of Mandy out of his head.

In an hour he returned and took a cold shower. Then he went to the kitchen and poured himself a stiff drink of bourbon and carried it outside to sit on the porch and gaze into the darkness.

What happened if they fell in love? When his marriage to Cherie had ended, he had sworn he wouldn't ever love again, but as time passed and his pain had healed, he had been more realistic about the future, feeling that some day far in the future, he might consider marriage.

Was Mandy right? Were they rushing headlong into disaster? He didn't think so, but he had to admit that they didn't know each other all that well yet. He sighed and stretched out his long legs, remembering totally how it had felt to hold her in his arms, to kiss her and caress her and feel her soft body thrust against his. He swore, knowing he wasn't one degree closer to sleep than he had been before his run. Was she sleeping peacefully? What had those kisses done to her?

Upstairs in her room, Amanda heard the floor creak and glanced at her closed bedroom door. Was Jeb still up? She looked at the clock and sat up in bed, staring at the door and then looking at the open door to Kevin's room, knowing his door to the hall was also open.

How easy it would have been to have yielded to passion tonight. Had she done the right thing? Was it really the smart thing to do? Or should she let go and see where passion took them?

Logic told her she was right in insisting that they slow down and get to know each other before they got into a physical relationship. Yet how difficult it had been to stop kissing him! She had wanted to close her eyes, let go and make love all night long. Instead, she went to the window to gaze outside, amazed that she was living out on a ranch and that Kevin now had a father—amazed that her life had changed completely.

This was the only wedding night she would ever have, and she was spending it alone.

A light knock on her door broke into her thoughts.

Her insides constricted and heat flashed in her while she fought with herself about whether to answer the knock or pretend to be asleep. Even as she told herself to pretend to be asleep, she crossed the room. She was aware of how short her cotton gown was and how scantily she was dressed.

"Jeb?" she said softly, and heard an answer from the other side of the door.

Yanking on a pale turquoise cotton robe, she opened the door to face him. He was bare-chested and barefoot, wearing jeans.

"I can't sleep, either," he said quietly. "Come sit with me outside and have a drink and we'll talk. I promise, only talk."

"I think you gave that promise that once before and didn't keep it."

"You can't fault a guy when the lady is irresistible."

She had to laugh.

"C'mon," he urged. "You can't sleep."

Again there was a quick mental battle between what she knew she should do and what she wanted to do, and what she wanted won. Nodding, she stepped into the hall. He moved away, leaving distance between them.

"At least Kevin can sleep. I've been for a run, showered and had a drink, but I still can't sleep and I wondered if you could. How about a glass of wine or beer or pop or lemonade?"

"I'll take lemonade."

"I looked at Kevin, and he's sleeping peacefully."

"He usually does."

She moved outside and they sat side by side. True to his word, Jeb kept a distance between them, but that didn't stop her acute awareness of him or the longing to reach for him.

"I'd like to teach Kevin to ride if it's all right with you."

"Kevin is only three!"

"He can ride around the corral. I'll watch him."

"Before I know it, you'll be taking him all over the ranch with you."

"Maybe, but I'll take care of him. Let's see how he likes it."

She studied Jeb and knew he was tough and strong. She wondered if he would expect too much of Kevin or take too many risks. So far he had been very careful about Kevin and hadn't done one thing she disapproved of, so she nodded. "All right, if he wants to."

"Stop worrying. You can come with us or come watch. Do you like to ride?"

"Actually, I don't think I've ridden a horse since I was a child and went on pony rides at birthday parties and that sort of thing."

"You're missing something. Mrs. Fletcher will be here to cook in the morning at half past five. Kevin knows her and can stay with her. Come riding with me and let me show you the ranch and we'll watch the sun come up."

"At five-thirty in the morning?" she asked, mildly horrified at the thought of getting up so early. "It's after three in the morning now."

"Then you'll sleep well tomorrow night," he said cheerfully. "Come on."

"I don't know a thing about horses."

"I'll show you. You just need to know the front end from the back end," he said, grinning at her. "Come on. The sunrise will be worth it. That and my company."

She had to laugh at him. "Such modesty!"

"I like it when you laugh," he said softly, reaching over to take her hand and lace his fingers through hers.

"It's usually nice when anyone laughs," she replied lightly, drawing a swift breath when their hands touched. "Tell me about growing up. When did you learn to ride?"

"I don't remember ever not riding," he said easily, and told her about his childhood on the family ranch. All the time they talked, she was aware of her hand in his.

They talked until four and he walked back to her bedroom door with her. "Well, I kept my word and kept my distance. See you in an hour and a half." He turned and sauntered to his room. She watched him until he reached his door and glanced over his shoulder at her. How close they were! And how easy it would be to fly into his arms.

She hurried into her room and closed her door, going to check on Kevin and then crawling into bed and smiling when she thought of some of the funny remarks Jeb had made. Then she drifted off to sleep, remembering dancing in his arms and repeating wedding vows. Mrs. Jeb Stuart.

By six the next morning, she was prickly with awareness of Jeb as she rode beside him, casting surreptitious glances at him and sometimes watching him openly. He looked totally at ease in the saddle, while she was as uncertain about the animal beneath her as she would have been in a spaceship. The horse seemed huge, but so far she had done nothing more than move along beside Jeb's black horse. He had given her Popcorn, the same small mare that Kevin rode, which suited her fine. But after the first few minutes, she forgot the horse because the man beside her took all her attention.

They crossed a stream and rode through tall trees along rolling country and came out on a green pasture that stretched away before them. When they halted, he looked at horses grazing peacefully. "I raise quarter horses. I can show you the papers on their bloodlines. I have some cattle, but what I love are the horses, and these are the cutting horses that cowboys use. You'll have to come watch sometime when I'm working and you'll see what they can do. You've seen them at the rodeo."

"Isn't this life harder and far more dangerous than what you did before when you worked in Houston?"

He gazed into the distance and shook his head. "Maybe, but I like it a lot better and I'm making a good living at it." He flicked the reins and moved on. She followed, catching up to ride beside him. They were in an early morning dusky light that caught the silvery drops of dew on the grass and leaves. Morning doves cooed softly and a hush was on the earth, and she had to admit that the ranch was beautiful at this time of day. They reached a swift-running creek, with clear water splashing over smooth stones and pools of green water where there were deep holes.

"You have a river on your ranch," she said, looking at the deeper places.

"It's only a big creek and it's great. I don't have to worry about water. I have wells, too."

"Kevin can't come out here. He's little and he can't swim. Last year he was scared of water, but he's gotten over that."

"Don't worry. If I take him out, he'll never be out of my sight."

She looked at Jeb as he urged his horse across a shallow part of the water. She followed, reassured by his promise.

They rode in an easy silence, moving through trees again and climbing a rise to stop beneath a spreading oak. He dismounted swiftly and took her reins. "Come down here," he said quietly, shoving his hat to the back of his head.

Aware of his watchful gaze and her fluttering pulse, she dismounted. His hands closed on her waist and he swung her the rest of the way to the ground. His arm circled her shoulders easily and he turned her to look at the view. Mist hung in the valleys and the first pink rays of the sun shone over the treetops. In the distance she could see the roofs of the house, the outbuildings and the stable, and the silvery ribbon of the creek winding across part of the ranch.

"It's beautiful."

"Very beautiful," he said in a husky voice, turning her to him. And then she was in his arms and it seemed the most natural thing in the world to be there and to be kissing him.

When he raised his head and looked at her, she opened her eyes.

"Someday, Mandy, we'll make love up here beneath this tree and you'll be my woman," he said roughly.

"You don't know that," she said, more shaken than she had been the night before. "You don't even know me that well or if you'll like me when you do get to know me." His dark eyes blazed and he looked as determined as he had the first day she met him. Even though she told herself that he couldn't know what would happen between them in the future, a thrill of excitement bubbled in her.

"I do know it." He lowered his head and his mouth covered hers. He spread his legs and his hand slid down over her bottom, pulling her up against him. She felt his hardness and his iron strength while her pulse roared from his words and his kisses.

She pushed against him, gazing up at him. "Let's go back."

He nodded. "What would it hurt if we fell in love?"

"It wouldn't—if we both fall in love, but if it's only a physical relationship for one of us, then the other one will get hurt."

"We took some vows."

"You know what a sham this marriage is."

"Maybe," he said cautiously, watching her. "But it doesn't have to be."

"You told me once that someday you want more children. I can't give them to you," she said flatly, the old empty feelings of inadequacy rising to haunt her.

He gave a dismissive wave of his hand. "We can adopt kids. You adopted Kevin and look how much you love him. And he's a good kid."

"You really wouldn't care if you didn't have any more of your own?"

"No. There are other important ties besides blood ties."

"Some men don't feel that way."

"I'm being truthful with you."

She gazed at the sprawling vista before her, yet was thinking of the past. "For a while I felt so inadequate. Actually, after my breakup with Darren, I felt undesirable. And then I got Kevin and I began to feel complete and a woman again and the physical impairment seemed blown out of proportion."

Jeb turned her to face him. "That's good, because you're one of the most desirable women I've ever known," he said quietly. "I want you, Amanda, and I'm willing to wait until you're ready, but we're already man and wife. It could be good between us."

He kissed her again and this time she let go of her reservations and returned his kisses until they both were half undressed and breathless. She pushed against his chest. "Jeb, I have to be more certain than I am now." She knew it was pointless to add that she wanted more than just to be desired, she wanted his love.

He released her, yanking on his shirt while she turned her back to dress with shaking fingers, too aware of him behind her, of his readiness, his desire.

He helped her mount and then swung easily into his own saddle, his horse prancing slightly before it settled into a walk. She watched Jeb, wondering about him and amazed by what he had said to her in the past hour. *"You're one of the most desirable women I've ever known."* His words strummed over her heart like a melody and warmed her. Yet too much was still left unsaid.

Her gaze ran over him swiftly, over his long legs

and tight jeans and broad shoulders, over the callused hands that could be so incredibly gentle. What did she feel for him? She knew she was falling in love with this tough cowboy. For the first time, she admitted that he had already taken part of her heart. And with every kiss, every hour together, she was more in love with him.

Would it be all right to let go, love him and give freely to him and see where love took her? Her pulse raced at the thought. She wanted to follow her instincts, wanted to let go, wanted him to make love to her mindlessly. *Wait, wait,* argued her logical mind. *Love him and let go,* argued her heart.

For the next two weeks, they lived under the same roof and she tried to adjust to her new life. Jeb seemed to take to it with the greatest of ease, and if he had rough moments, they didn't show.

But she was finding a lot of things a strain. She still worried about Kevin. She was beginning to trust Jeb and she had decided that he would be good to his son, but she knew he was going to let Kevin do things she considered dangerous and teach Kevin things she would worry about. Kevin was already riding in front of Jeb in the saddle when he left the house early in the mornings. And if Jeb didn't ride a horse, he buckled Kevin's car seat into his pickup and the two headed out to feed and check on animals.

She cut her practice back to two days a week, Wednesdays and Thursdays, because she didn't like the long drive into the city, she didn't like being away from Kevin, and, she had to admit, she didn't like being away from Jeb.

She knew she was falling in love with Jeb and had known that for weeks now, but should she let go and give him her heart completely? His words were heady, making her feel desirable, making her long for the real marriage that they were coming closer to each day.

On a Tuesday afternoon in early August, as she stood in the small bedroom they had turned into her office, she saw a pickup come sweeping up to the back door and Jake Reiner jumped out. He was bare-chested and in jeans, his hair wet and slicked back from his face. His long legs ate up the ground as he strode toward the house.

Suddenly alarmed that something had happened to Kevin, Amanda raced to the back door to meet him. Mrs. Fletcher stood at the kitchen sink peeling potatoes.

"Here comes Jake," Amanda said. The moment she swung open the back door, Jake grinned.

"Can you come with me? Kevin and Jeb have a surprise. They want to show you something."

Eight

"Now?" she asked, relief pouring over her and curiosity taking its place. She looked down at her cutoffs, her red T-shirt and her sneakers. "Like this?"

"That's perfect," Jake said, grabbing her hand and heading toward the pickup.

"I'll be back soon," she called to Mrs. Fletcher, and pulled the door shut behind her, laughing and wondering what Kevin and Jeb wanted to show her. Jake dropped her hand and opened the door to his pickup. She slid inside and watched him stride around the front. For the first time she noticed that his jeans were wet.

"You're all wet," she said when he climbed behind the wheel.

He grinned at her again with a flash of white teeth. "Yeah, and it feels good. It's hot enough today to go up in flames just standing still."

"And you're not going to tell me where we're going or what I'm going to see?"

"Nope. They want to surprise you."

"Everything about this ranch is a surprise," she said as they passed the small house where Jake lived. His Harley was parked beneath a shed.

"You like it here, don't you?" Jake asked her.

"Yes, I do and Kevin does. It's been good for him."

"He's a cute kid and coming out of his shell. Sorry, I didn't mean to sound as if something was wrong with him."

"That's all right," she said while the hot wind blew in the open windows against her. She had no idea where Jake was taking her or how he knew where he was going. It looked to her as if they were driving off across open country without following any road, but he and Jeb both seemed to know the ranch as well as she knew her own neighborhood.

"Kevin has never been around men and he was shy when we moved out here."

"He's the first kid I've ever been around. I know horses and bikes, but I don't know kids." He glanced at her. "You've been good for Jeb."

Startled, she looked at Jake, who was staring straight ahead again. "Thanks," she said, wondering when and how she had won the tough cowboy's approval. They hit a bump and she clutched the seat and forgot about Jake, wondering again about Kevin and Jeb.

In minutes they passed a stand of oaks and drove into the open, crossing a pasture to a tall oak where a shiny new stock tank stood in the shade. Jeb's black pickup was parked nearby. The tank was filled with water and Kevin was splashing merrily in it while Jeb sat in the water, leaning back with his arms stretched out on either side of him along the rim of the tank as he watched Kevin play.

Kevin spotted her and started jumping up and down excitedly, and she realized how much he had changed in the short time they had known Jeb. He had lost his quiet manner and was exuberant so much more often now.

She laughed as she stepped out of the pickup and walked over to them. "Is this what you rushed me out here to see? You're in a horse tank! That water can't be clean."

"Sure it is," Jeb said easily, eyeing her. "No horse has been near this tank. It's brand-new—I got it the day before you moved to the ranch. It's got fresh water in it and it's clean enough. Cleaner than the creek."

"Watch me, Mommy. Watch. I can swim!" Kevin exclaimed proudly, and moved to one side of the tank, poised as if he were diving in.

"I'm watching," she said, glancing at Jeb and then back at Kevin, who jumped in and thrashed his way across the tank to the opposite side.

Her heart fluttered because last summer when he was two, he had been frightened of pools. Surprise and joy filled her. Now he could halfway swim and his fear was gone. Enormous relief and pleasure at his happiness with his accomplishment filled her.

"Kevin, that's wonderful!" she cried, clapping her hands.

"Come in," Kevin urged.

"Yeah, come on in," Jeb drawled, and heat flashed in her as she looked at him and met his smoldering gaze. "Scared?" he challenged, and for a moment she forgot everything else as her body tingled.

Kevin splashed to the edge of the tank to look up at her. "Come swim, Mommy."

"Kevin, I don't want to get wet," she said, eyeing the tank and too aware of Jeb.

"Please!" Kevin called, and swept a big wave of water out, splashing her. Squealing, she jumped back and looked at Jeb, who gave her a mocking smile.

Impulsively, she took two quick steps, gave a leap and sailed over the edge and over Kevin, landing on her bottom and splashing water over all of them.

She laughed and came up while Kevin giggled and splashed her.

"Come on, kiddo," Jake said easily, picking up Kevin and swinging him to his shoulders. "Let's you and me go see Mrs. Fletcher about some chocolate ice cream."

Kevin squealed with delight and clutched Jake's hair as they turned toward Jake's pickup.

Amanda started to climb out to go home with Kevin, but Jeb reached beneath the water and took hold of her ankle.

When she turned to look at him, her heart missed a beat. His dark eyes burned with desire. He still had one muscled arm stretched lazily on the rim of the tank, but his other hand was sliding higher on her leg, stroking her below the surface of the water.

She glanced over her shoulder at Jake and Kevin, who were almost to the pickup and talking to each other. Jake buckled Kevin in his pickup and climbed in. Kevin waved, and she waved back.

"Did you tell Jake to take Kevin home so we could be alone?" she asked. Her words were breathless and she was too aware of Jeb, of his bare chest, that sparkled with tiny drops of crystal-clear water over skin that was deeply tanned. He had a smattering of black chest hair that tapered in a thin line toward his navel. She could see he still wore his jeans.

"No, I didn't. That was Jake's own idea. But a damn good one because it leaves you here with me."

"I don't believe you didn't set this up," she said as he closed his hand firmly around her calf and drew her toward him.

"Jake, this is out in the open in full view of anyone who happens by."

"Yeah, so many people pass this way," he drawled, teasing her. He reached out and pulling her to him, and then he kissed her.

She slid her hands over his warm, hard muscles, his chest that was rock solid. His mouth tasted of cool water and then his tongue ignited flames, and she closed her eyes and knew she had to make a choice now.

She wound her arms around his neck and clung to him, cold water rippling around them. How much longer was she going to keep telling him no when she didn't want to refuse him? Why not take some risks? Why not take a chance that he would fall in love with her?

Her heart pounded wildly as she kissed him, and she admitted to herself that she loved this tall, forceful cowboy with all her heart.

As he kissed her, Jeb stood easily, swinging her into his arms, splashing water when he stepped out of the tank.

She was only dimly aware that he carried her through some trees to a secluded grassy spot shaded by thick oaks. He set her on her feet and released her, his dark gaze riveting as he reached out with deliberation and caught the hem of her wet T-shirt and pulled it over her head.

His chest expanded and his appraisal was a warm caress that set her tingling. "You're beautiful," he said in a rough voice.

His hands shook as he unfastened the clasp of her bra, and then he leaned down and took her breast in his mouth, his tongue stroking her nipple.

She closed her eyes, clutching his shoulders, knowing she was ready to take any risk with him. Maybe this was living dangerously, but she wanted to reach out with heart and body and soul to make their marriage work and be a family for Kevin. And maybe win Jeb's love. She was in love with this strong cowboy who had stormed into her life and changed it completely. And she was ready to take some big risks to try to make a real marriage of their paper one.

He might not love her now, but he wanted her, and he seemed to like her. She hoped love would come as naturally as the sun rising. All their futures were at stake and it was a heady choice, but an easy one when it came down to this moment. Night after night she had thought about the attraction between them and where to go with it. To be wise and cautious and wait. Or to go for all she could and hope for the best.

When she tugged at his belt, he raised his head to look at her, questions in his gaze.

"I want you," she said quietly.

His chest expanded and something flickered in the depths of his eyes. "Not ever like I've wanted you," he whispered, pulling her to him to envelope her in his embrace and kiss her hungrily.

She unbuckled his belt and unbuttoned his wet jeans, pushing them away and then peeling down his wet briefs, freeing him.

His shaft was thick and hard and ready and she couldn't get her breath, looking at the perfection of him. He unbuttoned her cutoffs and shoved them away, then removed her lacy underwear. He pulled her down in the grass, leaning over her while he trailed kisses from her throat down across her breasts, stroking her nipple as he kissed her. Then he took her nipple in his mouth to suck and lick and tease.

Moaning softly with pleasure, bombarded by sensations that drove her wild, she trailed her hands over his strong body, discovering him, memorizing every texture, wanting him desperately. She sat up, pushing him down as she took him in her mouth to kiss him.

He groaned, his fingers winding in her thick hair. Then she was all over him, caressing him with her cool, soft fingers, trailing kisses over him. He yanked the ribbon out of her hair and all the fiery locks fell, darker with water, framing her face and curling on her bare, pale shoulders.

Jeb watched her and his heart threatened to pound out of his chest. She was magic and dreams and hot sex. She was all he wanted and had dreamed about since the night he met her. Her body was soft and pink and white. She was beautiful and wildly passionate, coming to him with a hunger that matched his own for her.

Sometime, somewhere she had made her decision about how they would live. This union was the lady's choice. Knowing she wanted him set him on fire even more. Then she lay sprawled across him, one hand playing over his chest, the other holding him while her tongue glided over his hard shaft. He felt he would burst with need and knew he couldn't wait much longer before his control was gone.

He swung her down and moved over her to kiss and stroke her in return while she looked up at him through half-closed green temptress eyes that were filled with desire.

He moved between her legs, his fingers caressing, finding her feminine places and stroking her until she was taut with need, clinging to him. Amanda's hips moved in an age-old rhythm and she shook, wanting him more than anything else.

"Jeb!" she gasped, and then she shuddered and spilled over a brink.

Spreading her legs, he towered over her, male, sexy, ready. And then he slowly lowered himself, the tip of his shaft touching her, setting her aflame all over again, and then gently entering her, filling her.

He went slowly, perspiration covering him, the only indication of the effort it was costing him to slow down and hold back for her.

"Mandy! My Mandy," he gasped, his voice grating and husky while one hand tangled in her hair and the other hand held her.

They moved together and she clung to his broad shoulders, her eyes closed while she was swept into an urgent spiral. Her long legs were wrapped around him and her hands played over his firm buttocks, down to his hard thighs as she pulled him even closer.

They rocked together, Jeb fighting to make it last, knowing he was losing all control. He was aware of her wildly thrashing beneath him while she clung to him tightly. Her hips arched and he could feel her body tense like a spring coiled tighter and tighter.

"Jeb," she whispered, turning her head. Shifting, he kissed her deeply as he thrust into her. She arched against him, her hips moving, and then he was lost, release exploding in him and shaking him, his pounding pulse shutting out all sounds.

Amanda cried out again, clinging to him, bursting with ecstasy as release came, moving with him in a blinding climax.

"Jeb, I love you," she whispered, unable to hold back the words, knowing she had made the fullest commitment possible to him this day. For better or for worse, she had given herself totally to him. Wife, lover, friend—she prayed she could be all three for him and that he would be husband, lover and friend for her.

They moved together, slowing, and then she was caught on another dizzying spiral, clutching him, her hips moving as his slow thrusts and withdrawals were setting her on fire once more.

"Jeb!"

Tension escalated in her, need rebuilding until she burst over another brink and melted into his embrace. He showered her with kisses and stroked her. When she opened her eyes to look up at him, she was shaken, too aware of how much of a commitment she had made, while he may not have made any at all.

Today she wouldn't worry about it. She would take what they had and cherish every moment and memory. She stroked his jaw, feeling the faint stubble, awed by the wonder of him and their union.

"You're beautiful and you're wonderful and you're sexier than I ever thought possible."

"That sounds like a man in the throes of passion."

"Nope. Just an honest cowboy and his awesome lady."

She laughed and picked a blade of grass to trail it over his face and down on his shoulder. "No one has ever called me awesome. You are still foggy from loving."

"*Foggy* isn't the right description," he said, rolling over and taking her with him so that they both lay on their sides facing each other. He brushed her damp hair away from her face. "I'm exhausted and too beat to even stand up."

"You didn't plan all this?"

"Promise. I'm telling the truth. Don't know why Jake decided to take Kevin and go—except Jake is a chocoholic. He loves chocolate ice cream and Mrs. Fletcher has some. Hon, if I was going to plan a seduction, it wouldn't have been in the horse tank."

She laughed and wrapped her arms around his neck, looking at him and wondering if she would ever get enough of touching him or looking at him or talking to him.

"I never would have guessed you'd take that flying leap into the water," he said, grinning at her. She stroked the corner of his mouth, thought about his kisses and pulled his head to her, tugging him closer to trail her tongue over his lips and then to kiss him.

"I intend to keep you guessing, mister," she teased.

"Let me guess how you like this," he drawled. His arms locked around her and he swung her up over him and in minutes she straddled him, sitting up straight to look down at him. His hands cupped her breasts and his thumbs drew lazy circles on her taut nipples while she closed her eyes and gasped with pleasure.

Then his hands slid to her narrow waist and he lifted her up, setting her on his thick rod.

"See what you do to me?" he said in a husky voice.

Hunger for him shook her and she slid slowly down on him, feeling him enter her again, and then they were moving, lost in another wild union that shut out the world.

He stroked her breast while his other hand went between her thighs, to stroke and touch her. She gasped with pleasure, intoxicated with desire and fulfillment and the knowledge that Jeb wanted her and wanted to give her pleasure.

They moved together until she cried out and fell across him, sprawling over his broad chest and thrilled to feel his strong arms wrapped around her.

"I don't want to ever go home," she whispered. "This is paradise."

"I don't want to go home for days because I want to keep making love to you all the rest of this day and night. And I'll want the same thing tomorrow." He rolled her over again and propped his head on his elbow while he stroked her hair away from her face. "Move into my bedroom with me."

"You're sure?"

"Yes."

She thought about all the move would mean and knew it was what she wanted, too. Her heart thudded with joy at his request and she nodded. "Yes, I will."

"Aah, Mandy. This is good. So damned good."

She wrapped her arms around him and pulled him closer. "I think so, too."

For the next half hour they lay in each other's arms and talked and then Jeb stood and carried her back to the tank, stepped into the water and lowered her into it with him.

His body was sleek and warm in the cold water and in minutes she could feel the change in him and knew he wanted to love again.

"Jeb, we're in the water."

"Yeah," he said, covering her mouth with his and stopping any conversation. He kissed her hard and long and she forgot any protests and in minutes he pulled her over him. She straddled him again and slid down on him, moving with him for another plunge into rapture.

This time when she sat beside him, she caught his hand as he started to caress her.

"We should go home."

"Why? Mrs. Fletcher will take care of Kevin. We have privacy and who do you need to see or talk to?"

"I guess no one if Kevin is all right."

"You know he is."

"You get your way again."

"I hope so, lady." He stood and picked her up again. "Come here."

He carried her easily to his pickup, opened a door and leaned down. "Get that blanket," he said.

She grabbed a light cotton blanket in multicolored stripes. When she covered herself with it, he grinned. "That isn't why I picked that up. If I had you to myself, I'd lock us in the house and throw all your clothes away."

"Thank goodness this is one time you can't and won't get your way! And you're making me blush again."

"That's no reason to blush. I'll give you a real reason to in a minute."

"Forget it, cowboy. Let your imagination cool down."

"It can't when I'm with you."

Her heart raced because she was having the most fun she'd ever had in her life. He was virile, sexy, exciting. His hair was dry now and locks fell on his forehead. He was confident and caring at the same time and she never wanted the day to end. She didn't have even the tiniest regret. Everything felt right and good and promising for a future together.

They reached the place where they had made love before and he set her on her feet, taking the blanket from her and spreading it on the grass.

"You can't tell me you didn't plan this," she said, watching his muscles ripple in his arms and back as he worked.

"I swear I didn't," he said. He straightened up, his grin fading as he looked at her standing nude before him, and she didn't care because she wanted to look at him and touch him and kiss him.

"Mandy," he whispered, drawing her to him and fitting her into his embrace, leaning down to kiss her hungrily as if it were the first time all over again.

They spent the late afternoon beneath the trees, making love leisurely, talking, touching, and she was in paradise.

"Jeb, we have to go home. I'll be so embarrassed."

"Shucks, honey, we're married! There's nothing wrong with a husband and wife disappearing for a few hours."

"I think it's more than a few hours, and Mrs. Fletcher will want to go home."

"I can remedy that. I'll call home." He was up and

striding away before she could answer. She watched him walk easily away, nude, confident, so sexy.

He was back in a few minutes. She felt ridiculous, lying on the blanket totally naked, and had flipped it over herself. He came striding back dressed in his jeans and carrying his phone, his watch and her T-shirt.

"These are dry. Your other clothes are back there. I called home and Mrs. Fletcher can stay with Kevin for another couple of hours and I told her we'd be home then."

"Jeb! That's downright decadent."

"I didn't tell her what we've been doing," he said, grinning at her. "I just said I was delayed and you were with me and could she stay longer. She didn't mind, so that's that. And I asked her if she could stay Saturday night. I want to take you dancing, although what I want most is just to be in bed with you."

His words thrilled her and she was excited by the prospect of going dancing with him. He stretched out beside her, unbuttoned his jeans and turned to take her into his arms. "Get this out of here," he said, tossing the blanket off her.

She saw that he wore nothing under his jeans and that he was aroused and ready for her again. She went into his arms eagerly, wanting him with an unending need that shocked her.

It was dusk when they dressed and he kissed her long and hard before climbing into his pickup to return to the house.

While Amanda talked to Kevin, Jeb talked to Mrs. Fletcher and then joined them. They spent the next hour with Kevin and put him to bed at nine.

As they tiptoed out of his room, Amanda took Jeb's

hand. "We haven't had any dinner yet. Mrs. Fletcher left a lot of food. There's some cold chicken and—"

Jeb picked her up and turned down the hall. "I'll tell you what I want—the wedding night we never had. Food can wait, lady. This is more important."

Her heart thudded and she wound her fingers in his hair to cling to him.

"You're a sex-starved, lusty cowboy."

"And you, ma'am, are the hottest wench around. What you do to me is magic and I can't wait," he whispered, closing his door and setting her on her feet.

Amanda gazed into his dark eyes and could hear only the pounding of her pulse. His gaze lowered to her mouth and her breath caught as he leaned forward. He wrapped his arms around her and kissed her, pulling her up against him. In seconds they were shedding clothes and moving to the bed together, all thoughts of dinner forgotten, as they made love again, consumed by wild passion.

At two in the morning as she lay in his arms in his big bed, he stroked her shoulder lightly. "I hear rumbles that I think are coming from my stomach. I didn't have lunch or dinner. That fruit and biscuit I had yesterday morning was the last food I've eaten."

"Are you complaining?" she asked in a sexy, languid voice, rising up on an elbow to look at him.

"Hardly," he answered, stroking her bare breasts and nibbling on her throat. "This is a lot better than cold chicken."

She laughed and rolled away from him. "Come on, cowboy. I'll feed you."

"And then we're coming right back to bed."

"Maybe," she said, slanting him a saucy look over her shoulder. "You'll have to entice me."

"I'll remember that, and it's a promise."

She scooped up her T-shirt and dropped it over her head. It came only to her thighs, but she knew they would have the house to themselves because Kevin would sleep soundly for hours longer.

She watched as Jeb pulled on his jeans and buttoned them, then came to drape his arm across her shoulders.

They ate cold chicken and a tossed green salad, and she heated steamed carrots. After dinner Jeb got a beer and poured iced tea for her, and they sat and talked at the kitchen table for another thirty minutes.

Jeb propped one foot on another kitchen chair and sipped the cold beer, feeling it go down his throat while he watched her. He knew she was wearing nothing except her provocative T-shirt and the thought was driving him wild. He marveled at himself; he had made love to her all afternoon and evening. He should be satisfied, and able to get his thoughts back to the ranch and everyday things. Instead, all he could think about was her body and how easy it would be to slip the red T-shirt over her head and how much he wanted to do so.

She was unbelievably passionate, something he had suspected she would be, but her eagerness still amazed him. All he had to do was start to think about this afternoon and he would become aroused again.

Would they have a real marriage after all? The thought cheered him. He wanted a family like the one he had known.

Right now, all he wanted to do was to go around the table, take her into his arms and pull off that red T-shirt.

Amanda was telling him something, but he wasn't hearing a word of what she was saying.

"Jeb, are you listening to me?"

"Sure, honey. Well, actually, I'm remembering this afternoon and thinking what I'd like to be doing right now."

She tilted her head to study him while he got up and left to turn on some music. He came back to take her hand and pull her into his arms to dance with her. She smiled up at him. "I don't do my best dancing when I'm barefoot."

"I think it's the best. I like it best when you're only wearing that sexy shirt that clings to you. Or no shirt at all."

"I'm not dancing naked."

As he chuckled, he pulled her closer and they slow-danced and she could feel his arousal. Desire was burning again in her. Then the song ended and a fast number came on and they danced together, Jeb turning her, his hand drifting lightly across her bare bottom when he got the chance.

The moment his fingers stroked across her bottom, her insides tightened and she wanted him as desperately as any time earlier. She locked both hands behind his neck and swiveled her hips against him and he groaned, pulling her tightly into his embrace. In minutes he carried her to bed and they made love long into the night, falling asleep a few hours before dawn.

"Jeb," she said sleepily in the first rays of morning light.

He stretched and then kissed her. "Yeah?"

"Kevin won't know where to find me."

"You can tell him today that you've moved in with me. He'll accept it and that will be that."

"I suppose you're right."

It was almost seven before Amanda was showered

and dressed and in the kitchen, ready to fix breakfast for all of them and expecting Kevin at any moment.

Jeb came striding into the room and kissed her, taking cups of coffee from her and setting them on the table.

"Kevin likes swimming so much, we might think about a pool in a year or two."

"That's a lot of work and expense."

"We can talk about it. It would be good for him."

"Are we arguing already?"

"Never."

Giddy with happiness, she laughed and Jeb grinned at her. She knew they were both on a high from love and she hoped it would last.

During the next weeks, into late August, Amanda was in paradise with Kevin and Jeb. The tall, tough cowboy came home early and played with Kevin, and as soon as Kevin was in bed each night, Jeb pulled her onto his lap or carried her to bed to make love.

One Monday afternoon Amanda heard a car coming up the road. She watched out the front window, wondering who was coming and thinking it must be someone for Jeb. To her surprise, it was a taxi.

"Who would come out here in a cab?" she asked herself aloud as she stared at the cab, unable to imagine who was in it. Jeb's mother always drove when she came.

It slowed and stopped and Amanda watched the driver get out and remove three large suitcases, but still no passenger had gotten out of the taxi.

Curious, Amanda went to the front door and swung it open to watch the driver hold the back door of the taxi. A long shapely leg appeared and then a woman stepped out. She wore skin-tight hot pink capri pants and a sleeveless, tight-fitting hot pink top. Her golden hair was almost white and framed her face in a mass of loose waves. As she started toward the house, Amanda stared in shock. Why would Cherie come to the ranch for a visit?

Nine

"I know I should have had my secretary call," Cherie purred, smiling broadly at Amanda as she approached her. She walked up and hugged her lightly, perfume assailing Amanda, and then she stepped back, smiling confidently.

Amanda stared at her, feeling the same deep shock as she had last June when she had opened the door to face Jeb.

"This is a surprise. And it'll be a surprise for Kevin, Cherie," Amanda said, worried about Kevin and how it would be for him to meet Cherie.

"May I come in?"

"Yes," Amanda answered carefully, still worrying about Kevin and what this was going to mean to him. At the moment he was away with Jeb, and she was glad he wasn't home. She needed time to discover what was behind Cherie's sudden appearance. And she was certain there was a purpose in Cherie's visit.

"Kevin isn't here right now, but since he's never seen you, this will be an adjustment for him."

Cherie smiled and looked around the room. "What a nice, homey place you've made this," she said, but her voice didn't sound convincing.

Amanda motioned to a chair and watched her cousin as she sat down. Show business had changed her, and she had a poise she hadn't had before. Her looks were even more spectacular with her big blue eyes and her lush figure. Diamonds adorned her fingers and wrist. Amanda became uncomfortably aware of her own appearance. Her red hair was up in a ponytail with locks that had fallen free around her face. She was dressed in a blue T-shirt and cutoffs and wore no makeup. She felt frowsy and plain next to Cherie, who sat with her legs crossed.

"Jeb isn't home?"

"No. And he's taken Kevin with him."

"Out riding the range with the cows and horses. How's your arrangement working?"

"Our marriage is fine," Amanda said uneasily.

Cherie laughed. "You don't need to pretend with me. Remember, you told me that you and Jeb did this to give Kevin a home." Her smile vanished and she leaned forward, suddenly looking solemn. "Amanda, I realize I've made some terrible mistakes."

A chill ran down Amanda's spine. She could guess what kind of mistakes Cherie had decided she'd made, but she wondered what was motivating her. Cherie couldn't have suddenly developed love and longing for a child she hadn't seen since the day he was born— a child she had been more than happy to give away.

"Jeb was a good husband. I've been married to two real jerks and my last marriage is over. I'm divorced and wiser, and I realize that I threw away the best man I've ever known."

Amanda's chill turned to ice because she knew that Cherie could charm any man if she set her mind to it. And Jeb was not only human, he had been married to Cherie and once upon a time was in love with her.

"We're married," she said softly.

"I can't imagine it really means much to either one of you. You yourself told me when you married him that it was for Kevin's sake. I know this is inconvenient—"

"Inconvenient? Cherie, we're a family."

"Not as much a family as Jeb and Kevin and I," Cherie said softly. "Amanda, I'm Kevin's blood mother. I was the wife Jeb was wildly in love with. Is he wildly in love with you?"

Amanda stared at Cherie, hurt and fear and anger springing to life in her.

"It might have just been for Kevin when we married," Amanda said stiffly, "but it's more than that now," she finished, the words having a hollow ring. She didn't know for certain the depth of Jeb's feelings for her. And she was too aware that he had never said he loved her. Not even in the throes of passion had the words crossed his lips.

She stared at her cousin and wondered if her paper marriage was going to crumble right here and be over before it had really started. "People fall in love fast sometimes, Cherie. I think you have yourself before," Amanda gently reminded her. To Amanda's horror, Cherie's eyes filled with tears that spilled over and she pulled a handkerchief from a purse and dabbed at the tears.

"I was wrong and did the wrong thing. I gave away my baby and tossed my husband aside. I shouldn't have done either."

"Cherie, I legally adopted Kevin. I'm his mother."

"I'm his real mother and Jeb and I can give him a real family."

Feeling numb, Amanda heard noise at the back of the house and, with a sinking feeling, realized that Jeb and Kevin were home. Once again, she wanted to wrap Kevin in her arms and protect him. She knew her cousin far too well to imagine that Cherie was suddenly struck with a longing for her child.

"Excuse me, Cherie, but I think I should tell Jeb we have company."

"Not company, Amanda. I'm family."

Amanda left the room, hurrying to the kitchen, hearing Jeb and Kevin laughing over something.

She stepped inside the room and Jeb glanced at her as he pulled his dusty shirt off. "Whoa—I'm hot, dirty and headed for a shower, and Kevin is, too." He frowned and became still, his voice changing. "What's wrong, Amanda?"

"Jeb, we have a visi—"

"Jeb!" came Cherie's voice as she brushed past Amanda, sweeping into the room and crossing to Jeb to stand on tiptoe and kiss him on the mouth, wrapping her arms around his neck. Extricating himself, he stepped back and frowned.

"Cherie?"

"Kevin, this is Miss Webster," Amanda said to Kevin, who was staring wide-eyed at Cherie.

"Don't be so formal, Amanda. Kevin. Little Kevin," she purred softly. "I'm your real mother."

"Cherie," Jeb said in a deadly quiet voice, sweeping Kevin into his arms and moving past Cherie to hand him to Amanda. "Want to start a bath for Kevin?"

"Yes," she said, looking into dark eyes that held all the rage she had seen that first day she met him. Kevin continued to stare openmouthed at Cherie. Amanda carried him out and heard Jeb moving around the kitchen.

Kevin looked up at her. "You're my real mommy," he said in a troubled voice.

"Yes, I am," Amanda said with certainty, feeling sure Cherie was up to no good. "Cherie is my cousin, Kevin, and she's the woman who gave birth to you, but you're my little boy and I'm your mother and Jeb is your daddy and we love you with all our hearts."

He hugged her and she knew she would be covered with dust, but she didn't care. She wondered what was happening in the kitchen.

Jeb yanked his dusty shirt back on and got himself a beer, turning to face Cherie. "What the hell is going on?"

She pouted and studied him. "That's not much of a greeting."

"Cherie, why are you here?"

"Jeb, don't be so harsh! I know I deserve it, but I made a dreadful mistake." Her eyes filled with tears, but Jeb's patience was short. She had caused him a lifetime of grief in the short time he had known her and he knew now how deceptive she could really be.

He had been charmed and burned once, he wasn't going to let it happen twice.

She dabbed at the tears. "When we divorced, I lost the best man I've ever known."

"Oh, please," Jeb said in disgust. "You can pack up and head back to wherever you live."

"Jeb, I'm sorry. I'm divorced and I've finally realized what I had with you," she said.

Jeb stared at her. "It's over, Cherie. I'm married to Amanda. I'm a very married man."

"You both did that for Kevin. She told me that herself. I know you as well as I know Amanda. You didn't come home and fall in love with her. You married her to give Kevin a father and mother. Tell me that isn't true," she accused, batting her eyes at him and moving closer. "Jeb, remember the fun times we had—"

"All I can remember are the bad times. They canceled out the fun times." Too well, he remembered how charmed he had been by her and how full of fun she had been when he met her. Now all he could see was the woman who had given away their son and never told him about her pregnancy.

"You can't be in love with Amanda. I know you and I know her. She's not your type."

"I do love her," he said firmly, realizing that he had never admitted it to himself, not even with all their lovemaking. Was he really in love with his wife? He had been so busy with getting to know her and living with her, he hadn't stopped to think about it. She was all he admired and found desirable in a woman. He didn't hear what Cherie was saying to him, as he gazed out the window and thought about making love to Mandy.

"Jeb?"

"Sorry, I was thinking about my wife, Cherie."

"Don't shut me out, Jeb," she said softly. "Give us another chance," she said.

"Not in the next six lifetimes," he said. "We're through, Cherie. I'm trying to forget."

She cried softly, and he noticed that she managed to cry without smudging her makeup, but he supposed it was something she'd learned to do. "But you're going to let me get to know my son, aren't you? Surely his blood mother has that right. I can go to court, you know."

"Don't threaten me," he said in a quiet voice.

"And don't hold my son from me," she snapped. "I can go to court and it will give me tons of publicity."

"Bad publicity for abandoning your baby, not telling the father you're pregnant and giving up your baby."

"There's no such thing as bad publicity. Do you know how much publicity a custody battle would get me?"

"Dammit, Cherie, don't you drag my—"

"Our son! Jeb, he's very much mine, too. Don't worry. I'm not going to court over him. I just want to see you both again." Her voice changed to warm honey and she moved close to Jeb to draw her fingers along his jaw.

"Will you let me get to know Kevin? That seems like something small to ask. I know I made terrible mistakes, Jeb. Don't make me keep suffering for them."

He wondered how much she meant what she said. She had lied to him so many times during their marriage that he found it hard to trust her, yet there was a chance that she was telling the truth. And he knew she could go to court and cause a lot of trouble for them because she was Kevin's natural mother.

"All right, but don't hurt him."

"I wouldn't think of it."

"Oh, yes, you would. What do you think you just did when you came bounding in and said, 'Kevin, I'm your real mother'?"

"Maybe I handled that poorly, but I was carried away. He's my baby, and I don't even know him."

"And that was your choice."

"You've gotten tough, Jeb. The army must have changed you."

"It wasn't the army, Cherie."

"You must still feel something for me or you wouldn't be so bitter."

"Cherie, I promise you, the only woman in my life is Amanda. I lo—"

Cherie placed her fingers on his mouth. "Don't say it. You're just saying things because you're angry, and I know I deserve your anger. But don't tell me what a wonderful marriage you two have. I know it was for Kevin."

"It's getting to be a good marriage," he said evenly. Cherie was a beautiful woman, fantastic to look at, yet facing her now, all he felt was a dull anger. Even the anger and bitterness had begun to fade. It was a relief to know he was over her.

"Can I stay and talk to Kevin a little?"

As he stared at her, wanting to refuse, she touched his chest.

"Please, just for a little while. Don't refuse me getting to know my child," Cherie said in a small, helpless voice.

He remembered how badly he had wanted to see Kevin and get to know him, so reluctantly, he nodded, knowing she was Kevin's mother and it was only right that she could see her son.

"Yes, but be careful. Don't disrupt his life."

"You're angry with me," she said, pouting. "I'm sorry, Jeb. I can't ever tell you enough how sorry I am. I know now what kind of man I was married to and I wish I could undo all my mistakes."

"The past is over and forgotten, Cherie. There's a bar in the family room and you can get a drink. I'm going to shower."

She ran her hand along his arm. "I haven't forgotten what muscles you have," she said softly, looking up at him. "I haven't forgotten anything."

"Well, I have, and what I didn't forget, I'm trying to forget." He moved past her and left, her perfume lingering in the air. He had felt nothing when she had touched him. He wanted her out of his house, but he knew he had to let her see her son. He strode down the hall, going to Kevin's bathroom.

Amanda was bathing him and he was laughing with her over something. She looked pale, and spots of color were high in her cheeks. Otherwise, she didn't look as if anything unusual had happened, but the moment her green eyes met his gaze, he could see the worry in them.

"Can he splash a minute?"

"Sure," she said, standing. "Now that he can swim, I don't worry as much about him."

"He's all right. You don't have a teacup of water in the tub, and we're right here and can hear him playing,'' he said as they stepped into Kevin's bedroom. Jeb placed his hands on her shoulders. "Cherie asked to stay and get to know Kevin a little. I can't deny her that."

Amanda looked at the open bathroom door and frowned. "I suppose we can't, but it's hard to believe she really cares about him."

"I agree, but there's a chance she's being truthful. And she reminded me that she can take us to court."

"Oh, Jeb!"

"I don't think it would do her any good, but it won't hurt to let her get to know him a little, so I told her she can stay."

Amanda had a sinking feeling, looking up into Jeb's gaze, which was as unreadable as ever. Was it as simple as he was saying—or had Cherie rekindled some spark in him? Cherie was a gorgeous woman with a fabulous career. What man wouldn't be charmed by her? Amanda nodded and turned back to get Kevin out of the tub.

"I'll get Kevin dressed," she said stiffly, wondering how much Cherie was going to disrupt their lives and how much she was going to try to win Jeb back.

Had he asked her to stay here at the house? Then Amanda remembered the taxi. Cherie couldn't get one to come back out here after six o'clock. Amanda glanced at her watch. Cherie would never get one later this evening.

Anger filled her. They would have to ask Cherie to stay or Jeb would have to drive her back to town to her hotel.

Grimly, Amanda helped Kevin dress. "Sweetie, Miss Webster wants to see you, so she'll be here with us for a little while."

"I'm hungry."

"We're going to eat as soon as you and your father get cleaned up enough to sit at the table," Amanda said, helping him dry and dress, while her thoughts were on Cherie and the evening ahead of them.

As they went to join the others, Amanda felt that her world had been invaded by a foreign presence. Cherie didn't belong in their home with them. She knew her cousin too well. Cherie had a nice side, but she was accustomed to getting her way and could get ugly when thwarted.

Cherie sat in the family room, looking poised for a camera, glancing up when Kevin and Amanda entered the room.

"None of us has had supper yet, Cherie. Would you like to join us?" Amanda reluctantly offered.

"Yes, I'd love that. Jeb asked me to stay," she said slyly. "I hope it isn't inconvenient."

"I hope not, too, Cherie. I'll get supper if you'll excuse us."

Cherie looked at Amanda with smug amusement. "Sorry, Amanda, but I am part of their lives. A very important part. Jeb and I had some wonderful times together."

"I'm sure you did," Amanda said quietly, and turned to go to the kitchen, anger shaking her.

Jeb had asked Cherie to stay. How would he be able to resist the woman? A star—gorgeous, sexy, charming when she wanted to be—how long would it take before he succumbed?

Dinner was quiet except for Cherie. Kevin had withdrawn into a shell, as quiet as he had been before moving to the ranch. Cherie had brought toys that fascinated him, including a toy fire engine and a model airplane that had a remote control. As soon as they finished eating, he began to play with his new gifts.

At half past eight Amanda put Kevin to bed. When she returned to the family room, she heard Cherie's peal of laughter and entered to see Jeb smiling and Cherie still chuckling. Amanda knew she was right, Jeb would never be able to resist Cherie for long.

"I suppose I should call a taxi now if you'll tell me where the phone is."

"You'll never get a cab out here, Cherie," Jeb said dryly. "I can take you back to town or you can spend the night."

"Whatever you prefer," she said, catching her lower lip in her teeth and looking directly at Jeb, ignoring Amanda. It was an hour-and-a-half drive into Dallas, and depending on Cherie's hotel, it could be even farther. It would take three hours for Jeb to come and go.

"Just stay. It'll be easier," Jeb said, glancing at Amanda, who looked away. She didn't want him to take Cherie home, but neither did she want Cherie moving in with them. "Someone can take you into town tomorrow," Jeb added. "I'll get your things," he said, standing and walking out of the room.

Cherie looked at Amanda and smiled. "You can't lose him," she said softly, "because you never really had him."

"Don't push it, Cherie. If you want to see Kevin, all right."

Cherie's brows arched. "This is a side to you I haven't seen, little cousin. You're in love with him, aren't you?" She laughed. "Small wonder. I'll get Jeb to show me where I sleep *tonight*." She put an emphasis on the word *tonight* and smiled again at

Amanda, who felt another flash of anger. Cherie was so confident where men were concerned, and small wonder. How many times in her life had a man not done what she wanted? There were three divorces, but in each of those, she suspected that Cherie had decided it was time for the divorce before the man had. Even with Jeb.

She heard them talking in the hall. It was twenty minutes before they returned, Cherie laughing again and Jeb smiling at something she had said.

They sat down and Amanda found it difficult to enjoy any light conversation while Cherie constantly flirted with Jeb and talked about her success as a singer. "I've signed for a movie deal," she announced smugly.

"Congratulations," Amanda said.

"That's great," Jeb said quietly. "What is it and who's producing it?"

They listened while Cherie talked about the movie plans and Amanda wondered what she really wanted. Why did she want Jeb back now? She still didn't think Cherie wanted Kevin, and with a movie deal, there was no way Cherie would want to live on the ranch. She studied her cousin, curiosity nagging at her.

The evening seemed interminable until Cherie announced she was turning in and left with smiles for Jeb.

As soon as she had gone, Jeb stood. "I'm getting a beer. Let's sit outside awhile. The air's thick in here. Want something to drink?"

"I'll come help. I'd like iced tea."

As soon as they had their drinks they walked out on the porch, where it was dark and cool and quiet. Crickets chirped and in the distance she could hear the deep croak of a bullfrog, but she couldn't enjoy the lovely night. She was too aware of the sexy woman asleep down the hall, a woman who wanted her husband and her child, a woman who was an intrusion in their lives.

They sat in silence, each lost in their own thoughts, and Amanda wondered whether Jeb was withdrawing from her. What was running through his mind? She had heard him laugh with Cherie, and she had listened to Cherie's outrageous flirting. Amanda touched her cold glass to her throbbing temple and prayed that Cherie wouldn't be with them long.

"She asked me if she can stay longer to get to know Kevin."

"Longer?" Amanda's dread deepened.

"I can understand how she feels about him. I know how I felt. I can't deny her getting to know her own son, Amanda. Neither can you. She's his natural mother, and that has to count for something."

"I'm the one who loves him and cares for him and sits up at night with him."

"I know she gave him away. Everything she did was wrong, but she's asked to stay a few days just to get to know him. I can't deny her that and neither can you. I don't want her here any more than you do."

"Don't you?" Amanda couldn't keep from asking.

"No, I don't," he said in a level voice, setting down his half-empty beer and reaching for her hand. "Come sit in my lap."

She went willingly and he pulled her to him to kiss her.

After a moment Amanda straightened to look at him. Black locks of hair fell across his forehead and she pushed them away. "She wants you back."

"I don't want her," he said firmly. He framed Amanda's face with his hands, looking at her for a long moment before he leaned forward to kiss her. His mouth opened hers, his tongue stroking hers, and then he wrapped his arms around her tightly and leaned over her, cradling her against his shoulder while he kissed her.

She returned his kisses, too aware of her throbbing head, the miserable day, Cherie in the house with them and Cherie wanting Jeb. A woman totally accustomed to getting her way with men wouldn't be one to give up easily. Then Jeb shifted, holding her tightly against him while he kissed her deeply and she forgot everything, clinging to him, wanting him with a huge ache in her heart.

In minutes he stood, holding her in his arms and carrying her down the hall to their bedroom. As he set her on her feet, he closed the door behind him. "She's at the other end of the hall."

"Then why do I feel her presence in here with us?" Amanda asked.

"Forget her. I can. And I'll bet I can see to it that you do."

"Oh, Jeb. All I can think is that she wants you back and no man has ever been able to resist her."

He ran his hands through Amanda's hair, framing her face. "I don't want her back, Mandy. Not now or ever."

She gazed up at him in the moonlit room and wondered if he could resist the seductive wiles of Cherie.

"I told you I can make you forget. Let's see how long it takes," he said in a husky voice, kissing her and pulling her into his embrace. She leaned away and shook her head.

"Jeb, my head is throbbing."

"I can cure that, too," he whispered, his tongue flicking in her ear, and then his warm breath was on her throat while he caressed her nape and trailed kisses to the corner of her mouth, his tongue sliding over her lower lip.

She inhaled swiftly, trying to catch her breath, desire blossoming in her. His tongue stroked hers and his hands moved over her, sliding up her rib cage, cupping her breasts. He pushed away her blouse and unfastened the clasp on her bra while he kissed her and then his thumbs lazily circled her taut nipples.

She moaned softly, moving closer against him while she wrapped her arms around his neck and kissed him with all the pent-up longing and love she had.

He leaned against the wall and spread his legs, cupping her bottom and pulling her up against his hard arousal.

She ached with wanting him, loving him. She fumbled with his buttons and belt, pushing away his shirt and then shoving down his jeans.

He peeled away her cutoffs and silk panties and lifted her into his arms while he kissed her hungrily. "Put your legs around me," he whispered, and nibbled at her neck.

She held him tightly as he slid into her, filling her, his heat melting her. They moved together, lost in sensation, and she clung to him, wanting to give to him, wanting to take from him, knowing that, at this moment in time, they were one and all was safe and well.

Ecstasy burst in her and she clung to him, hearing him say her name as he thrust wildly with his release. He slowed and held her tightly, kissing her throat, carrying her to their shower, where he set her on her feet and turned on the water.

After a quick shower they toweled dry and in minutes were in bed, loving again as he trailed kisses slowly over every inch of her. "I want to love you all night, to show you just a little of what I feel for you," he whispered. She trembled with love and joy at his words and tender kisses and slow caresses.

She clung to him tightly, loving him, wanting to hold him forever. "I love you, Jeb," she whispered, meaning every word, not certain about him. And then thoughts shattered and the world was mindless, sensations bombarding her, an insatiable need for him driving her to a frenzy until her release burst and she felt his shuddering release.

He held her tightly, showering her with kisses and rolling over to hold her close.

Exhaustion enveloped her and she lay locked in his arms, stroking his smooth back, sliding her hand over his firm buttocks, down to his muscled thigh.

Jeb fell asleep locked in her arms without another word about Cherie. Amanda lay staring into the darkness, Jeb's dark head on her shoulder while he slept. She stroked his hair and wondered if she would ever know what really ran through his mind. Amanda ran her fingers across her brow. Her headache was gone. True to his word, Jeb had driven it away and he had driven away every thought of Cherie for a time, but now the demon thoughts were returning to plague her. Amanda wondered how long Cherie would stay with them.

The next day Cherie stayed at the house all day, hovering over Kevin, giving orders to Mrs. Fletcher and taunting Amanda with biting remarks.

That night Amanda bathed Kevin, knowing Cherie was out on the porch flirting outrageously with Jeb.

When Jeb came home the following day, he slowed the pickup as he approached the house. Cherie was seated in the shade on the corral fence. She climbed down and came toward him, blocking his way. She wore a bright blue halter top and tight-fitting skimpy shorts, and she was even more beautiful than he remembered. She flagged him to a stop and walked around to his open window.

"Hi. I was waiting for you to get home."

Ten

"What do you want, Cherie?"

"Can we talk a few minutes? Get out. I know you're hot."

He climbed out, too aware that they were on the back side of the barn and out of sight of the house or any people. Cherie moved close to him to run her fingers along his arm. "Don't you feel something? Be truthful."

He looked at her wide blue eyes and flawless skin. "You're very beautiful," he said, thinking he would have to be dead not to have some kind of physical response to her attention. "But I'm not interested. I'm a married man, Cherie. Happily married."

"You're not in love."

"Yes, I am," he said evenly.

She shook her head, moving closer to him. "I don't

think you are. You don't act like a man in love. I should know.''

"I've changed and I love Amanda,'' he declared.

"Jeb, I can give you and Kevin so much. Remember how good it was when we made love? I remember exactly. I remember—''

"Cherie, I'm hot, tired and I want to see Amanda and Kevin. I'll see you at dinner.''

Not caring that anger snapped in her blue eyes, he climbed into the pickup and drove past her. He thought about his declarations of love. He had been so set against falling in love again, guarding his broken heart, that he hadn't stopped to really think about his feelings for Mandy. He had told Cherie he was in love with Amanda, but it had been a defensive answer. Not since the wedding had he stopped to sort out his own feelings.

Was he truly in love? he wondered. He remembered Amanda rocking Kevin and the tenderness in her voice. He thought about her beneath him, her softness enveloping him, her green eyes dark with desire. He knew she was a necessary part of his life, and he loved everything about her.

"I love her,'' he said aloud as he strode toward the house. He wanted to storm inside, find her, carry her to bed to make love to her and tell her all night long how he felt.

He looked at the house, lengthening his stride, and then he remembered that Cherie was living with them and how tense Amanda was. He would wait so they could have a special time when he told her.

He ran through what he wanted to do to surprise her. "I love her,'' he whispered to himself again, knowing that he did. Until today he hadn't stopped to acknowledge his feelings. Maybe he had been scared to look at them too closely. Was she as happy as he was? Twice in the throes of passion he had heard her say "I love you," and he hoped she did love him. Amanda had always been truthful with him. Impatience stabbed him.

They could put up with Cherie a little longer, but then Jeb wanted her to go. He wanted to take Amanda on a short trip where he had her all to himself to tell her he loved her. He would get her another ring—one that came with love this time. She hadn't had a honeymoon. She hadn't had several things she should have had.

He would wait and make it special when he said those three words, but right now, just thinking about her and his feelings for her, he wanted her in his arms desperately. He wanted to love and hold her. One thing—when he declared his love, it shouldn't come as any surprise. He knew he acted as in love as any man could.

He reached for the door, wanting to shout her name, grab her and carry her to bed and pour out his feelings, but they had to go to supper soon with Cherie and Kevin.

"Hot day?" Mrs. Fletcher asked as he walked through the kitchen. Kevin sat at the kitchen table coloring a picture, but the moment Jeb entered the room, he slid off his chair and ran to his dad.

"Hottest one yet," Jeb said, swinging Kevin into his arms and feeling another swell of love, this time for his son. "Hi, Kevin," he greeted him, hugging Kevin and relishing his small arms wrapped around his neck as he hugged Jeb in return. Kevin smelled soapy and clean and Jeb knew he was getting him dusty, but he didn't care. It was sheer heaven to come home and have Kevin throw himself into his arms. He shifted his son so he could hold him and talk to him, and Kevin rested one arm around Jeb's neck. "What's been happening here?"

Kevin merely pointed to his coloring book. "Will you color wif me?"

"After I shower," Jeb said, setting Kevin down. "I'm dusty now. I'll bathe and come back." As soon as Jeb stood and started to walk away, Kevin followed him.

Jeb knew he wasn't going to get Mandy to himself for a while because Kevin often tagged along with him around the house. "What did you do today?" he asked Kevin, looking down the hall and into the family room for Mandy, wanting to see her badly.

Maybe he shouldn't wait. Maybe he should just tell her now that he loved her. He debated with himself as he strode down the hall, but he decided to wait, to try to make that moment special.

And then he saw her coming out of Kevin's room with a pair of small jeans in her hands. She saw him and smiled and his insides constricted while heat flashed in him. She wore cutoffs and a T-shirt and was barefoot with her hair caught up in a ponytail. She looked incredible and he ached to scoop her into his arms and carry her to bed.

"Hi," he said, walking up to her and tilting her face up. He saw her quick searching glance and wondered how her day had been, but then her soft lips were beneath his. He knew Kevin was standing beside him, so he straightened up.

"I'm hot and dusty and going to shower." He

looked down at Kevin. "Are you taking a shower with me?"

Kevin shook his head and turned, running back toward the kitchen. Jeb laughed and looked at her. "I wonder how old he'll be before he minds getting a bath."

"When he notices girls, he'll want to bathe."

"Well, that's my case. I'm noticing one right now and I want to bathe with her. I missed you." He picked her up in his arms and she yelped softly.

"Jeb!"

"I know. I'll get you dusty, but that's just a penalty you pay for having a husband who can't wait to get you in his arms." Once again he was torn between telling her right now that he loved her or waiting to make it special. He strode into their bedroom and turned to swing the door shut with his toe. As he did, he glanced down the hall and saw Cherie standing at the end of the hall watching them.

"Jeb," Amanda said as the door closed and he leaned against it, setting her on her feet. "I feel Cherie's presence all the time. It's like she's here with us. I want her out of here."

"I want her out of here, too," he said solemnly, "but I think it's only fair to give her some time with Kevin."

"I don't think it's Kevin who's holding her here," Amanda said quietly.

"If I thought she didn't care about Kevin, I'd run her off the place right now." As Amanda started to move away, Jeb caught her, pulling her roughly against him. "Come here. This is what I've been waiting for since breakfast." Moving back to lean against the closed door, he bent his head to kiss her hungrily, wanting her and knowing he should wait until he showered, but thinking that then he might not be alone. He reached behind him to turn the lock on their bedroom door and then his hand slid to her cutoffs to unfasten them.

"I want you, Mandy," he whispered hoarsely, showering her with kisses, sliding his hand beneath the cutoffs and lace panties. Consumed with desire for her, he couldn't wait, kissing her hard and deep, his hand finding her soft, intimate places.

With a moan of pleasure Amanda melted into his embrace. The stiffness and worry and strain of Cherie being in the house evaporated. Jeb was dusty and sweaty, but she no longer cared. He was shaking with need, kissing her as if their kisses were his first in a year, his hands stroking her and driving every thought out of her head.

She was in his arms, being loved by him, and suddenly the world was right again. He was her man and he was showering her with love. He shoved away her clothing and pulled her T-shirt over her head, tossing it aside.

She wanted Jeb, all his hardness, his strength, his reassurance. She unfastened his jeans and shoved them away, peeling away his briefs and letting them fall around his ankles, wanting him with the same desperate urgency with which he seemed to need her.

He lifted her up and she wrapped her long legs around him and then his shaft slowly filled her. Sensations consumed her in scalding flames, and she clung to him while they moved in unison to a bursting release. "Jeb! My Jeb!" she cried softly, clinging to his broad, strong shoulders.

With ragged breathing, they slowed, and she slid

her legs down his, standing on her own feet. "Now I need that shower, too."

"We'll do that when I get out of these boots," he said with a grin. "I was a man in a hurry."

She rubbed against him with a purr. "I'm glad. It makes me feel wanted."

"You're wanted, all right," he said roughly, "and if you don't quit rubbing against me like that, we'll never get that shower."

"Mandy!" he yelled, struggling to get off a boot while standing with one arm still around her. He stepped away and she looked at him, naked, with his clothes shoved around his ankles while he tried to get off his boots, and she laughed.

"What a sight you are!"

He grinned at her. "You got me in this predicament and it's embarrassing, and if you don't stop laughing at me, I'll take some sweet revenge."

"Phooey!" She laughed as he hobbled to a chair and sat down, struggling to yank off his boots. He looked up at her and grinned.

"Just you wait!"

She turned and rushed to their bathroom to start the shower. In seconds he stepped in with her. "Now. I told you if you kept laughing, I'd get my revenge."

"You can't. We've got to show up at supper, and Kevin will probably come looking for us any minute now."

"Words, words," he said, running his hands over her hips and then up over her rib cage to cup her breasts.

She inhaled swiftly, but caught his wrists. "You don't get your way this time!" She stepped out of the shower swiftly, grabbed a towel and moved away from him.

Watching her, Jeb finished showering, knowing she was right but already wanting her again. Her green eyes sparkled mischievously and he was glad they'd made love because she looked far happier than she had when he had come home.

His mind jumped to where they could go for a delayed honeymoon. Tomorrow he would go into town and look at rings.

While he finished showering, Amanda pulled on a blue-and-white sundress, slipped on sandals and brushed her hair into a ponytail again swiftly. Jeb came out of the shower with only a towel wrapped around his waist. He was dark brown, hard with muscle, tall and lean, and she drew a deep breath at the sight of him. Just looking at him could turn her to jelly. With an effort she tore her gaze away and rushed to leave the room, afraid if he dropped the towel, she would walk right back into his arms.

"Mandy," he said softly.

She turned with her hand on the doorknob.

"You look pretty."

"Thanks. So do you."

He grinned and glanced down at himself. "That's a first, and something I never expected to hear."

"Pretty sexy, cowboy." She laughed and left their bedroom, closing the door behind her.

The next day it was half past six when she returned home from work. Jeb's pickup wasn't in sight, Mrs. Fletcher had asked for three days off, and Amanda knew Kevin was with Jeb. She wondered what Cherie had done by herself all day.

As Amanda opened the back door, she glanced over

her shoulder and saw Kevin riding Popcorn as Jake led the pinto around the corral. Kevin waved and she waved in return. She would change and then go join them. She wondered where Jeb was, but knew that Jake was capable of taking care of Kevin. She knew that none of them would leave Kevin in Cherie's care.

She moved through the silent house, wondering if Cherie was gone, too, but when she passed Cherie's bedroom, the door was closed, so she figured Cherie was in her room.

The moment Amanda entered her own bedroom, she paused, inhaling deeply. It was easy to recognize Cherie's perfume lingering in the air. Why had Cherie been in their bedroom?

Annoyed, Amanda unzipped her dress and stepped out of it, crossing to the closet to hang it up. She turned, looking at the room that appeared undisturbed, yet she was certain Cherie had been in it. If she hadn't have been looking, she might never have noticed, but she saw a tiny bit of pink under the edge of the bed. Crossing the room, she bent down, retrieved a bit of silk and held it up, looking at a pair of pink panties edged in lace. Amanda turned to ice, because she wasn't looking at a scrap of her own clothing. It was Cherie's.

Stunned, she sank down on the edge of the bed. Had Jeb and Cherie been in here? In the bed she shared with Jeb? Pain consumed her. How could Jeb have done that? But she knew instantly. Cherie was female perfection—physical perfection, at least. How could he resist her day after day and night after night when she was being her most charming with him, throwing herself at him, flirting with him. He would have to be made of ice to be impervious to her.

Amanda's stomach churned and anger and hurt battled within her. Her marriage was nothing but a paper promise, done for Kevin. Yet Jeb had acted like a man in love.

With shaking hands she flung the panties on the bed and rushed to yank on cutoffs and a T-shirt. She grabbed the panties and charged down the hall, flinging open the door to Cherie's room.

Stretched out in bed, Cherie sat up, her blue eyes widening.

Amanda flung the pink silk onto the foot of the bed. "You left that in our room today."

Cherie's face flushed and she yanked up the panties. "Amanda, I'm sorry," she whispered, looking guilty and smug at the same time. "We—I just—I'm sorry."

"Cherie, why don't you get out? You're not interested in Kevin. You want Jeb back even though he's married to me now."

Eleven

Cherie's eyes narrowed, her expression hardening as she swung her feet to the floor and stood, tossing the panties back onto the bed.

"Jeb loves me whether he'll admit it or not. And face it—what man wouldn't like two women fawning over him?" Cherie smiled at her. "It's like I told you, you haven't lost him, because you never really had him."

"We have a good marriage," Amanda said stiffly, wondering what she had now.

"Do you think if you had come into our house the third month of our marriage like I have yours, that you could have gotten him to show any interest in you?"

The question hurt, and Amanda struggled with her anger. "I want you to go."

"Amanda, you're the one who should leave. Jeb and Kevin and I are the true family. You're standing in the way of Kevin having the family he should have had. If you really loved him, you'd give him up."

Amanda drew a deep breath, remembering Cherie begging her to take Kevin, telling her she didn't want to see him or hold him after he was born.

"I'm Kevin's mother and the only mother he's ever known. And I'm Jeb's wife and we love each other."

"When I want to, I can make Jeb happy—make him happier than you'll ever make him. You're the one being selfish, Amanda. If you'd leave, we'd be a family. I'm Kevin's real mother. I'm the woman Jeb truly loves. I can give Jeb the children he wants and you can't. And I can give Jeb and Kevin a life that they'll never know otherwise because I'm making a fortune. Stop thinking of yourself and think of Jeb and Kevin and what I can do for them."

Her words cut like knives and Amanda wondered if she was standing selfishly in the way, blinded by her own love for Kevin and Jeb. Yet she couldn't forget Cherie's total disregard for Kevin when he was born. She shook her head, hot with hurt and anger.

"You're the one who should pack and go. You're disrupting our lives. You don't really care about Kevin, and the moment you stop showing interest in him, Jeb will lose all interest in you," she said.

Cherie glanced at the underwear on the bed. "He won't stop showing interest in me," she said slyly.

"You're wrong."

"If Jeb denies he was with you, I'll believe him. And I don't think he was," she said, suddenly realizing how easily Cherie could have put the scrap of clothing in their room. Thinking about it, she grew more certain and more angry. "You don't belong here, Cherie, and you're trying to hurt all three of us."

"Nonsense."

"If I walked out, you wouldn't want to live out here on the ranch with Jeb. You have a career."

"It would sound so good if I had a Texas husband to come back to. I could make my movies and come back here several times a year."

"And what about a mother for Kevin?"

She shrugged. "Children get used to anything. Jeb would take care of him, and when he's older, he can be sent away to school."

"That's a selfish view. Have you ever thought about anyone besides yourself?"

"It doesn't pay to. Except I'm thinking of Jeb now. You know I can make him happier than you can. Look at me. Do you know how many proposals I get a month?"

"Cherie, I've known you all your life. Stop and look at yourself. You're trying to tear up three lives on a whim. All your life you've done as you pleased—I've always known that—but down deep, I always thought there was a basic decency in you. Now I wonder."

Cherie blinked, staring at Amanda while all color drained from her face.

"You get out of my house. I love my son and my husband and you're not going to interfere. You pack and I'll drive you into town now. Our family ties are severed."

Amanda left to go to the corral to find Jake. Her hands were shaking with anger and she took deep breaths, trying to calm herself. Jake saw her and climbed over the fence while Kevin continued riding Popcorn around the corral.

"He's going to be a fine cowboy."

"Well, I hope not this year," she answered lightly. Jake's eyes narrowed and he studied her.

"Something wrong?"

"No. I just wanted to see if you can continue watching Kevin. Cherie's leaving, and I'm driving her into town."

"Want me to take her?" he asked.

She stared at him and thought about it, then shook her head. "No. I think I need to get away by myself for a little while. Jeb will be home before long, won't he?"

"Yep. He's mending a fence."

"I work in town tomorrow. I think I'll just stay at my house in town tonight."

Jake nodded. She passed him and climbed the corral fence to wave at Kevin and blow him a kiss. "Take care of my baby," she said softly.

"I will. Don't you worry."

"Thanks, Jake." She headed toward the house.

"Amanda," Jake said, and she turned. "Whatever happened today, Jeb hasn't been home since early this morning."

"I didn't much think he had, but it's nice to hear. Thanks." She turned and went to the house, wondering how much had shown in her expression and how much Jake had guessed.

She was sending Cherie packing, yet Cherie's words taunted her and hurt. Was she being selfish and standing in the way of Kevin and Jeb having so much more? She could never give Jeb more children and that knowledge hurt deeply.

She waited in the kitchen and then silently helped a white-faced Cherie carry her bags to the car. They rode in silence, and as she drove away from the ranch,

Amanda forgot Cherie's presence. Numb and hurt at the same time, she glanced in the rearview mirror as the home she had grown to love disappeared from view. *Kevin and Jeb were her life.*

"Just take me to the airport. I'm going to Nashville."

Amanda didn't bother answering, but drove to Dallas–Fort Worth International Airport and parked to let Cherie unload her things. Amanda got out to remove Cherie's bags from the trunk. When she slammed it shut and set the bags on the walk, she looked at her cousin. "Goodbye, Cherie."

Cherie turned abruptly and called for an attendant to help with her luggage. Amanda climbed into her car and drove away without looking back. Yet Cherie's perfume stayed in the car and her words lingered in Amanda's mind—words that hurt and worried her. Was she doing the wrong thing in binding Jeb to her in marriage? Was she being selfish with Jeb and Kevin? Particularly with Jeb because she couldn't give him more children.

Lost in her thoughts she drove to her home and let herself into the quiet house that now seemed so small and so terribly empty.

"Jeb, I love you," she said quietly, letting tears come and wondering whether, if she truly loved him, she would let him go.

In early evening at the ranch, Jeb slowed, stopped in front of the garage and climbed out of his pickup. He headed to the house in long strides. As he entered the kitchen, Jake and Kevin looked up. Seated at the table, Kevin was coloring and drinking chocolate milk while Jake sat across from him, nursing a beer.

"We made ourselves at home."

"That's fine," Jeb said, grabbing up Kevin, who had run to greet him. He hugged and kissed Kevin. "How's my boy?"

"Fine. I rode Popcorn all by myself."

"Good for you!" He set Kevin on his feet, and Kevin ran back to sit at the table and drink his chocolate milk and continue coloring.

"Amanda's not home from work yet?"

"Yep. She drove Cherie into town to the airport."

Startled, Jeb paused as he started to take a sip of beer. "Cherie's gone without saying goodbye?"

"Looks as if," Jake drawled, and Jeb glanced at Kevin, who was now looking at one of his picture books. Jeb motioned with his head and Jake followed him into the hall.

"What happened? That's not like either one of them."

Jake shrugged. "Dunno. Amanda said to tell you she's staying in town at her house tonight."

With foreboding, Jeb decided something was wrong. "I'm going to shower. Can you stay that much longer with Kevin?"

"Sure. I can stay all night if you want to go into town to see Amanda."

"Thanks, Jake. I'll give her a call. Have they had time to get there?"

"Yep, they have. Just let me know. I'll be in the kitchen with Kevin."

"Thanks. Get whatever you want to eat."

Jeb headed for his room, closing the door and going straight to the phone to call Amanda. He suspected something bad had happened for her to leave the way she had and to tell Jake she wouldn't be back tonight.

He listened to her phone ring and then got the familiar answering machine. Frustrated and worried, he left a message.

By eight o'clock, he had sent Jake home and he was getting worried about Amanda. Kevin had gone to bed, but Jeb was tempted to get him up and drive into town to look for her. Except he didn't know where to start.

When the phone rang, he grabbed the receiver and said hello. The moment he heard her voice, relief swamped him.

"Jeb, I just got home and heard your message," Amanda said.

"I was worried about you."

"Didn't Jake tell you that I was staying in town?"

"Yes, he did," Jeb answered, thinking she sounded stiff and cool. "What's wrong?"

There was a long silence and his sense of foreboding increased.

"Jeb, I need to think things through."

"What things?" he asked while a dull pain started in his middle. "How about I get Jake to come up and stay with Kevin and I come into town so we can talk? I hate talking over the phone."

"Not tonight. I want some time to myself."

He thought that over, wanting to be with her so he could find out what was troubling her and what had happened today.

"All right. Have dinner with me tomorrow night."

"I don't know. I want to think about our marriage and about Kevin. We rushed into marriage."

"Are you sorry?" he asked stiffly.

"I'll never be sorry," she said softly, and he wondered whether she was crying. Gritting his teeth, he wanted to swear because he needed to be with her.

"I have to stop and look at what we're doing," she said. "There are several of us involved and it's important to do the right thing for Kevin and you as well as me."

"You were pretty sure about Kevin not very long ago."

"I'll talk to you tomorrow evening, Jeb."

"Amanda, don't hang up," he said, and received another long silence.

"Sure you don't want me to come to town? I'd like to."

"Wait until tomorrow, Jeb. I'm going now. Good night."

He heard a click and then he was cut off. "Lady, what's wrong?" he asked the empty room. What had happened here today? he wondered. He went out to the back porch, staring down the road and wondering what was bothering her.

Amanda replaced the receiver gently, wiping at tears and staring at the phone. Cherie's words had shaken her. She didn't think Jeb would ever want to go back to Cherie, but she did think he would someday want a woman who could give him more children. *"You're the one being selfish, Amanda. If you'd leave, we'd be a family. I'm Kevin's real mother. I'm the woman Jeb truly loves. I can give Jeb the children he wants and you can't."*

The words rang in Amanda's mind. Was she being selfish or were they becoming a family? Each time she asked herself that question and thought about the happy times, the intimate moments with Jeb and her deep love for Kevin, she felt that their marriage was right and good. But then when she thought about Jeb wanting more children, a cloud darkened their future because she couldn't have any. He had blithely said they could adopt, but did he really feel that way?

She spent a sleepless night and found no satisfying answers to her questions.

Then at work she forgot her own problems as she talked with her patients, tested their hearing and fitted hearing aids. But when the day was over and she was driving home, excitement began to curl inside her, because at seven she would see Jeb. He had called her twice today, talking briefly each time. During the day he had taken Kevin to his mother's and she was keeping him for the next two days.

Amanda's pulse raced as she dressed. She wanted to see Jeb and be with him. She loved him, but she had to know his feelings because she didn't want to stand in the way of his happiness. Too well, she was aware that he had never told her he loved her. Yet he acted like a man in love, she reminded herself, thinking about their moments together.

Slipping into sleeveless, deep blue cotton dress, she pinned her hair on top of her head, put on a gold chain bracelet and decided she was ready. As she stepped into high-heeled sandals, the doorbell rang.

While her heart missed beats, she hurried through the house, opened the door and stepped back.

"Hi," Jeb said quietly, coming into the house and closing the door behind him. He was devastatingly handsome in his dark suit and crisp white shirt and dark tie. More than ever now that he was standing in front of her, she wanted to fling herself into his arms.

As she stared into fathomless dark pools, her breath caught. Tension sizzled between them, like tiny explosions in the crackling air, and she couldn't move.

"I missed you. Why did you go?" he asked.

"There are some things we need to discuss."

He reached out then and touched her, his hand sliding around her waist, and her heart thudded violently. Desire blossomed and she wanted to be in his arms. She was aching to hold him and be wrapped in his embrace and forget every worry nagging her.

"I have some things to tell you," he said solemnly. "I was going to take you to dinner and then come back and tell you, but I think I've waited too long already."

He drew her close and her hands were on his upper arms, feeling his smooth lightweight suit jacket and his hard muscles beneath it.

He leaned down to kiss her, his tongue sliding deeply into her mouth, stroking her, awakening too many feelings and needs as she moaned softly and trembled and wrapped her arms around his neck to kiss him in return. How could she walk away and give him up? He acted as though he were in love, and she wanted him so badly.

He pulled back to place his fingers against her throat, studying her. "Your pulse is racing," he said in a husky voice.

"You do that to me."

Something flickered in the depths of his eyes. "Look in my pocket. I brought something for you."

Mystified, she reached into his coat pocket and brought out a ring box, remembering the last time he had done the same thing. She already had a wedding ring and they were married, so, even more puzzled, she stared at the box. Opening it, she saw an emerald surrounded by diamonds.

"Jeb!" she gasped, surprised and uncertain.

Taking the ring from her, he held her right hand. "This is for the love we have now. I love you, Mandy. I love you with all my heart. You're the woman of my dreams, and this time, I'm damn sure."

"Jeb!" she cried, unable to talk as tears stung her eyes and she stared at him. "You're certain how you feel?"

"Absolutely," he said. "And I've waited too long to tell you."

"Jeb, that's why I left," she said quietly, looking at the deep green stone. "I can't give you more children and I know you want some."

"Mandy, we talked about that. We can adopt. You adopted Kevin and it's very good, isn't it?"

"Yes, but am I cheating you and Kevin both—"

"Oh, hell. Lady, I don't want to live without you. Last night was hell. Don't ever leave me again. If we can't adopt, I don't care. I have you and Kevin and that's my family and it's wonderful. I love you and I want you. You're my wife and I love you, now and always."

She let go of her worries. "I gave you your chance," she whispered, standing on tiptoe and pulling his head down to her. "I missed you incredibly," she said, kissing him and sliding her hands beneath his suit coat to shove it off his shoulders. Her heart pounded with joy that she had Jeb back. It was right and good, and she could get rid of doubts and go back to the life she loved on the ranch.

Her fingers fumbled with his belt and unbuckled it while he tugged down the zipper of her dress. While cool air spilled over her shoulders, he walked her back toward her bedroom. Clothes fell through the house until they reached the bed, and he shoved away the last scrap of lace and she peeled away his briefs to toss them aside.

Jeb picked her up and gently placed her on the bed, leaning over her to shower kisses down her stomach, trailing lower to her inner thighs. "I love you, I love you," he whispered over and over, kissing her, his hands stroking her, one hand moving between her legs while his other hand circled her nipple.

Amanda moaned with pleasure, winding her fingers in his hair and then caressing him, sliding her hands over his muscled back down to his firm buttocks. She sat up to take his thick shaft in her hands and stroke and kiss him until he moved her away to kiss her.

"Jeb, I love you," she whispered, and he kissed her, finally pulling back to wind his fingers in her hair and draw his other hand lightly across her lips.

"I love you, lady. I can't ever tell you how much I love you, but I'll spend a lifetime showing you. I'm sorry I didn't tell you sooner."

"Oh, Jeb!" she cried, joy and desire shaking her as she flung herself against him and kissed him hard and long.

Finally he moved between her legs, ready, devouring her with his heated gaze as he lowered himself into her, filling her and moving slowly in a sweet torment that drove her wild.

They moved together, Amanda's hips arching to meet him until release came and Jeb shuddered. "Mandy, I love you," he cried, and kissed her hungrily.

She clung to him, in ecstasy from their loving and from his words. They still moved together, slowing, trying to catch their breaths, coming back to earth to kiss and fondle each other leisurely now.

Later, as Jeb held her close against him, she looked again at her beautiful new ring. "I didn't know whether you loved me or not."

"How could you not know?" he asked, frowning. "I should have told you before now, but I didn't stop to think about what I felt until Cherie forced the issue, and then I wanted the right moment to tell you."

"The right moment?" she asked, frowning and rising up on an elbow to look at him. The sheet was tucked beneath her arms and draped across his hips as she stared at him. "*Any* moment is the right moment. How long ago did you decide you loved me?"

"I didn't want to tell you while Cherie was there. You know the evenings were tense. I wanted a special time and place and I wanted to get you a ring—"

"Oh, Jeb, all you needed to do was say it, just say the three little words! It would have been as thrilling whether it had been one night last week or now. It doesn't matter what or when—I just want to know how you feel."

He frowned and pushed wavy tendrils of her red hair away from her face. "I figured you'd know how I felt. Don't I act like a man in love?"

"Yes, you do, but you also act like a man in lust. How was I to know which one you felt?"

"Both, lady. Damn well both. I'm sorry, Mandy, if I should have told you sooner. Is that why you left last night?"

"That and worrying about being unable to give you children."

"Will you stop with that? Why don't we start adoption proceedings right now and then you'll never worry about that again."

She smiled and framed his face with her hands. "I don't think I'm ever going to worry about it again, anyway," she said, leaning down to kiss him, her heart overflowing with love.

Epilogue

Jeb sat with his long legs stretched out, his booted feet propped on the porch rail. In one hand he had a glass of iced tea. With his other, he reached out to take Amanda's hand. Summer shadows were long across the mowed green lawn as evening set in. Mrs. Fletcher sat knitting in the shade of an oak while seven-year-old Kevin tossed a ball to redheaded four-year-old Brad. Toddling back and forth between them was their two-year-old sister, black-haired Emily.

"Think I ought to rescue Emily? Those boys aren't paying any attention to her."

"She's happy just to be with them. That's the way women are with their menfolk around," Amanda replied, and Jeb grinned.

"Come sit on my lap."

As she moved over to his lap, he put his feet on the floor, holding her and stroking her arm. "A seven-year-old, a four-year-old and a two-year-old. It's pretty nice, isn't it?''

"It's the best, and so are you," she whispered, patting his face and leaning close to kiss him.

When the roar of a bike interrupted them, she looked around. "Here comes Jake to say goodbye."

"Yeah, to say goodbye again. He left four months after we married, came back a year later and now he's leaving again. I wonder how long before he's back."

She stood and Jeb came to his feet, draping his arm around her shoulders. "What drives him, Jeb, to keep moving? He's a wonderful man and half the women in this county are in love with him."

"I don't know. I've never asked and he's never said."

They walked out to the gate and Kevin and Brad came running, Emily slowly toddling along behind them. Jeb picked up Brad, and when Emily reached them, Amanda scooped her into her arms.

Jake slowed the Harley and cut the motor, joining them to greet the children first. Jake hunkered down to look at Kevin. "I'll miss you and I promise to come back to see you." He stood and swung Kevin into his arms to hug him. Then when he set him down, he said, "Be a good big brother, okay?"

"Yes, sir."

He picked up Brad. "And you be a good little brother," Jake said, hugging him.

"Yes, sir," Brad said, hugging Jake in return.

Jake set him down and looked at Emily. "And you be a good little sister," he said, winking at her. She smiled and wrapped her arms around Amanda's neck.

"You take care of him, because he needs some care," Jake said to Amanda, hugging her lightly, and she hugged him, kissing his cheek.

"You take care of yourself," she said. "There are a lot of ladies here who don't want to see you go."

He grinned and looked at Jeb, offering his hand. "You know I'll be back."

"I hope so. I'll miss you and my horses will miss you."

"Take care of your family and yourself. 'Bye, Mrs. Fletcher," he called and she waved. Jake turned and got on his bike and with a roar drove down the road toward the highway. Wind blew his long black hair and he didn't look back as he rounded a curve and disappeared from sight. The boys ran back to playing ball and Emily wriggled to get down and join them. Jeb and Amanda strolled back to the porch and quiet once again settled.

"I've got a good idea," Jeb drawled. "While Mrs. Fletcher watches the kids, come here and let me show you something." He took her hand and led her into the house.

"What are you doing?" she asked, and then laughed as he pulled her inside and closed the door, leaning against it and hauling her into his embrace.

"Let me show you how fast a Texas cowboy can get something done once he puts his mind to it."

"His mind my eye!" she said, laughing and wrapping her arms around his neck. "All right, cowboy, do your stuff."

Jeb pulled her close to kiss her. Amanda closed her eyes, standing on tiptoe, her heart filled with joy for this tall Texas cowboy and the wonderful family and love they had.

* * * * *

THE RANCHER AND THE NANNY

**by
Caroline Cross**

CAROLINE CROSS

always loved to read, but it wasn't until she discovered the romance genre that she felt compelled to write, fascinated by the chance to explore the positive power of love in people's lives. Winner of the prestigious Romance Writers of America's RITA Award for Best Short Contemporary, she's also been thrilled to win the *Romantic Times Magazine* Reviewer's Choice Award for Best Desire, as well as a WISH Award. She grew up in central Washington State, attended the University of Puget Sound and now lives outside of Seattle, where she *tries* to work at home despite the chaos created by two telephone-addicted teenage daughters and a husband with a fondness for home-improvement projects. *The Rancher and the Nanny* marks her tenth book for Silhouette. Caroline would love to hear from her readers. She can be reached at PO Box 5845, Bellevue, Washington, 98006, USA.

One

The shiny black pickup rocketed down the Bar M's gravel drive, raising a plume of dust in its wake.

Poised before the ranch house's back door, Eve Chandler turned as the vehicle swept past. Her stomach did a quick somersault at the sight of the big, dark-haired man behind the wheel.

It had been eight years since she last saw John MacLaren, but for an instant time seemed to melt away. All of a sudden she was seventeen again, and the way she'd felt whenever she was around him—hot, bothered, filled with yearnings that both enthralled and embarrassed her—came rushing back.

She shivered and took a step toward the stairs as if to flee, only to freeze a second later as her common sense kicked in.

Knock it off, Eve. You're no longer an inexperienced teenager, remember? You're twenty-five years old, the same age John was all those years ago. At least he doesn't have a clue how you felt back then— you made sure of that. Think how much harder this would be if he had.

The stark reminder of why she was here crashed over her like a breaker of icy water. And though she stubbornly refused to give in to the rising tide of panic that had been building inside her the past few weeks, she couldn't deny the irony of the situation. If someone had tried to tell her six months ago that she, the privileged granddaughter of Lander County's biggest rancher, would soon be forced to come begging favors from the sexy loner who once worked in the Chandler stables, she never would have believed it.

Yet here she was.

Thirty feet away, John pulled in beside the small red car she'd borrowed for the drive over. He switched off the pickup's engine.

She could hear her heart pounding in the ensuing silence. Determined not to let on, she deliberately struck a casual pose as he climbed out of the cab and shut the truck door. He began to walk in her direction, his long legs eating up the distance as he slowly yanked off his leather work gloves.

If he was surprised to see her, it didn't show.

He stopped at the foot of the stairs and inclined his head a scant inch. "Eve."

Taking a firm grip on her unruly emotions, she summoned her most confident smile. "Hello, John."

There was a distinct silence as they regarded each other.

Around them, the September day was much like any other. A pale yellow sun hung high in the vast blue Montana sky. The temperature hovered in the mid-fifties, while the summer-seared grass that covered the surrounding range waved gently beneath a light but persistent breeze.

Eve paid no attention. Her focus was completely claimed by the tall man standing before her. Despite her little pep talk, the fluttery feeling in her stomach got worse as he slowly rocked back on his heels and gave her an unhurried once-over. His gaze touched on her sunny blond hair, then raked her ice-blue cashmere sweater, gray wool crepe slacks and Italian leather shoes.

She'd chosen the expensive outfit deliberately. At the time, she'd told herself she merely wanted to look her best. Now, she realized that on some level she'd also hoped it would give her an edge, acting as a subtle reminder of their respective pasts. In the half second before his eyes hooded over, however, she caught a glimpse of something in their depths that seemed to be as much cool disdain as grudging appreciation.

Stung, she lifted her chin and studied him in turn. She had to concede the years had been good to him in ways that had nothing to do with his newfound wealth. He might be dressed in scuffed cowboy boots, jeans whitened at the hips and thighs, a faded black T-shirt and a weathered Stetson, but nobody would ever mistake him for a simple ranch hand.

Time had added muscle to his lean six-foot three-inch frame and character to the chiseled angles of his face. What's more, while he'd always possessed more than his share of virility, now he also radiated an air of leashed power. It was easy to see why women from sixteen to sixty turned to watch when he walked past. From the determined angle of his square jaw, to the compelling bite of his laser blue eyes and the deliberate set of his broad shoulders, he was all man.

The realization that she found him even more attractive now than she had when she was seventeen set off an alarm deep inside her.

"I was sorry to hear about Max," he said abruptly.

She jerked her gaze to his, heat rising in her cheeks as their eyes met. Horrified he might guess what she'd been thinking, she did her best to look cool and contained. "I received your card. Thank you."

He shrugged, the simple motion seriously straining the seams of his T-shirt. "He was a good man."

Off balance, and unable to think about the unexpected loss of her grandfather without a piercing sense of grief, she said merely, "Yes, he was."

"Rumor has it you're selling the Rocking C to some big Texas cattle consortium."

"That's true, I am. The deal will be final in just a few days."

He crossed his arms. "You sure didn't waste any time unloading the place, did you?"

Eve stared at his hard, handsome face, taken aback by his obvious disapproval even as she realized he'd just given her the perfect opening. All she had to do was tell the truth—that if she hadn't sold out to the Texans, she would have lost the ranch either to the bank or the IRS—and he'd know the gravity of her financial situation.

Yet she couldn't—she wouldn't—do it. Word of the disastrous investments her grandfather had made the last year of his life would no doubt eventually surface, since the Lander County ranching community was surprisingly tight-knit. But it wouldn't come from her. Just as Max Chandler had protected her in life, Eve would protect him in death. Because she'd loved him. And because it was the very least that she owed him.

"I guess that means you'll be taking off pretty soon," John said in the face of her silence. "Back to Paris or New York or—where is it you've been living lately?"

"London," she supplied automatically, trying to decide just how she was going to broach the reason for her visit.

She needn't have worried. In his direct, no-nonsense way, John took care of the problem for her. "So, you going to tell me what you're doing here or not?"

"Yes, of course. I was hoping we could talk. There's something I'd like to discuss with you."

He took a cursory glance at his wristwatch, then shocked her by shaking his head. "Sorry. I've got a prior commitment. We'll have to do it another time."

"But this won't wait!"

He shrugged, clearly unmoved. "It'll have to. I've got less than fifteen minutes before I have to be somewhere."

Struggling for composure, she turned to keep him in view as he strode up the stairs and brushed past her, trailing the scent of sunshine, horses and hard work in his wake. "Please, John," she said, swallowing her pride. "I promise it won't take long."

His hand froze on the doorknob. He turned, obvious reluctance warring with curiosity—and something else she couldn't define—in his eyes. "All right," he said finally. "I guess if you don't mind talking while I get washed up, I can spare you a few minutes." Pushing open the inner door, he disappeared inside.

She stared after him, feeling both relieved and annoyed, trying to convince herself that she shouldn't read too much into his being less than friendly. After all, he was simply treating her the way she'd treated him when they were younger.

And just like that, despite her every intention not to revisit the past, the memory of their first meeting came rushing back.

Once again it was a still summer morning. The air smelled clean and sweet, redolent with the scents of sunshine, hay and the bark chips beneath her feet as she stood in the doorway of one of the Rocking C's roomy box stalls, stroking the warm, satiny neck of Candy Stripes, her quarter horse mare.

The two had just returned from a glorious sunrise ride and Eve vividly remembered how she'd felt at that moment: happy, gloriously alive and totally pleased with her life.

But then, why shouldn't she be? Just seventeen, she was cherished and indulged at home and popular at school, where she was both a cheerleader and an honor student. It wasn't surprising she'd believed the world was hers to order.

And then she'd stepped blithely into the corridor, directly into the path of a big, dark-haired stranger—and everything had changed.

He swore as she smacked into the solid wall of his chest. Yet somehow he still managed to swing the hundred-pound sack of grain he had balanced on one broad shoulder to the ground at the same time he reached out to steady her.

Startled, she'd looked up into the bluest eyes she'd ever seen. And as she took in the rest of his features— the strong cheekbones, the blade-straight nose, the chiseled lips, the silky dark hair tumbling over his brow—something unprecedented happened to her.

Heat pooled between her thighs. Her nipples contracted into stiff, aching points. The starch drained from her knees, and she couldn't seem to remember how to breathe.

For one mad moment she wanted nothing more than to step closer, press her body against his boldly masculine one, bury her face against the pulse beating in the strong column of his throat.

She wanted to touch him and taste him... everywhere. And she wanted it so badly she ached with it.

The discovery shocked her. Confused, frightened, alarmed, she took a hasty step back, jerking away from the steely strength of his warm, calloused hand gripping her arm. "Who are you?" she demanded.

He didn't immediately answer. Instead, he looked her over, taking note of the way she was rubbing her fingers over the spot where his hand had been. His mouth compressed slightly, but when his gaze met hers, it was coolly polite—and nothing more. "John MacLaren."

"What are you doing here?"

"Working."

It was bad enough that her body was still throbbing, her throat dry, her heart pounding. But even worse, *he* seemed completely unaffected. She lifted her chin. "Since when?"

"Since I was hired yesterday. And if you don't mind my asking—" he shifted his weight onto one hip in a way she found both arrogant and enticing "—just who are you to be asking?"

She drew herself up a little straighter. "Eve Chandler. My grandfather owns this place."

"Huh."

He sounded completely unimpressed, and panicked by the storm of unfamiliar emotions roaring through her, she snapped, "And if you want to keep your job, I'd suggest you watch where you're going from now on."

He reached over and carelessly hefted the sack of grain onto his shoulder. "I'll keep that in mind." With that, he'd strode away.

Eve stared after him. At any other time in her life she would have been mortified by her rude behavior. But not at that moment. Not with him. Instead, she'd told herself that John MacLaren was an arrogant bore who wasn't worth her time.

Yet every time she'd seen him from that point forward she'd felt that same overwhelming arousal and attraction. It had embarrassed her, made her feel self-conscious and unsure of herself—a new and unwelcome experience. Worse, she'd lived in constant terror that he might discern how she felt. It was no wonder that she'd decided that it was smarter to invite his dislike than risk having him find out how vulnerable he made her feel.

And since she wasn't about to confess the truth after all these years, she could hardly expect him to fall all over himself, welcoming her, she reminded herself now. She'd simply have to do the best she could.

And try to remember that he was her last hope. That no matter what she felt, she couldn't afford to give up on him now.

She drew herself up and walked toward the door. Entering the house, she found herself standing in a spacious, sun-filled mudroom. She had a quick impression of a granite-tiled floor, of a wall covered with hooks that held coats, hats, chaps and all sorts of other equipment, of an alcove housing an oversize washer and dryer. To her left was even what appeared to be a spacious bathroom equipped with a glassed-in shower.

But it was the sight of John planted before a large utility sink with his back to her that commanded her attention. He'd tossed his hat on a nearby counter and yanked his dusty T-shirt out of his jeans. Now, he tugged the garment over his head and tossed it to the floor.

An unwitting voyeur, Eve stared at his smooth, sun-bronzed back, observing the muscles bunch and shift as he turned on the water, picked up the soap and proceeded to wash. When he bent to rinse off, the satiny hollow of his spine flattened out, exposing a ribbon of taut, pale skin at his belt line.

She was so transfixed that she almost didn't look away in time as he abruptly shut off the water, grabbed a towel and swiveled around. "Well?" He waited expectantly.

She forced herself to meet his gaze, trying to behave as if she wasn't acutely aware of his seminakedness. It wasn't easy to do, particularly when an unwanted ribbon of heat curled through her as he rubbed the towel down his neck and over the sculpted contours of his chest. "I had lunch with Chrissy Abrams last week," she began, ordering herself to concentrate. "She told me that you have a seven-year-old daughter who recently came to live with you. And that you've been trying since summer to find somebody to look after her."

"So?"

"So I'd like the job."

He went absolutely still, and then a faint smile curved his mouth. "You're joking, right?"

"No. No, I'm not."

The smile faded. He gave her a long, penetrating look. "Why would you want to do that?"

She'd known he was bound to ask and she was ready. Keeping her eyes steady on his face, she said with a lightness she didn't feel, "Because Lander is my home. I've missed it and I'd like to stay in the area. And now that I've sold the ranch, I need something to do."

"And you think working for me is it?" His face hardened and he slowly shook his head. "I don't think so, Eve."

Even though she'd suspected it was coming, his answer was crushing. She swallowed. "Why not?"

He tossed the towel onto the counter and headed for the dryer, where he retrieved a clean blue T-shirt several shades lighter than his eyes. Frowning, he peeled off a small white lace-edged sock that clung to it, tossing the stocking onto the washer top. He pulled on the shirt and strolled back toward the sink, stuffing the tail into his jeans as he went. "Let's just say I don't think you're the right woman for the job."

"But I am." She struggled to keep the desperation out of her voice. "I'm here, I'm available, I know my way around a ranch and I'm very, very good with kids."

He leaned back against the counter, looking singularly unconvinced. "Maybe. But it doesn't matter. Chrissy apparently didn't tell you that I need somebody who's willing to live in."

"Actually, she did."

His glorious blue eyes narrowed slightly. "And that's all right with you?"

Clearly now was not the time to admit it was the prospect of living with him that had made her exhaust every possibility of other employment first. "Yes."

"Well, it's not with me. This'll probably come as a shock to you, princess," his voice took on a distinctly sarcastic tone, "but I need somebody who can do more than just keep Lissy company. I don't have either a cook or a maid, so I'm looking for someone who can run a house, too."

She absolutely was *not* going to lose her temper. Still, she couldn't keep the tartness out of her own voice as she answered. "I think I can handle it, John. I know how to cook and clean. More importantly, as I understand it, your daughter's not having the easiest time fitting in at school—" she saw his mouth tighten and knew she was moving into dangerous territory "—and I think I can help."

"Chrissy Abrams talks too much," he said flatly.

"Maybe. But that doesn't change the fact that I have something unique to offer. I was just a little older than your daughter when I lost my parents and came to live with Granddad. I know what it's like to be uprooted, to lose one way of life and make the adjustment to another."

He shook his head. "Even if you have more moves than Mary Poppins, the answer is still no, Eve."

"But—" For one reckless moment she nearly blurted out the truth. *Please. I need this job. I've sold everything of value I can, I've got less than three hundred dollars to my name and in four days I'll be homeless—*

"I'm sorry." John coolly interrupted her frantic thoughts. "But it just wouldn't work."

The finality in his voice was unmistakable. Like a slap in the face, it brought Eve to her senses. A shiver went through her as she realized just how close she'd come to begging for his help and shaming her grandfather's memory.

Even so, she couldn't stop the hot wash of tears that prickled her eyes as her last hope died. She glanced quickly away and blinked hard, swallowing around the sudden lump in her throat. "I see."

It would be all right, she told herself fiercely. This was merely another setback, not the end of the road. Something was bound to turn up. The important thing now was not to make a bigger fool of herself than she already had by coming here.

She swallowed again. Raising her chin, she forced herself to face him. "Well." She managed a smile. "I guess I'm not going to change your mind, am I?"

He shook his head. "No."

She felt her lower lip start to tremble and glanced blindly at her watch. "Then I'd better let you go, or you'll be late."

To her relief, he shifted his gaze to his own wristwatch and she seized the opportunity to turn away. Although she suddenly wanted nothing more than to escape, she forced herself to stroll toward the door. Summoning up another surface smile, she glanced over her shoulder. "It was nice seeing you again, John."

He nodded, his expression impossible to read. "You, too."

"I hope you find someone soon."

"Sure."

And then she was out the door and crossing the porch. She made her way to her car, her steps deliberately measured. Climbing in, she turned the key she'd left in the ignition, backed out carefully and pulled onto the ranch driveway, resisting the urge to speed.

It wasn't until she reached the highway that she could no longer ignore the way her hands were shaking. Tightening her grip on the steering wheel, she pulled over and stopped the car, struggling to yank on the emergency brake as the shaking spread.

Stubbornly, she again tried to tell herself that everything was going to be all right.

Except that deep down, she no longer believed it.

She squeezed her eyes shut, but it was too late. A single tear slid down her face as she wondered what she was going to do now.

Two

The pickup rattled over the cattle guard with a muted thump of its heavy-duty tires.

Slowing the vehicle as he reached the highway, John turned to the left, pulled over onto the shoulder and braked. Squinting into the sun, he looked toward the west and quickly spotted the distinctive yellow school bus still well off in the distance.

He gave a sigh of relief, glad that he wasn't late. Rolling down his window, he switched off the pickup's engine and settled back to wait, aware, as he felt the tension in his shoulders, that he was strung tighter than seven feet of barbwire on an eight-foot section of fence.

He knew exactly who was to blame.

Although he'd promised himself he wasn't going to think about her, his thoughts zeroed in on Eve. You could have knocked him over with a feather when he'd pulled into the yard and seen her. After all these years, she was still as blond and beautiful as ever. Not to mention as self-assured. What was it she'd said about her job qualifications?

Oh, yeah. *I think I have something unique to offer.*

Well, she sure as hell was right about *that.* And for all he knew, she also wasn't half bad when it came to taking care of kids.

His mouth twisted caustically. He wasn't a man to hold a grudge but he wasn't a fool, either. He hadn't forgotten the way she'd acted toward him all those years ago, before she'd left for her fancy college. Slim and long-legged, with golden skin, clear gray eyes and the straightest, whitest teeth he'd ever seen, at seventeen she'd been an absolute charmer—with everyone but him.

Since there had never been anything wrong with his ego, he'd known damn well he wasn't without a certain appeal of his own. For whatever reason—his size, the innate aloofness that gave him an air of being hard to get, the fact that he was an orphan—women had been drawn to him since his early teens.

But not the lovely Ms. Chandler. She'd taken an obvious dislike to him at first sight. There had been no sunny smiles, none of the warmth or practical jokes or wry teasing she bestowed on the rest of the hands. Instead, although always faultlessly polite, she'd treated him as if he smelled bad.

He sure as hell hadn't appreciated her attitude. But he had needed the job, so he'd sucked it in and done his best to ignore her. He'd told himself she was nothing more than a kid. And that she was actually doing him a favor, since he'd known that Max Chandler would fire him in a second if he showed the slightest interest in her.

Still, it had rankled. And for all that he'd never let on, it hadn't been long before he'd itched to take her down a peg and wipe that superior look off her pretty face. Making matters worse, on some level he'd known that the urge sprang not from a need for respect or revenge but because he wanted her. He'd wanted to thrust his hands in her silky blond hair and taste her smooth pink mouth. He'd wanted to feel her slim, golden body under his. He'd wanted to touch her all over and make her cry out his name.

Spoiled or not, she'd made him ache.

Which was all water under the bridge, he reminded himself now. Sure, she still looked damn good, maybe even better than before. And yeah, there was still something about her—the husky timbre of her voice, the graceful way she moved, the silky-soft look of her hair and skin—that seemed to go straight to his groin and play hell with the fit of his jeans. But as for her suggestion that she come to work for him...

John's expression turned cynical. No matter how much he needed the help, or how appealing the thought of being Eve's boss, he had no intention of indulging the whims of the Rocking C's patrician princess.

She was all wrong for the job, for one thing. He needed someone who would take care of practical matters without caring if she mussed her hair. And that someone had to be warm, grounded and nurturing, not a spoiled social butterfly. What's more, she had to be willing to stick around longer than it took for a coat of nail polish to dry.

When it came to Eve, he especially doubted her

staying power. She could talk all she wanted about how she'd missed home and wanted to remain in the area, but he was sure it wouldn't be very long before she changed her mind. After all, what could Lander offer compared to New York or London or Paris? And why would she suddenly feel the need for a job, when she'd spent the past few years as a lady of leisure?

Unless... He shifted, feeling a trace uneasy. He'd heard rumors a few months back that Max Chandler was in financial trouble. At the time, he'd been too preoccupied with the discovery that he had a daughter to pay much attention. When he had bothered to think about it, he'd just assumed the gossips must be wrong. Although rising expenses and a downward trend in the price of cattle had bankrupted a lot of spreads over the past few years, he couldn't believe anyone as shrewd as Max would allow things to get out of hand. And yet, if he had, that might explain Eve's surprising desire for employment.

The sound of squealing brakes interrupted his speculations. Looking up, he saw the school bus had finally arrived. As he watched, the hinged stop sign swung out and the red and yellow warning lights flashed on. With a swoosh of escaping air, the door folded back and Lissy appeared.

John's heart squeezed as he took her in. She was barely bigger than a minute, with her skinny arms, pale little face and big blue eyes. And though her outfit was hardly stylish—he winced a little at the orange sweater, red-plaid skirt that fell to midcalf and the pink frilly socks with the white patent leather mary-janes—he didn't care. She was *his* daughter, his flesh and blood. He felt a rush of emotion—love, awe, tenderness—so strong, it was almost painful.

Not that it mattered, he was quick to remind himself as their gazes met and she sent him a brief, uncertain smile before glancing away. No matter how strongly he felt about being a father, he and his daughter were still strangers. Her mother—a woman he barely remembered—had made sure of that.

John's jaw tightened. He still didn't understand why Elaine hadn't come to him when she found out she was pregnant. Granted, the handful of times they'd spent together had been more a series of one-night stands than an actual affair. And by insisting on using protection, he had made it clear that he wasn't interested in a commitment.

But if she had just sought him out, told him that something had gone wrong and that she was carrying his child, he would have married her in an instant. He was a man who took care of his obligations.

Instead, she'd remained silent, even when she fell ill and left *his* child with her mother to raise. Hell, if the old lady hadn't gotten sick herself, he never would have known he had a kid.

He shook his head. Every time he thought about all the years he'd missed with Lissy, it made him a little crazy. He couldn't help thinking that maybe, if he'd had a chance to get to know her as a baby, to see her grow and get acquainted with her gradually, he wouldn't be such a bust as a parent now.

Then again, maybe not. The truth was, the Lander County Boys' Home hadn't prepared him for fatherhood, instant or otherwise. Nor had it taught him the first thing about being part of a family. No matter how hard he tried, he didn't know what to say or how to act, much less how to befriend a little kid—and a girl, at that.

And though he wasn't surprised, it ate at him. He'd long ago decided he'd never marry, since what he'd seen at the orphanage—boys left alone, whether by their parents' choices or by their parents' deaths—had convinced him that love couldn't be depended upon. But with Lissy it was different, since neither of them had a choice in the matter. She was here, and he was here, and he knew damn well that she deserved better than he was able to give.

Still, they'd managed all right during the summer. Due, no doubt, to the fact that his nearest neighbor's teenage daughter had been willing to baby-sit, leaving him pretty much free to go about his business as usual. Now that school had started and he and Lis were on their own, it wasn't so simple, however. In addition to having a twelve-thousand-acre ranch to run, he had to contend with baths, bedtimes, laundry and meals. And without someone to run interference, his normal reticence combined with his daughter's shyness was making for increasingly long and awkward silences.

Across the way, Lissy started down the bus's steep metal stairs. It was his signal to climb out of the truck, and he did, striding around to the other side as she walked up. "Hey, Lissy." Opening the passenger door, he reached for her bright red backpack and tossed it onto the truck's abbreviated back seat.

She glanced shyly up at him. "Hi."

He reached out and boosted her carefully onto the seat. She weighed next to nothing, making him acutely aware of his own strength. Straightening, he stepped back and waited for her to fasten her seat belt. Once she did, he shut her door, walked around and got in on his own side. As soon as the bus lumbered away, he started the truck, made a tight U-turn and headed back to the ranch.

Silence reigned as he tried to think of something to say. Finally, after more than a mile, he glanced surreptitiously at her. She jerked her gaze away from him and stared down at her lap, pink touching her cheeks as she began to pluck at her skirt with her pale fingers.

He cleared his throat. "So...how was your day?"

She shrugged one thin shoulder. "Okay."

"Anything interesting happen?"

Her fingers stilled. After a moment, she nodded. "Uh-huh."

He waited, but she remained silent. "What?" he said finally.

To his surprise, she suddenly sucked in a breath and turned to face him. "Jenny Handelmen asked me to come to her birthday party!"

He stared at her. Her usually sober little face was lit up like a Christmas tree. "She did?"

"Uh-huh. She wasn't going to—" her pleasure dimmed a fraction "—but her mom said she had to ask all the girls in the class."

John suppressed the urge to ask who in the hell had felt compelled to tell her *that*. "Yeah, well, the important thing is you got invited," he said awkwardly.

She appeared to think about that. "I guess." Her face brightened. "She's going to have pizza, and a Barbie cake and chocolate ice cream. And she said we're gonna play games!"

He frowned, surprised by the extent of her excitement. "That's good, huh?"

She started to reply, then appeared to reconsider. "I think so."

"Don't you know?"

She shook her head and her unruly mop of dark blond corkscrew curls bobbed around her shoulders, making him belatedly wonder what had become of the ponytail he'd struggled so hard to secure that morning. "I—I've never been to a birthday party before."

"You haven't?"

"Uh-uh."

"Why not?"

She shrugged, her expression suddenly uncertain. "Grandma always said no."

"Huh." He'd known Lissy's grandmother only briefly, but it hadn't taken him long to form an opinion about her character. He wondered if it had been disapproval of having fun in general or the price of a gift that had made the old lady deny the kid such a simple pleasure.

"So can I go?"

He started to say yes, then caught himself. "When is it?"

"Saturday."

"This Saturday? Tomorrow?"

"Uh-uh." She shook her head. "The next one."

His heart sank. "Are you sure?"

"Uh-huh."

"What time?"

"Six. Remember, I told you, we're gonna have pizza for dinner."

Great. The annual Cattlemen's Association banquet was due to kick off at seven the same night in Missoula, a hundred and twenty-five miles away. He'd already tried and failed to get a sitter, so he'd gone ahead and made a reservation for the two of them at the hotel. As outgoing president, there was no way he could miss it.

Yet something told him that Lissy wasn't going to see it that way. He glanced at her. For once she was staring straight at him. Her eyes—the same intense blue as his own—were bright with anticipation. "Can I go? Please?"

He swallowed a curse. "No, I'm afraid not."

She blinked in surprise, her long lashes brushing her translucent cheeks as all the joy drained from her face. "Oh," she said in a small voice.

"Look, I'm sorry." Even to his own ears, his voice sounded stilted. "I've got a meeting that night and I can't miss it."

"Oh," she said again. She swallowed hard, turning away to once more stare down at her lap. "It's okay," she said after a moment. "I—I didn't really want to go anyway."

It was clearly a lie. Yet try as he might, John couldn't think how to address it—much less what he could say that would make things better. Feeling guilty and frustrated, he looked away from her still little face and pretended to be absorbed in the road in front of him.

They traveled the last half mile to the house in total silence. Pulling into the same spot where he'd parked earlier, he stopped the truck and turned off the engine. "I've got to get some stuff from the barn," he said gruffly. He nodded toward the porch. "Why don't you go on in? Have a quick snack and then you need to change into some play clothes."

"What for?" she said dully.

"We need to run some salt licks up to the herd at Blue Ridge."

She still didn't look at him. "But…couldn't I stay here? Please?"

He considered. It was a good thirty miles to the ridge round-trip. It would be dark by the time he got back. If something were to happen to her... He shook his head. "No."

Silence. And then, with an air of utter dejection, she gave a faint sigh. "Okay." Without another word, she opened the door and climbed out, sliding the last foot to the ground before nudging the door shut and heading for the porch. She looked very small and very much alone as she trudged along, her shoulders slumped, her feet dragging in her scuffed white shoes.

John watched until she disappeared inside the house. For a moment he sat motionless. Then he let loose a curse and slammed his fist against the dashboard. *Damn it!* She deserved better than this. She deserved better than *him*. There had to be something he could do, some way he could make things better—

There is, you sorry sonofabitch. The solution was here earlier asking for a job—remember?

The thought froze him in place. He started to deny it, but in the next moment all his earlier arguments against hiring Eve seemed to fade away, replaced by the image of Lissy's sad little face. He sank back against the seat, his anger abruptly replaced by a sort of grim resignation.

Okay. So he didn't particularly like Eve. What did it matter? It was Lissy's happiness that was important. And it wasn't as if he had other options. If having Eve around would make things better, he could handle his feelings—couldn't he?

As for his unfortunate physical attraction to her... Big deal. It wasn't his way to let his feelings cloud his judgment, or his desires dictate his actions. And he certainly wasn't a stranger to deprivation. He'd lived most of his life without the sort of things—such as a home or family or even a close companion—that other people took for granted. He could handle himself.

As quickly as that, his mind was made up. For Lissy's sake, he'd do it.

And to hell with his gut, which was already warning him that Ms. Chandler was going to be nothing but trouble.

And that he was making a big mistake.

Three

"You ready?"

Poised in the open doorway of her childhood home, Eve considered John and his less-than-gracious greeting. He looked very big as he stood backlit by afternoon sunshine, the breeze ruffling the navy T-shirt tucked into his close-fitting jeans.

Very big, very remote—and far from friendly. The old adage "Be careful what you wish for" played through her head. Three days ago she'd been distraught when he'd refused to give her a job.

Now, face-to-face with him again, she felt distraught that he had.

A faint, self-mocking sensation curled through her. Clearly this was the time to remind herself that if not for John's change of heart, she'd be on a Greyhound bus right now bound for who knew where. And that no matter how much she might wish he were a different kind of man—more easygoing, more forthcoming, less attractive, less blatantly male—she owed him for giving her a chance.

"Yes," she said pleasantly. "I'm ready. And I really appreciate you coming to get me."

"No problem. That your stuff?" With a jerk of his chin, he indicated the matched set of luggage and the large cardboard box lined up on the porch to his left.

She nodded. "Yes."

Without another word he walked over, picked up a suitcase in either hand and headed for his truck.

Eve watched him stride away, telling herself that he was doing her a favor with his brusque, businesslike manner. Because, for reasons she was sure were solely attributable to some obscure facet of male-female chemistry, she had to admit that after all these years simply looking at him still made her a little breathless. She didn't want to think how she'd react if he ever displayed the least bit of charm.

Not that there appeared to be any chance of that. For which she was extremely grateful, she told herself firmly, forcing herself to look away from his retreating back. She needed this job. It would be the height of folly to let some juvenile attraction get in the way.

It was just hard to remember when John's presence was so unsettling. But then, she supposed in a way she owed him for *that,* too, since her extreme awareness of him seemed to overshadow everything, even her imminent departure from her childhood home.

She turned and took one last look at the familiar entry, the broad staircase, the living room that was never used, the long hall that led to the family room that was.

It had been a good place to grow up. Yet she wasn't

sorry to leave. Being here alone the past few weeks had made her realize that without her grandfather, the ranch was no longer her home.

She settled the strap of her purse on her shoulder and smoothed her suede vest into place over her white, open-neck shirt and slim-fitting jeans. Then she calmly pushed in the lock and stepped outside, pulling the door shut behind her. She was just in time as John came up the stairs again.

He nodded at the single remaining suitcase as he reached for the cardboard box. "You think you could grab that?" He straightened without any sign of strain, although Eve knew how heavy the box was since she'd needed help carrying it outside.

"Of course."

"Then let's go. I need to pick up Lissy and get back to work." He turned on his heel and headed back the way he'd come.

All right. So maybe he was making it difficult to be grateful. She still wasn't going to let him get to her. Chin up, she set out after him, approaching just as he finished setting the box in the bed of the truck. He turned but didn't say anything, merely reached for the suitcase. In the second before it occurred to her to let go, his hand pressed firmly against hers.

It was big, hard and warm, and Eve felt the contact clear to her toes. Startled, she jerked away, her gaze shooting to John's face as she wondered if he'd felt it, too.

If he had, it didn't show. His glorious blue eyes were hooded, his strong, masculine face expressionless as he gazed down at her. With a faint shock, she realized how close he was. Despite the breeze, she could feel the heat roll off of him, carrying with it the faint scent of soap and sweat. And she could see the beard that shadowed his smoothly shaven cheeks, as well as the faint lines that bracketed each side of his chiseled mouth.

Her own mouth suddenly felt desert dry. And still she continued to stare at him, riveted by the sensual curve of his lips—

He abruptly turned away, tossing the bag in the truck with a thump. Leaning over, he snagged an elastic cross tie and secured it across her belongings. Then he straightened, walked the few feet to the passenger door and jerked it open. Leveling a blue-eyed stare at her, he rocked back on his heels. "You getting in or not?"

Eve sucked in a breath. *Remember. You can handle this—no matter how he behaves.* "Of course." Deliberately taking her time, she strolled over and climbed unhurriedly into the cab. Looking out at John, she smiled her most gracious smile. "Thank you."

"Sure." He slammed the door, walked around and climbed in on the driver's side. Neither of them spoke as he started the truck and put it in gear.

Eve stared fixedly outside, watching the familiar landscape roll by. The sky was a vast expanse of cloudless blue that seemed to go on forever. On the far horizon, the mountains rose in shades of gray and plum, their jagged peaks frosted with snow. Closer in, a few head of cattle grazed, all that was left of the once vast Chandler herd.

Regret rocked through her. It came despite her confidence that the ranch would prosper again; the Texas consortium that had bought it had deep pockets and a good reputation. Nor did it seem to matter that in addition to making one year's guaranteed employment for the handful of loyal hands who'd opted to stay on a condition of the sale, she'd also seen to it that they received every dime of their back pay, the best she could do under the circumstances.

She just wished she knew what had prompted her grandfather to make that first risky investment. Or why, when things started to go sour, he hadn't simply accepted his losses instead of stubbornly throwing good money after bad.

She swallowed a sigh. If only she'd paid more attention, instead of blithely assuming that everything was all right. If only she'd come home last spring, instead of letting Granddad convince her the timing was bad. If only she'd behaved more responsibly, he might have felt he could confide in her, instead of believing he had to protect her the way he always had.

"Why didn't you tell me you were broke? That you had to sell the ranch?" John asked abruptly.

The question caught her off-guard. Her stomach twisted even as she gamely raised her chin. "Whatever makes you think that?"

"Don't try to snow me, Eve. I'd already heard some rumors. After you gave me that story about needing a ride today because you were 'between cars,' I got to thinking. I called Eldon Taylor and he filled me in."

Eldon Taylor was the president of Lander Savings and Loan. Eve had never particularly liked him, but until now she'd always thought he was discreet. "He had no right," she said woodenly.

"Maybe not. But the point is, he did." They rattled over the last cattle guard, then drove beneath the carved wooden arch that marked the ranch entrance. After checking for other traffic, John pulled out on the sparsely traveled two-lane highway and accelerated. "And you still haven't answered my question."

"Unlike Mr. Taylor, I didn't think it was any of your business," she said coolly. "I don't recall asking you for a loan. Or a handout." She glanced challengingly at him. "Or do you make everyone who works for you fill out a financial statement?"

A muscle flexed in his jaw. "I'm not entrusting 'everyone' with my daughter. I'm entrusting you. I think that entitles me to ask a few questions."

As much as it rankled, Eve had to concede he had a point. "All right. What is it you want to know?"

"I thought you had a trust fund, money that came from your parents."

"That's right."

"What happened? You blow through it already?"

Before, she'd only suspected he thought she was a spoiled brat. Now she knew. Yet she was darned if she'd defend herself. Not now, and not to him. She shrugged. "As a matter of fact, I did. But don't worry. I swear I won't steal your silver or anything. I'm not that desperate. Yet."

To her satisfaction, his mouth tightened.

Deciding to press her advantage, she added, "What made you change your mind about hiring me, anyway?"

One shoulder rose and fell dismissively. "I don't have time to run the ranch and also take care of a kid. Once I thought about it, I decided that any help was better than none. Even yours."

It was hardly a ringing endorsement, but Eve told herself she didn't care. His opinion wasn't the one that mattered. "What about your daughter? What does she have to say about this?"

He shrugged again. "I've got a meeting in Missoula this Saturday, the same time that one of her classmates is having a birthday party. Your being here means she can go, so I'd say she's for it." He paused, then added almost defensively, "She's not a real big talker."

Eve stared at him in surprise, suddenly wondering if there was something he wasn't telling her. Pursing her lips, she tried to decide how to broach the subject, when suddenly his whole big body stiffened.

"Damn," he said fiercely.

"What's the matter?"

"The bus must've been early."

A quick look around made her realize they were coming up on the entrance for the Bar M. But it wasn't until she followed his gaze that she noticed the forlorn little figure who stood half-hidden next to a large metal mailbox boldly marked MacLaren.

Eve wasn't sure what she'd expected, but it wasn't this.

John's daughter was small and pale, with big blue eyes set in a delicate face and a wild tangle of butterscotch curls that spilled from a bedraggled, off-center ponytail. She was also atrociously dressed in a pea-green nylon slicker, a too-big canary-yellow dress that sported an oversize Peter Pan collar, and a pair of sagging navy kneesocks.

Yet what captured Eve's attention was the way the child took several spontaneous steps forward when she saw the truck, then stopped, as if uncertain of her reception. She hesitated, then raised her hand in a tentative wave.

The vulnerability of the gesture tugged at Eve's heart.

She glanced at John as he pulled over onto the

verge. His face was granite hard as he slammed the transmission into park. He was out the door almost before the pickup had come to a full stop. Yet for all his urgency, he stopped several feet short of his daughter, and he made no attempt to touch her. "You okay?" Although his back was to Eve, his gruff voice carried clearly on the breeze.

The little girl nodded.

"Sorry I'm late."

"It's okay. I just...I thought you forgot."

There was a moment's silence. When he spoke, his voice was even more clipped than before. "I wouldn't do that." He reached down and picked up the small backpack that was lying on the dusty ground. "Come on." He straightened. "There's someone I want you to meet."

The child glanced toward the truck, apprehension suddenly filling her face. "Is that her? Is that the lady who's going to stay with me?" she asked anxiously.

Eve had heard enough. Propelled by an instinct she didn't question, she unlatched her seat belt, scrambled out of the truck and walked over to where father and daughter stood.

Ignoring John, she looked down at the child standing silently at his side. She smiled her most reassuring smile and waited.

There was a brief silence. Then, with an abruptness she pretended not to notice, John said gruffly, "This is my daughter, Lissy." He touched his hand to the child's shoulder. "Lissy, say hello to Miss Chandler."

The little girl looked soberly up at her. "Hello."

"I'm so glad to finally meet you, Lissy," she said warmly. "You can call me Eve, okay?"

The child hesitated, then nodded.

Eve's smile softened. Gently, she reached out and gave Lissy's shoulder a reassuring squeeze. "Good. I just know we're going to be friends."

For a second the child appeared startled. "You do?"

Eve nodded. "Uh-huh. And that's good because I could use a new friend."

"Oh." Lissy hesitated. Her big blue eyes seemed to search Eve's face, and then an uncertain smile trembled across her mouth. "Me, too."

In that moment, Eve lost her heart.

John's house was beautiful as well as functional.

Designed to conform to the surrounding land, the spacious, sprawling, single-story structure was shaped like a trio of rectangles stacked in a sideways stair step. The first block contained the mudroom, which Eve had already seen, and an airy, modern kitchen. A granite-topped eating bar angled along its far side and was open to the second, largest block, which held John's study and a great room. The third block housed the sleeping quarters, with the master bed and bath occupying half the space, three smaller bedrooms and two bathrooms sharing the rest.

Standing in the great room, midway between the kitchen, dining and living areas, Eve admired the huge stone fireplace and the open beams that arched across the vaulted ceiling. The far end of the room jutted out like the bow of a ship and was ribbed with tall windows, so that it seemed to blend with the vast sweep of land and sky outside. The effect was expansive and restful, a feeling echoed by the furniture that was simply but beautifully done using warm woods and soft fabrics in shades of camel, taupe, sand and blue.

"This is wonderful," she said sincerely as John appeared from delivering the last of her things to her room.

He shrugged. "It'll do."

Their gazes met. To her dismay, although he looked about as friendly as an iceberg, she felt a subtle but unrelenting tug of attraction similar to an ocean undertow.

"Where's Lissy?" he said abruptly.

"She went to change her clothes."

"Ah." He considered her for a moment, then headed for the kitchen. "There are some things we need to go over."

"All right." She turned as he walked past her and followed him as far as the eating bar.

Opening the door to the walk-in pantry, he took a set of keys off a hook on the wall. He shut the door, walked over and slid them across the counter to her. "I had the ranch Jeep brought in for you. It's not much to look at, but the engine and the tires are sound and the gas tank's full."

"Thank you."

A faint, slightly cynical smile touched his mouth. "Trust me, it's no Mercedes, princess. But it's safe and it'll get you and Lissy where you need to go."

She inclined her head, since there didn't seem to be anything to say to that.

"We can go over the school bus schedule and any questions you have later. Right now, all you need to know is that the freezer here is fully stocked—" he touched the stainless-steel front of the Sub-Zero next to the matching refrigerator "—and that I'd like to eat by six."

Before Eve could respond, the sound came of somebody knocking at the back door. John strode over to look into the mudroom, then turned back to her. "Sorry," he said, not sounding sorry at all. "That's my foreman. I'd better go see what he wants."

"No problem." She watched him walk away—until it dawned on her that she was admiring the way his jeans clung to his narrow hips and long legs.

Heat climbed into her cheeks. She turned away, wondering a little wildly what it was going to take to dim her awareness of him, only to realize she was pretty sure she wouldn't like the answer.

Irritated with herself, she set off to find Lissy, determined to put John, and her unfortunate reaction to him, out of her mind. Walking quickly down the hallway that fronted the bedrooms, she stopped at what she hoped was the correct door and glanced in.

Like her own room, this one was bright and spacious, with a large closet on one wall and a trio of arch-top windows opposite the door. Yet except for a battered stuffed rabbit propped on the bed, it also felt rather impersonal, like a nicely appointed hotel room. While the carved oak dresser, highboy and double bed with its blue, beige and white bedspread were lovely, they seemed far too old for a seven-year-old.

She spotted her charge lying on her stomach on a blue-and-white braided rug beneath the windows. Several sheets of paper were spread out around her, and a big box of crayons was tipped on its side by her right hand.

Eve knocked, staying put until the child looked up. "Hi. Can I come in?"

Lissy nodded and scrambled into a sitting position.

"What are you up to? Coloring?"

The child nodded again, her face registering near-comical surprise when Eve crossed the rug and sank onto the floor beside her.

"Is it all right for me to look?"

The little girl dropped her gaze, suddenly shy. "Okay."

Eve studied the drawings spread out before her. One was of a tall man with dark hair—clearly John—who stood so much larger than life that he dwarfed the mountain behind him. Another was of an eagle soaring across the sky. And the third, the one that Lissy was obviously working on now, was of a house at night, bright yellow light pouring from the windows beneath a star-spangled sky. Tellingly, there was a dark-haired man framed in one window and a little blond girl in another, both quite alone.

Eve's heart clenched, even as she managed a cheery smile. "These are lovely. Did you know, my friend Chrissy is the sister of your teacher, Miss Abrams?"

"She is?"

"Uh-huh. And I understand that Miss Abrams thinks you're one of the very best artists in her class. I can see why. You draw wonderful pictures."

"Oh." The little girl's face filled with surprised pleasure. "I like to color." She glanced down self-consciously at her lap.

Eve considered that small, bowed head. In addition to her comments about the child's artistic talent, Pam Abrams had also reportedly said that John's daughter could use a woman in her life. At the time, Eve had just assumed—foolishly, she now admitted—that the child must be a miniature version of her father, and what she needed was a civilizing influence.

It didn't take a genius to realize she'd missed the mark. Or to discern that in sharp contrast to her self-assured, self-possessed father, what Lissy was most in need of was someone to give her their undivided attention, to build her up, to boost her confidence and be her champion.

That—and a fashion makeover. Eve swallowed a wry grimace. Just as she'd told John, the youngster had indeed changed out of her school clothes. Now, instead of that awful yellow dress, she was wearing a drab red sweatshirt that sagged at the neck and fell nearly to her knees over a faded, too-short pair of faded pink leggings. The latter exposed her bony little ankles, which protruded above a pair of ruffled lavender anklets and worn white mary-janes.

Eve wondered what on earth John was thinking to allow his child to go around looking like a pint-size bag lady. For someone so prickly proud, it seemed out of character. Then again, she didn't really know him, a fact that was becoming increasingly clear with every hour that passed.

"Oh, I almost forgot. I have something for you."

The child's eyes widened. "You do?"

"Yes, I do." She reached into her vest pocket, pulled out a small, gift-wrapped package and handed it to Lissy. "It's something my granddad gave me when I came to live with him," she said softly, watching as the child carefully began to remove the pink and gold paper. "I thought, since you just recently came to live with your dad, that you might like to have it."

Lissy stared down at the small, velvet gift box she'd unwrapped. Chewing her lower lip in concentration, she pried up the top. "Ohhh!"

Lying on a bed of midnight satin was a small gold

horse pendant, threaded onto a sturdy but pretty gold chain.

Lissy looked at her, her eyes as round as pennies. "Oh, it's so pretty," she breathed.

Eve smiled. "Would you like to try it on?"

The child nodded. "Yes, please."

Eve picked up the necklace, opened the clasp and leaned forward. "Max, my granddad, told me—" she fastened the chain around the child's delicate neck, then sat back to admire the effect "—that wearing this makes you an official Montana cowgirl."

Lissy touched her hand to the necklace. "It does?"

"Absolutely."

"Even...even if you're afraid of horses?"

Eve considered the sudden hope on that little face and added *teach to ride* and *revamp wardrobe* to her quickly growing list of things to do. "Even then," she said firmly, rewarded by one of Lissy's shy, tremulous smiles.

She smiled back, then looked up as an inexplicable little tingle warned her they were no longer alone. Tall and imposing, John stood silently in the doorway. Their gazes met and to her shock, for the briefest moment she could have sworn there was something in his eyes that was dark and hungry.

As if she were seventeen again, her body responded instantly. Her breath caught, her skin flushed, her nipples beaded. Worse, she felt an overwhelming urge to climb to her feet, close the distance between them and indulge herself in the luxury of exploring that big, hard body—

"Look what Eve gave me!"

Lissy's awe-filled exclamation jerked John's gaze toward his daughter. As if released from a spell, Eve snapped back to reality. What on earth had just happened? she wondered, a shiver shuddering through her.

Whatever it was, Lissy thankfully seemed oblivious. Climbing to her feet, the child approached her father and shyly held up the pendant. "See?"

John looked from the necklace to his daughter's upturned face. "It's real nice," he murmured.

The little girl smiled with surprised pleasure and his own expression seemed to lighten fractionally.

He straightened. "I've got to get back to work but I shouldn't be too long." His blue eyes once again found Eve. They were cool and polite, nothing more. "Like I said before, I'd like to eat around six."

"Fine."

"If you need anything, my cell phone number's posted next to the telephone in the kitchen."

She forced herself to smile. "Don't worry about us. We'll manage, won't we, Lissy?"

The child's head bobbed. "Uh-huh."

"All right, then." With a brusque nod, he turned on his heel and left.

It wasn't very mature of her, but in light of her inability to control her rampaging hormones, Eve was glad to see him go.

Four

Eve was seated at the kitchen counter when John walked out of his bedroom Friday morning.

His step faltered as his gaze raked over her, taking note of the slender line of her back, the taut curve of her fanny, the bare feet he could see propped on the bottom rung of the bar stool. With her shining blond hair and sun-kissed skin, she looked all-American exotic, as if she ought to be hanging ten on a beach somewhere.

Not that he gave a damn. Shoving his shirttail into his jeans, he told himself that the sudden tension humming through him was nothing more than annoyance. Growing up at the orphanage, privacy had been nonexistent; in the years since he'd left it, he'd come to treasure his morning solitude.

Somehow he doubted Eve would understand, however. With her upbringing, she probably believed he'd be thrilled to see her. God knew, she hadn't held back from making her presence felt in the brief time that she'd been here. Small reminders of her were all over his house, from the bouquet of fall flowers in the center of the dining room table, to the flimsy Italian leather shoes lined up next to his boots in the mudroom, to the faint scent of her perfume that seemed to linger long after she'd left a room.

Still, he was willing to concede that so far she was managing a lot better than he'd expected. The house was clean and tidy. Dinner the past four nights had been delicious. Most importantly, she seemed to really be making an effort with Lissy.

And that was the only thing that mattered.

He crossed the room, his stride firm and purposeful as he walked around the end of the eating counter.

"Good morning," Eve said softly.

Her husky voice tickled along his spine. Deliberately taking his time, he poured himself a cup of coffee before he finally turned to face her. "What are you doing up so early?"

If she was taken aback by the curt question, it didn't show. "I've always been a morning person."

His opinion of that must have shown on his face because the corners of her mouth unexpectedly quirked up.

"I realize it doesn't fit my indolent image—" that tempting mouth curved a little more "—or square with the fact that I slept in the past few mornings, but it's true."

John stared at her. He could see that she'd already showered; her pale hair was still slightly damp. He could also smell her, a faint scent like raindrops on clean, warm skin. But it was the unexpected display of charm that gave him pause—it was as warm and seductive as the first sunny day after a hard winter.

It was also a first where he was concerned and something stirred inside him.

"Besides," she added, her manner abruptly sobering, as if she'd suddenly remembered just who she was addressing, "I also wanted to talk to you."

Ah, that was more like it. Leaning back against the counter, he tried to decide what her problem was likely to be. Would she announce that her bedroom was not up to her standards? Or admit that she'd prefer not to share a bathroom with a seven-year-old? Or would she complain that driving his old Jeep was beneath her? He set down his mug and crossed his arms. "So talk."

"Well, to start with, I have plans to go into town today. I thought I'd better let you know, since dinner may run a little late."

He should have known. "What's the matter, princess? Bored already?"

Her hand froze in the process of raising her coffee mug to her lips. She regarded him for a moment, then slowly shook her head. "No." She took a sip and gently set her cup down on the counter. "On the contrary. I've volunteered to work a few hours a week in Lissy's classroom and I thought I'd start today."

It was so far from what John had expected, it took him a moment to take it in. "You what?"

"I volunteered to—"

He silenced her with a curt wave of his hand. "What I meant was *why*."

"Why what?"

"Why would you do that?"

She began to look a little exasperated. "Oh, I don't know. Maybe because I hope it will make Lissy feel sort of special. And maybe because I hope that feeling special will give her a little added confidence."

Out of nowhere, a memory flashed through his head. He'd been six years old and in Miss Wakin's first-grade class, and it had been his birthday. He'd waited all day, secretly hoping someone from the Home would show up with cupcakes the way the other kids' moms always did. When nobody had, he'd finally accepted that being an orphan meant no one really cared about you.

He shoved the recollection away, wondering blackly what was wrong with him. This was about Lissy, not him. And no matter his feelings about Eve, he had to concede she had a point. "All right. What else?"

"Excuse me?"

"You kicked off this little discussion by saying, 'to start with.' What else have you got planned?"

Her chin came up a fraction. "Not much. I thought we'd pick up a gift for the birthday party tomorrow. And I also thought we might do some shopping. Not only does Lissy need a dress to wear to the party but her wardrobe could use updating. That is, if it's all right with you."

Despite her impeccably polite tone, there was no mistaking the glint in her clear gray eyes. And though he returned her stare with a steady one of his own, everything that was male in him rose to that unspoken challenge. As the seconds ticked past, he grew increasingly aware of the touch of pink high on her cheeks and the accelerated pulse beating at the base of her throat.

A coil of heat twisted through him. Out of nowhere, he found himself wondering what would happen if he thrust his hands into her pale silky hair, hauled her across the counter and sampled that soft pink mouth with his own.

The thought set off an insistent throb in his groin.

And an alarm in his head. For the second time in under two minutes, he wondered what in the hell his problem was.

But he knew. It was her. Eve. There was just something about her that made him want to cut loose and indulge his baser instincts without a thought to the consequences.

Or would, if he was stupid enough to give in to it.

Which he wasn't. He slapped his coffee cup down on the counter. "Get whatever you think Lis needs. You can sign for it—I've got an account at pretty much every store in town. And don't worry about dinner." He yanked his wallet out of his back pocket, peeled two twenties free and slapped them down on the counter. "As long as you're there, you might as well eat in town."

She looked from the money to him, a slight frown marring her patrician features. "All right," she said slowly. "That's very nice of you."

"Oh, I'm not being nice, princess. I'm just looking forward to some time to myself."

Once more their gazes locked. And though he tried to deny it, for an instant he again felt that unholy desire to wrap his hands in that silky hair, to run his lips over that satiny skin.

By sheer strength of will he forced it away.

Yet as he picked up his car keys off the counter and headed out to work, he found himself thinking it was a damn good thing he was spending the weekend in Missoula.

* * *

"Eve?" Lissy pursed her lips in concentration as she tugged a ruby red tulle skirt into place around Very Velvet Barbie's impossibly slender waist.

"Hmm?"

"Do you think Jenny really likes the present I got her?"

Seated across from the child on the floor, her back propped against one of the great room's oversize club chairs, Eve looked up from the cookbook she'd been perusing. So far she'd done all right, but she could already see that cooking five or six nights a week was going to put a severe strain on her limited culinary repertoire. Hence the cookbook and the pad of sticky notes in her lap. "Sweetie, she loved it. I heard her tell you that myself when I came to pick you up. Between you and me—" she leaned forward and dropped her voice to a confidential whisper "—I'm pretty sure it was her favorite."

The child still didn't look entirely convinced. "You really think so?"

"Absolutely. She got lots of Barbie dolls and stuffed animals, but only one sequined cape and rhinestone tiara."

Lissy considered, then gave a relieved sigh. "Yeah. You're right. All the other girls wanted to try them on. And Jenny did say she likes to play dress-up."

Eve swallowed a fond smile and went back to her cookbook. The past week had taught her that due to her sensitive nature, Lissy was a worrier. Yet she'd also found that with just a little gentle encouragement, the child's natural optimism eventually surfaced.

"Eve?"

"Hmm?"

"Are you sure it'll be okay with my dad for Jenny to come play tomorrow?"

"Of course. Why wouldn't it be?"

A slight frown crinkled Lissy's brow as she picked up a miniature pink comb and began to smooth Barbie's bangs. She gave a little shrug. "Well, my grandma always said that other kids were too loud to have around. She said all that chatter hurt her head."

Eve felt a familiar twinge of dismay. By now she had a pretty clear picture of Lissy's life with her grandmother and it wasn't pretty. As far as she could tell, the elderly lady had believed that children should neither be heard nor seen—and she'd made sure her granddaughter behaved appropriately.

According to Grandma, good little girls played quietly alone in their bedrooms. They didn't wear jeans or laugh too loud or get dirty. They always wore dresses to school, they didn't speak unless spoken to and they never, ever talked back.

Apparently, playmates were also on the forbidden list.

Until now. Just as she'd been doing each time she got the opportunity, Eve tried to reassure Lissy that the rules had changed. "I'm sure your dad won't object."

"Even when he finds out Jenny is going to stay for dinner?"

"Even then. He'll be pleased. You'll see," she said, crossing her fingers that she was right.

On the one hand, John really seemed to care about his daughter. There was just something in his voice whenever he said her name, as well as a subtle gentling in his manner whenever he dealt with her, that made Eve believe his feelings ran deep.

But then again, she could hardly forget the way Lissy had deflated like a punctured balloon when they'd gotten back from shopping Friday night and found the house empty except for a note from John saying he'd decided to go to Missoula a day early.

The child's disappointment had been painful to see, and Eve had been left to wonder whether John didn't know how much he meant to his daughter—or just didn't care.

Frowning, Lissy struggled to force a minuscule Lucite high heel onto one of Barbie's feet. "You're still going to ask him about the horse, aren't you?"

"Sweetie, I told you I would."

"But you promise not to tell him it's for me?"

"That's right." The little girl had been both thrilled and apprehensive when offered the chance to learn to ride. She'd immediately said yes—as long as it could be kept a secret from her father. Eve had reluctantly agreed once she'd realized that Lissy was afraid she might fail and disappoint him.

Barbie's shoe slid on. Lissy reached for the other, but before she could pick it up a flash of sunlight on metal sliced through the room and they both looked over to see John's black pickup roll by the far window.

The little girl's face lit up. "My dad's home!"

"Yes, it sure looks that way," Eve murmured. She tried to tell herself that the sudden kick of her pulse was merely a reaction to the child's excitement, but on some level she knew better.

It was anticipation, pure and simple.

In what seemed no time at all, she heard the back door open and close. Moments later, John strode into the room.

Eve tried not to stare—and failed. Dressed in charcoal slacks and a dove-gray linen shirt, with black boots and a dressy black cowboy hat, he looked heartbreaker handsome. And almost civilized.

Lissy jumped up, her Barbie forgotten. "Hi!" Her voice squeaked with sudden nervousness.

John didn't appear to notice. "Hey, Lissy." For a long moment his gaze lingered on his daughter's face. Then, almost reluctantly, he glanced over at Eve and inclined his head.

Although his expression was as impossible to read as ever, as their gazes met she felt the familiar jolt of his appeal. Only this time she was ready. Taking refuge in action, she climbed to her feet, using the time to compose herself. "Welcome back," she said evenly.

To her relief, he seemed completely unaware of his effect on her. "Thanks." He set his overnight bag on the floor and draped his suitbag over the counter.

"How was your meeting?"

He began to rifle through the previous day's mail. "Good. What about you? Everything go okay?" He didn't bother to look up.

"Everything went fine." She glanced at Lissy; the child was staring intently at him, managing to look both eager and uncertain all at the same time.

Setting the mail aside, he began to sort through his phone messages. A good half minute passed before he finally seemed to become aware of the expectant quality of the silence. He raised his head, a slight frown forming between his brows when he found both Eve and Lissy looking at him.

The silence stretched out until finally Eve couldn't take any more. "I bet you're wondering about the birthday party," she said mildly, trying not to be too obvious.

His expression abruptly cleared. "Yeah. Of course. I was just getting ready to ask." He folded the paper with his phone messages, slipped it into his pocket and turned fractionally toward Lissy. "So—how was it?"

Shyness suddenly tongue-tied the little girl. Digging one small, sneaker-covered toe into the carpet, Lissy gave a little shrug. "Fine."

He frowned. "Did you have fun?"

"Uh-huh."

His voice abruptly softened. "Well, that's good. I'm glad."

It was all the encouragement she needed. Raising her head, she blurted, "Jenny really, really liked the present I got her and her cake had three layers and Barbie on it and I got to wear a party hat and blow a make-noiser and we played pin the tail on the donkey and musical chairs and drop the clothespin and I won at musical chairs and I got this for a prize." Sucking in a much-needed breath, she reached up and touched the pink plastic headband holding back her burnished curls.

"Huh." To Eve's surprise, he didn't seem quite certain how to respond.

"Isn't it pretty?"

"Yeah."

They both fell silent. After a moment, he reached for his bag.

Lissy's face fell.

The next thing she knew, Eve heard herself saying, "She really did have a wonderful time. As a matter of fact, she had so much fun I hated to see it end, so

I invited Jenny to come home with Lissy tomorrow after school and stay for dinner. Isn't that nice?"

John straightened, the bag temporarily forgotten, and stared at her consideringly. "Yeah. Sure."

"Then it's okay?" Lissy said hopefully.

To Eve's relief, he shifted his gaze back to his daughter. "Sure," he repeated.

"Oh, good." A happy smile bloomed on Lissy's face.

The sight seemed to give him pause. He appeared to weigh his words, then said carefully, "You look different today."

Her smile got even brighter. "That's 'cause I'm wearing jeans. See?" With endearing awkwardness, she did a quick pirouette to show him. "I know they're pink, and they got lace and stuff—" scrunching up her face, she looked down at the delicate trim that edged the front pockets "—but Eve says that's okay. They're still jeans."

"Ah," he murmured neutrally.

"And I got my hair cut, too. This much." She held up her hands and marked off eight inches, twice as much as had actually been lopped off. "Now it doesn't get so tangled. And I got lots and lots of other new clothes, too. You want to see?"

He hesitated—and in the next instant the telephone rang. For a moment the sound seemed to freeze him in place, and then with a gesture to Lissy to wait, he walked over and picked up the receiver.

"MacLaren." He listened intently for a good thirty seconds before obvious satisfaction flashed across his face. "Of course my offer still stands, Marty. If you're really willing to part with those heifers, I'm definitely in the market to buy. Let me change phones, and we can go over the figures."

Punching in the hold button, he glanced at Lissy. "I'm sorry," he said to his daughter, as he replaced the receiver in the cradle and walked around the counter, "but I really need to take care of this."

"Oh." Her voice, so animated only a minute earlier, was suddenly subdued. "Okay."

"Good girl." He sent her a brief smile of approval and headed for his study.

Rooted in place, Eve swallowed an instinctive cry of protest. She longed to shake him until his teeth rattled but, of course, would do no such thing. She'd only been here a week, after all, and John was her employer. It wasn't her place to tell him how to run his life—or raise his daughter.

Yet as she turned toward Lissy, her heart nearly broke in two at the disappointment she could see on the child's face as Lissy watched her father walk away.

"Thanks, Marty. I'll give you a call later in the week after I get the transport arranged. It's been a pleasure doing business with you, too. Be sure and tell Maxine hello."

Pleasantries complete, John hung up the phone. Feeling the tension in his shoulders, he stretched, then leaned back in his oversize leather desk chair and took yet another look at the columns of figures on his computer screen.

He'd been trying to get Martin Hersher to sell some of his prime breeding stock for more than six months. Now, not only had the Oklahoma rancher finally agreed to part with more than a thousand head, but he'd agreed to do it for an extremely reasonable price.

And how did he feel? Was he pleased? Satisfied? Filled with a sense of triumph?

No. He felt empty, as if he'd just achieved the world's most hollow victory.

He shoved back his chair and climbed to his feet. The thick, hand-knotted Persian rug muffled the sound of his boots as he prowled restlessly around the room, finally coming to a stop at one of the tall, arched windows. Bracing his hands against the frame, he looked out.

With the suddenness so typical of fall, night had fallen in the hour that he and Hersher had spent hammering out a deal. The evening sky stretched overhead like a vast swath of dark velvet, studded with the first faint glimmering stars and a silver slice of moon.

Yet it was the land, vast and ruggedly beautiful in the moonlight, that drew his eye. How many nights had he lain in his narrow bed at the orphanage and promised himself that no matter what it took, someday he was going to amount to something?

Now, thanks to hard work and a talent for playing the stock market, he had all the things he'd once only dreamed about—his own ranch, financial security, a respected position in the community.

And none of it seemed to matter when measured against the happiness of one little kid.

His heart squeezed as he thought about the look that had come over Lissy's face when he'd blown off her offer to look at her new clothes. He knew damn well that a good father never would have done such a thing. A good father would have jumped at the invitation.

He would have told his caller, no matter how important, that he'd have to call back.

He would have put his daughter first.

But not him. Not John MacLaren, hotshot cattle rancher and businessman. As usual, he not only hadn't known the right things to say to her, but when presented with an opportunity for the two of them to spend some time together, he'd leaped at the first opportunity to pass.

And though he knew it was for her own good—that if he had gone to look at her clothes he'd either have said the wrong thing or not known what to say at all, letting her down even more—it didn't make her disappointment any easier to bear. About the best that could be said of the whole sorry performance was that it appeared he'd done one thing right. He'd hired Eve, who, if the cozy little scene he'd walked in on was any indication, seemed to have achieved over the past week the kind of bond with Lissy that he could only imagine.

So what if her unexpected rapport with his daughter also made him feel the way he had as a kid, like an outsider looking in?

He'd survive. He always had.

That is, if he didn't first expire from unrelieved lust.

A self-mocking smile twisted his lips. By the time he'd reached Missoula Friday night, he'd managed to convince himself that his recent reaction to Eve was nothing more than his body's response to being celibate for much too long. What's more, he'd decided a little grimly that it was past time he do something about it—a resolve that had lasted right up until last night, when he'd been approached at the hotel bar by an attractive brunette who'd made her intentions clear with flattering directness.

It had been an unpleasant shock to discover he didn't feel a shred of interest.

Frustrated, he'd gruffly tendered his regrets to the lady, pleading exhaustion while telling himself that he simply liked to be the one in pursuit. He'd almost believed it, too—until he'd walked into his own house, taken one look at Eve and felt the desire he'd just spent forty-eight hours telling himself wasn't reserved solely for her come roaring back to life.

"John?"

Eve's soft voice invaded his thoughts. For a second he thought he'd imagined it. And then she said his name again and he realized he hadn't. More than a little aggravated—she was the last person he wanted to see right now—he stayed where he was. "What?"

"Dinner's ready."

He'd never felt less like eating in his life. "Thanks, but I'll pass. I stopped in Drover on the way home and had a late lunch."

There was a lengthy silence. Yet with a sixth sense he didn't question, he knew she hadn't left.

Reluctantly, he turned. Sure enough, she stood just inside the doorway. And though he knew it was ridiculous, for a split second he could have sworn he saw a flash of longing, a glint of hunger in her eyes. In the next instant it was gone, leaving him feeling even more foolish and frustrated. "Was there something else?"

At his harsh tone, she drew herself up. "As a matter of fact, yes. I was going to talk to you at dinner, but— may I come in?"

He didn't want her here. Not now, when he already

felt dangerously on edge. Yet damned if he had any intention of letting *her* see such weakness. "Suit yourself."

She shut the door and approached. His mood deteriorated even more at the realization that the mere sight of her—the lithe way she walked, the way her pale hair gleamed in the lamplight—turned him on.

Stopping when only a few feet separated them, she glanced up at him. "I thought you might want to look over the receipts for Lissy's new clothes. That way—" her manner was as cool as her clear gray eyes "—you'll at least have some idea what we purchased."

There was no mistaking the censure in her voice. And though he knew he deserved it, coming from her it rankled. "Thanks. You can leave them on my desk on your way out."

"All right." She didn't move.

"Anything else?"

"Yes. I have a favor to ask." Despite the words, she didn't sound in the least like a supplicant.

"And what's that?"

"While I was at home, I got into the habit of riding a few hours a week. If you can spare a horse, I'd like to start again. I—I could use the exercise."

His jaw bunched at the irony of it. Here he was, feeling as if his life was spinning out of control, and she was worried about going horseback riding. "No problem, princess. I'll let them know down at the barn to expect you." He paused, unable to keep the sarcasm out of his voice as he added, "You'll have to be your own groom, though. I don't pay my wranglers to wait on anybody. Particularly not another employee."

Her chin ratcheted up another notch. "I think I can manage."

The hell of it was, he had no doubt she could. As galling as it was to admit, the way she'd handled things this past week had forced him to acknowledge that she wasn't nearly as spoiled or selfish as he wanted to believe.

Not that he'd changed his overall opinion of her. At least where he was concerned, she was still the original ice princess, as evidenced by the way she currently seemed to be looking down at him—no mean feat, given that he towered over her by at least eight inches.

It was just his bad luck that the very air of superiority that set his teeth on edge also made the more primitive part of him want to tame her—atop the nearest horizontal surface.

"Are you done?" he inquired brusquely.

She hesitated, then nodded.

"Good." He stepped around her, strode to his desk, sat down and began to go through a stack of papers. "If you don't mind, I've got work to do."

He felt her eyes on his back. Yet she didn't say another word, simply walked over, set down what he belatedly realized were Lissy's clothing receipts, and exited the room.

Telling himself he was glad she was gone, he took a deep breath to settle himself—only to discover too late that the air was laced with the faint scent of her perfume.

His body hardened, and in that instant he came to a decision.

From now until however long it took for his libido to come to its senses, he'd give Ms. Chandler some serious distance.

Five

"**I** think that went really well," Eve said to Lissy as they walked out of the barn and began the trek to the house.

"You do?" Lissy's voice was doubtful.

"Uh-huh." The breeze tugged at her hair, and she smiled, enjoying the play of crisp air against her face. Although the afternoon was sunny and mild, the snow line on the surrounding mountains was noticeably lower than it had been a week ago, a reminder that winter was on the way.

"Even though I start to fall off every time Clue trots?" Clue was the small pinto mare that Jeb, the old wrangler who oversaw John's horses, had selected for the child.

"Yes." Eve reached over and squeezed the little girl's shoulder. "You're still learning, sweetie. You just need to relax a little, give it some time—and stop being so hard on yourself. Don't forget, just two weeks ago you were afraid to even touch a horse. Now, after only a handful of lessons, you know how to saddle and bridle one, how to get on and off, how to walk and trot and make the horse go where you want. I'd say that's a lot."

Almost reluctantly, Lissy nodded. "I s'pose." Despite her agreement, she continued to look pensive.

Eve regarded her with a thoughtful look of her own. There had been a lot going on lately, and suddenly she wondered if perhaps it had been too much. In addition to the sessions with Clue and having Eve help out in her classroom, Lissy had had her new friend Jenny over to play twice in the past ten days. Eve supposed the child had every right to be feeling a little overwhelmed.

"Eve?"

"Hmm?"

"Do you think my dad's mad at me?"

The question was so far from Eve's thoughts that it stopped her dead in her tracks. She swiveled to look at Lissy, dismayed when the child looked back at her and she saw the worry in those big blue eyes. "Oh, sweetie, of course not. Why would you think that?"

"Because." Hunching her shoulders, the little girl stared down at the road, refusing to meet her gaze. "He never did ask to see my new clothes. And even though he said it was okay, he wasn't there for dinner either time that Jenny was. He hasn't even been around enough—" there was a sudden hitch in her voice "—to say good-night to me."

For a moment, Eve didn't know what to say. Then she leaned over and clasped the child's hand, tugging her around so that they were facing each other. "Lissy, listen to me. I am one hundred percent certain your dad is not mad at you."

"You are?"

"Yes, I am."

The child swallowed. "Then do you think...do you think that maybe he just doesn't like me?"

Eve wasn't sure whether to laugh or cry. "Oh, sweetie, no. *No.* Your dad *loves* you."

The child considered a moment. "Then how come he never wants to be with me?"

Eve hesitated. More than anything, she wanted to reassure Lissy. At the same time, instinct told her that if she wanted to retain the girl's trust, she had to tell the truth. "I know it may seem that way," she said slowly. "But you have to remember, he has this whole big ranch to run. But he does care. That's why he hired me. So I could be here with you when he couldn't."

"Oh." Some—but not all—of the misery on that young face lifted. "But how come, even when he is around the way he was before you came, he hardly ever talks to me?"

"Well...sometimes it's hard for grown-ups to know what to say to kids."

"It's not hard for you."

She smiled. "True. But then, you and I are both girls. Maybe what I should've said was that sometimes it's hard for grown-up men to know what to say to kids, particularly little girls."

"Was it hard for your grandpa to talk to you?"

Again, Eve hesitated. "Well, no, not really," she reluctantly admitted. She'd already told Lissy how she'd come at age eight to live with Max after losing her parents in a car accident. "But my grandpa was a different kind of person than your dad."

Lissy looked at her questioningly.

Eve tried to decide how best to explain Max's effusive, take-charge personality in a way that the child could understand. "With my grandpa, the problem was never getting him to talk...it was getting him to listen. He'd sweep into a room, give you a great big bear hug, and then he'd start telling you what he had planned for you."

"That sounds nice."

"Sometimes. But my grandfather could also be very stubborn. So there were times—" more times than Eve wanted to remember "—when you found yourself doing what he wanted you to, rather than what *you* thought was best for you." A faint frown marred her brow as she heard the truth in her own words.

Lissy, however, wasn't concerned with such distinctions. She gave a wistful little sigh. "I just wish my dad would give me a hug, even once. And that he'd talk to me. Even just a little."

There was such longing in the little girl's voice that Eve found herself reminded of the previous Sunday and Lissy's expression when John had chosen business over her. And suddenly she knew that she'd been wrong when she'd told herself that it wasn't her place to intercede with John on Lissy's behalf.

Wrong—and spineless.

Because she'd made a vow the day she buried her grandfather. She'd promised herself from then on, if she ever again cared about someone, she was going to pay attention to that person's hopes and needs.

She knew it didn't sound like much. At least, not until one took into account that for the past few years the only person she'd looked out for was herself. Thanks to her trust fund, she'd spent her time gliding through life like a leaf on a wind current. She'd skied in Switzerland, sailed the turquoise waters of the Aegean, observed endangered gorillas in Uganda and attended fashion shows in Paris. While it hadn't been a life-style that encouraged close relationships, she'd done what she wanted when she wanted, and she'd enjoyed every minute.

Everything had seemed perfect until she'd gotten the phone call informing her that Max had died from a massive heart attack. Grief-stricken, she'd rushed home—and crashed headlong into a massive wall of reality. While she'd been off enjoying herself, the man who'd always been her rock had been losing everything he'd worked seventy years to achieve. What's more, he'd deliberately hidden the truth from her, obviously believing she couldn't handle it.

Eve had been shocked, angry, heartsick. Yet as the weeks had passed and she'd had to grapple with the overwhelming financial mess that was her inheritance, she'd gradually come to accept what she couldn't change. And to acknowledge that even though she'd been doing what she'd thought her grandfather wanted, she'd let him down by not being stronger— and by living her life as if it were one endless summer vacation. It hadn't been much of a leap to see that it was time to stop playing and start acting like a grown-up.

That realization had led to her vow, which seemed especially meaningful now.

Because she cared about Lissy—more than she'd cared about anyone for a very long time. And, if she were honest with herself, she had to admit that she'd been selfish the past pair of weeks. Rather than worrying about the effect of John's absences on Lissy, she'd been secretly relieved he was making himself scarce because it meant she didn't have to deal with his effect on *her*.

Except this wasn't about her. And it was time she remembered that and got her priorities straight.

She looked over at Lissy. "I honestly don't know if your dad's ever going to be the kind of dad who gives lots of hugs," she said gently. "But I am sure, now that the weekend is here and he doesn't have to be somewhere the way he did last weekend, he'll set some time aside just for you."

As easy to read as a picture book, Lissy's face reflected a combination of skepticism and hope. "You are?"

"I am," Eve said firmly. She intended to make sure it happened.

No matter what she had to do.

John shrugged out of his coat and tossed it onto a hook in the mudroom.

A wedge of light poured through the door from the kitchen, cutting a path through the room's darkness. The house was quiet, for which he was profoundly grateful. Today, like every other day since he'd returned from Missoula, he'd worked a full eighteen hours, and he could feel it in every aching muscle. Still, it was worth it. He'd put some serious space between himself and Eve, just the way he'd intended.

He'd also managed to get quite a lot accomplished. Although his hired hands had grumbled that he was pushing too hard, almost every mile of fence that surrounded the ranch's perimeter had now been checked and mended as needed. The various feed stations were fully stocked, and the watering holes cleared of any debris and obstructions. Come Monday morning, they'd start moving the herd down from the summer pastures.

And after that? Well, in addition to normal daily chores, there was wood to be chopped for both this place and the bunkhouse, half a dozen vehicles to be winterized, gas generators and kerosene heaters to be cleaned and filled, food and emergency supplies to be purchased.

He expelled a tired breath. Hell, all he had to do was give it another month or two, and he might be worn out enough that the mere thought of Eve would finally stop making him ache.

With an exasperated shake of his head, he pulled his feet out of his boots, grabbed a pair of clean jeans out of the laundry basket and walked into the bathroom. Scant minutes later he stepped naked into the tiled shower enclosure, groaning with pleasure as the hot water poured over his back and shoulders. He let his head fall forward and gave himself over to the luxurious sensation.

It was a long time before he found the strength to reach for the bar of soap on the shelf in the corner.

Not until the water began to cool did he reluctantly turn the spigot off and climb out. Yawning, he did a haphazard job drying off and yanked on his jeans, not bothering to fasten more than the first three buttons. Scrubbing at his damp hair with a towel, he opened the door and ambled out. He walked several paces, the granite floor cool against his bare feet, before the realization that he wasn't alone brought him up short.

"I thought I heard you come in," Eve said softly.

She stood in the kitchen doorway. Her pale hair was loose, tumbling like a silken cape to her shoulders, and she was wearing a pair of leggings and a loose-knit sweater the same soft gray as her eyes. Backlit as she was, the enticing shape of her body was perfectly outlined.

He lowered the towel. "What are you doing up?"

"It's Friday."

"So?"

"So it's only 9:30. There's no school tomorrow, and I told Lissy she could stay up a little later on the off chance that you'd be home in time to say goodnight."

Annoyance over her bossiness couldn't compete with the guilt he carried about Lissy. While he didn't doubt that making himself scarce had been the right thing to do, there was also no denying that he'd missed not seeing more of his daughter. He'd looked in on her every night before he turned in, and again in the morning before he'd lit out for the day, but even he knew that watching her sleep wasn't the same as actually being with her. "Sure. I'd like that."

Approval—and something that looked oddly like relief—flashed across her face. "Good."

He waited for her to leave. She didn't.

Instead, her gaze remained fixed on his face. And though there was nothing even remotely provocative about her manner, her mere presence, along with the dim light, her husky voice and the unintentional display of her body, had desire slamming through him.

He came to a sudden decision. "As a matter of fact, I'll do it right now." Straightening decisively, he tossed the towel onto the washer and headed for the door, intent on reaching the lighted oasis of the kitchen before he did something irreparably stupid.

"But I also wanted to—John, wait!" she exclaimed as he brushed past her.

Out of the corner of his eye, he saw her reach for him. And just for an instant he was tempted to stop, to experience her touch, to find out if his reaction would be as intense as he suspected.

Except that he was very much afraid that one touch wouldn't be enough. Just as he was very aware that his control was marginal; already he could feel his body respond—and he was only *thinking* about having her hands on him, damn it.

He jerked sideways, out of her reach, careful to put a few feet between them before he finally turned to face her. "What? What do you want, Eve?" Self-imposed restraint made his voice harsh.

There was no way for Eve to know that, of course. Predictably, the lush line of her mouth thinned out in the face of his impatience. "I was just hoping that if you had a moment, we could talk."

"No." He was shaking his head before she finished the sentence. "Not tonight," he amended. "I'm beat."

She frowned. "Tomorrow then?"

"Sure." He walked away even as he said it, passing into the kitchen and quickly crossing the great room. He didn't slow until he reached the hall leading to the bedrooms.

Lissy's door was the first one on the right, well before his own. Taking a grip on his emotions, he thrust every thought of Eve out of his head, assumed a neutral expression and looked in.

Not only was the little girl still awake, but she'd clearly been watching for him. Although the room was heavily shadowed, illuminated only by a small lamp on her bedside table, there was no missing the uncertain little smile that flitted across her face. "You came."

Nodding, he stepped across the threshold.

"I was hoping you would," she murmured, burrowing deeper into the covers as he gingerly approached the bed. "Even though Eve said I shouldn't count on it 'cause you were real, real busy taking care of the ranch and everything."

He felt a pinch of surprise. Surprise that she'd missed him. And that Eve of all people would bother to make an excuse for him.

He reached down and awkwardly smoothed the blanket over one small shoulder. "It's late," he said gruffly. "You better get to sleep."

"Okay." Despite her ready agreement, she didn't close her eyes. Instead, she looked up at him with an air of expectancy, as if she were waiting for something.

Helplessly, he looked back. "What?" he said finally.

She ducked her head, looking very young and uncertain. "You—you can give me a kiss good-night, if you want to. Eve always does."

Squashing the image of Eve pursing her soft pink lips for a kiss, he cleared his throat. "Yeah. Sure." Exceedingly aware of how small and delicate Lissy was, and how small and delicate he wasn't, and suddenly self-conscious about his lack of a shirt, he carefully braced an arm on either side of her, leaned over and gently touched his lips to her brow.

She smelled of toothpaste, talcum powder and innocence. He squeezed his eyes shut, wishing yet again that things were different, that *he* was different, that he could be the kind of father who could actually gather her close and tell her how very special she was, instead of just thinking about it.

But she was only seven years old; such fierce emotion coming from him would probably scare her to death. And he'd cut off his right arm rather than scare her even a little bit.

Reining himself in, he straightened. "Good night, Lis."

There was a heartbeat of silence. Then she gave a little sigh that was so filled with disappointment even he couldn't miss it. "Night," she whispered. Rolling onto her side, she pulled the covers to her chin and closed her eyes.

John stood, rooted in place by the ache in his heart as he stared down at the still form of his daughter. Although he wasn't sure how, he'd clearly just let her down. For a second the pain was so great, he was unable to breathe.

Then, through an act of will, he shook it off and forced himself to move, bitterly aware that it wouldn't matter if he stood here forever—he still wouldn't have a clue what he'd just done wrong.

He reached for the lamp switch, only to freeze at a faint sound from the hallway. He swung around to find Eve standing in the hallway, staring straight at him. For a second their gazes locked, and then she hurried away.

Yet he knew from the look on her face that she'd been a witness to his failure.

With angry despair, he switched off the light and headed for his room.

Eve slid the last clean plate out of the dishwasher and added it to the pair in her free hand. Taking a secure grip on the trio, she carried them to the cabinet and put them away.

Outside, a heavy cloud curtain darkened the morning sky. Inside, the room was cloaked in shadows, giving it a somber feeling that perfectly suited her mood.

She returned to the dishwasher. Pulling the silverware holder free, she set it on the counter and began putting the various utensils away.

Although she was getting a late start on her morning chores, she'd been awake for hours, after a long night spent tossing and turning. And no matter how hard she tried to convince herself that she'd slept poorly due to frustration over her failure to speak to John about Lissy, she knew better.

The plain truth was, she couldn't quit thinking about the look she'd seen on John's face last night when she'd looked in and seen him gazing down at Lissy. In the brief time that she'd observed him, she'd seen tenderness, confusion, regret—and stark, unadulterated longing. It had opened her mind to the possibility that there was a whole other side of him.

And she didn't want that to be the case. Because, try as she might to pretend otherwise, even before last night her attraction to him had stubbornly been refusing to go away.

And she was darned if she understood it. So far he'd been brusque, aloof and shown her all the warmth of an ice cube. She didn't care for the way he treated his daughter. Heck, as far as that went, she didn't like the way he treated *her,* always assuming the worst about her character.

And yet, after three weeks under his roof, the magnetism he held for her hadn't diminished. Worse, there were some things about him she actually admired. He worked harder than anyone she'd ever known. He was generous to a fault, paying excellent wages and doing whatever it took to make certain working conditions on the Bar M were top rate. What's more, a chance remark by Mitch Mason, his foreman, had revealed that many of the ranch's hired hands came from the Lander Boys' Home, hinting at a depth of loyalty she never would have suspected.

Oh, and don't forget his other sterling quality, she thought dryly. *He can make your nipples stand up and pay attention just by walking into a room.*

She sighed, finally facing the crux of her problem.

She was twenty-five years old. And while she wasn't a virgin, so far in her experience she'd found sex to be highly overrated. Oh, she was willing to concede that under the right circumstances it might be pleasurable enough—if your tastes ran to being sweaty, undignified and having your privacy invaded.

So far, hers hadn't.

Of course, John was nothing at all like the men who'd pursued her in the past. Those men had been polished and sophisticated, with salon-cut hair and manicured nails. They'd approached sex like some sort of parlor game, as if it were nothing more than an entertaining way to fritter the time away. They'd been far too polite to press for a response she wouldn't, or couldn't, give.

John wasn't polite about anything. He was hard, tough, real, and every instinct she possessed insisted that making love with him wouldn't have a thing to do with either courtesy or restraint.

Not that she planned on testing her theory anytime soon, she told herself hastily. Or anytime at all, for that matter. Although she might be tempted if doing it meant she could stop thinking about it.

The sound of the back door slamming shut made her jump. Hastily putting the last pair of coffee cups away, she struggled to regain her composure as she heard the cupboards being banged open and shut in the mudroom. Seconds later John strode into the kitchen.

To her relief, he was so intent on his own thoughts he gave her only a cursory nod before he tossed his work gloves onto the counter, walked over to the open pantry door, hit the light switch and disappeared inside.

By the time he reappeared, she had herself and her intemperate thoughts well under control. "Good morning," she said with a polite smile.

He brushed past her and yanked open a door to one of the overhead kitchen cabinets. "Morning."

She turned to keep him in view. "What are you doing?"

"Looking for a Band-Aid. I thought there was a box of them in the mudroom. But I'm damned if I can find it."

"Oh." Skirting around him, she retrieved the box in question off the counter and handed it to him. "Sorry. I took them after I nicked my finger on a paring knife last night. I should have put them back."

"Don't worry about it." Taking the box, he pried open the top and dumped the contents on the counter.

It was then that she noticed the blood oozing angrily from an ugly gash in the back of his right hand. Ridiculously, she felt an immediate surge of concern. "What happened?"

He selected the largest of the adhesive strips and

shrugged, dismissing her worry. "I caught it on a nail. The damn thing keeps bleeding on everything." He removed the backing and awkwardly tried to position the rectangular bandage over the wound with his left hand.

Eve hesitated. The last thing she wanted to do was touch him. At the same time, they were both adults, he was hurt—and she'd rather parade naked down Lander's main street than behave in a way that made him suspect how unsettled he made her feel. "Here. Let me." She reached over and plucked the bandage away before she could lose her nerve.

His head came up and he glowered at her. "I can do it myself."

So much for that softer side. The man was as tough as nails. "I'm sure you can," she said evenly, determined not to lose her composure. "But don't you think you ought to disinfect it first?" Not waiting for an answer, she went and got the first-aid kit out of the cupboard.

Lips pursed, he didn't say a word as she opened it, motioned him over to the sink, cradled his hand in hers and poured a liberal amount of hydrogen peroxide over the cut.

As the seconds passed and she waited for the disinfectant to work, she discovered her resolve had its limits, however. She grew increasingly aware of his proximity, of the warmth radiating from his skin, of the size and strength of his hand. And she found herself wondering what those long, calloused fingers would feel like against her breast—

She released him as if scalded and said the first thing she could to fill the silence. "You were up early this morning."

He made a sound that could have been a yes.

Gesturing for him to step back over to where the Band-Aid pile was spread out on the counter, she gingerly patted the back of his hand dry with a paper towel and reached for the antibacterial ointment. "I'm sorry you cut yourself. Still, I'm glad you're here. We really do need to talk."

"About what?"

She tore open a bandage and carefully covered the deepest part of the wound before she answered. "Lissy."

She felt his arm tense beneath her fingertips a second before he pulled his hand away and took a step back. "What about her?"

"Well, you've hardly spent any time at all with her the past few weeks."

He stiffened. "I've been busy."

His stance, his expression, his tone—all warned her to back off. And though the voice of reason told her that it was the height of foolishness to press him, she couldn't seem to let it go. "When won't you be busy?"

"I don't know. Later."

"When later?"

"I don't know." Although his voice was even when he spoke, his blue eyes glittered with warning. "Maybe tonight. Maybe tomorrow. Maybe not until next week."

"Tomorrow's my day off."

"Yeah, well, I've been meaning to talk to you about that. There's this bull I need to take a look at over in Lager—"

"No."

One black eyebrow shot up. "What?"

"I have plans."

"So cancel them."

She stared at him in disbelief. Half a dozen pointed replies sprang to mind, but before she could settle on one that wasn't guaranteed to get her fired, a movement across the room caught her eye. She looked over and saw Lissy padding toward them. A quick glance at John showed that he, too, had caught sight of his daughter.

Her face still blurred with sleep, the child climbed up on one of the padded bar stools on the far side of the counter. She glanced from one to the other, looking endearingly sweet with her hair standing up in every direction. "What's the matter?"

John spoke without hesitation. "Nothing." The finality in his voice—and the warning glance he threw Eve's way—made it clear that as far as he was concerned, the discussion was over.

His autocratic manner set Eve's teeth on edge, and all of a sudden the thought of him having the last word—yet again—was intolerable. "Actually, we were just talking about tomorrow. It's my day off, but your father has some business he needs to take care of." Just for a second, she wondered about the wisdom of what she was about to do, then shrugged it off. She'd tried to appeal to John's reason; it wasn't her fault that he didn't have any. "That's why I'm going to take a few hours off today."

She felt John's gaze snap to her face. "What?" he demanded, in nearly the same breath that Lissy said, "You are?"

"Yes, I am," she said to the child. She turned to the child's father. "I haven't had a day off since I started," she pointed out in a level voice. "And there are some things I need to take care of."

He was silent. She crossed her fingers, praying he was going to be reasonable, only to have her hopes dashed when he said caustically, "What's the big emergency, princess? Chip your nail polish?"

Inexplicably, the words hurt—and that made her angry. She lifted her chin. "As a matter of fact, yes. How charming of you to notice."

To her satisfaction, his mouth clamped shut.

"But...when are you going?" Lissy again glanced between them. Her worried expression made it clear she sensed the tension that stretched between them like an invisible wire.

"Now." Suiting action to words, Eve picked up her purse off the counter.

"But I'm s'posed to go to Jenny's this afternoon to play and have dinner, remember?"

"Don't worry. I'll be back by three. That'll be plenty of time to take you."

"Oh."

"In the meantime, you and your dad can spend some time together."

"Oh." Again, Lissy glanced between them. Only this time, the gaze she sent John's way held burgeoning anticipation. "Okay."

It was enough to give Eve the courage she needed to leave.

Six

True to her word, Eve was back in plenty of time to take Lissy to Jenny's.

Staunchly ignoring the butterflies in her stomach, she parked the ancient Wagoneer next to John's shiny pickup and told herself—for what had to be the hundredth time in the past six hours—that she'd done the right thing.

Not that she was particularly proud of the way she'd backed John into a corner. Common sense—as well as a very clear memory of the look in his eyes when she'd announced she was leaving—suggested she would be wise to pursue a more diplomatic course in the future. Still, it wasn't as if he'd left her any other options. If he had, she wouldn't have felt pressed to take such drastic action.

With that thought in mind, she picked up her purse, climbed from the Jeep and walked resolutely into the house, letting the screen door slap shut behind her to announce her presence. Yet by the time she reached the great room, it was clear the place was deserted. She was puzzled for all of a second, until she realized that John wasn't the type to hang around inside under any circumstances—and certainly not to wait for her. Obviously, he and Lissy were out on the property somewhere. Although she knew it didn't speak well of her character, as she headed for her bedroom she felt a little surge of satisfaction at the thought of them together.

She hadn't walked more than a few feet down the hallway, however, when some primitive instinct warned her there was someone else in the house after all. Instinctively, she glanced over her shoulder, but there was no one there. She turned back around, shaking her head at her foolishness—only to jerk to a halt as John stepped out of his bedroom at the end of the corridor.

He, too, stopped short when he saw her. "You're back."

Her stomach plummeted at his cool, clipped tone. It didn't take a genius to realize he was still angry. "Yes." She took a calming breath, determined to remain composed no matter what. "I said I'd be home by now."

He didn't say a word, simply watched her.

"How did it go with you and Lissy?"

"We managed."

He didn't seem inclined to say anything more, and because she knew the child would fill in the details, she let it go. "That's good."

He crossed his arms. "You get your business taken care of?"

"Yes. I did."

Again, he was silent. Eve wondered if he was purposefully trying to intimidate her or if it was just a natural talent. She tried to inject some lightness into her voice. "So, is Lissy ready to go?" She took a step toward the child's closed door, only to freeze as John abruptly cut the distance between them in half.

"Not so fast." Although several feet still separated them, he suddenly seemed far too close. "There are a few things we need to get straight."

She lifted her chin, not liking his tone. And liking even less that she was far too aware of everything about him, from the way a gleaming lick of inky hair angled over his forehead to the manner in which the clearly delineated muscles in his arms and shoulders flexed beneath his black T-shirt as he leaned toward her. "Like what?"

"Let's start with the fact that *you* work for me. And what I say goes. If I tell you I'm busy, or I have something I need to do, that's it. *You* don't decide my priorities."

Eve opened her mouth to protest, then shut it again. While she hardly agreed with his take on things, she knew she'd pushed things earlier. Given that she'd accomplished what she set out to, and she still had her job, she could afford to be magnanimous. "Fair enough."

Incredibly, his eyes narrowed. "Don't patronize me, Eve. And just so there's no misunderstanding, don't you ever again try to use Lissy, or her presence, to manipulate me the way you did this morning. Because I swear, if you do—" he took another step toward her as if to underscore his point "—I'll fire you."

Well, that was clear enough. So was the realization

that she didn't like being threatened. But again, under the circumstances, she was willing to let it pass. "Fine."

There was another long silence as they considered each other.

"Is that it?" she said finally.

He nodded.

"I'd better get Lissy then. It's time for us to go."

"That won't be necessary." Once more his voice stopped her, this time as she reached for the doorknob. "She's not here."

"What?" She turned to look at him.

"She's already at Jenny's. I ran her over."

"When?"

His eyes hooded over, and she had a sudden premonition that she wasn't going to like the answer. "This morning. After breakfast."

"What?" Usually she was slow to anger, but now she felt her temper ignite. And as angry as she was at him, she was even angrier with herself as it dawned on her that while she'd thought she was so clever by forcing father and daughter together, the truth was she'd unthinkingly set Lissy up for another rejection. "Why?"

He drew himself up. "She'll have a hell of a lot better time there than she would here, hanging around with me."

"John! You're her father—"

"So? It's not like we have tons to talk about. She's not exactly interested in the price of hay, and I don't know jack about Barbie."

"But it doesn't matter! Not to Lissy. She just wants to spend time with you. Surely you must know that.

It's written all over her face every time she looks at you!"

"I don't want to discuss it," he said flatly.

She stared at him in amazement. "Well that's too bad, because I do, and as you were so kind to point out, I'm your employee—not your slave. What's more, I care about your daughter, and she happens to care about you, which you'd know if you'd just taken the time to talk to me the way I asked twice in the past twenty-four hours!"

"I was tired last night."

"I understand that. But you said we'd talk today—"

"Well excuse the hell out of me for not making you my first priority!" For the first time the icy control he had on his emotions slipped a little bit.

She threw up her hands. "Oh, for—! I want you to make Lissy your first priority! Good heavens, you're all each other has. She's starving for your attention, not to mention your affection—"

"Damn it, Eve! I don't need you to tell me I'm never going to be father of the year. But what I did was for Lissy's own good, and that's all I intend to say about it!" His face set, his mouth a straight line, he made to walk past her.

"No, John, wait!" Eve didn't stop to think; she simply reacted. "If you'd just listen to me, if you'd just take the time to really think about your daughter—" She stepped sideways into his path.

Unable to stop his momentum, he twisted sideways to keep from running her down, and wound up bumping her hip with his thigh. Thrown off balance, she reached out to save herself.

John wasn't prepared as her smooth, soft hand closed around the bare skin of his upper arm. Already dangerously on edge, he felt an explosion of warmth spill through him.

"Don't," he said hoarsely as all of his senses responded to her touch. He swung around to ward her off, but the action only served to send her cool, slender fingers skimming down his arm.

And then they were face-to-face, so close he could feel the warm whisper of her breath through the thin cotton molding his chest.

She made a faint little sound. He looked down, frozen in place as her gaze drifted over his torso and her lips promptly parted. A faint flush of color rose in her cheeks. To his shock, her nipples pebbled.

He ordered himself to move. To get away. Now, before he did something rash.

Then she looked up. He could see the agitation, the anger, the uncertainty in her eyes. But he could also see her awareness of him as a man. And—the sight made his throat go tight—something that could best be described as speculation, as if she were wondering what they'd be like together...

It was too damn much. All the emotions he'd been struggling to contain seemed to fuse into one overpowering need. He didn't want to think. He wanted to taste her. Just once.

He locked his arm around her waist and yanked her close, only to freeze as her hand came up to splay across his chest.

"No." Her voice was barely more than a whisper, but the pewter gaze she raised to his held a spark of determination. "Not unless you can accept that I'm not giving up on you and Lissy. That this conversation...isn't over. Just on hold."

His eyes narrowed, but she didn't flinch, and he felt

an unwanted kernel of respect for her. Slowly, he nodded, a jolt going through him as her voice became even huskier as she murmured, "Good."

Her hand rose, cupped his cheek, and the next thing he knew his mouth had found hers and he was lost to everything else as he claimed what he'd only fantasized about for so long.

Her lips were smooth and pliant, every bit as soft as he'd always imagined. For untold seconds he savored the sweetness of her taste, the breathy little moan she couldn't contain as his teeth claimed her full lower lip, the provocative way her mouth clung to his as he relentlessly deepened the kiss.

Then it was his turn to shudder as her arms came up and locked around his neck. One slender hand gripped the hair at the base of his skull, urging him closer as she molded her body to his.

The shock of it was almost more than he could bear. His mouth opened over hers and his tongue stabbed inside, instigating an evocative rhythm. He felt the erect tips of her breasts press into his chest and her foot start to climb the back of his thigh.

Heat scorched the last rational thought from his mind.

Wedging his hand between them, he slid it under her shirt. Her skin was warm, smooth, taut, like sun-warmed satin. Consumed with the need to touch her, he forgot to breathe as he cupped the ripe weight of one breast in his palm and rubbed his fingertips against the pebbled velvet of her nipple.

She whimpered and crowded even closer.

He couldn't hold back any longer. Releasing her breast, he reached down with both hands, gripped her high, round little fanny in his hands and lifted her up, rubbing her against the iron-hard ridge barely contained by the worn denim of his jeans.

The heated contact jolted through him, an overload of sensation so intense, he was almost able to ignore her breathless "oh" and the way she stiffened slightly in his arms.

Almost, but not quite. He wanted her, yes. But more than that, he wanted her willing; his pride dug in its heels at the thought of anything less. He tore his mouth away from hers. "What's wrong?"

Denied his lips, she slicked a kiss down the line of his jaw. "Nothing," she said breathlessly.

"Do you want me to stop?"

"No."

"Are you sure?"

"*Yes.*" Her mouth slid to his throat and settled over the pulse thundering there.

For half a second, he was riveted in place. And then his whole body caught fire. He picked her up, carried her into his bedroom, shouldered the door shut and set her down. Without a word, he began to strip off his clothes.

Eve drew a shaky breath and pressed a finger to her tingling lips. In some dim recess of her mind she realized this was going to complicate everything. And yet right now she couldn't bring herself to care. For eight years she'd wondered about him, about this. It had been John who, without so much as a touch, had awakened her burgeoning sexuality and fueled her every adolescent fantasy. It had been his image against which she'd measured every other man in the years since. Measured—and always found lacking...

She watched, unable to move, unable to breathe, as he stripped his T-shirt over his head. She was peripherally aware of the room around her, of the series of arched windows looking out toward the mountains, of the simple lines of the oak furniture, of the richly patterned blue-and-black comforter on the big bed.

It was the emerging sight of his bare chest that claimed her attention, however. She'd seen it before, of course. She'd seen the way the sun-bronzed skin stretched taut over his broad shoulders and the hard, sculpted muscles of his arms. She'd seen the carved slab of his pectorals and that flat, washboard abdomen punctuated by the shallow navel and the tantalizing line of fine, jet-black hair.

But this was the first time she'd had license to touch it, the first time she'd had license to touch *him*.

The realization shuddered through her, and then she was moving, closing the distance between them. Busy with the buttons on his jeans, he gave a jerk of surprise as she slid her fingers over the satin flesh of his sides, trapping his hands between the two of them. And then she was flush up against him. She gave into temptation and pressed her face into the smooth curve of his chest.

It felt like the most natural thing in the world to rub her cheek against all that hot, velvety skin, to part her lips and forge a chain of kisses along his collarbone, to run her palms up the steely curves of his arms. She vaguely registered his hands at her waist, tugging open her slacks, pushing them down, helping her as she toed off her shoes and slid her legs free.

There was nothing vague about her reaction as his hands slid up the back of her bare thighs and over her naked behind, however. Gasping, she buried her face in his throat and raised her arms as he slipped her

T-shirt up and over her head and pulled it and her bra away.

And just like that she was standing before him without a stitch of clothing. She might have felt shy, but she didn't have time as he reached down and tipped up her chin and she saw the look on his face.

His mouth was compressed, his eyes intent, the skin over his nose stretched tight with need while his eyes gleamed like twin slices of blue fire. It was the look of a conqueror, of a man who wouldn't be denied.

He reached around and released the clip holding back her hair. "Damn." With a gentleness totally at odds with that fierce expression, he spread her hair over her shoulders. "I always thought you were beautiful, princess. But I never realized..." Swallowing hard, he reached down, pressed the pad of his thumb to the stiff, aching point of her nipple and rubbed, his gaze never leaving her face.

Pleasure, unexpected and overwhelming, rocketed through her. She swayed toward him. "John. Please."

His control shattered. His arms came around her and the next thing she knew he was lifting her up. His mouth opened over her throat, hot and insistent as it slid hungrily downward over the notch of her collarbone and feasted on the slope of her breast.

She instinctively locked her legs around his waist as his lips latched onto her nipple. She cried out and arched her back. Weaving her fingers into the cool, heavy silk of his hair, she urged him closer as he began to walk toward the bed.

Seconds later he was bearing her down onto the king-size mattress. Only vaguely did she register the cool press of the comforter beneath her back. Her senses were fixed on John: the taste of him on her lips, the raspy sound of his breath, the solid wedge of his stomach between her thighs.

She watched, heart pounding, as he rocked upright and yanked at the fastenings on his jeans. With one violent shove, he shucked them down along with his briefs. A second later he was leaning forward. He slid his hands beneath her hips and she felt the broad tip of his erection bump up against her welcoming wetness.

"Oh." She couldn't contain the soft breathy sound as he pressed forward and she felt the first thick invading slide of him.

His head came up. Their eyes locked and then he was shifting forward, his mouth taking hers at the same time he thrust his hips and seated himself all the way inside her.

The pleasure was intense, immediate and totally outside the realm of her previous experience. She gave a cry of surprise and dug her fingers into the rock-hard curve of his buttocks, only to cry out again as he shifted and slid his hands under her hips, lifting her up to meet him as he began to thrust.

And then she couldn't breathe, she couldn't think, she could only feel. There was the hot brand of John's mouth at her throat, the cool brush of his hair against her jaw, the firm grip of his big calloused hands, the stomach-hollowing advance and retreat of his sex.

Just as she'd always suspected, there was nothing polite or restrained about what they were sharing. With every surge of his powerful body he was laying claim to her in the most elemental way, and everything that was female in her responded. She felt a heightened sense of urgency, a growing need that had her straining toward him, a building ache that made her dig her heels into the mattress and sob his name.

And then pleasure slammed into her. Her senses exploded. Somewhere off in the distance she heard herself scream with satisfaction. Yet before she could fully grasp the meaning of that sound, much less claim it as her own, another wave rolled through her, stronger and more explosive than the first. Locking her arms around John's neck, she arched upward, holding onto him for dear life as sensation after sensation rocked her.

He continued to thrust heavily into her. She felt her body contract around him, and suddenly he stiffened and his whole big body began to shake. He threw back his head, lifting her off the bed as he bit off a hoarse shout of completion.

Moments later he collapsed, holding her tight as he rolled onto his side. Tangled together, her head pillowed on his shoulder, they lay there, their breath coming in noisy gasps.

Minutes passed. Their breathing quieted. As it did, the pleasurable haze clouding Eve's mind slowly began to lift, while the reality of what had just happened began to sink in.

Beside her, she felt John shift. She bit off an automatic protest as he let go of her and rolled away, the mattress dipping beneath his weight.

With a reluctance she didn't want to analyze, she opened her eyes.

He was sitting on the edge of the bed, his broad, bronzed back flexing as he leaned down to yank off his boots and strip away his jeans. Straightening, he sat for a moment as if to compose himself before finally turning to face her.

To her surprise, although his expression was as guarded as ever, she would have sworn that there was a hint of vulnerability in those brilliant blue eyes. Yet before she could be certain, the phone suddenly rang, the bell shrill in the stark silence. With a look of exasperation, John twisted back around and snatched the receiver off the nightstand. "MacLaren."

Eve let out a breath she hadn't realized she was holding, grateful for the unexpected respite. Tuning out his one-sided conversation, she tried to sort out what she was feeling.

Not too surprisingly, her old self, the contained, self-protective, sane one, was urgently insisting they needed to talk about what had just happened, to agree at the very least that this had been a big mistake.

Yet her new self, a wild, elemental creature she barely recognized, refused to listen. *You've waited a long time to be with him,* it whispered. *Why not give it some time and see what happens? After all, you were wrong about him wanting you. Maybe you're wrong about other things, as well. You'll never know if you don't give it a chance....*

She looked over as he hung up the phone. "Everything okay?" she asked quietly.

"Yeah." He turned around. "That was Lis. She's going to spend the night at Jenny's."

She thought about it, but only for a second. "I suppose, under the circumstances, that's probably a good idea."

"Yeah. I guess it is." He cleared his throat. "So...are you all right?"

She nodded. "Uh-huh. What about you?"

"Me?" The question seemed to surprise him. "I'm fine."

"Good."

Silently, they considered each other. And then, as if he couldn't stop himself, his gaze slid over her naked body, leaving a trail of goose bumps in its wake.

There was no mistaking his appreciation for what he was seeing; his sex stirred to bold, flattering life. But even without that, she would have recognized the hunger suddenly burning in his eyes.

Because she felt it, too.

Yet it was also clear, from the suddenly austere set of his mouth, that he didn't intend to give in to it. "Eve—"

In that instant, she made up her mind. Reaching up, she pressed her fingers to his lips. "Don't. There'll be plenty of time to talk later."

He searched her face. "Are you sure?"

"Yes."

For a long moment he still hesitated. And then he turned his head and unexpectedly pressed his lips to the center of her palm. "All right."

She considered that exquisitely gentle caress, so at odds with his steady, dispassionate voice and felt her last little reservation melt away. With a soft sigh, she wrapped her fingers around the back of his neck and urged him closer.

And then he was rolling her beneath him and his mouth was on hers, hot and hungry, and everything else faded away.

* * *

John came awake with a jerk.

Momentarily disoriented, he lay in the darkness with his eyes wide open, waiting for his mind to catch up with the rest of his body. In the next instant it happened, and with sudden clarity he knew he was in his own house, in his own room, between the sheets of his own bed.

And that the silken shape curled against him was Eve's.

A glance at the digital clock on his dresser told him it was going on midnight. He blinked as he realized he'd slept nearly four hours. But then, he'd been worn down to a sliver after that last bout of lovemaking. Unlike their first explosive encounter, they'd gone slow, taking their time, letting the tension build and build as they explored each other. It had been exquisite torture—and the most intimate experience he'd ever had with a woman.

He slowly let out his breath.

For as long as he could remember, except for a short time as a very young boy when he'd foolishly believed his mother would recognize her mistake and come back for him, he'd dealt with life straight on, refusing to back away no matter how harsh the reality.

But this... Damn but it was hard to wrap his mind around. For so many years, Eve's dislike had been a given.

Yet lying here now, with her hand twined in his and her hair draped over his chest, he could suddenly see how it could be like one of the trick pictures his psychology teacher had sprung on him back in high school.

He'd been asked to look at an image; he had and

he'd seen a goblet. He'd been told to look again, and he'd seen the exact same thing. It hadn't been until it had been pointed out to him that he'd seen that his "goblet" could also be the silhouettes of two identical faces looking in opposite directions.

It had been so many years ago that he couldn't remember now exactly what that exercise had been meant to prove. But he suspected it had something to do with getting locked into a single perspective and seeing only what you expected.

Even though the truth might be more complicated. Like a beautiful girl who'd feigned antipathy to mask attraction. And a young man too proud to look beyond the obvious.

Still, it was old news. Instead of focusing on the past, he ought to be deciding what to do next.

The answer should have been easy, given that he never should have allowed this to happen in the first place. Having failed that, he should end things right now, before they became even more complicated. After all, he wasn't in the market for any kind of committed relationship, having long ago judged—accurately as it turned out—that his chances of making someone a good husband would be on a par with him being a good father. And there was no reason someone like Eve—beautiful, intelligent, educated—should settle for anything less.

His mouth twisted at the irony of him suddenly feeling protective of her. But then, tonight he'd found out that she was far more vulnerable and far less experienced than he'd ever imagined. He also now knew that he was the first man ever to give her pleasure. It made him feel all knotted up inside, as purely primitive male satisfaction warred with an unexpected sense of obligation.

A sense of obligation that was very likely misplaced, he reminded himself. Because it wasn't as if Eve had made any declarations of love herself. Hell, they'd barely talked. For all he knew, she might wake up at any moment, announce that she'd come to her senses and inform him that this had been a big mistake.

Which would probably be for the best. So why did he hate the idea?

He was damned if he knew. But then, he supposed he could be excused for feeling a little fuzzy-headed. It had been a long time since he'd been with a woman. And even if it hadn't been, he'd never experienced the sort of pleasure he had with Eve. Hell, he'd been so far gone during that first encounter that he hadn't even given a thought to birth control, which was a first for him—and a matter that ought to be a major cause for concern.

Only he didn't feel concern. Instead, like some sort of caveman, he felt an irrational surge of satisfaction at the thought of her carrying his child.

That scared the hell out of him. So did the notion that after just one night with her he didn't recognize himself.

Yet neither thought was as alarming as the realization that far from having his appetite appeased by the hours they'd just spent together, he still wanted her. Maybe even more than he had before.

Beside him, she shifted. Unable to help himself, he stroked his hand over the warm curve of her back, and in the next instant her breathing changed. With an instinct he didn't question, he knew she was awake.

Confirmation came half a dozen heartbeats later as she angled her head up to look at him. "John?" Her voice was a whisper, designed not to wake him if he were asleep.

"Yeah."

"What time is it?"

"A little past twelve."

"Ah." She pushed her hair off her face and settled back against him, resting her cheek against the slope of his shoulder. "Have you been awake long?"

"A while."

"I hope..." She fell silent, and then her breath sighed out. "I hope you haven't been lying here regretting what happened."

It was the perfect opening. All he had to do was claim that that was exactly what he was doing and that would be the end of it. Yet even as the thought entered his mind, he knew he wasn't going to do it. For a number of reasons, one of which was the hint of vulnerability he could hear in her voice. "No. I'm not sorry, Eve. But it does complicate things."

"Only if we let it."

He ignored the heat that coiled low in his stomach as her hand drifted over his hipbone. "You want to clarify that?"

"We're both adults. Why can't we agree not to make this complicated? To just...take it as it comes?"

He frowned. It was exactly what he'd been about to suggest. So why did the sound of it coming from her make him feel oddly dissatisfied? "It's not that simple."

"Why not?"

"It's just...not," he said, knowing he was being unreasonable but impatient at being pressed.

There was a long stretch of silence. Finally, in an exceedingly reasonable voice she said, "All right."

To his shock, she lifted her head off his shoulder and her hand off his stomach and sat up.

"What are you doing?" he demanded, coming upright himself as he felt the mattress give and realized she must have swung her legs over the edge of the bed.

"I'm going to my room." In contrast to his, her voice was soft.

"Why?"

"Because somehow I doubt you're about to propose. And if you don't want to just take things as they come, and you won't talk to me, that leaves us nothing, and I prefer to go without being asked."

He swore under his breath, wondering how he could have forgotten, even for a moment, her Chandler pride. "Damn it, Eve, don't."

"Don't what?"

"Don't make this harder than it is. I didn't mean we should break things off now. It's just—there are some issues we need to consider."

"Such as?"

"There's Lissy, for one. I wouldn't want her to get the wrong idea."

Slowly, she turned to face him. "Neither would I. I understand the need for discretion, John. I wouldn't be comfortable any other way."

"That's fine. But you also need to understand up-front that I don't intend to make any long-term promises."

"I'm not looking for promises," she said, still in that same, quiet voice. "These past few months...I've just started to learn the importance of living life on my own terms. I'm not interested in seeing that change."

He told himself—again—that he ought to be glad she valued her independence. After all, he'd had some experience with women wanting to stake a claim on him and he knew just how unpleasant things could get when one party wanted more than the other was willing—or able—to give.

So why, just for a second, did some perverse little part of him wish she were just a shade less reasonable, a touch less self-contained?

He didn't know. But this clearly wasn't the time to dwell on it. "All right. If you're sure you can handle it."

As if on cue, beyond the night-dark windows the moon suddenly slid free of the clouds, painting the room with enough silvery light that he could see her nod of consensus.

He could also see her full mouth and patrician features, the slender curve of her arms and shoulders, the rounded breasts with their small, rose-colored nipples. A drumbeat of need shuddered through him, gaining strength as she raised her chin and her rain-gray gaze met his.

He reached out and stroked his thumb lightly across her cheek, down the sensitive line of her jaw, over that delicate but determined chin. "Come back to bed."

She made a soft, needy sound. Parting her lips, she

caught his finger lightly between her teeth, then closed her lips around it.

His body rioted. Yet even as he pulled her into his arms, a part of him warned that he was making a mistake. He could kid himself all he wanted, it whispered, but the truth was he wanted more from Eve than just sex.

He pushed the thought away.

Seven

"Look, Eve! Look at me! I'm not falling off or anything!" Her two neat pigtails bouncing wildly, Lissy grinned as she circled the corral on Clue at a gentle trot.

Eve smiled back from her stance in the corral's center, making a small circle of her own on foot to keep the child in view. "You're doing great. Now sit down deeper in the saddle, ease back on the reins and tell her to walk, okay?"

Lissy pursed her lips in concentration and followed instructions, rewarded as the mare instantly eased into the slower gait. She glanced over again, her eyes gleaming with satisfaction. "How's that?"

"Perfect. Now why don't you turn around and try it in the other direction?"

"Can I canter after that?"

Eve swallowed a spurt of amusement. It hadn't

taken the little girl long to discover that it was much easier to keep her seat at the faster pace. "Yes."

"Good." Always eager to please, Lissy dutifully turned the horse and gave her the signal to trot.

Eve followed her progress, enjoying the pale October sun warming the top of her head and the sweet Montana air in her lungs. With a touch of surprise, she realized she felt relaxed, a minor miracle given that the last seven days had forever changed her view of the world, not to mention her image of herself.

She now knew that with the right man she was more than capable of being carried away by passion. That with just a look, a word, a single touch, she could be transformed into a woman who was openly needy and thoroughly wanton.

It was as heady as it was unsettling. Yet she took comfort in the knowledge that John seemed every bit as affected by her as she was by him. More than once this week she'd looked up in the middle of the day from some household chore to find him standing in the doorway. And no matter how valid his reason for being there, whether it was to grab his cell phone, change his shirt or get a bite to eat, he eventually found an excuse to touch her. And then one thing would lead to another....

She shivered with remembered pleasure, even as she acknowledged that like most things in life, it didn't come without a price. Hers was the growing awareness that when it came to living in the moment, the reality was considerably more difficult than the theory.

She blamed John for that. Because, as the week had unfolded, he'd not only proven to be a powerful, inventive lover, but had unwittingly revealed that there was a tender side to his nature, an unspoken need to be close directly at odds with his outward remoteness.

And it intrigued her, making her wonder what would happen if his guard ever truly came down. More times than she could count during the past days, she'd found herself not just thinking about him, but tempted to seek him out.

Not that she had any intention of giving into such desires. They'd agreed to take things easy, not to press, for one thing. For another, she was finally taking care of herself, making her own way in the world, and she was determined to keep it that way. She didn't want to make the mistake of depending on someone else for her happiness.

She also hadn't forgotten her vow to help Lissy. While things between father and daughter had already improved simply because John had been home more lately, he rarely took any initiative with the child. Eve knew it was ridiculous, but if it wasn't so at odds with his forceful personality, she'd swear he was afraid of saying or doing the wrong thing. Particularly since she'd now caught him several times watching Lissy with the sort of pained longing she'd first observed from the hallway last Friday night.

On the far side of the corral, Lissy brought Clue to a walk. "Eve?"

"Hmm?"

"What do you think my dad's gonna say when he sees me?"

"I don't know, sweetheart. But I think we're about to find out." Shading her eyes, she nodded toward the familiar black pickup coming lickety-split down the drive. "It looks like he got done checking out the truck Mr. Hansen has for sale sooner than he expected."

"But he can't do that!" Lissy wailed, staring in dismay at the swiftly approaching vehicle. "I'm not ready!"

Eve walked over to where the horse and rider had come to an abrupt halt. She gave the youngster's leg a reassuring squeeze. "Lissy, relax. You know what you're doing. And your dad *is* going to be pleased. I promise."

The child stared intently at Eve. Then, as if gaining strength from the conviction in her eyes, she took a deep breath and nodded. "Okay."

"Now, come on. Let's go say hello." With one last reassuring pat, she began to walk toward the fence, Lissy trailing behind her.

Tall and commanding, John climbed out of the pickup. His laser blue gaze found Eve, lingered for the merest moment, then shifted to Lissy. For a second his whole body stilled.

The child waved and urged the pinto forward. "Look, Daddy! It's me! I'm riding!"

"I'll be damned. You sure are." He headed in her direction as Eve slipped through the gate and walked around to join him at the fence.

Lissy's tentative smile grew a little brighter. "Are you surprised?"

"Absolutely."

She glanced at Eve, who gave her a nod of encouragement. "Do—do you want to see all the things I can do?"

"Sure."

Taking a deep breath, she straightened her narrow shoulders and carefully turned the pinto. After walking for a few paces along the fence, she nudged the animal into a trot.

John watched silently, but Eve didn't miss the way he drew himself up when Lissy momentarily lost her balance and slid sideways. "You sure this is wise?" he said abruptly.

Despite his brusqueness, she heard the concern in his voice. "Don't worry. She's fine."

As if on cue, the child settled more firmly into the saddle and some of the tension left John's posture. Propping an arm on the top of the fence, he looked over at Eve. "How long has this been going on?"

"A few weeks."

His eyes narrowed thoughtfully. "So that night in my study, when you asked about a horse to ride...?"

"It was for Lissy," she said easily, shifting her gaze back to her charge.

For the space of several long seconds she could feel him staring at her, but finally he, too, turned his attention to his daughter. "Yeah, well...you did all right."

"Thanks. But Lissy's the one who deserves the credit. She's worked hard to get over her fear of horses."

"I can see that." Uncharacteristically, he hesitated. "Did I forget to mention that I'm proud of her?"

John so rarely shared his thoughts or emotions that Eve felt oddly touched, as well as happy for Lissy. Without thinking, she reached out and squeezed his forearm. "I'm glad."

For a moment he seemed startled. Then he shrugged one big shoulder—but not before she saw the faint tide of color beneath his tan. The sight made her feel curiously off balance, and it was a relief when Lissy suddenly called her name.

"Eve? Can I canter now?"

"Go ahead." She watched as the child set the pinto

into a rocking-horse lope, making a circuit of the ring, giving Eve the time to gather her composure before she addressed John again. "You're back early. What did you think of Hansen's truck? Is it what you're looking for?"

"I don't know. It wasn't there."

"What happened?"

"Hansen's son broke his ankle skateboarding. So Hansen took his wife and the kid—and the truck—into town to the clinic."

"Oh. That's too bad. Is the boy going to be all right?"

"As far as I know. Hansen left word asking me to come back tomorrow." He frowned, rubbing his thumb over a nail protruding slightly from the fence post. "I know it's your day off, but I thought maybe you and Lissy might want to ride along. Afterward, we could grab a bite to eat."

She blinked, taken aback at the unexpected invitation. "I'm sorry, John, but I can't," she said with genuine regret. "Chrissy called earlier and asked me if I'd go to Missoula with her tomorrow, and I said I would."

Just for a second something flashed across his face that seemed to be as much displeasure as disappointment. Yet when he spoke, there was no sign of it in his voice. "I see. Maybe another time."

That was all there was time for as Lissy rode up. Bringing the pinto to a shambling stop, the child stared eagerly at her father. "Did you see me?"

"Yeah, I did." A little stiffly, he inclined his head. "That was real nice, Lis."

"Oh." Although she did her best to hide it, the child's whole body sagged at his lackluster praise.

Eve couldn't believe it. And she could see by John's suddenly taut expression that he knew he'd blown it. Wondering how such an intelligent man could miss the need to be more effusive when dealing with a child, she decided it was past time to give him a nudge in the right direction. "It *was* nice," she said warmly to Lissy. "As a matter of fact, your dad was just telling me how proud of you he is."

Lissy's gaze shot from her to John. "You were?"

Clearly aware he'd just been given a second chance, he said forcefully, "Yeah, I was. I *am*. A lot. You've worked real hard and it shows."

"Oh." The child's small face flushed with unmistakable pleasure.

There was a brief silence that might have grown awkward if Eve hadn't again interceded. "You know, sweetie, it's about time for me to get up to the house and get dinner started. So why don't you give Clue a good walk to cool her down and then take her on into the barn."

The youngster made a slight face. "Do I have to?"

"'Fraid so."

"Okay." With one last shy smile at her father, she turned the mare around and the two of them ambled off.

John watched her walk away. Not until she was all the way across the corral did he finally glance at Eve. "Thanks," he said simply.

She smiled. "It's not that hard, you know. If you'd loosen up a little and just talk to her, she'd do the rest."

He looked singularly unconvinced. "Yeah. I suppose."

She considered him for a moment, knowing he

probably wouldn't like what she was about to say, but was compelled to say it anyway. "About tomorrow..."

There was a glimmer of something that looked almost like hope on his face. "Yeah?"

"If you're just going to go off and leave her, I can take her with me."

For a moment he looked as if he wasn't sure he'd heard her right, and then his expression closed. "No. It's your day off. We'll manage." He glanced quickly at his watch. "I've got a sick heifer I need to check. I'll see you at dinner."

Eve couldn't decide if she felt pleased or exasperated at his answer. Before she could decide, he turned, strode over to his pickup, climbed in and roared off.

But suddenly she was glad that she'd accepted Chrissy's invitation. Not only would it be good for John and Lissy to spend some time alone together, but she clearly needed to get away. Because, despite her every intention to keep things simple, it was time she faced the truth.

Her feelings for John were far from casual.

Seated at the counter, John looked up from the Sunday paper as Eve walked into the kitchen the next morning. "You taking off?"

She opened her purse and began to rummage around inside. "Uh-huh."

He struggled to keep a scowl off his face. Dressed in slim black slacks and a pale pink twinset, with her hair done up in a French twist and a sleek black leather coat over her arm, she looked beautiful and sophisticated. Perfect for Paris, he thought sourly. All wrong for Missoula.

"There." Car keys in hand, she slipped the strap of her purse over her shoulder and smiled. "I guess I'll see you later. Be good, Lis," she called to the child, who was sitting on the floor in front of the TV set, quietly watching cartoons.

"I will," the little girl answered.

"Have a nice time," John murmured, turning his attention back to the paper. He sensed her gaze on him but he didn't look up. A few seconds later he heard the back door slap shut in her wake.

Released from the need for pretense, he pushed the paper aside and scowled, asking himself what the hell his problem was.

Unfortunately for his peace of mind, he knew.

It was Eve. God knew, he didn't begrudge her some time off; she worked hard and she deserved it. And he sure didn't expect her to double-check her every move with him, any more than he wanted her to seek him out every time she had a free moment.

But that didn't mean she had to take off to do the devil knew what with that airhead Chrissy Abrams. The two of them had been hell on wheels in high school, and he had no reason to think anything had changed now.

Yeah, that's right. Just think of all the trouble they can get into in Missoula on a Sunday. Why don't you admit it, MacLaren? The reason you're fried is because she made plans and they didn't include you.

He stood up abruptly and walked around into the kitchen to refresh his coffee. His movements were jerky as he told himself that last thought wasn't true and the contents of the pot splashed, stinging his hand. He swore.

"Daddy?"

Lissy's hesitant inquiry intruded on his unsettled thoughts. *"What?"*

"Is—is something the matter?"

He glanced impatiently at her, about to snap *no* when the apprehension in her eyes registered.

A wave of indignation shot through him, directed at himself. No matter how out of sorts he felt, it was no excuse for taking it out on his kid. He blew out a pent-up breath and did his best to wipe the scowl off his face. "Everything's fine. I just burned myself, that's all."

"Oh." Her big blue eyes studied him closely. "You know what?" Glancing away, she made a circle on the floor with one dainty finger.

He braced. "No. What?"

"I'm hungry."

Relief washed through him. "Okay. What are you hungry for?"

She looked up. "Pancakes."

Well, hell. That's what he got for asking. Cereal would at least be quick and easy. Ditto toast or your basic fried egg. Pancakes, however, took time. And with Lissy, time was always his enemy, stretching interminably as he struggled to behave like a proper father.

"I could help," she offered, clearly misunderstanding his silence. "I know how 'cause I help Eve all the time, even though she's a really good cook."

The ingenuous comment served to stiffen his spine. "All right."

"Really?"

"Yeah."

It was all the encouragement she needed. Leaping to her feet, she came around the end of the counter, darted into the pantry and emerged lugging a large yellow box of pancake mix. "It tells you how to make them right here," she explained, scooting up next to him and indicating the back panel.

"I know how to make pancakes."

"You do?"

He took the box from her. "Yeah."

"Oh."

Oddly enough, she looked crestfallen. Puzzled, John couldn't imagine what the problem was—until it dawned on him that her offer to help had been more than a mere courtesy.

Great. They'd been together all of five minutes and already he'd screwed that up. Frustrated, he tried to think of something he could say to retrieve the situation, but typically, the words refused to come.

"Daddy?"

"What?"

"I could get a mixing bowl for you. That is, if you want me to. I know right where Eve keeps them." She stared up earnestly at him, her expression an odd combination of resolve and uncertainty.

"Well, yeah. That'd be nice."

"Okay!" Just like that, she scampered happily toward the cupboard, smiling back at him over her shoulder. "Do you want me to get the eggs and the milk, too?"

"Sure." Bemused by her eagerness, he forced his gaze away from her innocent face and considered the back of the pancake box. He wasn't quite sure what had just happened, but he was grateful for it nevertheless.

Lissy set the bowl on the counter with a clatter. "Daddy?"

"Huh?"

"If you really know how to make pancakes, how come you're reading the directions?"

He started to shrug the question off with a noncommittal answer, then remembered Eve's admonition to loosen up. "Because I haven't done this since I was a teenager," he said, mentally cutting the recipe in half. "And then I was cooking for a dozen guys with big appetites."

"Oh." There was a slight pause. When she spoke again, her voice held a note of awe. "I guess that means you have lots and lots of brothers, huh?"

As the question sank in, he realized what he'd revealed and was appalled. Normally, he didn't talk about his childhood. With anyone. Yet as he glanced over and found her looking at him with open curiosity, he knew he couldn't let her think she had other family when she didn't. "They weren't my brothers."

A little V formed between her eyebrows. "They weren't?"

"No." He opened the cupboard and got out the measuring cups. "You know what an orphan is?"

She nodded.

"That's what I was. I lived with a bunch of other boys in a group home about fifty miles from here."

"Oh." There was a heartbeat of silence. "Who took care of you?"

"Different people. It changed over the years." Having already said more than he wanted to, he took a stab at changing the subject. "So. You gonna get the rest of the stuff for the batter or not?"

"Oh—oh, yeah!"

To his relief, she took the hint and bolted toward the refrigerator. In need of a moment to regroup, he retrieved the griddle and turned it on to heat. He was just beginning to feel more at ease when the refrigerator door slammed and he glanced over to see her clutching a gallon container of milk to her chest with one hand while gripping the basket holding the eggs with the other.

Off balance, she started toward him. His heart kicked into overdrive as her stocking feet slid precariously on the polished stone floor. "Damn it, Lissy, slow down!"

The instant he said it, even before she jolted to a stop and he saw the pink climb into her cheeks, he regretted it. Not the sentiment, perhaps, but the swear word, his harsh voice, his overbearing manner—and, most of all, his certainty that he'd just ruined an encounter that for once had seemed to be going right.

Angry at himself, he said curtly, "Look, I'm sorry. I shouldn't have snapped at you. But I was afraid you were going to fall and I didn't want you to get hurt, all right?"

To his amazement, instead of shrinking away she stared right back at him, the oddest expression on her face. "You didn't?"

He shook his head. "No."

"Oh." For a moment she almost appeared to brighten, and it seemed as if things were going to be all right. And then she suddenly bit her lower lip. "Daddy?"

His heart sank. "What?"

"Can you take the milk? It's heavy."

He closed the distance between them with a single step, took both food items and set them on the counter. "That better?"

She nodded. "Uh-huh. Only…"

"What?"

"Can I pour the batter when it's ready?"

In that instant, as he met the big blue eyes gazing steadily up at him, he finally saw what had been staring him in the face for the past two weeks. She'd changed. A month ago she would have bolted for her room at his first harsh word. But not anymore. Like a flower that was finally taking root, she was blossoming with newfound trust and confidence.

And he knew exactly who was to thank.

He cleared his throat. "Sure. Just let me grab the step stool—" suiting action to words, he dragged it out of the corner and set it by the counter with a clatter "—and you can help me make it."

Her eyes widened. "Really?"

"Yeah. Only take your socks off first."

"Okay!" She tore them off in a flash and clambered up beside him as if fearing he'd change his mind.

Taking turns measuring and pouring, they put the batter together. When it was ready, he pushed the bowl toward her and handed her a measuring cup. "You know what to do?"

"Uh-huh." She dipped the cup in the batter. Then she carefully lifted it up and poured a succession of lopsided circles onto the griddle.

"Pretty good," he murmured.

As compliments went, it wasn't much. Even so, her face lit up. The sight made him feel funny, and he shifted his gaze to the pancakes rising on the griddle, only to stiffen in surprise as she took a half step sideways and tentatively leaned her weight against him.

He tried to decide what to do. Yet it didn't take him more than a few seconds to realize he'd never forgive himself if she were to overbalance and topple off the stool. Gingerly, he settled her more securely into the crook of his arm.

She gave a contented little sigh. "Daddy?"

"Hmm?"

"I'm glad I'm not an orphan."

He kept his gaze firmly fixed on the rising pancakes, his throat suddenly tight. "Yeah. Me, too."

To his relief, his voice sounded steady and matter of fact. Yet for the very first time since Lissy had come to live with him, he felt a kernel of hope that there might be hope for him as a father after all.

Eight

"Lissy looks happy tonight," Pam Abrams said to Eve.

The teacher's low voice carried easily despite the din in Lander County Elementary's second-grade classroom, which was filled with kids and parents all gussied up for the school's annual fall parents' night.

"Yes, she does," Eve agreed, following the other woman's gaze across the room to where the child stood beside her tall, broad-shouldered father.

Something good was happening between John and his daughter. Eve had suspected as much all week. Although the changes had been subtle, John seemed to be a little more at ease, a little less aloof with the child than he had been in the past.

His behavior tonight was a case in point. Instead of keeping Lissy at arm's length, he'd devoted the evening to her, touring the classroom, inspecting her desk, listening attentively as she talked about what she most and least liked to study. While not everything had been clear sailing—John had looked distinctly uncomfortable when they'd first walked in and half a dozen giggling little girls had rushed over to say hello to Lissy—he seemed to be making a genuine effort.

The result could be seen in the happy glow on Lissy's face. Dressed in a fashionable pink jumper, worn with a lace-trimmed white T-shirt, white tights and pink tennis shoes, with her perky golden-brown curls caught off her face with a quintet of little pink butterfly clips, she bore scant resemblance to the bedraggled, sad-eyed little waif of a month ago.

Nor was Eve the only one to think so, as Pam soon made clear. "She's come a long way in the past month," the teacher commented. "She's lucky to have you."

"I'm the lucky one," Eve replied, knowing it was true. Above and beyond providing her with food in her mouth and a roof over her head, her job taking care of Lissy had given her a purpose. For the first time in years she felt useful, as though she were making a small but worthwhile difference in the world, and it felt good.

Perhaps that was why she felt no sense of foreboding as Pam walked away to greet another set of parents and Gus Bolt, the bespectacled young Lander attorney who'd handled the Rocking C's sale, approached.

"Eve. Nice to see you."

"Hello, Gus."

"I understand from Freddy—" he indicated one of Lissy's classmates, a thin, dark-haired little boy who was his spitting image "—that you've been helping in the classroom. I'm glad to see things are working out."

"Thank you." Bolt's gaze shifted momentarily and she turned to see John approaching. His eyes met hers for a moment as he stepped up beside her, before he turned his attention to the shorter, slighter man.

"Gus, you know John MacLaren, don't you?" she said easily.

"Of course." The two men shook hands and exchanged greetings.

Once the amenities were out of the way, Bolt's attention swung back to her. "I tried calling you earlier this evening, but apparently you'd already left for town." Again his gaze flickered to John, then came back to her. "Can you give me a call tomorrow? Something's come up that I need to discuss with you."

She hesitated, her curiosity piqued. "Surely you can give me a hint?" she said wryly. "John knows why I had to sell the ranch."

"In that case...I'm afraid I've been contacted by yet another gentleman claiming he had dealings with Max."

Her amusement died. "Oh."

"This one's name is Morris Chapman. He's from New Mexico, says he just learned of Max's passing and claims he has something important to discuss with you. Naturally, I explained I was handling matters and refused to give out your phone number. Unfortunately, that seemed to get his dander up and he said he'd be sending you some papers. I thought you might know who he is."

She shook her head, filled with dismay at the prospect of dealing with yet another creditor. Gamely, she tried to rise above it, but some of her distress must have shown on her face, as evidenced by the attorney's quick look of concern.

"I'm sorry, Eve. But I did warn you this was a possibility when you decided to use your personal assets to settle those last liabilities."

Beside her, she felt John stiffen and abruptly realized she'd never thought to correct his initial impression that she'd squandered all her money on herself.

Gus reached out and gave her hand a quick squeeze. "I debated whether to say anything until I have a better idea what's involved, but decided it would be best if you were prepared."

"Of course, Gus. You were right to tell me."

The attorney visibly relaxed and they spent the next few minutes discussing how well young Freddy was doing in school before he excused himself and went off in search of his wife and son.

Bracing herself, she turned to John. To her surprise, though there was speculation in his eyes, after a quick look around he seemed to decide this was not the right time to pursue answers. Instead, he said quietly, "You all right?"

Relieved, she smiled. "I'm fine."

"Good."

She looked around. "Where's Lissy?"

He nodded toward the cloakroom as she and three other little girls, including her best friend Jenny, emerged, chattering excitedly as they shrugged into their coats. "The Hendersens are getting ready to leave."

"Already?" Lissy was going home with Kristin Hendersen, who was having a slumber party; John and Eve had dropped her things off earlier on the drive into town.

"It's nearly nine o'clock."

"Oh." She stared at him in amazement, surprised at how fast the evening had gone. In the next instant Lissy came skipping up to say goodbye and to confide that she and her friends were going to stay up "really, really late" so they weren't to come get her before noon. John nodded, Eve told her not to worry, and a moment later she was gone.

There was a moment's silence following the child's departure. Then John's gaze found Eve's, and the banked heat she could see in those deep blue depths set off a throb of need inside her. "Let's go home," he said abruptly.

"All right." She went and got her coat, exquisitely aware of the light touch of his hand at the small of her back as they said their goodbyes and walked out of the school.

The October night was crisp and clear. Stars twinkled like silver sequins against the ebony fabric of the sky, their pale, shimmering light unaffected by the thin slice of an ivory moon.

Eve looked out at the familiar landscape and drank in the silence, awed by the vast beauty of the land, wondering how she could have stayed away as long as she had. With the sort of understanding that comes with hindsight, she realized the restlessness she'd felt so often the past few years had actually been homesickness. While she refused to regret those years, knowing they'd taught her a lot, she was glad to be home.

"You're awfully quiet."

John's deep voice brought her head around. She allowed herself a moment to appreciate his chiseled profile, illuminated by the dashboard lights. "So are you."

A faint smile curved his chiseled mouth. "I guess I am."

That unexpected smile made her feel warm all over. "I was just thinking about all the parties I used to attend and wondering how I stood all the noise."

"Don't you miss it?"

"The noise?"

He shot her a chiding look. "No. The parties. And the travel, the glamorous people, not having any responsibilities?"

She laughed softly. "No. I had fun, and I saw a lot of beautiful places, but this is where I belong. I just wish I'd figured it out before I lost Granddad. I keep thinking that maybe, if I'd come home, I could have done something to help him."

He shook his head. "Don't kid yourself, Eve. I liked your grandfather, but he'd been in charge too many years to suddenly relinquish his authority. Not to mention he was a proud man. He would've hated having you know he was in trouble."

Although she'd told herself the very same thing, the conviction in John's voice was strangely comforting. "I know you're right. But sometimes it's just…hard."

He nodded. "Yeah," he said quietly. "I suppose it is."

The understanding in his voice surprised her. Feeling closer to him than she ever had before, she asked, "Did you have a good time tonight?"

"I'm not sure a good time is exactly how I'd phrase it but, yeah, I did. Lis seems to like school. I'm glad she's doing well."

"What about you? Did you like school?"

He shrugged. "It was all right."

"I imagine it was hard, not having anyone to call your own."

He hesitated. And then, just when she'd decided he wasn't going to answer, he surprised her. "Yeah, it was. Kids don't like being different. Sometimes I used to wonder…"

"What?"

"Just…why me? But I got over it. I survived." John suddenly heard what he'd just said and grimaced. The last thing he wanted was her pity, and he deliberately changed the subject. "What did Bolt mean when he said you'd used your personal assets to settle some of Max's liabilities?"

"It's nothing."

"It's not nothing. I want to know."

She hesitated, as if weighing her answer, but finally gave a faint sigh, as if she knew he had no intention of letting it go. "After the rest of the creditors made their claims, there wasn't enough money left to pay the Rocking C's hands their back wages. I took care of that and a few other things."

"You took care of it," he repeated slowly, his mind working. "With what? The money from your trust fund?"

"Yes."

"Back wages took all of it?"

"Granddad hadn't paid payroll taxes for nearly two years. What with interest and penalties, it added up. And as trustee, he had the power to make investments." She paused and in the glow from the dashboard, he saw her shrug. "Some of them weren't very wise."

John felt something inside him shift as he listened

to her answer, which was notable for its lack of self-pity. Almost reluctantly, he admitted that despite the growing evidence to the contrary, up until tonight a part of him had continued to regard her as the spoiled, pampered princess he'd labeled her eight years ago. And though he tried to tell himself he wasn't sure why, on some level he knew it had to do with the unwelcome discovery that she was starting to feel important to him.

Not that he was falling in love with her or anything as foolish as that, he told himself firmly. Or that it would change anything if he did. He still wasn't suited for family life, or for the intimacy demanded by marriage.

It was just that he didn't like the idea of Eve worrying about money. And he did have a responsibility toward her. She was his employee, as well as his lover, and that meant he had an obligation to see to her welfare.

"I don't want you to worry about this new claim, if that's what it turns out to be," he said decisively.

"What do you mean?"

"Whatever this guy from New Mexico wants, I'll handle it."

"Pardon me?"

"I said, I'll handle it." He slowed and took the turn onto the Bar M road.

For a handful of seconds she seemed stunned. "That's very generous," she said finally. "But I couldn't possibly accept. It's my problem and I'll take care of it."

"Damn it, Eve—"

She leaned over and touched her hand to his arm to silence him. "John, please. I don't expect you to understand, but for so long I did whatever was easiest. Being responsible for myself is important to me. And I really don't want to argue about this.'' Her voice dropped even further, taking on a slightly husky note. "Not tonight."

Her touch was like a brand, making his blood heat, while that velvety voice stroked along his senses. She was such a contradiction, stubbornly independent one minute, a warm, yielding temptress the next. Although they'd been as intimate as a man and a woman could be the past pair of weeks, he still didn't quite know what to expect, a realization he found more than a little frustrating.

But then, he'd had a crash course in frustration lately. It had been more than a week since they'd last made love; first Lissy had been home with a cold, then Eve had spent the bulk of the remaining days at school helping Miss Abrams and the kids get ready for tonight.

And when they had made love, they'd been under a time constraint, forced by Lissy's schedule, Eve's obligations and his own work demands to limit their time together. Add to that the fact that his self-control seemed to be on a permanent vacation, that no matter how often he told himself he was going to take it slow there always came a moment when wildfire need overcame his formerly effortless self-discipline, and it was no wonder he felt edgy.

Nor had his state of mind been helped by the way she was dressed tonight, in thin, strappy high heels and a simple but elegant navy silk dress that had been driving him crazy since they'd left home three hours ago.

Still, he promised himself this subject wasn't over

even as he outwardly acquiesced. "All right. We'll drop it for now."

"Good."

He pulled up to the house and cut the pickup's engine, frowning as he saw that the porch light was out. "Stay put," he ordered as she reached for her door handle. Undoing his seat belt, he climbed out, went around, opened her door, leaned in and scooped her into his arms.

"John!" she protested, her hands locking around his neck for balance. "What do you think you're doing?"

He straightened and bumped the door closed with his hip. "It's dark out here. I don't want to take a chance on you falling in those heels." Only to himself did he admit that he simply couldn't wait to hold her a second longer.

Her body felt sleek and supple against his as he strode across the yard and up the steps, while her light, powdery scent teased at his senses. Stopping at the door, he gave in to temptation, lifted her higher and lowered his head as the desire he'd been keeping so tightly leashed broke free.

His mouth settled over hers, hot and demanding. To his gratification, her lips immediately parted, clinging hungrily to his. With a sweetly satisfying moan, she tightened her arms around his neck and twisted closer.

John drank in the taste of her, his body tight with need. In the back of his mind, he marveled at her powerful effect on him, which seemed to be growing rather than diminishing with time. Marveled, and felt the tiniest spark of alarm...

He broke the seal of their lips and set her on her feet, gritting his teeth as she leaned against him and he felt the slim, elegant curves of her body. He allowed himself the indulgence of rubbing his cheek against the fragrant silk of her pale hair before he straightened. "Come on. Let's go inside."

Keeping her close, he opened the door and ushered her in, their path illuminated by the soft glow of light from the kitchen. With a touch of his hand to her shoulder, he guided her through the house and down the hall to his bedroom.

He snapped on the bedside lamp and reached for her, pulling her close for another hungry kiss. By the time he raised his head, they were both breathing hard. Taking a firm grip on himself, he took her purse and helped her out of her coat, shed his own and tossed everything onto the big upholstered chair that took up most of one corner. Moments later, the rest of his clothing followed, until he was standing before her unabashedly naked. "Turn around," he said softly.

Her wide gray eyes searched his for a moment, then swept slowly downward, a faint flush of color rising in her cheeks at the proof of his desire jutting thickly from his body. For a moment he thought she was going to balk at his request, and then she dampened her lips and did as he bid.

Slowly, he unzipped her dress, exposing the silky line of her back, bare except for the coffee-colored lace of her bra and panties. Brushing her hair out of his way, he bent his head and pressed his mouth to her nape, stringing a chain of kisses a few inches down her spine.

"John," she protested weakly.

"Shh." He pushed her dress off her shoulders, feeling a distinct throb in his groin as it slid to the floor and he saw that her nylons came only to the tops of her thighs, held there by built-in lace bands. The sight of her smooth, bare legs rising out of them made his whole body go hard. "It's been a hell of a long week," he ground out, his breathing suddenly labored. "I missed touching you." He unclipped her bra, pushed it off her arms, and reached around to cup her breasts in his palms.

"Oh." Eve gasped, squeezing her eyes shut as he traced the shape of her tightly beaded nipples with the broad tips of his fingers while blazing a trail along the sensitive underside of her jaw with his mouth. Sensation streaked through her, hot and melting. Her knees felt weak, her body heavy.

She leaned back against John's big, hard frame. At moments like this she was acutely aware of the difference in their size and strength. And yet she felt no fear, but rather a delicious sense of her own femininity. There was no question that he was uncompromisingly, overwhelmingly male, but she trusted him to use all that raw, masculine power for her pleasure.

His right hand drifted down her midsection and over the satin of her panties, coming to rest between her legs. With wicked accuracy, he honed in with his thumb and began to stroke her.

Her whole body flushed. Pleasure twisted through her, stealing her breath, making her rock her hips in time to the rhythm he set. It was too much and not enough all at the same time. Needing more, she reached up, twined her fingers in the cool, black satin of his hair and tugged down his head to claim his mouth.

Lips parted, they kissed, tongues tangled, breath intermixed. With every brush of his hand, tension climbed higher inside her. Just when she was sure she couldn't take any more, his fingers paused, lifted, then skated beneath her panties and slid over her damp, aching cleft.

She tore her mouth from his. "John. Oh, oh please!" She came up on tiptoe, quivering as she felt the rigid weight of his sex nudging heavily into her back, the sure press of one fingertip at her opening. "I need, I want…"

"What?" His voice was raw, his touch sure and skilled as it slid over her, setting her on fire. "What do you need, Eve?"

"You. I need you."

A shudder went through him and the breath hissed out between his teeth. The next thing she knew he was turning her around, lifting her out of the pool of her dress and backing toward the bed, where he sank down with her standing between his thighs.

He cradled her hips in his hands, his fingers stroking the bare skin between her nylons and panties. "What the hell do you call these things, anyway?" he asked hoarsely, touching the elasticized tops of her hose.

She swallowed, searching to find her voice, no mean feat when her whole body ached for him. "Thigh-highs."

"Yeah? If I'd had any idea that's what you had on, we'd have been home a hell of a lot sooner." To her wonder, his hands shook slightly as he peeled her panties down her legs, leaving her in hose and heels and nothing else.

That telltale tremor in his big, competent hands made her bold. Trembling herself, she kicked off her shoes, stepped forward, locked her arms around his powerful neck and straddled his lap. He wrapped an arm around her waist and slowly began to guide himself inside her.

She rocked upward to accommodate him, squeezing her eyes shut at his unhurried entry, shuddering as he stroked his hand down her spine. Sensation overwhelmed her; the tantalizing brush of his hard warm chest against her breasts, the tickle of the hair on his legs between her thighs, the satin over steel play of flexing muscle as she braced her hands on his wide shoulders, the slow, heated pressure as he filled her.

"Eve." His voice whispered over her like rough velvet.

She opened her eyes and found herself transfixed by the intensity of his gaze.

John stared back, a fierce, totally male satisfaction filling him as they came together. He was acutely aware of the slenderness of her waist between his hands, the elegant fineness of her bones compared to his.

He knew, from a few things she'd said, that he was the first man to give her pleasure. Which seemed only fair, since she was the first woman for whom he'd experienced this all-consuming hunger. Each time he was with her he wanted more.

She moved, rocking upright, slowly sinking down, and he gave an unexpected groan, the sound torn from the very heart of him.

Satisfaction stole across her face. "Do you like that?"

"What do you think?" Although his body was already screaming for release, he fought the urge to grip her hips, to quicken the tempo, determined to let her set the pace.

Perspiration beaded his forehead as she did just that,

settling into a protracted rhythm that seemed guaranteed to drive him mad. Desperate for a diversion, he found her mouth with his own, but the sweetness of her lips as they parted for the hot slide of his tongue did nothing to relieve his building tension.

And then he heard her breathing quicken and felt her soft, inner muscles begin to tighten. Gritting his teeth against a rising flood of pleasure, he brought his hand around and lightly rubbed his fingertip over the swollen center of her desire.

She tore her mouth from his as her whole body shuddered. "Oh. Oh, John!" Sobbing, she clung to his shoulders as the velvet glove of her body clenched around him again and again. "Don't stop, don't stop!"

He couldn't hold back any longer. With a guttural cry of his own, he gripped her hips and drove into her, his back hollowing as his own pleasure slammed into him.

It was long minutes later before he found the strength to lift his head. Gathering her close, he twisted around and lay back on the bed with her sprawled against him. Her hand came up and stroked gently over his face, then her thumb feathered lightly over his parted lips.

A surge of possessiveness went through him and he reached up, caught her hand in his and kissed her palm. She was his. And while he might not be the marrying kind, neither did he have any intention of giving her up, not in the immediate future.

What's more, he intended to take care of her.

Whether she wanted him to or not.

The phone rang before dawn. Eve came awake long enough to hear the sharp concern in John's voice and to make sympathetic noises when he climbed out of bed and began to pull on his clothes, brusquely explaining that the call had been from one of his men reporting that his favorite gelding had gotten out of his stall and into the grain bin and appeared to be foundering.

The next thing she knew, the clock read five after nine, sunshine was streaming in the windows, and John still wasn't back.

She stretched, bunched the pillow under her head and turned onto her side, grimacing at the slight soreness in her thighs. Taking stock, she realized that the skin on her face and chest felt tender and her lips slightly swollen, but overall what she felt was a sort of bone-deep languor.

Which wasn't surprising since she and John had made love three times last night.

What was surprising was the discovery that he'd been gone only a few hours and she missed him.

She immediately told herself not to be foolish. Of course she missed him. She missed his embrace, and the hard strength of his body against hers and the chance to make love again before it was time to go get Lissy.

Yet it was more than that, and she knew it. She missed his deep voice. She missed lying quietly in bed and talking the way they'd talked last night. She missed his smile, the way his glorious blue eyes darkened when he looked at her and the sense of safety she felt when his arms were around her.

Suddenly restless, she tossed back the covers and climbed out of bed. Despite the sunshine, the early morning air felt cool against her bare skin. Rubbing her arms, she glanced at her wrinkled dress, but the idea of putting it on didn't appeal.

With sudden decision, she walked over to John's dresser, telling herself he wouldn't begrudge her a T-shirt. Trying not to feel as if she were prying, she began opening drawers. Her first forays yielded underwear, jeans and socks until finally she found a stack of cotton T-shirts.

Shivering now, she drew the top one off the stack and pulled it on, sighing as the soft cotton slid over her. Although it was probably her imagination, since the shirt was freshly laundered, she would have sworn she could smell John's scent. Hugging it to her, she leaned over to shut the drawer when a swatch of bright red cloth at the very back of the drawer caught her eye. Intrigued—she didn't think she'd ever seen him in a shirt that wasn't navy, black or plain white—she reached in and tugged the garment free, frowning as she realized it was wrapped in a thin layer of tissue paper.

The tissue fell away and she saw that the item wasn't a T-shirt at all, but a small child's faded corduroy jacket. For a moment she assumed it was Lissy's, but as she unfolded it she realized it was far too small and that the style had to be several decades old.

She stared at the small rectangle of paper pinned to the front with a large safety pin. The writing on it was faded but easy to read, done in the large, loopy handwriting so often favored by teenage girls.

His name is John. Tell him I loved him and I'm sorry, but I tried and I just can't take care of him.

Eve's heart seemed to still as she realized the coat must have been the one John had been wearing when he'd been abandoned as a little boy. That the note could only have been written by his mother. And that John—outwardly so tough and so very unsentimental—had kept the item all these years.

Emotion swept her. Heartache for the defenseless, innocent, no-doubt bewildered child he'd been. Pride for the hurdles he'd faced and the man he'd become. And, as she smoothed the thin paper with trembling fingers, carefully refolded the coat and replaced it in the drawer, a mixture of elation and dread.

Because as she slowly shut the drawer and straightened, she knew why she missed him and why she'd found such pleasure in his arms.

She loved him. It was probably a mistake and he'd probably break her heart, but she also knew that didn't matter.

She loved him, now and forever, with everything that was in her heart.

Nine

Eve pulled the heavy roasting pan out of the oven and set it on the larger of the two front burners. Lifting the lid, she inhaled the rich aroma of simmering meat and vegetables. Although the past few days had been sunny, the temperature had been falling steadily in the week and a half since the school open house, and the hot, savory meal seemed perfect for a chilly fall evening.

She turned up the heat on the oven and slid a pan of biscuits inside. Reaching to set the timer, she heard the back door slam and the approaching stamp of footsteps. A few seconds later, a familiar male voice said, "Whatever you're cooking, it sure smells good."

She looked over to see John lounging in the doorway, and her heart beat a little faster. Dressed in boots, jeans, a navy henley and a quilted black vest, his hair ruffled from the breeze and the day's beard shadowing his lean cheeks, he looked vital, virile, the quintessential male. "It's pot roast."

"Could've fooled me. It smells like heaven."

She smiled. "I take it you're hungry."

"Yeah. You could say that." His gaze met hers, and there was a spark in his eyes that suggested he wasn't talking only about food. "How are you?" he asked quietly. "And how'd it go with Lissy at Dr. Edger's?"

"I'm fine and so is she, although she wasn't very happy about having to get her finger pricked for the blood sample."

"Is everything all right?"

"Doc said she seems perfectly healthy. He signed her health card, and we dropped it off at the rec center on our way home." Much to Lissy's delight, one of the local guilds was offering a ballet class for kids age six to ten. "She can hardly wait. Especially since the teacher told her they're going to have a Christmas recital."

"That's great."

It was clear he meant it, and Eve felt a wave of tenderness go through her. Most of the men she knew would roll their eyes at the prospect of an evening spent watching a bunch of little girls twirl around a stage pretending to be snowflakes or sugar plums, but not John. He might not always know the right thing to say to Lissy or how to act, but there was no longer a single doubt in her mind that he genuinely cared about his daughter.

As if he'd read her mind, an uncharacteristic flash of self-consciousness registered on his face and he promptly changed the subject. "You hear anything from Bolt about that Chapman fellow?" he asked a tad gruffly.

"No, not yet."

"Huh." For a second she thought he was going to pursue it, but then he seemed to think better of it. "So how long until dinner?"

"I still have to make the gravy and set the table." She calculated. "Say, ten minutes?"

"I'll go wash up."

She nodded and went to get the flour and an instant gravy packet out of the pantry as he walked away. Yet he remained the focus of her thoughts as she mixed the items together in a measuring cup, added water and stirred until smooth.

He'd changed. Granted, it was subtle, more a general easing of his manner than an actual shift in attitude, but he was different just the same. Overall, he seemed more relaxed and less guarded with both her and Lissy, and it made her happy. While she was doing her best to take things day by day, she couldn't deny that her heart felt a little fuller each time he revealed another facet of his complex personality.

Turning the heat on the burner to a medium temperature, she lifted the lid on the roasting pan and poured in the gravy mixture, blending it with the beef broth she'd added earlier to the roast's natural juices.

By the time the liquid started to bubble a few minutes later, John was back. This time he'd shed the vest and his sleeves were pushed back. Crossing the kitchen, he grabbed three of the place mats stacked in the middle of the table and set them in place. "Where is Lis, anyway?"

"In her room. She finished her homework right before you came in and went to put it away. She has a surprise for you." He glanced at her curiously, and she tried to look angelic. "Sorry. I promised not to tell." Grabbing a hot pad as the buzzer rang, she retrieved the now golden biscuits and diplomatically changed the subject. "How was your day?"

He came back around the counter and opened the silverware drawer. "Productive. We moved the last group of stragglers down from Gull Creek, replaced a few tons of hay that went bad and got the last of the horses reshod." Gathering knives, forks, spoons and a trio of napkins, he headed back toward the table.

"Is that the farrier's rig that's parked out in the yard?" The deluxe cherry-red sport-utility vehicle had been there when she'd returned from picking up Lissy at school. At the time she'd thought it was odd that it should be at the house rather than the barn, but then she'd promptly forgotten about it.

There was the slightest hesitation before he answered. "No."

"Oh. Well, whose is it?"

"Mine."

She glanced over at him in surprise. "You got rid of your pickup?"

"No." He put the last fork into place and turned to face her, anticipation suddenly lighting his deep blue eyes. "I bought it for you to drive."

For a moment she just stared at him. "But it's brand-new!"

He gave one of those expressive shrugs she'd come to know so well. "So? It's not like I can't afford it."

"Well, yes, but..." She broke off, suddenly realizing that if she wasn't careful she was going to hurt his feelings. "I just...you shouldn't have. It's too much."

Nobody's fool, his eyes narrowed. He studied her for a moment and when he spoke his voice had gone quiet. "What's the problem?"

It was a good question. Eve tried to decide how to explain her uneasiness. "I suppose," she said honestly, "it's a little like the coat—"

"Aw, hell." His frustration was obvious as he stalked back into the kitchen. "We're not going to get into that again, are we? You needed a decent winter coat instead of that thin little leather thing you've been wearing, so I bought you one. You insisted on paying me back out of your next few paychecks, and I agreed. End of story.

"As far as the Explorer's concerned, it's not the same at all," he went on. "The title's in my name. And one way or another I was going to have to replace the Wagoneer anyway." He let out a sigh and abruptly changed tactics. "The thing is fifteen years old, Eve," he said more reasonably. "It's fine for getting around the ranch, but the heater's not always reliable and the four-wheel drive doesn't always engage. What with the forecasters saying we may get snow by the weekend, and you driving back and forth to town as much as you do, I need to know that Lissy and you are safe."

It was hard to argue with that. Particularly when he'd actually made the effort to explain himself, which was a rarity in itself.

Besides, what exactly *was* she protesting? Yes, he'd bought her a beautiful coat. But in all fairness, at the time they'd been shopping for a new parka for Lissy, and it had been the child who'd insisted that Eve needed one, too. It wasn't as if John had intended to buy it for her when they'd set out. And, as he'd pointed out, the vehicle *was* in his name, and she could hardly fault him for being concerned about his daughter's safety.

This wasn't like the situation with Max, she assured herself. John wasn't trying to run her life or tell her what to do. Yes, he was looking out for her, but given her feelings, she'd do the same for him if he'd let her. Instead of complaining, she ought to be glad that he was concerned.

She slowly let out a breath and managed a smile. "You're right. I'm sorry. I just don't want you to think I expect you to buy me things."

"Believe me, I don't." Catching her off-guard, he leaned over and kissed her, softly at first, and then with more and more heat. By the time he raised his head, her breathing was shaky and her knees were weak.

He tucked a stray strand of hair behind her ear. "I think we'd better eat." His mouth twisted ruefully. "While we still can."

Lips tingling, she nodded and went to put dinner on the table.

Lissy's surprise for John turned out to be herself, decked out in tights, leotard and tutu. With her delicate torso and skinny legs, the large froth of yellow netting billowing around her middle made her look a lot like an overripe dandelion he decided as she twirled around the living room demonstrating her ballerina moves.

"Come on, kiddo, that's enough." Eve set the biscuits and a bowl of peaches next to the steaming platter of roast and vegetables and sat down at the table. "You're going to make yourself so dizzy you won't be able to eat."

Lissy slowly teetered to a stop. "Okay," she said breathlessly. Cheeks flushed, her hair a froth of curls, she swayed, then righted herself and headed for her place.

"Do you need to wash your hands?" Eve asked gently.

The little girl gave a gusty sigh. "Yeah, I s'pose." She trotted into the kitchen and gave herself a quick wash at the sink.

"You probably should take off your tutu," Eve suggested to her as she rejoined the adults.

"Do I have to?"

"No. But I don't think you want to take a chance on spilling anything on it, do you?"

Lissy considered, then quickly shook her head. She slipped the tutu off and carefully set it on one of the club chairs as Eve filled her plate.

The next few minutes were devoted to taking the edge off all their hunger. Like everything Eve cooked, the meal was delicious, John thought, as he swallowed a bite of moist, succulent beef.

"Guess what, Daddy?" Lissy looked over at him, her big blue eyes soft and trusting. "I got a hundred on my spelling test."

"Well, good for you."

"*And* Miss Abrams picked one of my pictures to go in Mr. Adams' showcase."

"Hey, that's great." Mr. Adams was the principal, and from parents' night John knew that it was an honor to have your work shown in the big glass display outside the school office.

"Uh-huh. Eve said I should be really proud of myself, didn't you, Eve?"

"I sure did."

Lissy beamed. "So I am."

John watched as the two females exchanged smiles, grateful for their obvious fondness of each other. He cleared his throat. "I understand you were a pretty brave girl at the doctor's today."

Lissy's brow crinkled. "I was?"

"For your blood test."

She instantly shook her head. "I was scared," she admitted guilelessly. "I cried and wouldn't put out my hand 'cause I was afraid it was going to hurt, but then Eve said they could do it to her first, and after that...it wasn't too bad."

His gaze flickered to Eve's hands, and for the first time he noticed the small adhesive strip adorning one of her fingertips.

He raised an eyebrow and she shrugged. "It seemed like the thing to do."

He considered her serene face, knowing it was a solution that never would have occurred to *him*.

But then it was becoming clearer with every passing day that he didn't understand her nearly as well as he'd once thought he did.

Her reaction to the Explorer was a case in point. He'd picked it out with her in mind, choosing the deep red paint and champagne leather interior as the perfect foil for her sunny beauty. But had she been excited by his surprise? Impressed by his thoughtfulness? Happy to have a new vehicle to drive?

Not so you'd notice. Oh, she'd been gracious enough, but in a restrained, I'd-prefer-you-hadn't-done-this sort of way. Which, he reminded himself, was better than her reaction when he'd bought her the parka. Initially she'd flatly refused to take it. He'd insisted, and they'd been locked in a stalemate until, out of sheer frustration, he'd suggested that if it made her feel better she could pay him back a little out of each paycheck. Clearly recognizing he was making a major concession, she'd agreed.

He had no intention of taking her money, of course. And though part of him had to admire her thorny pride, mostly he felt annoyed. She didn't seem to have any trouble spending his money when it came to Lissy. If he could afford nice things and wanted her to have them or, even more importantly, wanted to take care of a situation like the one with the mysterious Mr. Chapman, what was the problem?

He was damned if he knew. The only thing that was clear was that for someone he'd once considered a pampered princess, Eve was turning out to be a real challenge to spoil.

"John?"

"What?"

"Is everything all right?"

He glanced from her to Lissy, suddenly aware that both of them were staring curiously at him.

"Sure. I was just thinking about what needs to be done if we actually get the snow they're forecasting. Why?"

She smiled. "I've asked you twice already—would you care for some dessert? It's blueberry cobbler."

"Thanks, but I think I'll pass, at least for now."

"I want some!" Lissy was quick to assert.

Eve's smile widened. "Somehow, that doesn't surprise me." Climbing to her feet, she picked up their dishes and headed for the kitchen.

Eyes hooded, John watched her retreat. As if of its own volition, his gaze lingered on the elegant line of her back, noted the way her waist nipped in above her long, slender legs, recorded the feminine sway of her hips. Desire, always close to the surface where she was concerned, surged through him.

He tried to tell himself it was the sole cause of the ongoing frustration he felt but he knew it was a lie. Although it had only been a few weeks, he was fed up with having to constantly be discreet, sick of meeting resistance each time he tried to do something for Eve, annoyed that he didn't have more say in her life.

He'd worked hard to make a place for himself in the world where he was in charge, yet when it came to their relationship, none of that seemed to matter.

And he didn't like it. Even worse, he was damned if he knew what to do about it.

Eve took a firm grip on the ladder's side rail. Careful not to dislodge the plastic bottle of glass cleaner tucked under her arm, she leaned sideways with a wad of paper towels and scrubbed at the filmy streaks some enterprising bird had left on the outside of the great room's cathedral window.

Normally, washing windows was one of her least favorite tasks. But today it suited her mood. Although it was only a little after noon, the laundry was done, the house clean and in order, the pantry and freezer fully stocked since she'd shopped earlier in the week. She'd already started dinner, and it wasn't her day to be at school. She'd felt restless, in need of something physical to do, and hauling out the ladder, getting out in the fresh air and having a go at the windows fit the bill.

She just hadn't counted on it also leaving her plenty of time to think about John.

But then, lately he seemed to be on her mind most

of the time. Eve's mouth curved ruefully. She was starting to understand all the poems and songs dedicated to being in love, which she was finding tended to consume a person.

In her case, it was also making it increasingly difficult to stand by her principles and take things as they came, as she and John had agreed to do the first time they'd made love. She missed sleeping with him all night and waking up next to him in the morning. She wanted to feel free to seek him out, to claim him as hers in public, to spoil and fuss over him occasionally. Most of all, she wanted to tell him she loved him.

Except she was afraid of his reaction. There had been no compromise in his voice when he'd told her not to expect any long-term promises. All she could do was wait and hope that if she gave it enough time and didn't press, he'd change his mind and see how much he had to give. And he'd also see, she added a little grimly, glancing over at the gleaming Explorer peeking out of the parking shed, that she wanted him for him, and not for his money or because he could make her life easier.

A sudden gust of wind shook the ladder. Frowning, she decided she'd better finish while she still could and applied herself to the job with fresh vigor.

"What in the hell do you think you're doing?"

The unexpected sound of John's voice made her jump so she nearly lost her footing. Clutching the ladder, she swiveled around to find him standing below her, his hands on his narrow hips. "Good grief, you scared me." Despite her racing heart, she started to smile, happy to see him.

He glowered up at her. "You ought to be scared. Get down from there. Now."

Her smile vanished as she took in the steely expression that said he expected to be obeyed. Annoyed—he really was a slow study when it came to figuring out that she wouldn't put up with being ordered around—she said tartly, "Gee, John, it's nice to see you, too. I'll be down in a minute. I'm not quite done." With that, she resumed her task.

The next thing she knew, she felt the ladder flex and an arm like a steel band clamp around her middle. To her disbelief, a second after that she found herself tucked against John's side, being carried downward as if she weighed no more than a feather.

The minute her feet touched the ground, she wriggled free and turned to confront him. "What on earth do you think you're doing?"

He gave her a long, shuttered look and stooped to pick up his hat off the ground. "Getting you off that ladder before you break your neck."

"I'm perfectly capable of getting down under my own power if that's what I wanted—which I didn't."

"Tough. I'm not paying you to do this sort of labor."

She couldn't believe she'd heard him right. "What does that have to do with anything!"

"It has to do with the fact that you could've fallen through the damn window!"

Like a veil being torn away, she suddenly heard the anxiety beneath his anger. With dawning surprise, she realized she'd scared him, which opened the way for another, equally unexpected perception. "What are you doing here, anyway? I thought you had a meeting in Missoula."

"I canceled it."

"Why?"

He shrugged. "Because I felt like it."

"Why?" she persisted.

"Because." His voice held a telltale combination of belligerence and defensiveness. "The front they've been talking about all week finally seems to be moving in, and I didn't want to take a chance on leaving you and Lissy here alone, all right?"

The admission stripped away the last of her irritation and flooded her with tenderness. She could feel her face soften as she looked up at him. "All right." Her smile was back, tugging at the corners of her mouth. "And I'm sorry I scared you."

He scowled. "I wasn't scared. I just don't want you taking stupid risks."

"Right. I'll try to restrain myself in the future. After all, who needs clean windows? It's not as if we need to see out..."

He gave her a sour look. "You done?"

"Not if I can help it."

They considered each other. Later, she wasn't sure who took the first step, not that it mattered. John shook his head and murmured, "Damn, but you make me crazy," and then she was in his arms.

Eve drank him in, the knowledge that he cared warming her as much as the hot, drugging pressure of his lips. She sighed with pleasure as he cupped the side of her face with one big hand, lost in the contrast between his calloused palm and his gentle touch.

Everything around her faded away. She couldn't hear the breeze that made the fir trees creak overhead or feel the cold. Only John mattered, and by the time he took a deep, sustaining breath and lifted his head, she'd lost all sense of time. "No," she automatically protested as he took half a step back.

He looked down at her, and the skin at the edges of his eyes crinkled. "It's cold out here," he said with a rough edge to his voice. "Let's go inside."

"Yes."

He quickly pressed another brief kiss to her throbbing lips, then walked over, wrestled the ladder onto its side and propped it against the house. That task completed, he claimed her hand and headed for the porch. He didn't touch her anywhere else, but she could feel his tension, just as she could feel the need that now flowed wordlessly between them.

Once through the door, she started to reach for him but he shook his head. "No, not here," he said tersely. "Anybody could look in."

He twisted the lock. Boot heels ringing on the stone floor, he led her into the kitchen. The house felt warm after the frigid outside air and was filled with the delicious aroma of the stew she'd started that morning.

Neither of them paid any attention. Instead, they had eyes only for each other as John pressed her back against the nearest cabinet, winnowed his hands into her hair and kissed her again.

His hands and his face were cold, but his lips were warm. Eve groaned at the sweetness of it, wanting all of him that she could get. She slid her hands into his open coat and crowded closer. Tugging his shirt free of his jeans, she stroked the warm hollow at the small of his back and pressed her aching nipples against his hard chest.

He made a low sound deep in his throat. His mouth feasted on hers, making promises that made her temperature rise. He was so incredibly male, from the clean scent of his skin to the air of leashed power that was uniquely his. She skimmed her hands up his smooth, sleek back, glorying in the firm bulge of muscle beneath her palms. Need twisted through her, setting off an ache only he could satisfy.

He raised his head, breathing hard.

"John." She pressed her mouth to his throat.

Angling back, he unzipped her coat, unbuttoned her moss green flannel shirt and peeled both garments back. She opened her eyes and looked down, her pulse throbbing at the sight of his bronzed fingers against her paler skin. His hands were steady as he undid the center hook on her white lace bra and cupped her bare breasts in his palms.

He lowered his head and she gasped as he rubbed his cheek against her tender flesh a second before his mouth latched onto one distended nipple. The ache at her core grew as he suckled, drawing on that sensitized morsel, while his fingers shaped its mate. She forgot to breathe, her head falling back as his cool, dark hair tickled against her and his clever lips built on her need.

"John," she whimpered. "Oh, please."

He released her, resting his head for a moment against the slope of her breast before he straightened. "I know, princess. I want you, too." His eyes gleaming like a slice of midnight, he worked at the snap of her jeans while she toed off her shoes. His fingers found the zipper, tugged, then gripped her waistband and slid the soft denim down. As her jeans hit the floor, he lifted her onto the counter.

Freeing himself from his own clothing, he wrapped an arm around her waist and guided himself inside her. She clutched his shoulders, unable to contain a moan as his body sank into hers, hard, hot and deep. "Yes. Like that." She gripped his shoulders tighter.

He tangled his hand in her hair and tugged, baring the long smooth line of her throat to his questing mouth. The slow slide of his lips made her shiver as he painted a trail of fire from her jaw to her collarbone. And all the while, they rocked together, slowly at first, and then faster and harder.

Eve wrapped her legs around him, unable to contain another soft cry as she realized she was on the verge of exploding. With a sudden sense of urgency, she cupped his chin in her hand and guided his mouth to hers, needing to kiss him, to try and tell him without words all that was in her heart.

And then, like a swimmer caught by an incoming wave, pleasure slammed into her, lifting her up, tossing her toward an exquisite shore. She felt herself tighten around John, felt the fullness as he pressed deep inside her, heard the cry he couldn't contain as her climax triggered his own. Mouth to mouth, heart to heart, they tumbled together on a crest of pleasure that seemed to go on forever.

It was long minutes later before Eve slowly surfaced. Feeling deliciously boneless, she lay nestled against John, her head on his shoulder, her body anchored by the muscular strength of his arms.

Slowly, she opened her eyes and a smile lit her face. "John?"

"Hmm?"

"Look." She raised her head and gestured to the window. "It's snowing."

Ten

Snow swirled in the pickup's headlights, a curtain of white against a tar-black night.

John clenched his teeth and did his best to ignore his wet, clammy clothing. He concentrated instead on holding the pickup steady against the gusting wind and told himself to be grateful for small favors. Like the line of reflectors topping the fence posts that marched along both sides of the driveway.

Still, he couldn't deny he'd like to have ten minutes alone with the irresponsible fool who'd lost control of his car on the highway, taken out a portion of Bar M fence and then driven off without alerting anybody.

Thank God the ranch was as remote as it was. That most folks from these parts had better sense than to go out in a snowstorm. And that one of the few who didn't was Mitch, his foreman, who'd been on his way back from town when he'd come across a dozen head of Bar M cattle standing in the road.

As long as he was counting his blessings, John supposed he should also be glad that the beasts were now all safely corralled, the fence temporarily shored up, and it looked as if he was actually going to make it home before he succumbed to frostbite.

Home. Just the thought of it brought a kick of anticipation. He tried to shrug it off, only to abruptly sigh. It was no use kidding himself. For the first time in his life he actually had somebody—or rather, two somebodies—waiting for him. And try as he might to tell himself not to be foolish, it made him feel warm inside.

But then, he'd felt that way for the better part of the day, and not just because of what had happened once he'd gotten Eve off that damn ladder. As fiercely as he'd enjoyed their lovemaking, he'd also discovered he trusted her to manage during the storm, to take care of Lissy and do what needed to be done around the house, leaving him free to concentrate on making sure the ranch was in order.

It was a nice feeling, if a little strange. He'd never had anyone to rely on before. But then, there were a lot of things about his relationship with Eve that were new for him. Not the least of which was that lately he'd found himself thinking about her at odd moments in the day, wishing she were there to talk to, wondering what she'd say about one thing or another. If he didn't know better, he might actually think he was starting to depend on her.

It was an unsettling thought, and he shook it off as he peered through the windshield. Unfortunately, what he could see of the surrounding landscape looked like a foreign country thanks to the blowing snow. Instinct told him he should be close to the turnoff for the house, but he still would have missed it if not for a bobbing circle of light up ahead. Frowning, he eased the pickup to the left, and his headlights illuminated a slender figure hunched against the wind, waving a Coleman lantern.

Eve. He swore under his breath, his anticipation replaced by aggravation as he eased past her, turned into the yard and pulled into the dark garage. The sight of her outside in such treacherous weather made him feel a little crazy, the way he had earlier today when he'd caught her up on the ladder. Face grim, he climbed from the truck as she walked up, her slim figure buffeted by the wind.

"Hi." Ignoring his thunderous look, she stepped close and gave him a quick hug.

"What the blazes are you doing out here?" He had to raise his voice to make himself heard.

She retreated half a step. "The power's out. I was afraid you'd drive right past the house."

He sent her a look of disbelief. "So you were just going to stand out in the road until I showed up?"

"Of course not. Mitch called and said you were on your way, so Lissy and I've been watching for your headlights." She looked up at him, her gray eyes level despite the snowflakes frosting her thick lashes. "It's getting late. I was worried about you."

Her unexpected admission rekindled that warm feeling in his gut. Disconcerted, he took refuge in action and started herding her toward the porch. "I can take care of myself," he said gruffly.

"I know you can. But—" she broke off as they struggled up the stairs and he wrestled open the door

"—that doesn't change how I feel." The last words were said as they knocked the snow off their boots and jeans and hurried inside.

He grunted, still not knowing what to say, when a small figure emerged out of the semidarkness and hurled herself at him. "Are you okay, Daddy?"

He looked down to find Lissy clinging to the front of his jacket, gazing anxiously up at him. Apparently both the females in his life had a low opinion of his ability to take care of himself. It would have been humiliating if it weren't so damned endearing. "I'm fine, honey."

"He just needs to get warmed up." Eve set the lantern on the counter and stripped off her gloves, hat and coat. She laid her hand on his arm, only to recoil. "Your clothes are wet!"

"Yeah. I noticed."

"What happened?"

"Steer knocked me into the ditch." Though the house felt warm after the air outside, he couldn't entirely quell a shiver.

She sucked in her breath. "Good grief, John. You're lucky you don't have hypothermia. Lissy, why don't you get your dad a cup of the hot chocolate we made while he gets out of these clothes."

"Okay!"

The child darted out of the room before he could object, so he turned his frown on Eve, uncomfortable with being fussed over. "I don't need any hot chocolate," he protested. "And if I did, I could get it myself."

"Of course you could. But Lissy needs something to do. She's been worried about you, too."

There didn't seem to be anything he could say to

that, so he settled for unbuttoning his coat, only to find his hands were clumsy with cold.

"Here. Let me." She brushed his ineffective fingers away and had him stripped down to his long-john bottoms in no time.

He might be tired and half-frozen, but her touch had its usual effect on him. Need curled like a fist low in his belly, and only the thought of Lissy's imminent return gave him the strength to catch Eve by the wrist when she reached for his waistband. "I'd better take it from here."

Her gaze flew to his face, and whatever she saw there had her struggling not to smile. "Spoilsport," she murmured.

He tried to look stern but couldn't entirely hide the answering smile that tugged at his lips. "You're dangerous."

Lissy walked slowly back into the room, an oversize mug clutched carefully in both her small hands. "Here, Daddy."

He started to tell her he really didn't care for chocolate, only to fall silent at the expectant look on her face. With a sigh, he took the mug and raised it to his lips. To his surprise the rich, hot drink tasted wonderful. He drained the cup before he finally looked up. "Thanks. That was great."

Lissy beamed.

"Now why don't you two clear out and give me a second to change?"

Eve pulled off her boots and set them out of the way. "All right. There are dry clothes for you on top of the dryer."

"Okay." He reached over and snagged the navy thermal weave top she'd set out as she and Lissy headed into the other room. He pulled on the soft garment, trying to convince himself his sudden sense of contentment stemmed merely from being home, and not from Eve and Lissy's warm reception. Yet he found himself hurrying to finish dressing, and he knew damn well it wasn't merely because he was anxious to cozy up to the fire.

Once clothed, he picked up the lantern and headed for the other room, pausing just past the kitchen. In the time that he'd been gone Eve and Lissy had hauled out the sleeping bags, quilts and pillows and laid them out in front of the fireplace. A log burned hot and steady in the grate, while a trio of automatic lanterns augmented its soft, flickering light. With the snow swirling outside the big windows at the far end of the room, the atmosphere felt intimate and cozy.

"Come on, Daddy." Already ensconced in her sleeping bag, with Eve seated on her left, Lissy patted the space to her right. "I get to be in the middle. Eve said."

"She did, huh?" His gaze found Eve's, and to his amusement she gave a slight, apologetic shrug. Despite the unfortunate sleeping arrangements, he didn't hesitate, however. The truth was he still felt chilled to the bone, and the lure of the warmth from the fire, not to mention the company, was more than he could resist. He crossed the room and gingerly lowered himself onto the makeshift bed. Scooting back, he followed Eve's example, propping his back against the couch and stretching his legs out toward the hearth.

The second he was settled Lissy gave an enormous yawn and scooted closer to him. "Daddy?"

"Hmm?"

She rested her head against his chest. "Do you think we'll be able to go outside tomorrow?"

"I don't know. Why?"

"I want to make a snowman."

"You do, huh?" The scent of her came up at him, lemon shampoo, talcum powder and freshly laundered flannel. She felt incredibly small and vulnerable as she lay against him. Without thinking, he slid an arm around her.

"Yeah. I've never made one before."

"You haven't?"

"No." She yawned again. "Grandma always said the cold made her bones ache, so I had to stay inside."

"Well, you won't have to tomorrow."

"Really?"

"I promise."

"I love you, Daddy."

The words caught him totally unprepared. Everything inside him seemed to go still for a moment, and then from a distance he heard someone with his voice say quietly, "I love you, too, Lissy."

"I know." With a happy little sigh, she burrowed a little closer and without further ado drifted off to sleep.

He gazed down at her slack face, amazed by the whole exchange. For a moment he wondered if he'd simply imagined it, and then he felt the touch of Eve's hand on his arm. He looked up and her expression told him he hadn't. "You okay?" she asked softly.

"Sure."

"Good."

He was the first to look away, shifting his gaze back to Lissy. "You think she'll wake up if I move her?"

"I think you're safe."

Reassured, he twisted sideways, carefully cradling the child's limp upper body in his arms as he slid her deeper into her sleeping bag. Without so much as a murmur, she rolled onto her tummy, buried her head into her pillow and settled more deeply into sleep.

He started to straighten, only to still as Eve reached over and gently brushed his hair off his forehead. She smiled. "I'm glad you're home."

He caught her hand and pressed it to his cheek. "Yeah. Me, too." They leaned toward each other, careful not to disturb Lissy as they came together for long, lingering kiss.

Desire rose in him like an incoming tide. But tonight it was wrapped in a layer of contentment that gave the ache in his body a certain sweetness. Cupping Eve's face in his hand, he broke the seal of their lips to press kisses over her chin and cheeks, luxuriating in the satin warmth of her skin, the silkiness of her hair, her light, pleasing fragrance.

It was with a sigh of regret that he finally straightened. Neither of them spoke. As their gazes met, there didn't seem to be a need for words. Linking her fingers with his, he settled back and lay down on his makeshift bed, bunching the pillow under his head.

The heat from the fire settled over him like a blanket and his eyes grew heavy as the long day caught up with him. And yet he felt a sense of peace and belonging he'd never felt before.

His last thought as he drifted to sleep was that this must be how it felt to be a part of a family.

It was the quiet that woke John.

He stared blankly into the darkness. The only sounds in the room were the steady rhythm of Eve's and Lissy's breathing and the occasional pop of the log in the fireplace.

With a start, he realized the wind had stopped. Craning his head, he looked out the window to find that it was no longer snowing and that the sky beyond the glass was an expanse of navy-blue studded with stars. He glanced at the luminous dial on his watch. It was just coming up on four o'clock.

He rolled onto his back. Then, driven by a need he didn't question, he turned to consider Eve. She was lying on her side, her cheek resting on her arm, her lovely face serene. Her other arm was curved protectively over Lissy, who was cuddled against her.

Watching her, he felt an unfamiliar swell of emotion. He might not love her, he realized, but he cared. More than he'd ever cared for a woman. More than he'd ever cared for anyone except for his daughter. In addition, he liked her. He liked her independence and her wry sense of humor, her courage, her integrity and her obvious femininity. He also knew that she was good for him, bringing a balance to his life he'd only recently begun to understand that he needed.

If he had any sense at all, he'd marry her.

The instant the thought registered, he dismissed it. Yet as he continued to lay there, his gaze on Eve's face, the idea persisted, refusing to go away.

Why *not* marry her? he asked himself slowly.

He knew she loved Lissy. He also thought her feelings for him ran deep. And not only were they extremely sexually compatible but he was genuinely fond of her.

A union between them would benefit everybody. Lissy would get a mother she adored. He'd get the security of knowing his home and his daughter were in good hands, as well as the freedom to indulge this compulsion he had to take care of her. As for Eve, once again she'd have someone to provide for her the way her grandfather had. She'd be able to buy pretty clothes, drive a nice car, do all the things she couldn't afford on her salary as his nanny.

There were worse things on which to base a marriage.

Not that he expected it to last, not forever. Eventually, inevitably, she'd leave. But by the time she did, he'd be ready. The sexual fire that blazed between them now would no doubt have burned down, if not flamed out. This inexplicable need he had to be with her, to touch her and talk to her and protect her, would have faded away. And Lissy would be older....

In the meantime, however, the benefits clearly outweighed the drawbacks.

Still, he continued to debate with himself, weighing the pros and cons, going over it again and again.

Eventually, however, the decision was made. And when it was, a profound sense of peace settled over him and all the frustration he'd felt recently seemed to drain away. Settling his head more deeply into the pillow, he knew as he finally fell back asleep that he was doing the right thing.

The morning sunshine sparkled on the snow that stretched as a vast white blanket in every direction.

Ignoring the slight ache in her lungs from breathing the frigid air, Eve narrowed her eyes against the dazzling light and watched as John lifted Lissy up so she could put her snowman's head in place. Once the oversize ball was securely situated, he set the child on her feet and took a step back to consider their creation. "What do you think?"

Lissy considered, her small face grave. "It's perfect," she said solemnly. "Only..."

"What?"

"It doesn't got a face."

"Good point."

Eve smiled. "I think I can help with that."

Lissy turned eagerly toward her. "You can?"

"Uh-huh." She dug into her coat pockets and pulled out the items she'd gathered before venturing outside. "I thought these would work for eyes—" she handed the child a plastic bag holding a pair of Oreo cookies "—and I brought a carrot for the nose and—" She held up another bag, "I thought we could use chocolate chips for the mouth."

"Perfect," Lissy crowed. "But what about the buttons for his coat?"

"I thought we could use gravel from the drive." She smiled sweetly at John. "Your father can get it."

"Thanks a lot." His attempt to look forbidding failed miserably, given the way his blue eyes gleamed with good humor.

But then, he'd been in a good mood all morning, Eve thought, as she watched him stride over to the driveway and begin digging through the snow. From the moment Lissy had shook them awake to excitedly inform them the sun was shining, he'd seemed uncharacteristically lighthearted. And though she couldn't help but wonder at the source, she also couldn't deny that it made him seem younger and even more wildly attractive.

Lissy tugged on her coat. "Will you lift me up, Eve, so I can do the face?"

"Sure." Tearing her gaze away from John, she did just that, and by the time he rejoined them, they were almost done.

Not that he seemed impressed with their progress. Frowning slightly, he reached over and plucked Lissy out of her arms and into his. "You shouldn't be lifting her. She's too heavy," he said as the child put the last chocolate chip into place.

"I'm stronger than I look," she replied demurely.

He didn't comment, just set Lissy on the ground and handed her the rocks he'd collected. Both of them watched as she promptly used them to decorate the snowman's midsection.

"Are you happy now?" He asked his daughter when she was done.

She nodded. "Except…"

"Now what?"

"He looks sort of…naked."

John raised his eyes to heaven. "Well, yeah. He's a snowman."

"I know. But he ought to have on something."

"You're right." Smothering a smile, Eve unwound her muffler and wrapped it around the snowman's neck. "There. How's that?"

Lissy bit her lip. "But won't you get cold?"

Before she could answer, John surprised them both by removing his hat and plopping it on Eve's head. "Not as long as I'm around. That'll help. So will this."

Without warning, he reached out, caught her in his arms and kissed her soundly.

"Daddy!" Lissy let loose with a shriek that was half protest and half excited little girl giggle.

With an exaggerated air of reluctance, he broke off

the kiss and looked down at his daughter, eyebrows raised. "What?"

"You kissed Eve!"

His mouth twitched. "Yeah, I know."

"But how come?"

"Because I like her."

"You do?"

"Yeah. Don't you?"

"Of course!"

Without further ado, he reached over and pulled the child close, so she was cuddled between them. "That's because you're a MacLaren." He looked down, gave her small body a gentle squeeze, then looked straight back at Eve and grinned. "And we MacLarens have exceptionally good taste."

Eve looked at his incredibly handsome face, her heart melting, as for the first time ever, she saw the deep groove—in anyone less masculine she would have termed it a dimple—that bracketed the left side of his mouth. "I'm not going to argue with that," she murmured, smiling back. And because she couldn't help herself, she wrapped her hand around the back of his head, leaned forward and kissed him again.

The feel of his warm lips in the cold air was delicious. What's more, there was a kind of tender possessiveness in his touch today that made her stomach hollow and her breath hitch. Leaning into him, she lost all track of time as the world seemed to narrow to the taste of his mouth, the grip of his hand, the slippery softness of his hair beneath her fingertips.

"Gosh." Lissy's voice held a note of awe. "Don't you guys need to breathe or something?"

John's mouth curved against hers, and then he pulled back and chuckled. In all the time she'd known him, it was the first time Eve had ever heard him really laugh, and the sound seemed to fill her like champagne, making her dizzy.

Looking into his laughing face, she was overcome by her feelings for him.

She loved him. And it was past time that she told him.

Eleven

Eve shut the Explorer's door and started up the walkway to the house.

Although the temperature was only in the high thirties, most of the weekend's snowfall was gone, thanks to three days of weak but steady sunshine. The one exception was Lissy's snowman, which continued to grace the yard with its cheerful, if now decidedly lopsided, presence.

Careful to watch for icy patches, Eve pattered up the porch steps. Juggling her purse, a bag of groceries and a stack of mail, she opened the door and stepped inside. She proceeded into the kitchen, set down her burdens, shrugged out of her coat, then put it and her purse away. Next she unloaded the groceries, checked on the chicken she'd put in the oven earlier and, on a whim, started a fire in the fireplace.

Finally out of obvious things to do, she slowly approached the kitchen counter, carefully stacked John's mail next to the telephone and reluctantly considered the large manila envelope she'd picked up from Gus Bolt's office earlier in the day. The return address label left no doubt as to who sent the package—Morris Chapman's name was there in bold printing, as was the listing of a post office box in Two Pennies, New Mexico.

Eve sighed. The past few days had been magical. Not only had John's good mood persisted but he seemed finally to be at ease with Lissy, and the improvement in their relationship had been dramatic. And even though the world seemed to be conspiring to make sure she and John never got a moment alone, Eve didn't mind.

It didn't seem right that reality had to choose now to intrude. But then, hadn't she learned by now that life wasn't always fair? And that bad things didn't go away, no matter how long one procrastinated?

Squaring her shoulders, she picked up the envelope, walked over to the table and sat. Taking a calming breath, she tore the flap and pulled out a sheaf of papers.

She loosened the clip holding them all together. On top was a letter. She set it aside and thumbed through what appeared to be a mining company prospectus, only to dislodge a rectangle of pale green paper.

It fluttered to the tabletop, and she stared at it in amazement. It was a check, issued by the Two Pennies Mine. And it was made out to her, in the amount of sixty-five thousand dollars.

For a moment she couldn't breathe, could only stare.

Finally, however, the worst of her shock passed. With an almost steady hand, she picked up the letter, which proved to be short and to the point.

According to Mr. Chapman, her grandfather had invested in his struggling silver mine seven years ago. After nearly a decade of barely breaking even, the mine had hit pay dirt nine months ago, when a huge vein of silver had been discovered. The enclosed check was the first return on Max's money. Mr. Chapman sent his assurances that there would be more to follow.

Eve sat motionless, the words blurring on the page as she tried to take it in. After all her worry, it appeared she didn't owe Mr. Chapman money after all. On the contrary, she'd come into a windfall, with the promise of more to come.

She shook her head, as if to clear it, and considered what this would have meant to her a few months ago.

She never would have come begging to John for a job. She would have left Lander without ever coming to know—or love—him and Lissy.

Just the idea made her shudder.

And now? she asked herself.

Now it didn't matter. She was where she wanted to be, with the two people she loved most in the world. The only difference was that now she'd have some added security. And—she couldn't contain a smile—she'd be able to indulge herself. Come Christmas, not only would she be able to afford the super-deluxe Barbie house Lissy had seen in the Sears catalog but she'd also be able to get John the exquisitely beautiful saddle she'd seen the last time she'd been to Missoula.

Just the thought made her smile.

Her head came up as she heard the back door open and close, followed by the familiar sound of John's footsteps. Without thinking, she gathered the check, the letter and the rest of the papers, turned them over and stacked them on top of the envelope. She'd tell him about her good news, but later, after she'd had more time to absorb it herself.

There was something far more important she wanted to tell him first, if only she could find the right time.

"Hey," he said, looking big and vital as he strode into the room.

"Hey yourself." Unable to help herself, she climbed to her feet, closed the distance between them and went up on tiptoe to give him a welcoming kiss. For a second he stiffened, and then his arms came around her and the pressure of his mouth increased. She couldn't contain a soft sound of pleasure at the solid strength of his chest against hers and the muscular press of his arms.

It was awhile before they separated.

When they did, John took an audible breath and leaned his forehead against hers. "That was nice. Where's Lis?"

"Having dinner at Jenny's. I told Lois I'd pick her up around eight."

A gleam ignited in his eyes at the breathlessness in her voice. "In that case..."

To her consternation, he put her away from him and headed purposefully for the mudroom. Gathering her scattered wits, she was about to ask what he was doing when he reappeared, a sleeping bag tucked under his arm.

She watched as he unzipped the thick bedroll and spread it out before the fire. Leaning against the back of one of the club chairs, he yanked off his boots, set them out of the way and straightened, his hands going to his shirt buttons. His gaze played over her, his eyes looking very blue in the light as a lazy smile transformed his handsome face. "I've been thinking about making love to you in front of the fire ever since Friday night," he informed her.

His smile, still so new, made her knees feel ridiculously weak. "In that case, I suppose it's all right to admit that so have I." Her gaze never leaving his, she began stripping her own clothes away.

"You have?"

"Absolutely."

He made no effort to hide his satisfaction at her answer. Tall and straight, his wide shoulders, washboard stomach, narrow hips and long lean thighs outlined by the fire as dusk filled the room, he simply waited.

Naked, she stepped toward him.

He looked at her one endless moment. "You're so damn beautiful, Eve." He slid his hands into her hair, holding her still as he lowered his head. "Say my name," he whispered. "I need to hear you say my name."

"John." She slid her hands over his satiny shoulders and gazed steadily at him. "John."

With a groan, his mouth settled over hers, hot and sweet. Her pulse leaped. An insistent ache bloomed between her thighs as the kiss went on and on, their only point of contact, until finally he wrapped an arm around her waist and carried her down to the sleeping bag.

Never relinquishing her mouth, his hands found hers and he twined their fingers together as he stretched her arms above her head. "Sweet," he murmured fiercely. And then, as his body rocked, sliding home between her open thighs, he whispered, "I need you. Damn it, I need you too much."

With a sob, she arched beneath him, the unexpected words igniting her blood with fire. In that instant the love she felt for him was overwhelming, and despite the suddenness of his possession, she was more than ready, her body already trembling on the verge of release.

Sensation flooded her as he surged into her, thick and hot. She couldn't get enough. Not of the strong grip of his hands holding hers, the way his back hollowed as she wrapped her legs around his waist, the delicious pressure of his chest rubbing against her sensitized nipples. Not of the feel of him as he drove into her over and over, and heat seemed to scorch her from the inside out.

She strained against him, crying out. "Yes. John. Yes...." She struggled for the absolute pleasure that beckoned tantalizingly just out of reach, wanting that completion even as she longed for their union to go on. "I love you." She couldn't hold back the words any longer, any more than she could stop the feelings that ran so deep inside her. "I love you so much."

For a second he went still, and then he shuddered as the last of his control vanished. Sobbing for breath, his hips driving like a piston, he thrust full into her, crying out as she clamped down around him and his whole body tensed with his climax, triggering her own. Wave after wave of pleasure poured through her.

Holding tight to each other, they clung together for so long that Eve lost track of time. All she knew was that she'd never felt this way about anyone before in her life, as if they were one body, one breath, one heartbeat.

John raised his head minutes later. Carefully shifting his weight onto his elbows, he looked down at her. "You all right?"

A languorous smile tugged at her mouth. "Uh-huh."

To her dismay, she could have sworn there was a shadow in his eyes that hadn't been there before. There was no hint of it in his voice, however. "Good. That's good," he said as he rolled onto his back, keeping her close.

Telling herself she must have imagined it, she nestled closer and waited for her heart to quit pounding, savoring the feel of him against her, all warm and densely muscled.

Outside, the sky had darkened to charcoal as day slipped inexorably into night. Inside, the fire had burned down to a steady wave of flame that bathed the room in a rosy light. As the minutes passed, she relaxed. Pillowing her head on his arm, she sighed with contentment as she pressed a kiss to the bend of his elbow. Slowly, her breathing evened out. Her eyelids grew heavy, and she decided it couldn't possibly hurt to close them just for a moment.

When Eve awoke, the room was dark and John was sitting beside her, his back propped against the couch.

At some point he'd pulled on his jeans and covered her with a blanket. Warmed by his thoughtfulness—not to mention the compelling picture he made as he stared into the fire—she lightly touched her hand to his bare chest. "Hi."

He looked down at her, and there was a look in his eyes she'd never seen before. "Welcome back."

"How long was I out?"

"About an hour."

"What?" Clutching the blanket to her breasts, she sat up. "Dinner must be a cinder."

"Relax." He stroked his hand down her exposed spine. "I turned down the oven a while ago."

"Oh." She settled back next to him. "Well, thanks."

He shrugged, watching as a piece of the log in the fireplace gave way and sent up a shower of sparks. The silence stretched for several seconds before he shifted and gave her a long, searching look. "Did you mean it when you said you loved me?" he asked abruptly.

Somehow she'd known the question was coming. "Yes. Of course I did."

Some of the tension left his face. "I think we ought to get married."

She was so stunned that for a moment she forgot to breathe. She wasn't sure what she'd expected, but it wasn't this. "You do?"

"Yeah. I know we haven't been together that long, but as much as I like these stolen moments—" he took a pointed look around at their temporary nest "—they're not enough. I want people to know you're mine. Just like I want the right to take you to my bed at night and wake up beside you the next morning."

Her heart squeezed. Until this very moment, she'd had no idea how much she wanted to be his wife. But she did. She wanted to spend the rest of her life with him, have his children, be the one he turned to with his hopes and dreams, his disappointments and his triumphs.

Misreading her silence, he went on persuasively, "Think about it, Eve. You'd get a nice home. A kid who's crazy about you. And you wouldn't have to worry about money. I can give you everything that Max did and more, so you'll be able to have the sort of luxuries you did before. Except for the travel, you'll have your old life back."

With every word, the warm glow she'd felt just seconds earlier dissipated. "Is that what you think I want?" she asked slowly.

"I suppose I could dress it up in prettier words, but yeah—why not? You're a beautiful woman. You deserve nice things. And why would anyone bother to get married if it wasn't to their benefit?"

"I see. And in this case, you get sex and I get money?" Her voice sounded remarkably calm. Which was a surprise, given that she felt as if her heart were breaking. Suddenly chilled, she looked around but her bra and panties were nowhere to be found, so she simply pulled on her sweater and jeans without them. "I believe there's a name for that, John. And it's definitely *not* 'marriage.'" She stood and stepped into her shoes.

He climbed to his feet as well. "Damn it, Eve, don't twist what I'm saying! It's not that I don't have feelings for you. I do. But if you're waiting for some big romantic declaration, you'd better accept that it's not going to happen.''

Ignoring the hurt his words brought her, she raised her chin in challenge. "And why is that?"

"Because it's not who I am. I gave up on all that happily ever after stuff as a kid. There's nothing like growing up the way I did to teach you that the whole love thing is highly overrated. From what I've seen, it doesn't last. Give me a well-crafted business deal any day.''

She stared into his stony face, appalled to realize he believed what he was saying. Rubbing her arms, she paced across the room, not turning until she reached the table. "But how can you say that? Look what's happened with you and Lissy. I know you love her—"

"That's different," he said sharply, stalking toward her.

"Maybe it is. But you had no way of knowing it was going to be. So why did you ever agree to take her in the first place?"

"Why the hell do you think? She's my flesh and blood. There was no way I was going to turn my back on her, not after—'' He abruptly caught himself and broke off, the familiar shuttered look appearing on his face.

"Not after what?" she persisted.

"It doesn't matter."

She didn't believe him, not for an instant. She replayed his words and out of nowhere found herself completing his sentence in a way that made what was happening between them fall into place. "You couldn't turn your back on Lissy the way your mother did on you," she said slowly. "Isn't that what you were going to say?"

"I told you it doesn't matter."

"I think it does." Her mind continued to work, and she decided to take a chance. "Do you remember the morning the horse got loose?"

He looked at her woodenly. "What about it?"

"When I got up, I was cold, so I decided to borrow one of the T-shirts out of your dresser. I didn't mean to pry, but I found the jacket and the note your mother left you."

"You had no damn right—"

She ignored him. "At the time, I thought you'd kept those things because they were all you had to connect you with her, but now...I wonder..."

"You wonder what?" His voice was colder than a mountain creek in the dead of winter.

"I wonder if you kept them to remind you that people who claim to love you can't be trusted, that they'll hurt you in the end."

"You don't know what the hell you're talking about." His movements stiff with undisguised anger, he started to turn away, and his thigh bumped the table, sending the papers from Morris Chapman fluttering to the floor. Swearing, he stooped down to gather them up, only to suddenly stiffen as his gaze zeroed in on the check. He picked it up and gave it a long look, and as he did, a veil seemed to come down over his eyes.

Straightening, he tossed the check and the rest of the papers onto the table. "So much for true love," he said scornfully. "No wonder you're not interested in marrying me."

"What?"

"Apparently you've come into some money. At least you could have told me the truth instead of putting us both through this farce—"

"You're a fool if you believe that," she said flatly.

"Am I?"

"Yes. I love you, John. And no matter what you say or how badly you behave, that's not going to change."

"Yeah, right."

His sensual, arrogant mouth compressed into a mulish line.

She walked over and picked up her keys and purse. "I'm going to get Lissy now. But when I get back..." She considered his hard, closed expression and suddenly feared that no matter what she said, he wasn't going to listen.

Still, she had to try, even if it meant trying to shock him into reason. "When I get back, I'll pack my things and go." Holding her breath as she waited for his reaction, she headed for the door.

He didn't say a word.

"Daddy?"

John looked up from his computer screen to find Lissy standing just inside the study doorway.

He'd heard her and Eve come into the house more than an hour ago but had deliberately opted to stay in his office. For one thing, he had a ton of paperwork to catch up on since lately—due to certain distractions—he'd let things slide. More to the point, what could possibly be gained by another confrontation? He and Eve had said more than enough. And he was damned if he'd expose Lissy to something he felt strongly shouldn't concern her.

Except it was obvious from the child's stricken expression that Eve hadn't shown the same discretion. With a mixture of anger and dismay, he considered his daughter, noting the eyes jeweled with tears and the ominously trembling lower lip. Despite her cheerful outfit of pink flannel pajamas and bunny slippers, she looked as if she'd just lost her very best friend.

Or learned she was about to. "What is it, Lissy?"

She hesitated for the briefest instant, then dashed across the thickly padded rug and flung herself into his arms. "Eve's leaving," she cried, dissolving into tears.

So. She was really going through with it.

A heavy weight seemed to press against his chest. Stubbornly, he shook off the sensation, telling himself that what he was feeling was merely concern for Lissy. He patted her small, shaking back and tried to find the words to reassure her. "I know she is. But you don't need to worry about it. We'll be fine without her, baby, I promise."

She raised her tear-streaked face to his. "But I d-don't want to be without her!" Swallowing hard, she took a long shuddering breath, struggling for control over the sobs still threatening to overwhelm her. "She says she'll see me at school and she'll come to my dance recital, but it w-won't be the same." Her voice rose. "Can't you make her stay?"

The old, familiar frustration at not knowing the right thing to say swept him. "Lissy..."

"Please, Daddy?" Tucked against his shoulder, she

looked up at him imploringly, her blue eyes huge in her small face.

For an instant he wavered, wishing he could grant her her desire. But then an image of Eve walking out the door flashed through his mind, and he felt a fresh rush of anger. After all, his only crime was that he'd offered her a mutually advantageous marriage, and what had she done? She'd thrown it back in his face, making it clear that what he had to offer wasn't good enough.

Which only proved what he'd known all along: when push came to shove, love wasn't worth much. His face hardened. "I can't, Lis."

"But why not? Did—did you guys have a fight?"

He regarded her earnest little face and realized that this, at least, was a reason she could understand. What's more, in its simplest sense, it was true. "Yeah. You could say that."

"Oh." Biting her lip, she contemplated her slippers and appeared to consider his answer. After a moment she let out a shuddery breath and said in a small, uncertain voice, "If we have a fight, will I have to go away?"

Aw, hell. "No. *No.*" He tightened his arms around her. "Nothing you could do would ever make me send you away," he said forcefully. "You're my kid, and you're here to stay. Okay?"

She looked up, relief mixed with consternation on her face. "But I know Eve loves you. She said so. She said you and me mattered most to her in the world. And you're making *her* go away."

"No, I'm not. She made the choice—"

"But you won't even try to make her stay," she insisted with perfect, seven-year-old logic.

He searched for patience. "Look, you remember how I told you I grew up in an orphanage?"

She nodded solemnly. "Uh-huh."

"Well, it taught me some things. And one is that you can't always trust what people say."

Her brow puckered. "You mean they lie?"

He frowned. Somehow it didn't sound quite the way he'd intended said straight out like that. "Well, yeah."

"But why would Eve do that?"

He gazed down at his daughter, into those eyes that were the exact same blue as his own, and abruptly realized he didn't have an answer.

Two days ago—hell, two hours ago—he would have said Eve was just deluding herself, claiming she loved him because it was easier than admitting she wanted the security he could give her.

But that explanation didn't hold up very well in light of her newly acquired sixty-five thousand dollars.

Still, there had to be some logical reason, he assured himself. He was just too damn fed up with the whole subject to think of it at the moment. "I don't know," he said brusquely. "What I do know is what I learned when I was even younger than you are now. And that's that you can't depend on anyone but yourself."

The crease between Lissy's eyebrows deepened. "But that was a long time ago, Daddy." She worried her lower lip. "You're a grown-up now. And I depend on *you*. Or aren't I s'posed to?"

It was such a simple question, yet it pierced him to the core. Meeting his child's worried gaze, he felt the foundation he'd built his world on crumble as he gave her the only answer possible. "Well, sure. Of course you are."

She relaxed and nestled against him. "Good."

He barely heard her for the roaring in his head. Hell. He *was* a grown-up, he thought dazedly. The only problem was, he suddenly knew that on one particular subject he hadn't been thinking like one for a long, long time.

Eve had been right. She just hadn't taken it far enough. He *had* kept the note and the coat as a reminder of his mother's abandonment. Just as he'd taken what he'd seen in the orphanage and used it as proof that love, no matter how well-meaning, couldn't be counted on.

As a consequence, he'd spent his entire adult life avoiding emotional entanglements. But it wasn't because he didn't believe in love, he realized now.

It was because he did, since he'd seen its power and known firsthand what a toll its loss could take. Not to put too fine a point on it, but he'd been afraid.

And then Eve had shown up. And though he'd known she was a threat to his indifference right from the beginning, he'd been unable to resist her. But still he'd tried, throwing up every sort of barrier.

Now, however, he could see her clearly. And, among other things, he knew that when it came to money, she really didn't care. He was the one who'd put such a priority on it, because taking care of her had been his excuse for getting close while maintaining his emotional inaccessibility. All along he'd been secretly afraid that if she didn't have to depend on him financially, she'd leave him the way his mother had.

And in the end he'd managed to drive her away anyway.

"Daddy? Are you okay? You look funny."

He cleared his throat. "I'm fine, honey. I just...I do want Eve to stay. But I think I hurt her feelings and I don't know if I can make it right."

She patted his shoulder. "It's okay, Daddy. No matter what, Eve will forgive you."

He wasn't so sure, but as he stood to carry her into bed, he prayed she was right.

That's the last of it, Eve thought without the slightest trace of satisfaction, as she placed the last stack of her underthings into the largest of the two suitcases open on her bed. But then, it was hard to get too excited about being an efficient packer when you were preparing to leave a place—and the people— you'd come to love.

She squeezed her eyes shut, wondering yet again what had possessed her to push things with John the way she had. She should have been more diplomatic. She should have heard him out and told him she needed time to think about his proposal.

She should have done anything but what she had, rejecting his offer, calling him a fool, telling him she'd leave while praying he'd call her bluff. He was a proud man, and she'd painted him into a corner. If only she'd pretended to go along, she might have been able to talk to him later when they were both calmer—

Right. And at what cost? Or don't you remember what happened with Granddad when you chose to just "go along"?

She let loose a sigh and reluctantly faced the idea

that she'd done the only thing that she could. It had taken John more than thirty years to get where he was, and it was foolish of her to believe that anything she could say—today, tomorrow or a year from now—would make a difference. She knew better than anyone that change had to come from inside. It couldn't be dictated, or wished into existence.

For that reason alone, it was kinder by far to accept things the way they were and to let everyone involved get on with their lives. Even if she did feel as if her heart was breaking...

A faint sound came from the hallway. With a sixth sense that she didn't question, she knew it was John even before a quick glance at the doorway confirmed it. She looked away, wondering what he wanted, and praying that whatever it was, she could get through the encounter with her dignity intact.

She waited for him to say something. When he didn't, she flipped the larger suitcase shut, doing her best to appear calm. "There. That's everything, except for Lissy's pictures." She gestured in the general direction of the stack of drawings on her dresser. "I thought I'd put them in a paper bag and carry them so they won't get wrinkled." When he remained silent, she found herself chattering on. "Chrissy's coming to get me." She glanced at her watch, then closed and zipped the second suitcase. "She should be here within the hour. Is Lissy in bed?"

He spoke at last. "Yeah. I tucked her in a few minutes ago."

"Oh. I'll just go give her a good-night kiss then." Bracing herself, she turned. Unfortunately for her peace of mind, nothing had changed in the past few hours; he looked as tall, rugged and uncompromisingly male as ever, and she suddenly understood what it meant to love someone so much it hurt.

"I'd appreciate it if you'd hold off a minute." To her surprise, he shifted his weight onto his heels and shoved his hands into his back pockets in a way that, if he were any other man, would have made her think he was nervous.

Which was ridiculous. She'd seen John in all sorts of situations, and not once had he ever lacked for confidence. "I really don't think—"

"Please, Eve. Just listen."

Everything inside her protested; she didn't think she could bear to hear him tell her again that he'd never love her. On the other hand, he showed no intention of leaving, so short of trying to wrestle him out of the doorway it appeared she had no choice but to listen. "Okay."

"I want a second chance."

Her heart gave a painful lurch. "You do?"

"Yeah." He cleared his throat. "You were right about that stuff from my mother. I did keep it to remind me of the way she'd left me, and that love couldn't be trusted. I told myself I was just being honest, facing a truth that other people didn't have the guts to." A touch of irony colored his voice. "I didn't think of it as protecting myself. I just thought I was being independent.

"Then you showed up. And no matter how hard I fought it, I wanted you. Physically at first, it's true, but it didn't take long before I wanted more. Except that I was damned if I'd admit I was falling in love with you, because as long as I denied it, I thought I couldn't get hurt." His mouth twisted in a parody of a smile. "Only it doesn't work that way—I know that now. Because no matter what I call it, being without you would be like being without the best part of myself."

She blinked back the tears that were suddenly threatening to overflow. She wanted to stop him, to tell him he didn't need to go on, that she'd meant it when she said there was nothing he could do that would make her stop loving him. But she forced herself to remain silent, instinctively knowing he needed to get this out, no matter how difficult it was.

"I love you, Eve. I think I've loved you from the first time I saw you and I know I want us to spend the rest of our lives together. I'm not promising it'll be perfect. I'm not an easy man to live with, and I've been on my own for so long that I'm not very good at sharing my thoughts or my feelings. But if you'll stay, and give me a chance, I swear I'll do my best. Say you'll marry me, sweetheart. Please."

"Yes. Oh, John, yes." Unable to wait a second longer, needing to touch him, she started forward, but before she could take more than a step he was moving toward her. He pulled her into his arms, and the feel of him was like heaven.

For a moment they just stood, holding each other. Eve could hear his heart pounding, and the physical evidence of his vulnerability only heightened the aching tenderness she already felt. "I love you," she said quietly.

His arms tightened around her. "Say it again."

She smiled. "I love you."

He let out his breath. "Thank God. I love you, too."

Again, they were silent, savoring their closeness. It was minutes later before either of them spoke.

"I suppose I'd better call Chrissy." Eve rubbed her cheek against the smooth cotton covering John's chest, glorying in his warmth and strength.

His grip on her didn't change. "Good idea."

"And we probably ought to go talk to Lissy."

"Yeah. Probably." He stayed right where he was. "But first I'm going to kiss you. Maybe more than once."

She leaned back so she could see his face. His blue eyes blazed as he looked down at her, all of the emotion he'd suppressed for so long plainly visible for her to see.

She smiled. "That sounds like a good idea."

And it was.

* * * * *

*Look for RITA Award-winning author
Caroline Cross's next novel,
HUSBAND—OR ENEMY?
part of
FORTUNE'S CHILDREN: THE GROOMS,*

on sale in May 2002

SILHOUETTE® DESIRE™

0202/51a

AVAILABLE FROM 15TH FEBRUARY 2002

MADE FOR LOVE

COWBOY FANTASY Ann Major

When Melody Woods slipped from North Black's bed, innocence intact, and left town it fuelled North's desire. Now, Melody was back…and she wanted North. But he'd *never* tangle with that spitfire again… *would* he?

MORE TO LOVE Dixie Browning

When hard-edged playboy Rafe found himself stranded with delectable Molly Dewhurst, his usually strong control shattered. Molly refused to believe that his intentions were true. So Rafe was determined to show her that she was every inch the woman for him!

MILLIONAIRE BACHELORS

TYCOON WARRIOR Sheri WhiteFeather

Millionaire's Club

Wealthy Dakota Lewis wanted one thing—his wife. Kathy was still his, but she was not under his roof…in his bed. Acknowledging his mistakes, Dakota was now determined never to leave her side again…

MILLIONAIRE HUSBAND Leanne Banks

Millionaire Justin Langdon had sworn off marriage…until the day Amy Monroe saved his life. She had dangerous curves and, even more dangerous, dependants! So why was Justin getting an inexplicable urge to show Amy he was husband material?

TO WED A ROYAL

Two Royally Wed Stories

CODE NAME: PRINCE Valerie Parv

Meagan Moore had never intended to get caught up in her brother's plot to overthrow the throne, or fall for the man thought to be the enigmatic Prince Nicholas. Now, danger lurked everywhere and Meagan is torn between her family and her Prince Charming…

AN OFFICER AND A PRINCESS Carla Cassidy

Lieutenant Adam Sinclair readily agreed to help Princess Isabel carry out her brilliant plan to rescue her father. But he hadn't counted on the feelings that accompanied a reunion with the only woman he'd ever loved—or that posing as a married couple would feel so…right.

AVAILABLE FROM 15TH FEBRUARY 2002

SILHOUETTE®

Sensation™

Passionate, dramatic, thrilling romances

OUT OF NOWHERE Beverly Bird
NAVAJO'S WOMAN Beverly Barton
THE ENEMY'S DAUGHTER Linda Turner
THE AWAKENING OF DR BROWN Kathleen Creighton
EVERY WAKING MOMENT Doreen Roberts
THE MAN FOR MAGGIE Frances Housden

Special Edition™

Vivid, satisfying romances full of family, life and love

A BUNDLE OF MIRACLES Amy Frazier
HER UNFORGETTABLE FIANCÉ Allison Leigh
FATHER MOST WANTED Marie Ferrarella
WIFE IN DISGUISE Susan Mallery
AT THE HEART'S COMMAND Patricia McLinn
WHEN LOVE WALKS IN Suzanne Carey

Superromance™

*Enjoy the drama, explore the emotions,
experience the relationship*

BECCA'S BABY Tara Taylor Quinn
EXPECTATIONS Brenda Novak
A MESSAGE FOR ABBY Janice Kay Johnson
MR ELLIOTT FINDS A FAMILY Susan Floyd

Intrigue™

Danger, deception and suspense

BAYOU BLOOD BROTHERS York, Hingle & Wayne
THE HUNT FOR HAWKE'S DAUGHTER Jean Barrett
THE INNOCENT Amanda Stevens
STRANGER IN HIS ARMS Charlotte Douglas

Labour of Love

sharon sala

marie ferrarella

leanne banks

Three adorable bundles of joy are en-route in this trio of heart-warming and sexy love stories

Published 15th February

Available at most branches of WH Smith, Tesco, Martins, Borders, Eason, Sainsbury's and most good paperback bookshops.

Fortune's Children: THE GROOMS

Welcome back to the Fortune dynasty

The drama and mystery of Fortune's Children continues with a new 12-part book continuity series.

Fortune's Children: THE GROOMS
and
Fortune's Children: THE LOST HEIRS

The drama, glamour and mystery begins with Fortune's Grooms, five strong, sexy men surrounded by intrigue, but destined for love and marriage!

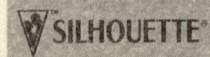

SILHOUETTE®

Fortune's Children: THE GROOMS

March	Bride of Fortune
April	Mail-Order Cinderella Fortune's Secret Child
May	Husband-or-Enemy Groom of Fortune

Fortune's Children: THE LOST HEIRS

June	A Most Desirable MD The Pregnant Heiress
July	Baby of Fortune Fortune's Secret Daughter
August	Her Boss's Baby Did You Say Twins?!
December	Special Christmas Anthology Gift of Fortune

SILHOUETTE INTRIGUE

Eden had been named as paradise, but evil had come to call...

EDEN'S CHILDREN

A powerful new trilogy by
AMANDA STEVENS

THE INNOCENT	March 2002
THE TEMPTED	April 2002
THE FORGIVEN	May 2002

Innocent young lives are in danger...
Can the power of love carry them home?

SILHOUETTE INTRIGUE
is proud to present

1201/SH/LC27

TOP SECRET BABIES

These babies need a protector!

THE BODYGUARD'S BABY
Debra Webb - January

SAVING HIS SON
Rita Herron - February

THE HUNT FOR HAWKE'S DAUGHTER
Jean Barrett - March

UNDERCOVER BABY
Adrianne Lee - April

CONCEPTION COVER-UP
Karen Lawton Barrett - May

HIS CHILD
Delores Fossen - June

Unwrap the mystery

SILHOUETTE DESIRE

is proud to present

Millionaires Galore!

Rich, renowned, ruthless and sexy as sin

Millionaire's Club - January

MILLIONAIRE MD by *Jennifer Greene*
WORLD'S MOST ELIGIBLE TEXAN by *Sara Orwig*

Millionaire Men - February

LONE STAR KNIGHT by *Cindy Gerard*
HER ARDENT SHEIKH by *Kristi Gold*

Millionaire Bachelors - March

TYCOON WARRIOR by *Sheri WhiteFeather*
MILLIONAIRE HUSBAND by *Leanne Banks*

Millionaire Marriages - April

MILLIONAIRE BOSS by *Peggy Moreland*
THE MILLIONAIRE'S SECRET WISH
by *Leanne Banks*

SILHOUETTE SUPERROMANCE

is proud to present

nine months later

Friends... Lovers... Strangers...
These couples' lives are about to change
radically as they become parents-to-be

HER BEST FRIEND'S BABY
CJ Carmichael
January

THE PULL OF THE MOON
Darlene Graham
February

EXPECTATIONS
Brenda Novak
March

THE FOURTH CHILD
CJ Carmichael
April

Join us every month throughout the whole of 2002 for one of these dramatic, involving, emotional books.

FREE!

1 Book
and a surprise gift!

We would like to take this opportunity to thank you for reading this Silhouette® book by offering you the chance to take another specially selected title from the Desire™ series absolutely FREE! We're also making this offer to introduce you to the benefits of the Reader Service™—

- ★ FREE home delivery
- ★ FREE gifts and competitions
- ★ FREE monthly Newsletter
- ★ Books available before they're in the shops
- ★ Exclusive Reader Service discount offer

Accepting this FREE book and gift places you under no obligation to buy; you may cancel at any time, even after receiving your free shipment. Simply complete your details below and return the entire page to the address below. *You don't even need a stamp!*

YES! Please send me 1 free Desire book and a surprise gift. I understand that unless you hear from me, I will receive 2 superb new titles every month for just £4.99 each, postage and packing free. I am under no obligation to purchase any books and may cancel my subscription at any time. The free books and gift will be mine to keep in any case.

D2ZEB

Ms/Mrs/Miss/Mr .... Initials ....

BLOCK CAPITALS PLEASE

Surname ....

Address ....

....

.... Postcode ....

Send this whole page to:
UK: The Reader Service, FREEPOST CN81, Croydon, CR9 3WZ
EIRE: The Reader Service, PO Box 4546, Kilcock, County Kildare (stamp required)

Offer not valid to current Reader Service subscribers to this series. We reserve the right to refuse an application and applicants must be aged 18 years or over. Only one application per household. Terms and prices subject to change without notice. Offer expires 31st May 2002. As a result of this application, you may receive offers from other carefully selected companies. If you would prefer not to share in this opportunity please write to The Data Manager at the address above.

Silhouette® is a registered trademark used under licence.
Desire™ is being used as a trademark.